DAWN OF DESIRE

Cole awoke slowly to darkness and a feeling of contentment. He couldn't recall when he'd felt so at peace. The woman in his arms was warm and sweet-smelling. A firm breast filled his hand and he fondled the nipple pressing impudently against his palm.

Morning Mist.

He almost said her name aloud until he remembered. Morning Mist was dead. The woman beside him was named Dawn. Dawn, with long black hair and innocent blue eyes that held the ageless knowledge of Eve. Vulnerable Dawn. She had known many men yet gave the impression of being untouched.

His hand moved against her breast, stroking her gently, restless, wanting. A groan slipped from his throat when he felt her nipple harden against his palm.

Other *Leisure* books by Connie Mason:

FLAME
PURE TEMPTATION
THE LION'S BRIDE
SIERRA
WIND RIDER
TEARS LIKE RAIN
TREASURES OF THE HEART
A PROMISE OF THUNDER
ICE & RAPTURE
BRAVE LAND, BRAVE LOVE
WILD LAND, WILD LOVE
BOLD LAND, BOLD LOVE
TEMPT THE DEVIL
FOR HONOR'S SAKE
BEYOND THE HORIZON
TENDER FURY
CARESS AND CONQUER
PROMISED SPLENDOR
MY LADY VIXEN
DESERT ECSTASY
WILD IS MY HEART

CONNIE MASON

SHADOW WALKER

LEISURE BOOKS   **NEW YORK CITY**

To my wonderful family,
for all their love and support.

A LEISURE BOOK®

June 1997

Published by

Dorchester Publishing Co., Inc.
276 Fifth Avenue
New York, NY 10001

Printed in the United States of America.

Prologue

Colorado Territory—1872

Straight as an arrow, tall and broad-shouldered, Shadow Walker braced muscular legs upon the ground where his beloved wife, Morning Mist, had lost her life. Lofty, snow capped mountains soared above him, making his own imposing form seem insignificant in comparison. During his years with the Sioux, Shadow Walker had shared their pain, their joy, their sorrow, but deep within his heart he knew his future lay elsewhere. His body had hardened, matured, adjusting to the harshness of the weather and the capriciousness of nature. Regrettably, the time to leave had arrived.

Running Elk was moving his people to the reservation, and Shadow Walker realized his life must take a different course. The People didn't belong on a reservation any more than he did, but he, at least, had a choice.

Shadow Walker turned his face toward the sun, savoring its warmth upon his wide, bronzed chest. He wore an eagle feather in his mahogany hair, which had darkened with the passing years, changing from bright red to a rich, deep auburn. Shadow Walker wondered if his twin sister's hair had darkened also, or if it still glowed like living flame. It was time he found out, he decided. A visit to Oregon City was long overdue.

"You appear troubled, Shadow Walker."

Shadow Walker turned to greet his brother-in-law, Running Elk. "I can no longer delay the inevitable. I must leave the People."

Running Elk nodded sagely. "It is time. Where will you go?"

"I long to see my family in Oregon. I will visit Ashley and Tanner first, then look for work."

Fond memories assailed Running Elk, and he smiled as he fingered the hank of bright red hair woven among his own dark locks. "I still mourn the loss of the woman called Flame. But the Great Spirit chose her for another. Tell Flame that her strong medicine continues to protect me after all these years."

"I will tell her. I will always treasure my years with the People," Shadow Walker said. "I have learned a great deal from the Sioux. Knowledge that will serve me well in the White world."

"Have you learned how to live without a woman? You have repeatedly refused to take another wife from among our maidens and widows. Do you prefer a White wife?"

Shadow Walker's rugged features hardened. "I prefer no wife. I will never love any woman the way I loved Morning Mist. No woman can compare with her. I take my pleasure where I find it and leave with my heart intact."

Running Elk found Shadow Walker's words worrisome. "Morning Mist walked the spirit path four winters ago. It is time for you to move on. Men need to father strong sons and daughters to honor them in their old age. You are wasting your seed, Shadow Walker. Find a good woman to warm your mat and bear your children."

Shadow Walker turned his emerald green gaze toward the towering snow-peaked mountains. "Morning Mist was pregnant with my child when she was slain. I have vowed that no other woman will bear a child of mine. I will spend my seed on Mother Earth before giving it to another woman."

Distressed, Running Elk shook his head. "You have carried your grief long enough, brother. I, too, miss my little sister, but no amount of wishing will bring her back. I have consulted with Dream Spinner about you. He says the signs are favorable that you will find a woman to take Morning Mist's place."

"No!" His denial was swift and decisive. "I will never take another wife."

"Laughing Brook will be devastated. The widow has shared your blanket many times during the past four years."

"I made Laughing Brook no promises."

Running Elk nodded, in no way condemning

his brother-in-law. He had almost forgotten that Shadow Walker had skin several shades lighter than his own and a White name. "Go, then, Shadow Walker. But mark my words, one day you will return, and then we will see if your vow was spoken in earnest. Every man needs a woman to ease his body and bear his children."

Running Elk's entire band was on hand to bid Shadow Walker good-bye when he left two days later. Laughing Brook gave him a misty-eyed smile and brushed away tears as she waved farewell. Shedding his familiar breechclout and moccasins, Shadow Walker had donned buckskin trousers, flannel shirt, leather vest and supple boots. He was mounted upon the faithful sorrel gelding he had acquired several years before, after he left the army.

"Farewell, Shadow Walker," Running Elk said solemnly. "May *Wakantanka* watch over you until your return."

"Farewell, brother. I will be forever grateful to you and the People. Because of your friendship I am now able to return to civilization and make a life for myself, a life without Morning Mist, a life without love. May Wakantanka protect you."

A faint smile stretched the corners of Running Elk's mouth. Intuition told him that Shadow Walker's words would come back to haunt him. Shadow Walker would find love where he least expected it.

Chapter One

Dodge City, Kansas—August, 1875

Cole Webster crouched in the underbrush, his rifle balanced on a rock as his sharp green eyes narrowed on the crude log cabin on the bank of the Arkansas River. Adrenalin pumped through his veins. It was always the same, he reflected. During the three years he'd worked as a Pinkerton detective, the chase and capture never failed to instill a wild excitement within him.

No one tracked better than he. He'd been taught by the Sioux. His skills had served him well in the job he had taken after visiting his sister and her husband in 1872. Detective work satisfied the restlessness that had churned inside him ever since the death of Morning Mist. He enjoyed traveling to wherever he was needed to investigate a crime or recover stolen goods. Currently he had been hired by the railroad to recover money stolen from the Union Pacific in a daring raid near Dodge City by the notorious Cobb gang. Operating in and around Dodge City, the Cobb gang had recently pulled off several train robberies and continued to elude the law.

It hadn't taken Cole long to close in on Billy Cobb, the leader of the gang. After several days of scouting, he had located Cobb's hideout in a remote area west of Dodge and was fairly certain Cobb was alone in the cabin now. Cole stared at the run-down cabin, pondering whether to rush it or wait to nab the bastard when he came out. It wasn't necessary to bring in Cobb alive as long as Cole recovered the loot from the train robbery that had taken place a week before. Four men had pulled off the robbery. One of the conductors had recognized Cobb from a Wanted poster he'd seen. After the robbery the gang had split up. Cole had tracked Cobb to his hideout on the bank of the Arkansas.

Suddenly Cole tensed as he heard a muffled scream coming from inside the cabin. His grip tightened on the rifle. The scream turned to pitiful whimpering, but Cole maintained his position. He'd been so certain Cobb was alone in the cabin, he would have bet money on it. The unexpected sound had unsettled him, something that rarely happened. His sojourn with the Sioux had taught him to conceal his emotions and remain calm no matter what.

Cole rose to his haunches, preparing to sneak up to the cabin, when suddenly the door burst open and Billy Cobb stormed out. His ugly face was like thunder as he flung himself atop his mount and took off, riding hell-bent for leather. Cole sprang to his feet and ran for his own mount tethered nearby. If Cobb had the money on him, Cole couldn't afford to let him get away.

Cole's horse shot out of the narrow forest that grew along the riverbank onto a flat grassy prairie surrounded by low hills and rocky outcroppings. Cobb was nowhere in sight. Cole spit out an oath and reined in sharply, realizing immediately that he had blundered into an ambush. Cobb must have heard Cole pounding after him and hidden behind the large rocks scattered on either side of the trail. Cole felt a prickling at the back of his neck when he saw the sun reflect off a shiny object a short distance to the left. Cobb's rifle? Digging in his spurs, Cole let out a Sioux war cry and flattened himself against Warrior's sleek withers. The animal surged forward beneath Cole's expert handling.

Bullets whizzed past Cole as he pinpointed Cobb's hiding place. Lesser men would have called him excessively reckless, others fearless, but in truth Cole was inured to danger and accustomed to taking chances with his life.

Removing his rifle from the saddleboot, Cole knew he was close enough now to return Cobb's shots with some accuracy. He didn't want to kill Cobb if he didn't have to. He needed Cobb alive to tell him where to find the train loot if he didn't have it with him. Unfortunately, one of Cole's bullets ricocheted off the rock behind Cobb and entered his heart through his back. Cobb died instantly.

"Dammit to hell!" Cole cursed when he reached Cobb and saw that his bullet had killed him. "Just my luck," he muttered sourly after a search of Cobb's saddlebags yielded nothing except a small amount of money and a gold bracelet set with rubies. Draping Cobb's body over the back of his horse, Cole took him to Dodge City, turned him over to the undertaker, and stopped by the sheriff's office to report the death.

"There's a reward out for Billy Cobb," Sheriff Tayler said.

"I'll be around to collect it after I recover the railroad loot. Cobb didn't have it on him, so I suspect it's still at his hideout. I'm heading out there now."

Sheriff Tayler appeared stunned. "Don't tell me the bastard has a hideout nearby? I never would have guessed he'd hole up so close to Dodge. What about the rest of his gang?"

"They split up. My partner is on their trail."

"Maybe Cobb gave the loot to one of his gang."

"I'd bet my last dollar Cobb took it with him when the gang split up. I reckon they'll turn up before long for their share. You'd best be on your guard."

"I'll keep my eyes peeled, Webster. I always cooperate with the railroad. The railroad brought prosperity to Dodge, and we all appreciate it. I hope you find the money. I'll form a posse to track down the rest of the gang members. I've been looking for them for months. They disappear as soon as they rob a train and don't turn up again until they pull off another robbery. Do you want me to go out to the cabin with you?"

"That's not necessary. I'll find the loot if I have to turn the cabin, outbuildings and grounds upside down to do it."

Tayler nodded. "You know where to find me if you need me."

"Oh, one other thing, Sheriff. If my partner shows up, tell him where to find me. His name is Sandy Johnson."

Cole gave the sheriff directions to the cabin and then took his leave. He had no idea how long it would take to locate the money, but he sure as hell wasn't going to leave until he recovered every last dime.

Cole approached the cabin cautiously. The noises he'd heard earlier, before Cobb left, warned him that someone was inside. A close inspection of the outbuildings revealed a swaybacked mule in the lean-to, but no horses. He paused before the cabin door, his hand inches from his gun. He lifted the latch and pushed it open. At first glance the one tiny room appeared empty. Then he saw her, backed into a dim corner like a frightened doe.

The woman's waist-length black hair fell across her face in a wild tangle, obscuring her features. His mind spun dizzily as he stared at her. He was reminded of another woman with hair as black as midnight. A woman he'd loved more than his own life.

"Morning Mist . . ." The name slid past his lips like a caress. Speaking his beloved's name aloud jerked him back to reality. "Who are you? What are you doing here?"

The woman in the shadows seemed to collapse inwardly. Cole couldn't tell whether it was from relief or fear. He motioned her forward, but she remained firmly planted within the shadows.

"I'm not going to hurt you. Can't you talk? Who are you? What are you doing here?"

He heard her sigh, saw her straighten her shoulders. "I can speak. I thought you were Billy." Her voice was soft and breathy; the sound slid over him like warm honey.

"Come out where I can see you."

"Are you a friend of Billy's? I haven't seen you before. Billy's not here."

"I know he's not here. You can rest assured I am no friend of Billy Cobb's. Are you his woman?"

She hesitated. "I'm his wife."

Cole let loose a string of oaths. Cobb had had a wife! If that didn't beat all. He supposed it was up to him to tell her he'd just killed her husband. He hoped she didn't go all hysterical on him, for he doubted he could deal with it.

The woman stepped out from the shadows; her face was all but hidden behind the thick black veil of her hair. "Are you the law?"

"In a manner of speaking. What is your name?"

"Dawn. Are you going to take Billy to jail?" She looked small and defeated, and Cole felt a pang of pity for the woman. He'd pity any woman who'd had to put up with a man like Cobb.

Though he could see little of her face, Cole was captivated by the rare smoky quality of her husky voice. He shook himself free of its enchantment.

"There is no way to soften this, Mrs. Cobb. Your husband is dead."

Dawn's head shot up, giving Cole the full benefit of her vivid blue eyes . . . and his first glimpse of her battered face. He exhaled sharply. Both of her eyes were black, and the high ridges of her cheekbones bore purple bruises. Her swollen, split lips still oozed blood.

"Don't call me Mrs. Cobb! I hate the name."

"Son of a bitch! Did Cobb do that to you? He died too easily," Cole said fiercely. "You need a doctor."

Dawn shook her head. "No, I'll heal. I always have before. Are you sure Billy is dead?" Her voice trembled with burgeoning hope.

"By now he's planted in Boot Hill. I took his body to the undertaker myself."

"Who killed him?"

Cole flinched. Did she love a bastard like Cobb? Obviously, this wasn't the first beating he'd given her. What made a woman stay with a man like that?

"I did. I'm sorry. I didn't mean to kill him. I would have preferred him alive."

Dawn gave him a mirthless laugh. "Don't be sorry. I'm glad." Deep inside she was more than glad. She was quietly, joyfully grateful. Her eyes glinted with a fierceness that bordered on madness. "The man was a vile beast, I hated him!" Her painfully thin body was taut with pent-up emotion, and something else.

Elation.

"Why did you marry a man you hated?"

"My father sold me to Cobb five years ago. The

17

only way Pa would let Cobb have me was if he married me."

"Had you no choice in the matter?"

"In case you haven't noticed, mister, I'm a half-breed. Indians don't have much choice these days."

"What about your mother? Couldn't you go back to her people?"

"My mother is dead. She was Sioux. Crow warriors captured her in a raid and eventually sold her to my father. She was his squaw; he never married her. I know nothing about Indians except for the Sioux tongue, which my mother taught me."

"Why did Cobb beat you? Obviously, it's not the first time."

Dawn stiffened. "I don't wish to talk about it. Why are you here?"

She moved away from the corner. Cole noted her stiffness and wondered if Cobb had beaten her about the body as well as the face.

"My name is Cole Webster. I work for the railroad. A few days ago your husband's gang robbed the Union Pacific somewhere between Dodge City and Garden City. A great deal of money was taken. I tracked Cobb to this cabin in hopes of recovering the loot. I saw him leave the cabin earlier today and followed. There was an exchange of shots. Cobb was killed but he didn't have the loot with him. I've come back to search for it. Do you know anything about the missing money? We're pretty sure Cobb carried it away when the gang split up."

Dawn's expressive blue eyes slid away from Cole. "Billy never told me anything. I was merely his slave. I cooked and cleaned and served as his punching bag."

"And warmed his bed," Cole added with a hint of sarcasm. The moment the words left his lips, Cole wished them back. He gazed into Dawn's haunted eyes and saw bleak despair. He had no cause to remind a woman of her husband's brutality in bed or out of it. Her battered face was visual proof of her suffering.

Dawn regarded Cole through hollow eyes. Then, sullen and uncommunicative, she turned away.

Cole studied Dawn through narrowed lids. Her shoulder bones made sharp ridges beneath the bodice of her faded, far-too-large dress. He could see no visible indication of waist or hips beneath the shapeless garment. Only the telltale rise of firm, rounded breasts gave hint of the womanly form beneath the worn fabric.

Dawn flushed beneath Cole's scrutiny. She knew he thought her a scrawny excuse for a woman, but she didn't care. The less she had to do with men, the better she liked it. She was fiercely glad that Cobb was dead; she had thought of killing him herself many times during the past five years. She was grateful to this man for doing what she had feared doing herself, but the sooner he left, the better. As for the money. . . . it was hers. Billy owed her for all she'd had to endure as his wife. The money would help her to forge a new life for herself.

"Are you sure you know nothing about the train loot?" Cole repeated sharply.

"Billy didn't confide in me."

She was lying. Cole knew it. Yet he couldn't

fault her for wanting the money for herself. Lord knows she deserved it. But he had a job and was honor bound to perform it to the best of his ability. Compassion had no place in the life he lived. At one time it might have, but losing Morning Mist had changed him forever.

Cole pulled out a rickety chair, one of two that rested on uneven legs beside the scarred kitchen table. "Sit down, Mrs.—er—Dawn. I think you know more than you're willing to reveal. Keeping that money is a crime even if you didn't participate in the robbery."

Dawn sidled around him warily and perched on the edge of the chair Cole indicated. "I told you, Billy didn't confide in me."

"Did you know about the train robbery?"

She looked up at him, studying him just as he had studied her a few minutes before. She had never before seen a man with hair the color of his. He was tall and strongly built. Though he was a White man, his skin was almost the same creamy tan as hers. Obviously, he was no stranger to the sun. Nor to vigorous exercise, judging from the well-developed muscles of his legs and torso.

The taut width of his shoulders stretched the material of his plaid shirt, and his snug-fitting tan pants emphasized the solid muscular thickness of his long legs. A silk neckerchief, leather vest and scuffed boots completed the blatant display of masculinity that would have impressed any other woman but Dawn.

"I asked you a question, Dawn," Cole said harshly. "Did you know about the train robbery?"

Dawn nodded jerkily. She moistened her

bruised lips with the tip of her tongue, reminding Cole that she was hurt, possibly more than he realized. Only a heartless bastard would interrogate an injured woman, and he hadn't fallen that low yet.

"Do you have some salve in the cabin?" he asked. "Your face needs tending."

Dawn gave him a look that spoke eloquently of her distrust of him. "Why do you care? Billy never did."

Cole swore with enough venom to make Dawn recoil in fear. "I'm not Cobb. I told you I wouldn't hurt you and I meant it. Where's that salve?"

Beyond speech, Dawn pointed to the cupboard. Cole reached it in two strides, found a round jar of salve inside and little else. He opened cupboard after cupboard and found nothing in the way of food, nothing edible at all. With difficulty he contained his anger. It wasn't his custom to frighten helpless women. The girl had been brutalized and abused, making her distrustful of all males. If the lack of food in the house was any indication, Dawn had been starved as well as beaten. Dimly he wondered if Cobb's gang had used her sexually. He thought they had.

Cole returned with the salve and set it down on the table. "Is there water in the cabin?" Dawn nodded toward a bucket on the dry sink. "What about clean cloths?"

"In the drawer. You don't need to bother, I can do for myself. I always have."

"Just shut up and sit still." Dipping the cloth in the water, Cole gently bathed Dawn's face, surprised at the dirt accumulated there. When the

21

grime came away, he discovered a smooth golden complexion that promised to be without blemish once the bruises healed. He carefully dabbed at the drops of blood gathered at the corners of her split lips, and when she flinched he had the unaccountable urge to kiss the hurt away.

Dawn squirmed uncomfortably beneath Cole's gentle ministrations. Never had a man touched her with such tenderness or caring. Of course, she knew why he was doing it. He wanted the stolen money and would go to any lengths to recover it, even to treating a no-account half-breed with kindness and consideration, something she'd never had from any man.

Cole dipped his fingers into the jar of salve and spread it over her bruises. The hardness of his expression and the cold calm with which he performed the chore did nothing to ease Dawn's nervousness. She thought Cole was much too controlled, too tautly coiled, and waited for the explosion.

Cole worked quietly beneath the skewering intensity of Dawn's blue eyes. Conflicting emotions warred within him. He felt pity, compassion and, surprisingly, admiration. He strongly suspected that Dawn was lying about her knowledge of the train robbery and where the money was hidden. If she refused to tell him where it was, he'd be obliged to conduct a thorough search of the premises despite her objections.

Cole stood back and regarded Dawn solemnly. "There. If the salve works, your face will be as good as new in a few days. Why did Cobb beat you?"

"You wouldn't understand."

"Try me."

She shook her head, spreading a curtain of tangled black silk around her back and shoulders. Cole appeared mesmerized, reminded once again of his beloved Morning Mist. Dimly he wondered if Dawn would turn out to be the beauty he suspected her to be. The facial bones beneath the bruises and swelling were good. Her cheekbones were high and cleanly defined, her blue eyes exceptionally clear and bright, and her lashes were so long and thick he was amazed that she could hold them up. He wrinkled his nose, thinking a little soap and water would do wonders for her appearance.

"Very well. I'll let that go for the time being, since you're so reluctant to talk about it. It's getting late. If you're up to it, perhaps you can fix us something to eat. Tomorrow I'll start searching for the money in earnest. Unless," he said, regarding her solemnly, "you save us both a lot of trouble and tell me where it's hidden."

"I told you, Billy . . ."

". . . Didn't confide in you. I know. Very well, have it your way. What about that grub?"

"I . . . there's not . . ." She gave an eloquent shrug and refused to meet his eyes.

"I think I already know what you're trying to say. There's no food in the cabin, is there? Cobb rode away without a thought for your welfare. Look at you. You're skinny as a rail. How did you feed yourself during his absences?"

Dawn wondered herself. It hadn't been easy. Between Billy's irregular visits she'd had to fend for herself. He never left any money, so it would have been pointless to go into town. After a time she'd realized that Billy left her penniless for a purpose. He didn't want her wandering around the countryside raising suspicion and alerting the law. He usually brought food with him when he returned, and that had helped.

"I fish, and I trap small game when I can. Usually Billy brings food with him, but this time he arrived empty-handed. He couldn't afford to go into town after pulling off robberies for fear of being recognized."

"There's food in my saddlebags. I'll bring in what I have, and you can put something together for us. It's not much, but it will keep us until I can bring supplies back from town."

"Don't bother. You won't be here that long. There's no money hidden here. Billy must have given it to one of his gang for safekeeping."

Cole snorted in derision. "You know Billy better than that. The loot is here, Dawn, I'd stake my life on it." He left the cabin, still chuckling to himself.

Dawn rose stiffly from the chair. Her back hurt dreadfully from the strapping Billy had given her. He had tried again to be a man with her without success. It was always the same. Nothing had changed during the five years of their marriage. Instead of placing the blame on the injury he had received during a bank robbery before they were married, he accused Dawn of not being woman enough to arouse him. The results were unmentionably vile. He assuaged his lust by pummeling her with his fists, and when he tired of that, he removed his belt and used it on her back and buttocks until he grew bored with the sport.

Thank God Billy rarely returned to the hideout, Dawn thought as she measured out the last bit of coffee in the can, poured it into the iron coffeepot, and fired up the stove with the last of the firewood.

The one luxury in the tiny cabin was the cookstove, and Dawn constantly blessed the previous owners for leaving it behind. It provided welcome warmth in the winter when wind-driven snow blasted through the cracks in the walls and shuttered windows.

Cole returned with a knapsack and placed it on the dry sink. "It's not much. A few potatoes, an onion, bacon and beans. I think there's a bit of flour and sugar, too. Can you manage?"

Dawn laughed without humor. "It's far more than I'm accustomed to."

Cole turned away, unable to hide the pity he felt for her. "I need to tend to my horse. I'll put him in the lean-to with your mule. Is there hay inside for Warrior?"

"There's plenty of hay. Billy treated his animals better than he did me."

Cole grunted, oddly distressed by the picture her words conjured. What had the bastard done to her besides use her for a punching bag? he wondered as he left the cabin. What had he allowed his men to do? Dawn was as skittish as a young colt, distrustful of men and hurt in ways few people would understand. She was like a fragile, broken doll, her spirit destroyed and her soul injured beyond repair.

Dawn knew what Cole was thinking but didn't care. Let him think she was helpless; it served her purpose. Let him believe she was broken in spirit and sick at heart. She'd have the last laugh when she left here with the money Billy had stolen. After Billy's vicious beating today, Dawn realized she couldn't continue like this. She had spied on him when he hid the train loot the day he'd arrived at the cabin, and prayed for him to leave on some errand or other so she could retrieve it and run away.

Unfortunately, Billy's hand had been heavier than usual and it had taken her longer this time to recover from his beating. By the time she'd roused herself from her stupor, Cole Webster had arrived and temporarily put her plans on hold. It was imperative now that she get rid of the lawman before the members of Cobb's gang arrived for their share of the loot.

Dawn worked efficiently and silently, using the ingredients Cole had provided for their meal. She fried the bacon and used the grease to fry together the potatoes and onion. There was enough flour for a batch of biscuits, and she shoved them into the oven to bake. Supper was on the table by the time Cole walked through the door. They ate in silence, each consumed with their own thoughts.

"That was good," Cole said, leaning back and draining the last of his coffee.

"Thank you," Dawn said as she sopped up a bit of grease with her biscuit and popped it into her mouth. One biscuit remained on the plate and she eyed it hungrily. But she'd been conditioned by Cobb not to take anything he might want for himself. Sometimes he made her watch him eat just to humiliate her for her failure to please him sexually.

Cole saw the direction of her gaze and swallowed the lump of pity forming in his throat. "I couldn't manage another bite. Go ahead and eat that last biscuit. I'll ride into Dodge for supplies first thing in the morning. Look for me around lunchtime."

Dawn nodded agreement. Pride was for fools to indulge in, and she was no fool. She was a survivor. She would survive long after Cole was gone. And she'd have money to buy all the food she could eat.

"I have no money to pay for food," Dawn said, licking the last bit of crumbs from her fingers.

Cole's body reacted in a way he'd never expected at the sight of Dawn's pink tongue lapping over and between her fingers until she'd cleaned them of every last crumb. He shifted uncomfortably and tried not to think of all the other things she could do with her tongue. The girl was an outlaw's woman, for God's sake. Willing or not, she had lain with Cobb and God only knew how many others. She'd lied about the money, and for all he knew she was as much a part of the gang as the other members.

"Did I ask for money? I don't expect you to provide my food while I'm here. Your cupboards are bare, you can't even feed yourself. Of course," he hinted, "you could save us all a lot of trouble if you would show me where Cobb hid the money."

"I'd tell you if I knew," Dawn said, giving him a sullen glare. "Go ahead and search, you'll find nothing. Why don't you leave now? Searching is a waste of time."

"Nice try, Dawn, but it won't work. I have a keen sense about these things, and my gut tells me the money is here. I'm being paid to recover that money, and I'm damn well going to do it. It would be a lot easier on both of us if you cooperated. You have no reason to remain loyal to Cobb after what he did to you. What do you plan to do, turn the loot over to the gang members after taking Cobb's share for yourself?"

No, I'm going to keep all of it, Dawn thought fiercely. Aloud, she asked, "How long do you intend to remain here?"

"For as long as it takes." He turned toward the door. "I'll bed down in the shed. Good night, Dawn."

Dawn watched Cole leave, the corners of her mouth turned downward into a scowl. Just when something good happened to her, that brash railroad man had to show up and spoil everything. For five long, desperate years she'd prayed for Cobb's death. Twice she had tried to run away and twice she'd been dragged back and beaten until she couldn't walk. Now that she had the opportunity and means to leave this vile place of pain and humiliation, Cole Webster was going to take it all away from her.

Dawn paced the cramped confines of the cabin, too nervous to sleep, too restless to remain cooped up. The night was exceptionally balmy, the moon bright and inviting. She knew the river would be warm and soothing on her abraded back and buttocks, and on the spur of the moment she decided to slip out and bathe. During the times Cobb used the cabin as a hideout, Dawn deliberately made herself appear unappealing to her husband and his cohorts. She would let days go by without combing her hair, changing her clothes or washing. Only when Cobb was gone did she groom herself with any care, not that it mattered. She rarely saw another living being during Cobb's absences.

Dawn found a ragged piece of linen, a sliver of soap and a clean dress only slightly less threadbare than the one she wore. Cobb wasn't one to spend his money on unnecessary fripperies. She slipped barefoot through the front door and followed the well-trodden path to the river.

Cole awoke with a start. Trained by the Sioux to hear a twig snap even in sleep, he peered through the darkness for the source of the almost silent footsteps. He saw a wraithlike figure heading toward the river, and alarm bells went off in his head. Rising as quietly as a shadow, he followed noiselessly.

Chapter Two

Dawn stood on the sloping riverbank, pausing in a rare moment of delight as a million silvery moonbeams danced upon the water's dark surface. It was so seldom that anything in this life gave her joy that she savored the unique feeling. Had she a romantic soul she would have said that this was a night for lovers. The air was warm and humid, scented with the aroma of prairie flowers.

But Dawn had never believed in fairy tales. Happiness didn't exist in this life, and love was for dreamers. Only fools dared to dream. Since Dawn was a half-breed and the wife of a brutal outlaw, she couldn't afford to indulge in fantasies. Sighing with visible regret, Dawn cleared her mind of foolish thoughts and pulled her baggy dress over her head. She wore nothing underneath.

Cole hovered discreetly behind a clump of

bushes, watching, waiting, convinced that Dawn intended to retrieve the train robbery money from its hiding place and disappear into the star-studded night. His lungs emptied harshly when he saw her pull off her ragged garment and toss it aside. She was naked.

Poised on the sloping bank, Dawn raised her face to the moon. Cole tried to look away but couldn't. She was thin, too thin. He hadn't realized that she was so fine-boned, so delicate. Her back was long and shapely, her buttocks taut and . . . His gaze jerked back up to her back, then down again to her buttocks. Sweet Lord! Her back and buttocks were scored with raw welts. Earlier Cole had speculated on whether Cobb had abused Dawn's body as well as her face, and now he knew.

Suddenly Dawn turned slightly, providing Cole with a tantalizing view of her breasts. He sucked his breath in sharply. They were perfect. Round, lush and golden, with nipples the color of dark honey. They tilted impudently upward, delicious and tempting. Cole's mouth went dry and he turned away. When he looked back, Dawn had waded into the water and was rubbing herself briskly with soap. He could see the lather bubbling on her skin and imagined himself rinsing it off her sweet body with his hands.

Cole's eyes turned a predatory green as he watched Dawn wash and rinse her long black hair, fascinated by the graceful arching of her body. His own body hardened and he stifled a groan as she waded to shore and rubbed herself dry with a scrap of cloth. His disappointment was keen when she donned a clean dress and traced her steps back to the cabin. He didn't follow until much later, after he'd taken a dip in the bracing water to cool his heated flesh.

Who would have thought a skinny, abused wretch, a liar and possibly a thief, could make him feel things he hadn't felt since Morning Mist's death? He shook his head to clear it of Dawn's image. He had lived too long with the memory of his dead wife to replace it with that of another woman.

An outlaw's wife.

Cole made his way slowly back to the shed and went to bed, but for some reason sleep eluded him. His mind kept returning to the river and the golden, shimmering figure with perfect breasts poised upon the bank. The sight of her whip-lashed flesh had angered him to the point of violence. It made him wish he could bring Billy Cobb back to life and tear him limb from limb, slowly, inflicting great pain.

Cole slipped from his bedroll just as dawn kissed the sky, and rode to Dodge. His first stop in town was the grocery store. He was waiting outside the door when it opened at eight. After placing his order, he went to the livery stable to retrieve Cobb's horse. He figured Dawn needed it more than he did. He left Dodge a few hours later with two gunnysacks bulging with supplies slung over the withers of Cobb's horse. Since he wouldn't have time to hunt, he had purchased salted and cured meats as well as dried and canned foodstuffs, flour, sugar, salt and coffee. Enough to last two weeks.

Cole didn't want to concern himself with Dawn's

future, or wonder what would become of her after he left. It wasn't his worry, he told himself, that Dawn had no money, no family, nothing. He decided to treat this assignment like any other he'd worked on. Once he recovered the stolen money, he'd forget that Dawn had ever existed.

Dawn slept later than she would have wished. When she finally roused from sleep, Cole was already gone and the sun was rising in the eastern sky. She had lain awake a long time last night, planning her escape with the train robbery money. She'd been overjoyed when Cole had said he was riding into Dodge this morning for supplies. With any luck he wouldn't return for several hours. In his absence she would have sufficient time to retrieve the money from its hiding place and light out of here on Old Betsy, the swaybacked mule that had carried her here five years ago as Billy's reluctant bride.

Using the last of the water in the bucket, Dawn washed her hands and face and cleaned her teeth. Still moving somewhat stiffly from the beating she'd received the day before, she walked outside into the sunshine. She paused on the doorstep, experiencing a moment of guilt. She knew that taking money that didn't belong to her was wrong, but she was desperate. She smiled in anticipation of her flight.

"Howdy, Dawn."

The smile melted from Dawn's face as she stared in horror at her unwelcome visitor. Duke Riley! She had hoped the other gang members wouldn't show up so soon. Duke grinned at her as he boldly approached the cabin.

"Hello, Duke. What brings you around?" Calm, stay calm, Dawn cautioned herself.

Duke Riley was young, no more than twenty-five, but as mean and ornery as any of the three outlaws who rode with Billy Cobb. He was tall, lean, and not too bad looking. He considered himself something of a ladies' man, and Dawn had always been wary of the hungry looks he gave her when Cobb wasn't watching.

"Where's Billy? Am I the first to arrive? Can't wait to get my hands on my share of the loot."

Dawn blanched. She had to get rid of Duke quickly or miss her chance to leave before Cole returned.

Dawn wiped her sweaty palms on her skirt and swallowed uneasily. "Billy is dead, Duke. He was ambushed by a lawman when he left the cabin yesterday."

Duke's expression turned ugly. "Dead! Shit! Where's the money? Cobb wasn't dumb. He must have hidden the money somewhere." His eyes narrowed on Dawn, his gaze sliding down her body with insulting intensity. "Be real good to me, and I'll see that you get Billy's share."

Dawn's mouth went dry. She wanted nothing to do with Duke Riley, or any other man. "I don't know about any money. Billy didn't confide in me."

Duke's eyes went murky. Closing the distance between them, he grasped Dawn's wrist and pulled her up against him. "Are you sure, darlin'? Damn sure?"

Dawn's chin rose defiantly. "I'm sure."

His voice was rough and low with implied promise. "If I give you a little lovin', will you remember where Cobb hid the money? You always did fancy me. I know I fancied you. I remember how Cobb always bragged about how hot you were. How you hollered and cried and dug bloody grooves down his back when he was rutting between your legs. He said you couldn't get enough, that you had to have it all night long. Hot damn!" He licked his lips. "I could use a little of that."

His hands settled on her waist, dragging her so close she could feel the hard ridge beneath his trousers.

"Let me go!"

"Not on your life." His mouth jammed down hard on hers. When he tried to push his tongue into her mouth, she bit down hard on it. "Ow, you little bitch! Don't play hard to get with me. Your man's dead. You got no one to take care of you. You ain't no beauty. It ain't gonna be easy findin' another man.

"Look at you." His gaze slid over her with barely concealed disgust. "Look at your face. You're a mess. Why did Billy beat you? Be good to me and I'll be good to you. Let's go back inside. The ground's a mite hard for what I got in mind."

Dawn resisted vigorously, finally pulling free. "If I'm no beauty, why do you even bother with me? There are plenty of willing women in Dodge. I thought you came for your money. You can't find it doing what you have in mind."

"You can stop pretending. You know I want you. You've been teasing me for years, parading around in them baggy clothes, making me guess what you got underneath besides those sweet little titties. I'm gonna have you, lady. And I want you wild beneath me, just like you were with Billy. But you're right, it will keep. After I find that train loot we'll spread it out on the bed and roll around on it while we have us a good old time."

Dawn was too grateful for the reprieve to say anything. She needed time to think. No man was going to make a victim of her again, she thought fiercely. She'd kill Duke Riley before she'd let him use her. Billy Cobb was dead. She had earned her freedom. The shackles binding her to a life of pain and degradation had been severed forever. Something had snapped inside her during Billy's last beating. If Cole Webster hadn't killed Billy, she would have done it herself.

"Go fix us some grub. I rode all night to get here. Had to make sure the law wasn't following me. Billy always kept the loot until we could meet back here and divide it. Claimed he'd found a hiding place for it close to the cabin." He glanced around him, saw the shed and smiled. "I'll start with that shed over yonder. Call me when the grub's ready."

Dawn knew with a certainty that Duke would not find the sack of money in the shed. She knew where Billy had hidden it, and it was where no one could find it.

While Dawn sliced bacon, put beans on to cook and made biscuits with the last of the flour, she worried that the handsome lawman would return and, unsuspecting, walk into a dangerous situation. Unfortunately, there was no way to warn Cole. He could return at any time. Knowing Duke as she did, he wouldn't leave until he found the money, and that frightened Dawn. Cole could be walking right into a trap.

Dawn was faced with a dilemma. Should she lead Duke to the money so he'd leave before Cole returned? Would telling him make any difference in what he intended where she was concerned? The answer to that was a resounding no. She'd recognized the look in Duke's eyes. He meant to have her whether he found the money or not. And without the money, Dawn had nothing. She'd be forced to seek work in a brothel. Whenever Billy was displeased with her, he'd threatened to sell her to a madam he knew in Garden City.

Suddenly the door crashed open and Duke stormed inside. "I tore that damn shed apart and didn't find a thing. Is the grub ready? I'm starving."

Dawn nodded jerkily and started to turn away. Duke stopped her, grasping her roughly by the shoulders. He gave her a slow smile. "You look mighty fetching today, Dawn. Don't recollect ever seeing you look so pretty."

Dawn flushed, sorry now that she'd bathed the dirt and grime away last night in the river. Her midnight black hair spilled straight and thick down her slender back and over her narrow shoulders. Her cornflower blue eyes were as large as saucers in her bruised face. But Duke's gaze did not linger on her face. They fastened greedily on her breasts.

Dawn gasped and spun away when Duke brought his hand to her breast and squeezed. "I thought you were hungry."

He leered at her. "I am. Food first, then I'll satisfy my other appetite. Loosen up, Dawn. I know you want me. Women always want me."

Dawn wanted to gag. His vile touch sickened her. The only good thing she could say about Billy was that while he was alive he had kept his men from her. Without Billy's protection, Dawn realized she'd be fair game to every outlaw in the territory. She needed the train robbery money to get as far away from here as possible. If she felt any guilt over taking the money, it disappeared when she considered her alternatives. Working in a brothel or scrubbing floors in a saloon. Either way she'd end up on her back, spreading her legs for strangers.

With trembling hands Dawn set the food down on the table and took a seat opposite Duke.

"Where's the coffee?" Duke growled.

"There isn't any."

"Water, then."

Dawn stood up in a rush. "The bucket is empty. I'll go down to the river and fetch us some."

Duke lashed her with a narrow-eyed look of disdain. "I ain't no fool. Once you get down to the river you'll keep going. Sit down and eat, I can do without."

Dawn sat back down, swallowing her disappointment but little else. The lump of food that lodged in her throat grew bigger and bigger. She finally summoned the strength to swallow but gave up trying to eat. She watched with barely concealed contempt as Duke wolfed down his portion of the food.

"Ain't you hungry?" Dawn shook her head. Duke

reached over and emptied the contents of her plate into his. "I am," he mumbled around a mouthful of beans.

Duke ate fast and without manners, not that Dawn expected any from the crude outlaw. When every last scrap of food had been consumed, Duke sat back and gave a loud burp.

"That's better. I feel like I could hump all day and night now. I wouldn't want to disappoint you after all Cobb told me about your stamina in bed." He rose abruptly, grasped her arm and pulled her to her feet. "Come on, honey, let's give that corn-husk mattress a try. I'm as horny as a billy goat."

Dawn wanted to scream, but she knew that no one would hear her in this isolated place. Fear was her enemy; she couldn't allow herself to succumb to it. She had to be on guard every minute. Men liked to hurt women, and if Duke knew she was afraid of him, he would use that knowledge to inflict even more pain.

Dawn felt like a rabbit caught in a trap as Duke dragged her to the cornhusk mattress in the corner and shoved her down. She landed on her back so hard the air exploded from her chest. Before she could catch her breath, Duke fell on top of her and shoved her dress up to her waist. Dawn struggled fiercely, to no avail. Duke was a strong man, too strong for her frail resistance.

"I like it when you fight me, honey," Duke said hoarsely. He shifted between her legs, and Dawn cried out as his gun dug painfully into her hip. He hadn't bothered to remove either his gunbelt or spurs, unconcerned about the damage they could inflict upon her tender flesh.

Something snapped inside Dawn. She'd been a victim of men's depravities once too often and she'd die before letting it happen again. The moment she felt the cold metal of Duke's guns biting into her flesh, she knew what she had to do to save herself. She grasped his gunbelt, trying to find the butt of his pistol. Duke mistook her desperate groping for impatience and gave her a leering grin.

"Hang on, honey, you're gonna get all the humpin' you can handle just as soon as I get these damn pants unbuttoned." Straddling her hips, he raised himself up on his haunches and fumbled clumsily with the opening of his trousers.

Her face pale beneath the yellowing bruises, Dawn acted with a determination born of desperation. While both Duke's hands were occupied, she found the butt of his pistol, pulled it free of the holster and aimed it at him.

"What the hell! Give me that. You shouldn't play around with a man's guns. No wonder Billy enjoyed beating you. When I'm through with you I'm gonna put bruises in places Cobb never thought of."

He grabbed for the gun at the same time that Dawn fired.

Cole was a few hundred yards from the cabin when he heard a single gunshot. The blood froze in his veins. Strangely, he wasn't worried for himself. It was Dawn he worried about. He hadn't noticed a gun in the cabin, but he supposed there could have been one hidden somewhere beyond his notice. His gut told him something was wrong, and he spurred Warrior forward. Cobb's horse, laden with supplies, followed close behind.

Cole saw a horse tethered to the stunted tree in the front yard, and alarm bells went off in his head. Dawn was in danger, he knew it! He cursed himself for leaving her alone. Leaping from his mount, he approached the cabin with both guns drawn. He wasted no time in preliminaries as he kicked open the door and stormed inside. The sight he encountered made his blood run cold.

Dawn lay supine on the cornhusk mattress in the corner, her legs spread obscenely and a man lying between them. He saw no movement from either occupant of the bed, and that frightened him. Who was the man and what had he done to Dawn? Willing his feet into motion, he reached the bed in three long strides.

Dawn's eyes were closed. A smoking gun lay beside the tangled bodies. Then he saw the blood and went wild.

Shoving his guns into his belt, he grasped the man by the shoulders and tossed him aside like a rag doll. Then he began tearing off Dawn's clothing, searching for a wound.

Dawn clutched the torn material to her breast, opened her mouth and screamed. "Don't, please don't!"

"Dawn, it's me, Cole. I'm not going to harm you. Where are you hurt?" His hands shook as he rid Dawn of her dress.

Dawn's eyes opened slowly, so grateful to see Cole that she clutched his shirtfront and refused to let go. "He was trying to . . . He wanted to . . ." She couldn't go on.

41

Cole had only one thought. "Where did the bastard shoot you? Are you in pain?"

Dawn swallowed several times before she could speak. "He . . . he didn't shoot me, I shot him. Is he dead?"

"The blood . . ."

"It's Duke's blood. I couldn't let him . . . do that to me. Oh, God, I shot a man. Did I kill him?"

Cole sent a quick glance at Duke, saw that he was writhing on the floor, and decided the bastard was very much alive. "It's all right, sweetheart, he's not dead. Don't trouble yourself over it." Before he realized what he was doing, he pressed a kiss to her forehead. Then he pulled the blanket over her shivering form and turned his hard-eyed gaze to the man who had tried to hurt her. "What are you doing here?"

Duke stared at Cole through pain-misted eyes. "The bitch shot me. I'm bleeding. Get me to a doctor before I die."

Cole dropped to his haunches and probed the wound high up on Duke's shoulder. "It's not life-threatening, more's the pity. The bullet shattered your collarbone. I would have aimed lower." Duke screeched and passed out. Satisfied that the man was in no danger of dying, Cole returned his attention to Dawn.

"Are you all right, Dawn? I shouldn't have left you alone. Who is that man?"

"His name is Duke Riley. He's one of Billy's men. He's come for his share of the money."

"And a share of you, unless I misjudged the situation. Why did you shoot him? Didn't you like

42

the way he was pleasuring you?" The moment he spoke, he wished he could call back the words. Dawn didn't look at all like she had enjoyed being mauled by Duke. She looked terrified. How many times in the past had Duke assaulted her with Cobb's approval? he wondered bitterly.

"Bastard!" Dawn hissed from between clenched teeth. "You have no right to judge me when you know nothing about me or my situation. You're just like the others."

Cole felt like a callous bastard. No one had the right to condemn Dawn for things she had no control over. "I'm sorry, I had no call to say what I did. Obviously, the man was hurting you, otherwise you wouldn't have shot him. Did he . . . ?"

"No. I shot him before he could finish what he started."

Duke started to moan and whimper, and Cole spit out a curse. "I'll get the bastard out of here so you can get dressed."

"What are you going to do with him?"

"Tie him up and lock him in the shed. He'll keep until I take him to town tomorrow. That's two down and two more gang members on the loose to worry about. One by one they'll turn up here for their money. Did Riley have time to search for the loot?"

Dawn nodded. "He tore the shed apart but found nothing."

He sent her an oblique look. "Why didn't you tell him where to find it?"

"I wouldn't tell him even if I knew."

Cole let that remark pass. Intuition told him that Dawn knew exactly where to find the money.

"What happens when the others show up for their share of the money, Dawn? I might not be here to protect you."

"I don't need you. I handled Duke just fine by myself."

"You were lucky. You might not be the next time."

"I'll manage."

Deciding not to push the issue, Cole prodded Duke to his feet and herded him out the door. Once Cole was gone, Dawn's bravado fled. She had never shot a man before, never even held a gun in her hand. What if she had killed Duke? Not that the low-down snake didn't deserve to die after what he had tried to do to her. Still shaking over her close call, Dawn rose and searched for something to wear.

The blood-stained dress Cole had ripped from her was beyond repair. She owned only one other dress and she couldn't bear the feel of the filthy garment she had worn yesterday, and many days before that, against her clean skin. She did the next best thing. She found a clean pair of trousers and plaid shirt in Billy's trunk. Even after she'd tucked the shirt into the waistband of the trousers, they were in danger of sliding down her narrow hips.

Cole returned, saw Dawn holding up her trousers with a bewildered look on her face, and gave a hoot of laughter. "Is that the best you could do?"

Dawn's chin lifted fractionally. "It's better than running around in the raw."

Cole's eyes sparkled mischievously. "In your opinion, maybe."

Dawn fumed in silent rage. "If you were a gentleman you'd find me a belt to hold up my trousers."

There was laughter in his voice. "Pardon me for forgetting I'm a gentleman." Casting around for a solution, Cole spied a rope hanging from a hook. He retrieved it handily and presented it to Dawn with a flourish.

Dawn seized the rope, threaded it through the belt loops and pulled the ends into a tight knot. "Thank you."

"Now that you're decent, tell me about Duke Riley. Has he always ridden with Cobb? Have you and he . . . never mind, it's none of my business. Just tell me what you know about the man."

Dawn shrugged and started clearing off the table. "Duke is one of Billy's gang. Other than that I don't know a thing about him. He hails from Oklahoma, I think."

"How thoroughly did he search the shed?"

"He said he tore it apart."

"It would be easier for both of us if you'd just tell me where to find the money. Sooner or later I'll find it, you know."

Dawn remained stubbornly mute.

"Very well, have it your way." He headed out the door.

"Where are you going?" It wasn't as if Dawn wanted him to stay, she told herself. She just felt safe with Cole nearby.

"To unload the supplies. I brought Cobb's horse back with me. If you don't want him you can sell him. He's a good animal, should bring a good price."

Cole was still unloading the supplies when Dawn walked outside with a bucket in her hand. She started down the river path. "Where in the hell do you think you're going?"

Dawn didn't even spare him a glance. "I need water."

He easily caught up with her. "I don't want you wandering away by yourself. What if Sam Pickens or Spider Lewis show up for their share of the loot and catch you alone? Will they be any more 'gentle' with you than Riley? Is that the kind of man you want for a protector?"

"I don't need a protector. I can take care of myself. I just proved it with Duke, didn't I?"

Cole stared at her, at her bruised face, so proud and defiant, at the stubborn set of her narrow shoulders, almost too slender to carry the burden she had borne during her years with Billy Cobb, and he felt something stir inside him. Undeniably she had suffered. Yet despite Cole's original assumption about Dawn's character, Cobb had definitely not broken her spirit. Bent it, perhaps, but not shattered it. The little half-breed had more spunk than he'd given her credit for. The very idea of Dawn suffering Cobb's abuse over the course of five years made him cringe inwardly.

"Very well, if you're not back in ten minutes I'm coming after you."

Dawn set out at a leisurely pace for the river, determined to show Cole Webster that she had a mind of her own. Nevertheless, she was back at the cabin within the time allotted her. She walked through the door to find Cole pulling up floorboards with a crowbar.

"What are you doing? You're wrecking my home."

"This wouldn't be necessary if you'd tell me where Cobb hid the money," Cole said, grunting from the effort of prying up a particularly stubborn floorboard.

"It's not in the cabin."

"How do you know?"

"Because Billy made sure I never watched when he hid the loot from his robberies. He always made me stay inside the cabin. I can truthfully say you won't find the money here."

Cole searched her face and realized she was telling the truth, at least about this. "Dammit! I've already questioned Riley, and he swore he hadn't found it in the shed. Did Cobb bury it outside? What about the lean-to? You must have some idea where to find it."

Dawn's lips flattened. "I can tell you nothing."

Cole's eyes went murky as he tossed the crowbar aside and grasped Dawn, bringing them nose to nose. "Why don't you trust me? I'm not going to hurt you."

Dawn went still as she stared into the brilliant emerald of his eyes. She felt the caress of his breath upon her cheek and was moved by the strangest temptation to touch his lips with hers. *To just touch him*. Her fingers tingled. Her palms itched.

Cole must have felt the same urge, for his arms tightened around her, bringing her hard against him. His gaze fastened hungrily on the soft pads of her bruised lips. They were lush and red and parted, as if waiting in anticipation of his next move. Lured by the misleading innocence of her blue-eyed gaze, Cole sensed the depth of her yearning, felt her reach out to him in mute appeal, and reacted instinctively. He tasted the sweet corners of her mouth, tempted her lips apart. His tongue slid inside, rasping against skin as slick as satin. Then he gently sucked on her pouting lower lip before tasting her more deeply.

Cole shuddered. He couldn't recall how long it had been since he'd held a woman in his arms, and his body responded powerfully. The heat of her breasts, belly and thighs scorched him, and he groaned low in his throat.

Dawn closed her eyes, forcefully moved by the intimacy of his touch. No one had ever touched her with such tenderness and warmth. She felt helplessly ensnared as she was drawn into his kiss, savoring this brief moment of madness. Shameful excitement raced through her, drawing her into its sizzling heat until all rational thought fled.

Abruptly Cole tore his mouth away and stared at her, his expression a mixture of confusion and anger at his loss of control. He hadn't meant to take advantage of Dawn's vulnerability, but he hadn't been able to control himself.

"I'm sorry. I didn't mean to do that."

Cole had no idea what had possessed him to kiss Dawn. The way she had looked at him, all misty-eyed, her mouth soft and trembly, God, he'd hated to stop.

Dawn swallowed convulsively, suspended in some faraway place by his kiss. Had any man but Cole kissed her, she'd be reacting far differently. She'd suffered through Billy's clumsy kisses and brutal pawing by willing her mind to another place. Then Cole Webster walked into her life. After one kiss he made her yearn for impossible things, made her dream of tenderness and . . . love.

She stared at Cole through long, feathery lashes. The planes of his handsome face were taut with tension, and she could see a pulse beating hard and fast at the base of his throat.

Swallowing convulsively, she forced her mind to sweep away fantasy and confront reality.

Chapter Three

Dawn backed away from Cole, her eyes watchful as she touched her lips with her fingertips. "Why did you do that?"

"Kiss you?" Cole shrugged. "Because you wanted me to, I suppose. Why else would a man kiss a woman?"

"To hurt her!" Dawn blurted out. "And to humiliate her," she continued, remembering Billy's cruel kisses.

Cole went white beneath his tan. "Did Cobb and his friends kiss you because they wanted to hurt you?" He cursed violently. The more he learned about Billy Cobb, the more he wished his death had been a slow and painful one. "I can assure you I have no intention of hurting or humiliating you. I kissed you simply because I wanted to."

"Why?"

He touched her cheek, lightly skimming the vivid bruises marring her flesh. Her skin was warm and satiny beneath his fingertips. It was hard to believe that anyone so young could have survived five years of brutality and rape by Cobb and his men and still retain an air of innocence and vulnerability.

"Why did I want to?" He hesitated so long Dawn thought he wasn't going to answer. Then he said, "I suppose it's because you remind me of someone I cared about."

Dawn went still. Suddenly she recalled the name Cole had blurted out the first time he'd seen her. "Morning Mist," she said softly.

Cole went still. "How did you know?"

"You called me by her name the day you burst into the cabin. Who is she?"

Cole's expression was unreadable. "Morning Mist was my wife. She's dead."

"I'm sorry." She didn't know what else to say. Obviously, Cole Webster had loved his wife a great deal. What surprised her was the knowledge that Morning Mist was an Indian name. "Was Morning Mist an Indian?"

"Her father was Sioux, her mother was White."

She bit her lip, wanting to know more. "Did she—"

"We've discussed my life long enough, I'd rather hear about yours. Does your father live nearby? Can you go to him now that Cobb is dead?"

Dawn gave an inelegant snort. "I wouldn't go back even if he were still alive. He'd just sell me again to someone like Billy Cobb, or worse." She turned and began putting away the supplies Cole had just carried in.

"How old were you when Cobb married you?"

"Fifteen."

"Damn! The bastard was old enough to be your father. What kind of parent would sell his daughter to a man like Cobb?"

Dawn shrugged, trying to pretend it didn't matter that her father had cared so little for her. "After Mama died I was in the way. He brought another woman home. She didn't like me. I was a half-breed. Pa never married my mother. She was his squaw. When Billy offered to buy me, Pa agreed, as long as Billy married me first. In Pa's eyes that made everything all right."

"You said your mother was Sioux."

"She was. She was captured by a Crow raiding party when she was a young girl and sold to my father. Pa was a trapper. He needed a woman to see to his needs. Things weren't so bad when Mama was alive. She sent me to a government school for Indians on a nearby reservation. She tried to protect me from Pa's temper while she was alive. He didn't much like children."

"Sounds like a real bastard," Cole said sourly.

"After Mama died I kept house for Pa until he brought home another woman. Then he struck a deal with Billy. You know the rest."

"Not everything," Cole said softly. "Why did Cobb beat you? Did it happen often?"

Dawn flushed and looked away. She couldn't talk about the things Billy had done to her. They were too shameful. "He beat me when I . . . didn't . . . please him. Or when I made him angry. Don't

52

ask me anything else. I . . . I don't want to talk about it ever again."

"What are you going to do after I leave here? Where will you go? You can't stay here. Sooner or later the other two members of the gang are going to show up for their money."

"I'm not going to wait around for them to show up," Dawn declared.

"Do you have any money?" Cole knew the answer to that question even before he asked it. If Dawn had money of her own she wouldn't be wearing rags or starving half to death.

"Billy wasn't a generous man."

"There's a reward for both Cobb and Riley. I'll see that you get the money."

"No! I don't want your charity."

Cole gave a snort of disgust. "You should be able to find work in a brothel with little effort. Is that what you want?" Cole hated to be so blunt, but Dawn had to understand she couldn't survive on her own. She'd become prey to every predator in the area. She'd been forced to endure abuse from Billy and his cohorts, but now she was free of that kind of degradation.

The breath hissed from Dawn's lungs. "I'm no whore. My mother was my father's whore, and I know what it's like."

"I never said you were. I was just trying to talk some sense into you. Your options are limited. You're a woman, you're young, and you're a half-breed. How will you support yourself? You could find another husband, who will—"

"No! No man will ever touch me again. All men are beasts. Just go away and leave me alone."

Cole wished he could do just that. He was becoming too involved in Dawn's life. He shouldn't care what happened to her, he told himself. During all his years as a Pinkerton detective he'd never been moved to pity before. Yet he wouldn't call what he felt for Dawn pity. Certainly he felt compassion for her sad plight, but something about her moved him as he hadn't been moved in years. He wasn't sure he liked the feeling.

"I can't leave until I recover the money." He turned toward the door. "I'm going to search the lean-to. If the money isn't there, I'll dig up the yard until I find it."

"What are you going to do with Duke Riley?"

"Feed him, for now. His wound isn't serious. I'll take him into town tomorrow. This time you're coming with me."

"No, I . . ."

Her protest made little impact on Cole, who had gone without a backward glance.

Dawn watched Cole from the front door of the cabin as he literally tore apart the lean-to. When he failed to find the money, he grabbed a shovel and began digging randomly in the yard. By supper that night he was dirty, tired and out of sorts.

"I'm going down to the river to bathe," Cole said when Dawn called him in to supper. "Fix up a plate for Riley. I'll take it to him when I return. Don't go near him, he's a mean-mouthed bastard and not too happy right now."

Dawn had no intention of approaching Duke. After what he had tried to do to her, she couldn't stomach the sight of him.

For supper Dawn had fried slices of smoked ham, boiled up a pot of potatoes and opened a tin of peas. She used some of the dried apples Cole had purchased in town to bake an apple pie. Her mouth watered hungrily. She couldn't count the times she'd dreamed of eating food like this, but Billy had provided only bare essentials such as bacon and beans and potatoes. Vegetables consisted of dandelion greens she'd dug up in the yard. And fresh meat was unheard of unless she managed to trap a small animal.

Cole returned to the cabin in a foul mood. He picked up the plate Dawn had prepared for Duke and took it out to the shed without a word. He returned twenty minutes later with the empty plate. Dawn had dinner on the table. He sat down and dug in with gusto. His mood lifted when Dawn brought the pie to the table.

"I can't recall when I last had a piece of home-made pie," he said, sniffing appreciatively at the warm apples and cinnamon.

"Neither can I," Dawn said as she served them both generous slices.

Between them they finished off half the pie. Afterward, Cole offered to help with dishes. Dawn looked at him as if he'd just grown horns. No man had ever offered to help her with anything. She shook her head, too moved by his offer to speak. He helped anyway, drying while she washed.

"Think I'll turn in," Cole said, yawning hugely. "It's been a long day. I imagine you're tired, too." He headed for the door.

"Wait!"

"What?"

Dawn flushed. "I mean . . . You can bring your bedroll inside tonight if you'd like. The lean-to is all but destroyed, and I don't suppose you'd get much sleep in the shed with Duke. Besides, it looks like rain. You'll get soaked sleeping outside tonight."

"Am I hearing right?" The invitation nearly floored Cole. He knew how intensely Dawn distrusted men.

Dawn fidgeted restively. It was the first time she could recall asking a man for anything. Even when Cobb beat her she hadn't begged or pleaded with him to stop. "I don't want to be alone tonight. What if Duke frees himself? What if Sam or Spider show up tonight and you don't hear them?" She was being foolish, she knew, but couldn't seem to help herself.

Something stirred inside Cole. He didn't dare examine his feelings for fear of finding something he wasn't prepared to deal with. "You'd trust me inside the cabin with you?"

Her chin rose fractionally. "You haven't hurt me yet. I suppose I trust you as much as I trust any man."

Cole smiled thinly. "That's not saying a lot."

"Well, maybe I do trust you more than the others, but that doesn't mean I'm inviting liberties."

"Did I ask for any?"

"You kissed me."

"You wanted me to kiss you. I'm over thirty years old. I think I know when a woman wants to be kissed." He sighed raggedly. "Go to bed, Dawn. I'll check on Riley and get my bedroll. That should give you ample time to ready yourself for bed."

When Cole returned fifteen minutes later, Dawn had scrambled into a threadbare cotton nightgown that could have wrapped around her three times with material to spare and was in bed with the covers pulled up to her chin. Cole spread out his bedroll in front of the door, extinguished the lamp and settled down to sleep.

Dawn tossed and turned for over an hour, listening to the even cadence of Cole's breathing, aware of the exact moment he fell asleep. Only then did she succumb to slumber herself. The dream came much later. It was vivid in its clarity. She felt the horror, relived the pain, suffered unspeakable humiliation at the hands of her cruel husband as he pounded her face with his fists and wielded his belt with ruthless dexterity against her tender flesh.

She refused to beg; she had learned long ago that he enjoyed her groveling. She forced back a scream but could not restrain the small cries gathering deep in her throat. She thrashed against the cornhusk mattress, wishing for a gun, imagining herself emptying the chambers into Billy's wiry body.

Cole awoke with a start, trained to react instantly to the slightest noise or disturbance. He reached for his gun. A survivor of many dangerous situations, he knew enough to keep it within reach at all times. Nothing seemed amiss, but he was taking no chances. Then he heard some rather pitiful noises coming from the bed and realized immediately what had awakened him. Dawn was tossing about on the bed, making pathetic sounds that reminded him of a wounded animal.

"Dawn."

No answer.

"Dawn. Are you awake?"

Silence.

Cole leaped to his feet, reaching the bed in three long strides. Once his eyes adjusted to the darkness, he saw that Dawn was in the throes of a nightmare. Not wanting to startle her, he reached out and gently shook her shoulder. She reared up, fighting, lashing out.

"No! Not again! Never again! Haven't you hurt me enough?"

"Dawn, wake up." Cole didn't want to restrain her forcibly but he had no choice. He feared she would hurt herself if she continued like this. He held her down with the weight of his body. "It's Cole. No one is going to hurt you."

Dawn opened her eyes, felt hard male flesh bearing her down onto the mattress and screamed. "Damn you, Billy! It's not my fault. Go back to your whores. Let them satisfy you. The pain . . . The pain . . ."

"It's Cole, Dawn. You're having a nightmare."

Suddenly Dawn went limp beneath Cole's weight. "Cole? What are you doing?" She tried to dislodge him. "Get off me!"

"I'm trying to keep you from hurting yourself. You were having a nightmare. Are you all right now?"

"I . . . yes, please get off me . . . Oh, God, it hurts."

Cole lifted his weight from her, struck a match to the lamp and settled down beside her on the bed. "Does your back hurt?"

Dawn stared at him. "How did you know?"

"It's obvious from the way you've been carrying yourself that you're hurt. Lie on your stomach. I'll get the ointment."

"No, please, just leave me alone."

"I'm sorry, I can't do that."

"It isn't proper."

Anger suffused Cole's rugged features. "How can you think about proper after all you've endured? Was it proper for Cobb and his cohorts to rape you? Was it proper for Cobb to beat you?"

"But Billy didn't—"

"Just turn around, Dawn, and don't try to deny what's obvious. Don't you think I've got eyes?"

Dawn shouldn't have been surprised that Cole believed Billy had used her sexually. She'd been his wife. Billy had had every right to use her. She was the only one who knew the truth. Billy hadn't been able to function as a man with her. He'd blamed her for his failure to please him, accusing her of being cold and ugly, but she'd learned the truth one day when he'd gotten drunk and told her about his injury. He'd paid whores to pleasure him in other ways, ways that sickened Dawn when he bragged about them. But no amount of beatings could induce her to duplicate those wicked things.

Cole returned with the jar of ointment, saw that Dawn hadn't moved from her back and gently turned her over. "I'm going to raise your nightgown. I'll try to be gentle."

Dawn heard the sudden intake of Cole's breath and could well imagine what her back looked like. Billy hadn't spared her this time. He'd been drunk and demanded sex when he had returned to the cabin after a month's absence. But nothing had changed. He hadn't been able to perform and took his frustration out on her.

She felt Cole's hands on her flesh. Gentle. So gentle she wanted to cry. The warmth of his fingertips spread over her and through her like tongues of pure flame. Healing. The heat settled in the pit of her stomach and lower. She'd never felt like this before. It frightened her beyond reason. She moaned and arched into his touch as his fingers massaged ointment lower, onto her bruised buttocks.

"Am I hurting you?"

"No. It . . . it feels good."

"So do you," Cole muttered beneath his breath.

He swallowed the groan rising in the back of his throat and cursed his body's reaction. He had hardened the instant he'd touched her silken flesh. Beneath the bruises and welts her golden skin was smooth and supple. Her body was thin but shapely. He recalled how she'd looked poised on the bank of the river, reaching up to the moon, her nude body and perfect breasts a feast for his hungry eyes. He'd seen women more shapely and beautiful. Morning Mist came to mind. But something about Dawn captured his senses. She called forth all his protective instincts.

His hands moved slowly over her bottom, spreading ointment and warmth with them. The taut mounds flexed beneath his touch, and he had the crazy urge to bend down and kiss away her hurt. With regret he set aside the ointment and pulled down her nightgown. If he touched her a moment longer he'd be tempted to do more. "There, is that better?"

"Much better," Dawn said, rolling over onto her back. She couldn't look him in the eye. Allowing this particular man to look upon her ugliness made her sad, and she didn't know why.

Billy had delighted in goading her about her ugly dark skin and unattractive body. He ruthlessly called her a bag of bones, letting her know how lucky she was to have him. She'd tried to ignore his insults, but after a time she'd come to believe she truly was homely and unlovable. Not even her father had loved her.

"Get some sleep, Dawn. We'll leave for town after breakfast tomorrow."

Cole lay awake until he was sure Dawn had fallen asleep. Then he closed his eyes and drifted off. In that brief moment before sleep claimed him, he was shocked to realize that his fingers still tingled from touching her sweet flesh.

After breakfast the next morning Cole boosted Duke Riley onto Old Betsy's back and waited for Dawn to come out of the cabin. She had tried to convince him to leave her behind, but Cole wouldn't hear of it. It occurred to Cole that Dawn was unnaturally reluctant to go to town, and he blamed Cobb for her lack of confidence. If Dawn was to make her own way in the world after he left, she had to learn how to mingle with people. Taking her into Dodge was a start.

She finally appeared in the doorway. Cole was pleased to note that she wasn't walking as stiffly as before and assumed the ointment had done its job. He helped her to mount and they rode off. Duke complained bitterly the entire time it took to reach Dodge. Riding the mule, his hands tied to the saddle horn, he swore so long and so loudly that Cole had to stuff a gag in his mouth. Cole had checked Duke's wound just this morning and was pleased to note that it showed no sign of infection. Two men had been killed during the train robbery, and Cole wanted Duke to live long enough to hang for his crimes.

The closer they got to Dodge, the more nervous Dawn grew. Isolated as she'd been at the cabin, she'd never cared about her appearance, but being among people changed everything. She looked like a ragamuffin dressed in Billy's cast-off clothing. The fact that she'd been married to an outlaw wasn't going to endear her to anyone, she realized. The only way she could make a new life for herself was to go where no one knew her. And that took money.

The jailhouse was the first stop for the three dusty riders.

"So you got another one," Sheriff Tayler said as he met them at the door.

"So it seems," Cole said dryly. "This one needs a doctor. He's Duke Riley, a member of Cobb's gang. Showed up at the cabin looking for the money. That's two down and two to go."

Tayler untied Duke, locked him in a cell and sent his deputy for the doctor. Then he rummaged through his Wanted posters and found one for Duke Riley.

"There's a two-hundred-dollar reward for Riley. The five hundred for Cobb hasn't arrived yet, so

I'll just add this to it. The money to cover both rewards should arrive on the next mail train."

"Give it to Cobb's widow," Cole said, indicating Dawn, who had tried to blend into the woodwork while Cole conducted his business.

Dawn hadn't escaped Tayler's notice. He couldn't help wondering why she avoided looking at him. He admitted to being damn curious about the identity of the skinny woman wearing cast-off men's duds sizes too big for her but decided to bide his time. But the shock of learning that Billy Cobb had had a wife was clearly evident in his incredulous expression.

"Cobb was married? Well, I'll be damned." He tipped his hat. "Howdy, Mrs. Cobb."

Dawn raised her head slightly, her eyes wary as she nodded to Tayler. "Please call me Dawn. I don't care to be identified with Billy Cobb."

If Tayler was shocked by the livid bruises on Dawn's face he didn't show it. "Can't say as I blame you. Cole says the reward money is to go to you. I'll see that you get it."

Dawn said nothing, but inside she was fuming. Damn Cole Webster for assuming she'd take his charity! She had money, plenty of it, if he'd just go away so she could claim it.

"Have you recovered the train loot yet?" the sheriff asked.

"No, but I will," Cole said fiercely. "I've never failed yet. I might have to dig up the whole damn yard but I'll find it. If you have no further need of us, Sheriff, Dawn and I have business to conduct."

"What business do we have in town?" Dawn asked as they rode away from the jailhouse.

"First off we're going to visit the general store and buy you something decent to wear."

Dawn reined in sharply. "I don't want your charity."

"It's not charity. When I killed Cobb I cut off your only means of support. It's no more than right that I make amends. Buying you a few new duds isn't going to beggar me. Later you'll have the reward money, but unfortunately it won't last forever."

Dawn's blue eyes flashed with resentment. "That's another thing. I won't accept the reward, it's yours."

Cole grinned. "You sure are one stubborn woman." He grasped her reins and took off down the street. Dawn's mount followed obediently behind him. Its rider was not so docile.

Cole dismounted in front of Cartwright's General Store, swung Dawn from the saddle despite her protests and tethered their horses to the hitching post. Dawn balked when Cole took her hand and led her through the door but finally acquiesced when she saw people staring at them. The last thing she wanted was to bring attention to herself.

"Can I help you, mister?"

Cole smiled at the proprietor, a middle-aged man with thinning hair and a potbelly. "Are you Mr. Cartwright?"

The proprietor's chest expanded proudly. "That I am. What do you need?"

Cole pulled Dawn out from behind him. "New clothes for the lady. From the inside out. And boots. Everything she might need."

Cartwright peered owlishly at Dawn, adjusting his spectacles to make sure he was seeing right. "She's a half-breed, ain't she?"

Dawn stiffened, but Cole seemed unperturbed. He gave Cartwright a daunting look. "That's right. So what? Are you refusing my money?"

"Joseph Cartwright! You have no right acting like a self-righteous prude. Go about your business, I'll take care of things here."

Cartwright skulked off, obviously intimidated by his forceful wife.

"I'm Lucinda Cartwright. You'll have to excuse my husband, he can be a mite thick-headed at times." A round little woman with rosy cheeks and a sweet smile, Lucinda Cartwright was a staunch advocate of women's rights. Be they red, white or black, Lucinda believed that all women deserved consideration from the opposite sex. And the right to vote.

"Now then, I believe you said you'd like your wife outfitted properly," Lucinda said, sizing Dawn up with a practiced eye. "She's a mite skinny, but I'm right handy with a needle. I can alter anything that doesn't fit."

Startled to hear herself referred to as Cole's wife, Dawn raised her head and looked Lucinda in the eye. "I'm not his wife."

Lucinda saw the yellowing bruises marring Dawn's pale cheeks and gave Cole a look that would have slain lesser men. "Oh, my, you poor child. What happened to you?"

"I fell," Dawn said before Cole could form a reply.

"Of course you did," Lucinda said, sending Cole

another lethal glance. "Come with me, child. We'll find you something pretty to wear."

"She's to have a complete outfit from the skin out," Cole said. "Nothing fancy. And a spare of everything. And boots and shoes. Better throw in a warm wrap, too. Winter's coming on. Add anything else you think she'll need. Oh, if you have any of those split riding skirts, she'd probably appreciate one of those."

Lucinda nodded, her face still grim. She blamed Cole for Dawn's bruises and was hanging on to her temper by a slim thread. This was the kind of abuse she abhorred. If she could, she'd take a horsewhip to every man who beat his woman.

"I'll return in a couple of hours. Is that enough time?"

Lucinda nodded jerkily and directed Dawn toward the women's section of the store.

Two hours later Cole returned to the store. Lucinda Cartwright met him at the door, her face mottled with rage. "You animal! You pig! How dare you beat that poor child? Did you think I wouldn't see her back? She's a mass of bruises. I have a good notion to take a horsewhip to you."

"Hold on a darn minute, lady. I didn't touch Dawn. I've never beaten a woman in my life. Her husband did that to her."

"Then it's her husband I'd like to horsewhip. I hope she's not going back to him."

"Her husband is dead."

Lucinda gave him a speculative glance. "Did you kill him?"

"I did."

66

"Good riddance. Dawn will be out in a minute. She's so thin I had to take in nearly everything she selected. Once she puts a little meat on her bones she can let out the seams."

Suddenly Cole's gaze shifted past the rotund Lucinda to where Dawn had just emerged from behind a curtain. His breath caught in his throat. He'd suspected that Dawn was lovely but he hadn't realized just how lovely. Her slimness was eased by the fullness of her breasts. She wore a split riding skirt of butter-soft doeskin that hugged her hips and flared around her ankles. Her blouse was made of practical cotton in a blue color that matched her eyes. Cole could tell by the way the material hugged the curves of her breasts that she wore no corset. Senseless objects, actually, but many women set store by them. On Dawn, a corset would have been as useless as tits on a boar.

Dawn's hair had been combed back from her face and tied in place with a blue ribbon. Her golden skin and exotically tilted blue eyes utterly captivated Cole. He couldn't help staring. He knew then that he wanted her.

"She looks lovely, doesn't she?" Lucinda said admiringly. "I've wrapped her other purchases and tied them with string so they can be attached to your saddle."

After Cole settled the bill, Dawn bade the kindly Lucinda good-bye and followed Cole from the store. She was troubled by the way Cole had stared at her. Had her new finery changed her so much? She was astute enough to realize that Cole wanted her. His hunger was clearly visible in the volatile depths of his green eyes.

Chapter Four

Conversation was sparse during the ride back to the cabin. Cole was having difficulty adjusting to feelings he didn't understand and liked even less. Pity and compassion he could deal with. But another emotion that had nothing to do with pity was plaguing him and it made him uncomfortable.

Dawn's thoughts paralleled Cole's. In the general store Cole had looked upon her with desire. She'd seen desire in the gazes of Billy's cohorts and had learned to fear it. Yet she didn't fear Cole. He'd been nothing but kind and thoughtful to her, considering how she'd lied to him about the train robbery money. Dawn knew she was no beauty. She was skinny, her skin was golden instead of milk white, her mouth was too wide, and her eyes tilted at the outer corners. She looked foreign and exotic, certainly not beautiful.

Dawn glanced covertly at Cole, admiring his tall form and easy grace in the saddle. Though his hat covered most of his mahogany-colored hair, she recalled how it turned to flame beneath the relentless prairie sun. His skin was tanned, but she suspected that, like most White men, it was pale in places the sun didn't touch.

"The cabin is just beyond those trees," Cole said, breaking into her reverie. "Unless you tell me where the money is hidden, I reckon I'll start digging again."

Dawn bit her lower lip in consternation. How could she let him take the money when she needed it so desperately? *How can you keep it when it doesn't belong to you?* her conscience challenged.

They came out of the trees into the clearing. The cabin sat basking in the midday sun, serene and peaceful. Suddenly Cole pulled up sharply; Dawn reined in beside him.

"What is it?" Did Cole sense something she didn't? she wondered.

"I don't know. Instinct tells me something is wrong. Take cover in the woods. I'm riding in. Don't leave until I tell you it's safe."

Cole rode toward the cabin. Everything seemed just as they had left it, but the jangling of Cole's nerves told him otherwise. Living with Indians had taught him many things. One was to follow his intuition; it rarely failed him. He dismounted several yards from the cabin, tethered Warrior to a post and paused near the shed to study the situation. He heard nothing out of the ordinary. Saw nothing amiss. Cautiously he crept toward the cabin and kicked open the door.

The cabin was empty. Cole felt a rush of relief, but it was short-lived. His gut still hurt and the hair prickled at the back of his neck. Maybe he was getting old, he thought, spinning around and directing his gaze to the yard and beyond. He stood in the doorway, alert, his narrow-eyed gaze skimming the surrounding area. He saw an arm and head poke out from behind the shed a second too late. He drew his gun and crouched slightly to the left. It saved his life. Had he been standing, the bullet would have entered his heart. Instead, it struck his left shoulder and exited his back, lodging in the doorjamb behind him.

Cole staggered, regained his balance and remained on his feet through sheer will. Seconds later the gunman recklessly exposed himself, expecting to see Cole laid low by his bullet. Cole was ready. Raising his gun, he aimed and fired. Cole's aim wavered slightly, but his bullet hit solid flesh and bone. The man gave a yelp of pain and ducked back behind the shed. Cole heard the gunman galloping away just as he began a slow spiral to the ground.

Dawn had heard the first shot and watched in growing horror as Cole's body jerked and he struggled to remain upright. She had no idea how he found the strength to aim and shoot, but it appeared that he had wounded his attacker. Suddenly Dawn saw a man on horseback burst from behind the shed and beat a path toward her. She had the presence of mind to remain hidden as the man pounded hell for leather past her. He was bent low over the saddle, a bright blossom of blood staining his shirt, but she recognized him instantly as he thundered by. It was Sam Pickens, a member of Billy's gang.

She didn't give Sam a second glance as she broke her cover and rode toward the cabin. She slid from the horse before he came to a full stop and dropped to her knees beside Cole.

"Cole! How badly are you hurt?" She opened his shirt to find his wound. Her panic subsided somewhat when she saw that the bullet had entered his shoulder and exited without shattering bone. Blood was everywhere, but that in itself was good, for blood would cleanse the wound.

Cole groaned and opened his eyes. He tried to move, but an explosion of pain plunged him to the edge of darkness. He swallowed hard and tried to focus on Dawn. She had ripped the tail of his shirt, made a pad from the material and was pressing it to the wound. She appeared to know what she was doing, so Cole concentrated on controlling the pain.

"The bullet went clear through," he said through gritted teeth. "Make sure there are no pieces of cloth in the wound."

Dawn nodded. "Can you get to your feet if I help you? You need to be in bed. I've done this for Billy before. Do you have some whiskey? Billy always said whiskey was the best disinfectant."

"In my saddlebag. If I hang on to your shoulder I think I can get up. Damn that bastard! Did you see who it was?"

Dawn bent and placed his arm over her shoulder. "It was Sam Pickens. He came for the money. I think you wounded him."

Cole grimaced. "He'll be back. So will Spider Lewis."

"All right, easy does it. Up."

Cole flexed his knees and lifted himself to his feet, trying not to put too much of a burden on Dawn. She was far too frail to bear his full weight. The pain was bearable, but nevertheless he was damn glad to reach the bed.

"I'll remove your boots and get the whiskey," Dawn said, concern coloring her words.

Cole thanked God he wasn't badly injured but was upset at his carelessness. Now this pesky wound was going to put him out of commission for a day or two. He shifted against the cornhusk mattress and closed his eyes, willing away the pain.

Dawn returned with the whiskey and stopped short of the bed when she saw Cole lying so still with his eyes closed. Fear spiraled through her. Upon first glance she thought he was . . . No, she thought, giving herself a mental shake. Cole's wound wasn't serious. He was a strong man. Billy had received wounds more serious than this and survived. So would Cole. Then she saw the steady rise and fall of his chest and chided herself for a fool. Of course Cole would live.

Dawn approached the bed and set the whiskey bottle down on the floor. "I'm going to take off your shirt and cleanse the wound," she said as Cole sensed her presence and opened his eyes.

Cole cooperated by lifting his torso so she could take his arms from the sleeves.

"This is going to hurt like the devil. Billy always had one of his men hold him down."

He gritted his teeth. "Go ahead. I'm no stranger to pain."

Dawn caught her lower lip between even white teeth and angled the whiskey bottle over Cole's wound. He jerked at the first spill of the amber liquid against his raw flesh and then went utterly still.

"Are you all right?"

"Fine." His taut voice and pain-darkened eyes betrayed his agony. "Just get it over with."

Dawn continued to pour. "Turn over, I need to disinfect the exit wound."

Beads of sweat gathered on Cole's forehead as he slid to his side, then onto his stomach. "You . . . make . . . a . . . good nurse."

"You're a better patient than Billy. He didn't dare go to a doctor and expected me to treat his wounds. I've dug a bullet or two out in my time." She worked quickly and efficiently. Once the area was clean, she tore her only spare sheet into strips and bound his wound securely. When she finished, she raised the whiskey bottle, saw there was an inch or two remaining and said, "There's some left, perhaps you could do with a healthy swallow."

Cole tried to rise but couldn't. "I'm going to need help."

Dawn poured the whiskey into a battered tin cup, lifted Cole's head and held it to his lips. He drank until the cup was empty. Then he lay back with a sigh and closed his eyes. Tomorrow he'd feel stronger. Tomorrow he'd be out of bed and able to resume his search for the money. He hoped to God that Sam and Spider wouldn't show up until his strength returned.

Cole wanted to sleep but couldn't. He knew there was something he was forgetting. Something he had to tell Dawn. With great effort he opened his eyes. Dawn was still there, out of focus, but still there. He remembered what he wanted to say.

"The gun. Get it."

"If Sam or Spider show up while I'm still under the weather, take my guns and shoot to kill. They're vicious men. They'll stop at nothing to get that money."

"I can take care of myself," Dawn said. "Go to sleep. I don't think Sam will be back any time soon. I don't know how, but you managed to wound him."

Cole tried to concentrate on Dawn's words, but they seemed to be coming from a long way off. The whiskey was beginning to take effect, and he slipped into a fitful sleep.

Dawn sat on the edge of the bed a long time, staring at Cole's bare chest. His body looked so fit, so hard. His upper torso was as tan as his arms and face. Few men removed their shirts long enough to tan that part of their bodies. But Cole was different from most men.

Dawn rose abruptly and began pacing the confines of the small cabin, her mind working furiously. Cole was unlikely to awaken for several hours. If she was going to leave, now was the time. She could remove the money from its hiding place, take one of Cole's guns and light out of here for parts unknown. Cole's wound wasn't serious, he'd heal in time, so it wasn't as if she'd be abandoning a helpless man. When he awakened he'd probably be well on his way to recovery.

Still she hesitated, recalling how kind he had been to her, how tenderly he'd cared for her when she'd been hurting. *Go!* a voice inside her urged. She looked longingly toward the door, but her feet refused to move. What was this strange feeling? Whatever it was, intuition told her to resist.

"This is ridiculous," she chided herself. Forcing herself away from Cole, she started gathering up her meager belongings. Except for what she wore, she had few possessions and nothing of value. Deciding it wouldn't be right to keep the things Cole had purchased for her in town today, she left them. She'd have money to buy her own clothes once she left this place.

She was ready to leave. The door beckoned to her. The money was close, so close. Then Cole moaned. Dawn froze, trying to block the sound from her mind. He moaned again. Dawn was torn. Her conscience demanded that she check on Cole one last time. It proved to be her undoing.

Cole's face was bathed in shiny pearls of perspiration. His skin was flushed with fever and torrid to the touch. Dawn knew with grinding certainty, and no little amount of disappointment, that she couldn't leave him. Not now. Only someone reprehensible would abandon a man too sick to help himself.

Sighing in resignation, Dawn shoved all thoughts of the money from her mind and set to work. She went to the river for a bucket of cool water and bathed Cole's face and torso with endless patience. Again and again she ran the cloth over his heated flesh. His chest was furred with red curling hair, so soft Dawn felt a wicked desire to set the cloth aside and run her fingers through it. His skin was smooth and firm beneath her fingertips. She was startled to realize that touching him gave her pleasure.

Day turned into night. Dawn returned to the river several times for cool water. Exhaustion finally took its toll and she was forced to rest. Cole was cooler now, his skin no longer burned beneath her touch. Briefly she considered leaving now, as she had planned, but she wondered how Cole would cope if his fever returned. She tried to harden her heart against the railroad detective who had burst into her life without warning, but she could not. Knowing she'd regret her decision, Dawn spread Cole's bedroll on the floor beside the bed and lay down. Sleep came almost instantly.

Cole reached across the bed for Morning Mist and wondered why she wasn't lying beside him. He needed her. They were kindred spirits, meant to love one another into eternity. Why had she left their mat?

"Morning Mist! Where are you, my love?"

Dawn heard Cole cry out in his sleep and came instantly awake. Had his fever returned? Worry gnawed at her. She had no medicine, nothing with which to ease his pain. She recalled her mother gathering herbs from the forest for medicinal purposes but had no idea what they were.

"Morning Mist! Come back to me."

Dawn rose and went to Cole. She placed her hand on his forehead and found him hot to the touch. His fever had returned, just as she'd feared.

"Morning Mist."

When he started to thrash about, Dawn feared he would hurt himself and tried to calm him. "I'm here, Cole. Your Morning Mist is here."

Cole appeared to hear her and quieted immediately. He sighed and spoke to her in the Sioux tongue. Dawn understood some of the words, for her mother had taught her the language years ago. "Lie beside me, my love. It's where you belong."

Dawn was startled when Cole reached out and pulled her down to lie against his uninjured side. He stroked her long black hair and crooned love words to her. Dawn made no attempt to free herself, since it seemed to calm him. Warily she relaxed against him, stunned by her thoughts. She wondered what it would be like to sleep in Cole's arms every night.

And she was a fool who dreamed impossible dreams.

Scant moments before Dawn fell asleep, she imagined she heard Cole whisper her name.

Cole stirred, cautiously testing his limbs. He felt stiff and sore throughout his entire body, but it was nothing he couldn't handle. He wondered why his arms felt strangely empty. Then he remembered. He had awakened during the night and been pleasantly surprised to find Dawn nestled beside him. The warmth and scent of her still lingered.

Light flooded the cabin; he could feel it against his eyelids. He opened his eyes slowly. When the haze before them cleared, he saw her. She was standing by the stove, wearing a new yellow dress. She looked like a ray of sunshine, all bright and golden, her cheeks flushed from the heat. She'd been to the river to bathe, and her hair was still damp and curling around her face. She must have sensed his eyes upon her, for she turned to look at him. She smiled shyly.

"You're awake! How do you feel?"

"Like hell, but tolerable. I can't remember much after you bandaged my wound."

"You slept. Fever set in, but I think the worst of it is over. I had no medicine to give you but I did what I could."

"What was that?" Cole asked curiously.

"I sponged you with cool water until the fever subsided. Are you hungry?"

He grinned. "Matter of fact, I am."

"Good. I found a rabbit in one of my traps. I skinned and cooked it while you were sleeping. The broth will give you strength. You lost a considerable amount of blood."

She ladled out a portion of broth and set it on a small table next to the bed. When Cole reached for the spoon, his hand shook so badly he couldn't bring the spoon to his mouth without spilling the liquid. Pushing his hand aside, Dawn sat on the edge of the bed and carefully spooned the broth into his mouth.

"That's good," Cole said, feeling stronger by the minute. "Once, a long time ago," he reminisced, "when I was sick, my twin sister fed me broth just like you're doing right now."

"You have a twin sister?" Dawn asked eagerly. She was anxious to learn more about this man who had made such an impact upon her life in so short a time. "Where is she now?"

"Ashley and her husband Tanner are living in Oregon with their two children. I visited them in '72 but haven't seen them since. We correspond regularly. I've been wanting to pay them another visit but haven't found the time. I have a nephew I've never seen."

"Does Ashley look like you?"

"She's much prettier," Cole joked. "We both have green eyes, but her hair is redder than mine. She came West with a wagon train in '66 to join me at Fort Bridger. I was in the army at the time. She asked Tanner to marry her because the wagon master wouldn't allow a single woman to join his train. Tanner is from the South. He had a grudge against all Yankees, but my sister managed to tame him. Running Elk saw Ashley and stole her from the wagon train. Remind me to tell you the story sometime."

"Running Elk," she repeated. "Who is he?"

"He's chief of a band of Sioux. I lived with the People for a time."

"Is that where you met Morning Mist?"

Cole's green eyes turned dark with remembrance. "Morning Mist was Running Elk's half-sister. I think we loved one another from the first moment our eyes met. Unfortunately, our time together was brief. Circumstances forced me to leave the village shortly after our marriage. In my absence the village was attacked by Crow raiders. Morning Mist was among those slain."

Dawn's heart constricted with sympathy. The raw pain reflected in the green depths of Cole's eyes told her that he still loved his dead wife. It must be wonderful to be loved like that, Dawn thought dreamily. She had never known love. Her mother had been afraid to show too much affection for her daughter. Dawn's father had been a jealous man who demanded all of Winter Sky's attention. To know, just once in her life, the kind of love Cole had felt for Morning Mist would be pure bliss. But Dawn knew better than to wish for things that could never be.

"I'm sorry."

Cole shrugged. "It happened a long time ago. I stayed with Running Elk four years before realizing I could no longer shut myself off from the world. I don't regret my years with the People. I learned to act, think and live like the Sioux. That knowledge has aided me in my work, and in many instances saved my life."

"Why have you never remarried?" Dawn regretted the question the moment it left her mouth. It was none of her business. Once Cole left, she would never see him again.

Cole looked away, visualizing Morning Mist on the day they had parted. Her eyes had been misty with tears, but her smile had said she knew he would return to her. Their love had been preordained and would endure until the end of time.

"No one could ever replace Morning Mist in my heart," Cole explained. "Someday you'll love someone like that and understand."

Dawn gazed at Cole and feared she already did understand. She was afraid of the things Cole made her feel. But rather than delve too deeply into her heart for an explanation, she rose abruptly. "Would you like some more broth?"

"Not right now. But I am feeling better. By tomorrow I should be fit enough to resume my search. I need to recover the money before Sam and Spider turn up." He searched her face, waiting for her to say something, and was disappointed when she remained stubbornly mute.

Dawn turned away. She knew what Cole wanted from her. But she just couldn't give him the money. It could mean the difference between life and death for her.

Cole watched Dawn as she went about her chores. She had changed since he'd first set eyes on her several days ago. Her eyes no longer had that haunted look, and the sharp edges of her facial features had eased. She appeared more sylph-like than gaunt now, and more in control of her life. Sometimes she seemed almost innocent and childlike. And vulnerable. It was difficult for him to believe she had been intimate with Cobb and his cohorts.

Cole wondered what Dawn would do when he left. It wasn't difficult to imagine why she continued to deny knowledge of the train robbery money. Unfortunately, there were few options open to a woman with no money and no prospects. The stolen money would go a long way in securing a normal life for Dawn. In a way, he couldn't blame her for denying knowledge of it.

But he had a job to do; sentiments did not apply here.

By suppertime Cole felt strong enough to go outside to relieve himself and sit at the table to eat. He washed up in a bucket of water Dawn had placed outside the door for that purpose and took a seat at the rickety table. When Dawn set a bowl of savory rabbit stew and dumplings before him, he dug in with gusto. Tomorrow he hoped to continue his search for the money, and he needed to build his strength as quickly as possible.

"How is your shoulder?" Dawn asked conversationally.

"Hardly hurts at all," Cole said, though in truth he felt more than a twinge of pain.

"You take the bed tonight. It's more comfortable than the bedroll."

"We could share the bed like we did last night." His words told her he'd been more aware than she had given him credit for.

Dawn's spoon clattered against her bowl. "I . . . that is, we . . . You couldn't have remembered."

"I remember," Cole said huskily. "I remember how empty my arms felt when I awakened and you were gone."

"You thought I was Morning Mist."

"I knew exactly who you were, lady. Besides, what can it hurt if we share the bed? I'm too weak to do either of us any good."

Dawn's eyes slid over him assessingly. He didn't look weak. He looked amazingly fit for a man who'd been shot and had survived a fever. He must have the constitution of an elephant.

"I'll take my chances with the bedroll," she replied shortly. Dawn trusted Cole more than she did any man but not enough to lie beside him all night. Or was it herself she didn't trust?

"No! *I'll* take the bedroll," Cole said in a voice that brooked no argument. "Either we share the bed or I'll sleep on the floor. It's your choice."

"Sleeping with a man is . . . It's not—"

"I'm not Billy Cobb. I won't hurt you. Unlike your husband and his men, I don't take women unless they're willing. All I'm suggesting is that we share the bed. Otherwise, I'll make do on the floor."

When Dawn remained silent, Cole rose somewhat stiffly. He'd been up too long, he thought as he staggered toward the corner to retrieve his bedroll. The dull ache in his shoulder was now a painful throbbing, and if he didn't lie down soon he'd probably fall down.

Dawn watched Cole stagger across the room with a twinge of guilt. Sharing the bed was a logical solution, so why was she acting like a foolish child? Had he allowed her to use the bedroll, there would be no argument, but Cole was too much of a gentleman to take the bed while she slept on the floor.

"Wait! We'll share the bed. But only until you're well enough to sleep on the floor yourself."

"Deal," Cole said as he changed directions and stumbled to the bed. To his credit, he fell asleep shortly after his head hit the pillow.

Since Cole had fallen asleep so soon, Dawn decided not to awaken him to change his bandage. Briefly she considered sleeping in her dress, but couldn't bear the thought of her beautiful new gown being reduced to a mass of wrinkles. Fearing that Cole would awaken while she was undressing, she pulled her voluminous nightgown over her head and undressed beneath it. Then she crawled into bed, pushing herself as close to the edge as possible.

Sleeping in Cole's arms last night had proved something to Dawn. Sleeping with a man could be wonderfully pleasant and comforting, if he was the right man. Sleeping next to Billy had revolted her. Whenever Billy returned to the cabin, he usually tried and failed to perform as a man. Then he would curse and beat her and kick her out of bed, forcing her to sleep on the bare floor. She was eternally grateful for Billy's frequent visits to the cabin.

Even in slumber, Cole sensed Dawn beside him. He felt her warmth, inhaled her sweet, natural scent, and turned toward her in his sleep. He reached out, gathering her in his arms and pulling her against him. Half asleep, Dawn resisted briefly, then cuddled into the curve of Cole's body as if it were the most natural thing in the world.

Cole awoke slowly to darkness and a feeling of contentment. He couldn't recall when he'd felt so at peace. The woman in his arms was warm and sweet-smelling. A firm breast filled his hand, and he fondled the nipple that pressed impudently against his palm.

Morning Mist.

He almost said her name aloud until he remembered. Morning Mist was dead. The woman beside him was named Dawn. Dawn, with long black hair and innocent blue eyes that held the ageless knowledge of Eve. Vulnerable Dawn. She had known many men, yet gave the impression of being untouched.

His hand moved against her breast, stroking her gently, restless, wanting. A groan slipped from his throat when he felt her nipple harden against his palm. Unable to stop himself, he eased her on her back. Dawn made a sleepy sound and tried to return to her side. Cole held her fast, wanting her, needing her so much that sweat gathered in the small of his back and an aching began low in his stomach.

Dawn stirred. She felt hot; her body was heat-flushed and restless. She wasn't quite awake but neither was she asleep. She felt strange, so very strange. Unfamiliar sensations made her limbs feel heavy and lethargic. She shifted restively, seeking something so close yet beyond her reach.

Cole held Dawn until she lay still in his arms once more. Then he eased slowly down her body, his mouth finding her breast through her threadbare nightgown. His lips closed over her nipple and he suckled her. He smiled when he heard her breathy moan. Then he felt her shudder violently and knew she was fully awake.

She shoved at his chest. "What are you doing? Dear God, what are you doing to me?"

Cole lifted his head and looked at her. Her features were clearly defined in the moonlit room, and he was startled to see her eyes open wide with terror.

"Awakening you to ecstasy. Don't be afraid, I won't hurt you."

85

A tiny, trembling sound escaped Dawn's lips. It was Cole's name. It was enough to burn through the restraint of Cole's best intentions.

Cole turned her face toward him with the gentlest of touches. Her lips were lush and wet. He swept her back into his arms, his open mouth slanting over hers. Her lips tasted of sultry sweetness and mystery. Of innocence and splendor. He deepened the kiss, driving his tongue past the barrier of her teeth into the satiny warmth of her mouth.

Dawn tried to think beyond the scorching, searing heat of Cole's kiss, but all coherent thought had been thoroughly blotted out. She had to stop this insanity. It wasn't right. This feeling was so wonderful it had to be wicked. Then, like a dash of cold water upon her senses, Dawn suddenly realized that Cole was seducing her, employing his considerable charm to make her reveal where Billy had hidden the money.

When he finally lifted his mouth from hers, she saw passion shimmering in the depths of his emerald eyes.

"I want you, Dawn. Trust me, I won't hurt you."

Chapter Five

Dawn drew back in anger. "Seducing me won't get what you want. Go away and leave me alone."

"Is that what you think? You believe I'm using seduction to wrest your secret from you? You couldn't be more wrong, lady. I want you for myself. I'm fully aware of the hell Cobb put you through. I want to show you a gentleness you've never known. There can be joy in mating. For both men and women. What Cobb and his men did was rutting. I want to make love to you."

His words sounded so sincere that Dawn wanted to believe him. She knew nothing of kindness or pleasure. She had no idea that women could enjoy the disgusting act Billy had tried to perform with her. She hadn't any doubt that Cole's loving would be exactly as he described, maybe better. But she was not a child, harboring dreams of love and happiness. She had learned the hard way that fantasy did not exist. There was only reality, and with reality came pain, disillusionment and loneliness.

Dawn moved a comfortable distance away from Cole, more wary than afraid. She didn't think Cole would hurt her, but she knew from experience that men's dispositions changed when they didn't get what they wanted. How did she know that Cole wasn't like Billy in that respect?

"No. I'm not going to let you do that to me."

"Are you afraid I'll hurt you? I told you I'd never force an unwilling woman."

Cole felt the tension ebb from her and wondered what Billy had done to her to produce such terror of physical contact. She'd been beaten, he knew that. But there had to be other things, too horrible to talk about. He moved away from her even as she retreated to the edge of the bed.

"I'm sorry, Dawn. I don't want to add to the hell your life has been. Go to sleep. I won't bother you."

Dawn relaxed, acutely aware of Cole's hard body resting beside her. Though Cole's words eased her fears considerably, the feeling of disappointment lingered. Deep inside she knew she was missing something wonderful by denying Cole, but she couldn't bring herself to surrender to him. Intuition told her he'd be good at it, but after suffering Billy's crude fumbling, she couldn't bear the thought of intimacy. She'd happily spend the remainder of her life celibate if it meant being free of a man's domination.

"I'm sorry, too, Cole, but that's the way it has to be. I can't bear to be touched like . . . that."

Cole thought differently but kept his own counsel. When he had touched Dawn intimately, her body had responded hungrily. She was ripe for loving. He wanted to show her how good it could be between a man and a woman when the man gave his woman pleasure. But he wouldn't force the issue. His body was still hard and pulsating; he had wanted Dawn more than he'd wanted any woman since Morning Mist. He closed his eyes, groaning in frustration.

Dawn heard Cole's moan and felt a twinge of guilt. But it didn't last long. She knew that Cole considered her a whore. He'd hinted often enough about her supposed intimacy with Billy's cohorts. God, if he only knew, she thought bitterly. Billy's lies about his sexual appetite and her enjoyment of his prowess were contemptible. He was too proud to admit he couldn't perform sexually. He had prevented his men from sharing her favors simply because he feared his men would learn she was still virginal, ruining his image as a virile man.

In the last minutes before sleep claimed her, Dawn felt a tiny nudge of curiosity. Some part of herself wanted to experience the things Cole had promised. However, the rest of her feared what those feelings might do to her. After Cole left she'd be totally alone, with no one but herself to rely upon. She didn't want to grow dependent on Cole, or learn to need him. Common sense told her she'd never be the same if she allowed Cole to make love to her.

Do you want to go through life never knowing the joy of making love with a gentle, caring man? a voice inside asked.

She fell asleep before the answer became clear.

The next morning when he awakened, Cole was still weak, yet determined to resume his search for the train loot. He'd already spent more time on this case than usual and he was anxious to move on. The longer he stayed with Dawn, the harder it would be to leave when the time came.

"Surely you don't intend to start digging again," Dawn questioned when Cole rose from the breakfast table and jammed on his hat. "You're not strong enough. Your wound will start bleeding."

"I'll take my chances," Cole said tersely. Their gazes met and clung. "I've already overstayed my welcome. I realized that last night. Things between us could become . . . something neither of us is prepared to deal with if I remain much longer."

Dawn could find no reply. What Cole had said was true. If he stayed much longer, her resolve would crumble beneath Cole's powerful allure. She'd never felt so helpless before. Not even during Billy's beatings, when she had managed to retain full control of her senses. Being with Cole made her lose all sense of reality. She feared that when he left he'd take a part of her with him.

Cole wielded the shovel with grim determination. The morning sun rose high in the cloudless sky and still he dug. Sweat beaded his brow and ran in rivulets down his back. He stopped once to remove his shirt and hat and wipe the sweat from his brow with his kerchief.

At mid-morning Dawn brought him a cupful of cool water. She felt more than a little guilty for allowing him to dig when she knew it would gain him nothing but a sore back. The money was not in the ground, nor had it ever been.

Cole dug like a man possessed. He had exhausted every potential hiding place he could think of, yet his gut told him the money was nearby. It had to be. Cobb hadn't had time to take it anywhere else. Logic told him Cobb had hidden it in or near the cabin. Setting his teeth against the gnawing pain in his shoulder, he continued to dig.

Toward the hottest part of the day Cole began to feel the strain. When Dawn brought him lunch and another cup of water, he drank the water but waved the food away. His wound throbbed painfully and his stomach felt as if buffalo were stampeding inside it. He knew he should stop, but some perverse demon drove him unmercifully. A demon named desire.

Cole was angry and disturbed by his feelings for Cobb's widow. He shouldn't want Dawn the way he did. He shouldn't let another woman interfere with his memories of Morning Mist. More importantly, he should force Dawn to tell him where the money was hidden. Other men in his position wouldn't be so generous with the outlaw's wife, Cole reflected. They would have forced Dawn to reveal the hiding place or suffer the consequences.

Dawn couldn't bear watching Cole dig until he was ready to drop. When she saw blood seeping into the new bandage she had put on just this morning, she knew the time had come to let go of her dream of using the stolen money to start a new life for herself. Anyone as stubborn as Cole deserved honesty.

When Dawn saw Cole stagger toward the cabin, she ran out to help him. "Why are you being so stubborn about this? The money isn't yours."

"Recovering the money is my job. I hate failure," he said from between clenched teeth. "Just as soon as I rest up I'll start digging again. That money has to be here somewhere, I can smell it."

"It is," Dawn said as Cole lowered himself into a chair.

At first Cole thought he'd misheard. "What did you say?"

"I said the money is here."

His angular profile hardened. "Why in the hell did you wait so long to tell me? For God's sake, lady, I could have recovered the money and been out of your hair by now!"

Dawn's chin rose a little. "Billy gave me nothing but pain and heartache. He owed me. He's dead now; why shouldn't I have something for all the misery he's caused me?"

"For starters, the money didn't belong to Cobb and it doesn't belong to you."

Dawn's blue eyes flashed pure fire. "Who gave you the right to play judge and jury? You don't understand, do you? You can't possibly know what I've had to endure these past five years. I was fifteen when Billy bought me, a child who'd never known love and kindness. That money could have provided me with a life far better than any I have ever known. Without it I have nothing."

She began pacing, growing more agitated by the minute. "You can leave now. I'll show you where the money is and you can get out of here."

"What will you do?" Cole asked, feeling decidedly glum despite the fact that he was about to find what he'd come for. This was his job, dammit, didn't she realize that?

"I understand there are several whorehouses in Dodge. I reckon I can find a place for myself. Or," Dawn spat out, glaring at him, "I could just wait here for Sam or Spider to show up and try to explain why their share of the money is missing. If I'm lucky, they'll keep me on as their whore."

Cole shot to his feet. He couldn't bear hearing Dawn refer to herself in such a demeaning manner. He reached her in two strides, grasping her shoulders and shaking her roughly. "Dammit, Dawn, don't talk like that! You'll have the reward money for Cobb and Riley. Perhaps I can get you a reward from the railroad for recovering the money. There's no need for you to sell yourself."

"I'd sell myself before accepting your charity."

His steady gaze held her immobile. "What in the hell did I ever do to you?"

You made me want things I had only dreamed about. You made me long for gentleness, for caring . . . for love. But she did not say those things.

"You came here," she said aloud. *And nothing's been the same since.*

Cole couldn't help admiring Dawn's courage. She was so brave. So full of life and passion. Not even Cobb's cruel domination had subdued her spirit.

"I had a job to do, Dawn. Recovering stolen goods is my livelihood."

She stared up at him, her expression belligerent, her eyes sparking with challenge. "What about my livelihood?"

The challenge didn't sit well with Cole. Why did Dawn's plight prick at his conscience when it shouldn't have made a dent upon a hardened man like himself? Rather than search his mind for an answer, he tilted Dawn's face upward and stared at the lush velvet of her lips for the space of a heartbeat before bringing his mouth down on hers. Once their lips touched, he seemed to go up in flames. He kissed her boldly, thoroughly, his tongue probing, tasting, unable to get enough of her.

Dawn shivered as little fingers of flame stirred her senses and ignited her dormant passion. Their tongues met, fenced and parried, nibbled and tasted. She made small noises deep in her throat but couldn't find the will to stop him. Her body burned beneath his hands as he hefted a breast, making it swell and feel heavy. His fingers pulled at her nipple, making it elongate. She made a gurgling sound as his hands moved lower, cupping her elegantly rounded bottom, bringing her flush against his arousal. Dawn felt it and panicked, dragging her mouth away from his drugging kisses.

"No, please! I don't want this!"

"You could have fooled me," Cole said, his voice ragged with need. "There's a name for women like you. Men call them teases."

Dawn inhaled sharply. "That's not fair. I'm not like that."

The urgency of his need was beginning to subside, and with it came the return of Cole's good sense. The heat of her body, the swift rise of her passion, her sweet scent, had made him forget she wasn't his for the taking.

"I know you're not like that," Cole said. Reluctantly he released her and she stepped back. "I'm rested now. Tell me where you've hidden the money. The sooner I leave, the better off we'll both be." He searched her face, his expression grim. "You're a temptation I can't seem to resist. I'm sure you know I want you. I don't like it but I can't help myself."

Dawn shivered, feeling the heat of his touch recede with his withdrawal. What was wrong with her? She hated being touched by any man, yet she'd allowed Cole to kiss and fondle her as if it were the most natural thing in the world. Even more frightening was the realization that she wanted everything Cole had promised he would do to her and make her feel.

Cole wanted to make love to her.

Dawn didn't even know what making love consisted of. Cole said it had nothing to do with rutting. He said she would enjoy it. What if . . . ?

"Are you ready now to tell me where to find the money?"

Dawn nodded jerkily. "Follow me."

Her back stiff, Dawn swept past Cole and out the door. Cole followed close on her heels. Skirting around the numerous holes he'd dug in the yard, Dawn led him along the path to the river.

"Cobb hid the money this far from the house?" Cole wondered aloud.

"Yes. I followed and watched where he hid it. I intended to retrieve it and take off after he left the cabin or got too drunk to awaken when I left. Unfortunately, he beat me so severely I couldn't leave right away. I was ecstatic when Billy left the cabin. Then you showed up and ruined everything."

Cole saw nothing to give away the place where the money was hidden. "Well, where is it?" he asked curiously, plopping down on a hollow log to rest. His shoulder was throbbing something fierce. All that digging had just about done him in.

"You're sitting on it."

Cole leaped to his feet. "What!"

Dropping to her knees, Dawn reached inside one end of the hollow log and wrested out a canvas bag. She shoved it at Cole as if it contained something offensive.

"Here, take it! You've got what you want, now leave."

Spinning on her heel, she stomped back to the cabin, leaving Cole holding the money and staring after her with a confused look on his face. The money was his sole purpose in being here. Nevertheless, he felt like a heel. Why did he feel as if he were taking candy from a baby?

Heaving a sigh, Cole followed Dawn more slowly. When he entered the cabin, she was busily fixing supper.

"Are you going to leave now or wait until morning?" Dawn asked tonelessly.

Cole had to think about that one. There were circumstances to consider, decisions to make. It wasn't as simple as Dawn had made it sound. How could he just go off and leave her, knowing what was likely to happen after he was gone? If Dawn didn't starve to death, she would become prey to human predators. All manner of riffraff would soon be sniffing around the cabin. The thought that Dawn might seek employment in a brothel set his teeth on edge. Dawn was no whore. She had simply done what she had to do in order to survive.

"If it's all right with you, I'll stay the night. All that digging has done me in."

Dawn turned her concerned gaze on him. His complexion was ashen. She saw blood staining his shirt and knew his wound was bleeding again. Stubborn man.

"You're bleeding. Sit down, I'll change your bandage and see how much damage you've done to yourself."

Cole obediently seated himself on one of the two rickety chairs while Dawn turned back to the stove and poured warm water from the kettle into a bowl. She brought the water to the table and found a clean cloth.

"This might hurt," she said as she peeled away a layer of bandage that had adhered to his wound. Once the wound was bared, Dawn sucked her breath in sharply. The edges were raw and red.

"Is it infected?" Cole asked, wincing as she removed remaining remnants of the bandage.

Dawn bit her bottom lip as she studied the wound. "You've certainly aggravated it, but I don't think it's infected. All that digging—"

"You could have prevented it with a simple word."

She met his gaze unflinchingly. "Yes, I could have. Hold still while I apply a clean bandage."

She worked in silence. She could tell that Cole was exhausted so she didn't attempt conversation. Not that he would be very interested in what she had to say now that he had what he wanted. Common sense told her that his kindness and his caring had been but a ploy to recover the money. Men were all alike. Not one of their intentions was pure. Everything they did had ulterior motives.

"There," she said, stepping back and surveying her handiwork with a critical eye. "Don't move. Supper will be done soon."

"Thank you." Cole wanted to say more but had no right. He wanted to tell her he'd protect her, but that wasn't true. He wanted to say she'd be all right after he left, but lying wasn't his way. He wanted . . . Oh, God, when he thought about what he really wanted from Dawn, he grew hot and cold at the same time.

Supper was consumed, and Cole rose to help Dawn carry the dishes to the sink. It had grown dark, and a kerosene lamp chased shadows from all but the darkest corners of the room.

"Don't bother," Dawn said curtly. "You're tired. Go to bed. I'll take the bedroll tonight."

"Dawn," Cole said, turning her around to face him. "That's not what I want and you know it. I want you to come to bed with me. I want to make love to you."

His hands were hot upon her shoulders, igniting flames throughout her body. She gazed up at him.

The sharp angles of his cheekbones were stark beneath his taut skin, making his features harsh in the flickering light, and his eyes glowed a pure emerald green. Dawn recognized his hunger and was frightened by it.

"Are you afraid of me, Dawn? You shouldn't be. I understand that you've known nothing but pain from men, but I want to change that. Come to bed with me. Let me show you that all men aren't animals. Do you know what I want to do to you?"

Dawn's eyes grew round with dismay. She couldn't speak, couldn't think. All she could do was shake her head from side to side.

"Let me tell you," Cole said, bringing her between his thighs so she could feel the proof of his need. "There will be no pain, only pleasure." His eyes fell to her chest. "You have beautiful breasts, did you know that? I saw you nude once." She gasped loudly as he continued. "I followed you to the riverbank and watched you bathe. I want to caress you all over with my hands and lips. I want to taste every inch of you. I want to take your breasts into my mouth and suckle your nipples. I want to hear you moan and cry out my name with joy, not pain.

"I want to bring you to climax with my mouth and hands. Do you know how wonderful that could feel? No, I can see by your expression that you don't know what I'm talking about. But you will if you let me show you. But the best will be when I come inside you." He closed his eyes, his hands tightening on her shoulders. "When I'm inside you I'll bring you slowly to climax, and it will be sweeter than anything you've ever known."

"No! Stop!" Dawn said, clapping her hands over her ears. "You lie! You have what you want. Why are you tormenting me?"

"Damned if I know," Cole said, wishing he could taste her mouth. "Unless it's because being near you torments me."

"I'm ugly and skinny and . . . and a half-breed."

Cole shook his head. "You're beautiful." He took a handful of her long hair, brought it to his mouth and let it slide through his fingers. "Your hair feels like silk. Black as midnight and sweet smelling." He kissed her full on the lips. "Your lips are full and lush, I could go on kissing them forever." He stared into her eyes. "Your eyes are so blue they rival the sky." He touched her cheek, then let his hand slide down to cup her breasts. "Your skin is smooth and golden. It's true you're a tad thin, but your breasts are perfect. Wouldn't you like to know how wonderful it would be to lie with someone who appreciates you?"

Dawn shook her head to clear it of the wicked images Cole's words built in her mind. They turned her insides to liquid fire. She felt her body grow soft and tried to deny the tingling centered between her legs. Pleasure with a man? Was there such a thing? She doubted it, even though her body wanted it. Obviously, Cole had been without a woman too long, and since she was handy . . .

"I don't believe a thing you've said," Dawn replied as she pulled herself free of his arms. Being so close to him was too distracting. She couldn't think clearly.

"You should," Cole said with profound regret.

"I can't," Dawn protested as she turned back to

the dirty dishes. "You're leaving tomorrow. Even if all those things you said were true, I can't do what you want. I'm not a whore. Billy didn't . . ."

"Billy didn't what?"

Dawn shrugged. What purpose was there in telling Cole she was technically still a virgin? "Never mind, it isn't important."

"Did Cobb and his men hurt you?"

Dawn sent him a sidelong glance. "Why do you care?"

Her question caught him off guard. Why, indeed? He hadn't known Dawn long enough to care. But, surprisingly, he did care about Dawn.

"I'm not a heartless bastard. I had a job to do and I did it."

Dawn stared at him, her expression unreadable. "If you intend to leave tomorrow you should get some rest. You're not as strong as you think. You've lost a lot of blood."

"You're probably right," Cole said, turning away. He was having difficulty convincing his body that he didn't want Dawn. "I'll take the bedroll tonight. This is your cabin and your bed, I have no right to take it from you. Good night, Dawn."

Dawn didn't trust herself to speak. She was still flustered by what he'd said to her. Just thinking about those things filled the lower regions of her stomach with butterflies. While he was telling her what he wanted to do to her, she'd found herself longing to feel what he was describing just once in her life.

Dawn kept her face carefully averted as Cole stripped and crawled into his bedroll. After putting away the last plate, she blew out the lamp, slipped into her nightgown and sought her bed. The night was exceptionally warm, and Dawn tossed and turned, unable to find sleep. She waited until Cole's steady breathing indicated he was sleeping before rising. With little effort she located a sliver of soap and a towel and left the cabin.

Cole heard a stealthy footfall and came awake instantly. He opened his eyes in time to see a billow of white ease through the door. Dawn. His gaze flew to the moneybag lying beside him. It was still there. Dawn had made no effort to steal it. Rising, he quickly donned his pants and boots and followed. It took only a moment for him to realize she was going to the river.

Dawn paused on the riverbank, admiring the play of moonbeams upon the diamond-studded surface of the water. It was an almost magical sight. She lifted her face to the balmy breeze, welcoming the coolness against her skin. Her nightgown was plastered against her body, outlining every curve and indentation.

Cole reached the river and halted, realizing that Dawn had come here simply to bathe. He tried to convince himself to leave. Then Dawn stripped off her nightgown and all his good intentions fled. She looked like a golden goddess, her head thrown back, her moon-kissed face lifted high. Moved by the vision, Cole sighed as she waded into the river.

Dawn ducked her head beneath the placid water and used the soap to work up a lather. Her eyes were closed and she didn't see Cole walk to the water's edge and sit on the log that had until recently held Billy Cobb's ill-gotten gains.

She's as graceful as a gazelle, Cole thought as Dawn arched her back and dipped her hair into the water to rinse it. Cole lost his breath when she lifted her hands and splashed handfuls of water over her breasts. Driven by fierce need, he stripped off his pants and boots and waded into the river.

Dawn heard a noise behind her and spun around, flinging her long hair from her eyes with a sweep of her hand. She saw it was only Cole, and her first reaction was one of relief. Against her will, her gaze fell to his groin, and relief turned to shock. He was hard, heavy and fully aroused. She traced with her eyes the curling pelt of red hair that narrowed from the breadth of his chest to his taut belly, her gaze finally settling on his sex, where it rose thick and high against a nest of dark red.

"May I join you?" Cole asked as he waded through the water to reach her. "A bath sounds wonderfully refreshing."

"I thought you were sleeping."

"I was, until I heard you leave the cabin. Would you like me to wash your back?"

"Certainly not! The river is all yours. I'm finished." She started toward the shore, careful to avoid him. Suddenly she slipped into a deep hole and went under. She came up sputtering.

Cole reached for her, steadying her while at the same time bringing her up against him. "Are you all right?"

"I will be as soon as you let go of me." Suddenly

her gaze fell on the bandage covering his wound. "I wouldn't get that wet if I were you. Infection is always a danger to open wounds."

Cole's reply was to sweep her into his arms and carry her to the shore.

"What are you doing?"

"Avoiding infection."

"Put me down."

Dawn's skin burned where it touched Cole's. She felt feverish and unsettled. She'd never felt desire before and didn't know how to handle it.

He gave her a wicked grin. "Very well." His gaze was intent as he let her slide down his nude body, giving her the full benefit of his hardened sex.

Then he kissed her, lifting her face and covering her lips with the heat of his mouth. He kissed her long and hard, licking the seam of her lips until Dawn opened her mouth to admit his tongue. The kiss seemed to go on forever as his tongue imitated the thrust and withdrawal of his hips grinding against her loins. She'd never known a kiss could be like this, could feel like heaven.

When he ended the kiss, Dawn was trembling so badly her legs refused to move. She looked longingly at her nightgown lying a few feet away on the ground. Cole saw her dilemma, scooped up the garment and handed it to her.

"I don't think you're as immune to me as you think, lady. Why are you trembling?"

I'm trembling because you make me yearn for things I don't understand. "I'm cold," Dawn said in a muffled voice as she flung her nightgown over her head and settled it over her nude body.

"You're a liar," Cole challenged. "You want me but you're too cowardly to admit it."

Dawn stared at him in total confusion, then she turned and fled.

Chapter Six

Cole entered the cabin and saw Dawn standing beside the bed. She stood poised in a golden circle of lamplight, her expression frightened and uncertain. Cole's heart nearly stopped beating when she approached him slowly, with a purpose and determination that took his breath away.

Dawn was aware of what she was offering Cole. She had arrived at a rather startling decision during the few minutes it had taken to reach the cabin from the river. She wanted Cole to teach her about passion. She wanted to learn about loving from a man as different from Billy Cobb as night was from day. She had no idea what life held for her after Cole left and she wanted to give her virginity to a man of her own choosing. Someone who would take it gently instead of ripping it from her by force.

Dawn had reached Cole's side now. Shyly she tugged his hand and brought it to her breast. A ragged groan slipped past Cole's lips. His sex jerked and swelled and grew instantly hard. He seemed to be walking around like that a lot lately.

"What's this all about, Dawn?"

Dawn licked her dry lips. Never in her wildest dreams had she imagined willingly giving herself to a man. "I . . . I want all those things you promised me, Cole. Once in my lifetime I want to feel pleasure."

Cole was astounded, and so aroused by her words, he had to forcibly stop himself from tossing her on the bed and thrusting himself into her hot center. Luckily, his good sense prevailed. Judging from Dawn's words, he felt certain she had never experienced pleasure and he wanted to be the one to bring her to climax, slowly, with gentle coaxing and tender caresses. He prayed for the fortitude to withhold his own pleasure until she attained hers.

"Are you sure, sweetheart? I won't force you."

Dawn looked straight into the blinding depths of his green eyes and was never more certain of anything in her life. "Yes, very sure."

Cole's breath whooshed out. "Let's get rid of your nightgown," he said as he pulled the garment from her body and tossed it aside. For several long minutes he merely stared at her.

Dawn felt the heat of his gaze slide over her and wanted to hide herself from him. She knew she wasn't shapely, and Cole was quiet for so long she feared he thought her ugly. Her hands flew to her breasts, and she looked longingly toward her nightgown. This was all a mistake. Whatever had made her think she could compete with the other women Cole had known?

"No, don't hide yourself from me," Cole whispered as he pulled her hands away from her breasts. "I meant it when I said you are beautiful."

Dawn's eyes never left his face. "Thank you for lying. You make me feel beautiful."

"I want to make you feel so much more," Cole whispered earnestly as he swept her from her feet and followed her down onto the bed. He searched her face in the dim light, then touched her cheek with his fingertip. "Your face is nearly healed and you're as lovely as I knew you'd be."

"I'm not really lovely."

"To me you are. Is your back still sore? I'll try not to hurt you. If I do anything you don't like, you've only to tell me and I'll stop. I want you to feel only pleasure this night."

"My back is nearly healed," Dawn said, more than a little bemused by his words. She found it difficult to believe that a man could actually care about the pleasure and needs of the woman he bedded. It was a concept that boggled her mind after her experience with Billy.

"I'm going to kiss you, Dawn," Cole said, smiling into her eyes. "Open your lips for me."

He took her into his arms and lowered his face to hers. Dawn parted her lips, dimly aware that his chin and cheeks were shadowed with rust-colored stubble. His beard looked soft, not bristly like Billy's unshaven jaw, and she ran her finger tentatively down one side of his face. She shivered with awareness. Touching him was pure magic.

108

Cole's mouth covered hers. Little tongues of fire licked at her flesh as his kiss deepened. She felt his hands on her body, cupping her breasts, his fingers plucking her nipples, making them hard. She groaned in disappointment when his hands left her breasts, then gasped as they moved lower, dancing teasingly across her skin, pausing to explore her navel, sending fingers of raw flame across the sensitive flesh of her stomach.

For the first time in her life Dawn wanted to please a man, but she didn't know how. She wanted to make him feel the same wonderful things she was feeling. Almost shyly she used her own small hands to caress Cole's flesh, ringing his flat male nipples, running her fingers through the soft red hair on his chest. His body differed from hers in so many ways. His stomach was ridged with rippling muscles, and her exploring fingers discovered bulging tendons on his smooth back.

Dawn knew she must be doing something right, for Cole lifted his mouth from hers and groaned. There was a rough note in his voice as he bent to kiss her breasts. "Oh, God, love, your touch drives me wild."

A thousand glittering sparks ignited inside her as his mouth tugged gently at her nipple. She closed her eyes, savoring the moment as Cole coaxed indescribable sensations from her body. She arched against him as his burnished head moved from one peak to the other, lavishing them with the rough wetness of his tongue.

"Do you like that?" Cole asked as Dawn writhed beneath him.

Heat enveloped her from head to toe. "Oh, yes, it feels . . . wonderful."

"There's more, love, much more."

As if to prove his words, his hand slid lower down, into the thatch of dark curls at the juncture of her thighs. She stiffened, but relaxed again when he kissed her, letting the heat of his mouth soothe her fears. She had barely recovered from his kiss when she felt his finger slide inside her, traveling on the slickness of her desire. He pierced her so deeply she began to tremble all over. His mouth sucking vigorously at her breasts and his fingers moving inside her drove her mad with wanting.

Firm, warm lips moved restlessly over her body, his mouth and tongue creating havoc wherever they touched. Her breath came in harsh, panting gasps. She could think of nothing but Cole and the wonderfully arousing things he was doing to her.

"You're hot and wet for me, sweetheart," Cole whispered against her lips as his hands tested her hot center. He found a place she hadn't known existed, a place where a single touch produced exquisite pleasure. She shuddered and cried out. "You're ready for me, love."

"I didn't know it could be like this," Dawn whimpered between gasps.

"It gets better." Cole slipped a second finger inside her, and she moaned so loud he went still.

"Did I hurt you? You're awfully tight." A vague warning nagged at him, but he shook it off.

Dawn shook her head. "It's not pain I feel but something . . . something that defies words." She wet her lips, wondering if she should tell him she was still a virgin. She was ignorant when it came to sexual matters. Would he know? Or even care? Her thoughts became distracted. She couldn't think while Cole's hands and kisses fueled the fires of passion inside her.

His stroking grew more frenzied. Dawn jerked and panted. His palms and fingers brushed her between her legs again and again, his fingers piercing her, his hands wet with her sweet essence as he brought her to the pinnacle of some great discovery.

A brilliant explosion wracked Dawn. Her body arched off the bed. Moans fell from her lips.

Intensely caught up in the very first climax of her life, Dawn was barely aware when Cole removed his trousers, parted her legs with his knee and rose above her, his face stark with need. She clenched her teeth when she felt his sex probe between her legs, demanding entrance into her tight sheath. He cupped her buttocks, raising her high off the bed as he thrust inside her. Dawn bit her lip to keep from crying out as his fullness stretched her. She feared he would break her in two.

Cole encountered resistance and frowned. Something was wrong. It was almost as if Dawn was a . . . but no, that couldn't be. Dawn had been a wife for five years. He pushed harder, shoving himself deeper inside her. She stared up at him, her blue eyes stark with shock and pain.

Cole went still. But Dawn wouldn't permit him to stop now, before she found the answer to all her questions. The pain didn't matter. Cole had given her a taste of heaven and she wanted more.

Wanted it badly enough to endure the brief pain of his entry into virgin territory. Grasping his buttocks, she urged him to continue, refusing to let him withdraw.

Cole appeared confused. "Dawn, I don't understand." But the heat of her exploring hands and the walls of her tight sheath squeezing him produced feelings too overwhelming to question. Nothing but sudden death would prevent him from forging ahead, thrusting himself inside her sweet warmth and bringing them both to a pleasurable conclusion.

Flexing his hips, Cole thrust forward. His body was hugely aroused; a fine sheen of perspiration beaded his forehead. He reached the barrier of her maidenhead and went still, staring down at her, his eyes hard, stark, determined. Her face contorted with pain, Dawn stared back, offering no excuses, no explanations.

"Sweet Lord! You're a virgin! It's too late to stop now, love." His words were strained, as if speaking was an effort.

Then he plunged into her, breaking through her maidenhead, stretching her with his thickness and filling her with a single powerful thrust. Dawn whimpered, gripping his shoulders as pain exploded through her. Cole soothed her with tender words until she quieted. Then slowly, carefully, he began to stroke inside her. Dawn felt herself stretching to accommodate him, the pain lessening with each successive stroke. Soon her body became accustomed to his size and hardness and she moved her hips experimentally. It was all the invitation Cole needed.

He thrust once, then again, one after another, until Dawn found herself meeting him stroke for stroke, pushing her hips upward against him as he rode her hard and deep. Release came abruptly, plunging Dawn into a chasm of blinding pleasure. It was more intense, more shattering than what she had experienced a few moments ago when he used his hands to send her over the edge. Cole drove in and out relentlessly, one pounding thrust after another as wave after wave of rapture engulfed her. Never in her wildest dreams had she expected mating with a man to be like this. Then she felt him go rigid, heard him cry out, felt his seed splashing hotly inside her, and still he continued.

Finally his frantic thrusting movements ceased and he collapsed against her, his arms holding her as if he'd never let her go. Several sweet moments passed before he moved off her and onto his back. Once his heart slowed, he rolled onto his side and propped himself up on one elbow. His eyes narrowed as he stared intently at her.

"You owe me an explanation."

Dawn pretended to misunderstand. "I . . . don't know what you mean?"

"I think you do." He rose abruptly, lit a lamp and brought it close to the bed. Then he spread her legs, staring at the smear of blood staining her thighs, then at his own sex, still wet with her virgin's blood. "You were a virgin, lady. You're not a wife. You've never been a wife. Why in the hell didn't you tell me?"

Dawn cringed beneath Cole's accusations. "I didn't think it mattered. You said you'd show me pleasure and you did. Forget the virgin part."

"I wish to hell I could." He set the lamp on the bedside table and settled back down beside her. "I'm waiting."

Dawn sighed, reluctant to bare her shame to Cole but unable to prevent it. Billy had accused her of being inadequate, but Cole had just proven him wrong. She had responded explosively to Cole, received pleasure and given pleasure. At least she thought Cole had enjoyed what they'd done together.

"Billy was never a husband to me," Dawn blurted out. "He blamed me for his inability to perform. He said I wasn't woman enough to please him. But the blame lay wholly with him. Once, when Billy was roaring drunk, he told me he had been wounded during a bank robbery. It happened a long time ago. He was wounded in a place that made it impossible for him to . . ."

Cole was stunned. "I get the picture. Cobb couldn't function sexually."

Dawn flushed and looked away. "There were certain things whores did to him, but I refused to do them."

"So Cobb beat you when he couldn't bed you properly," Cole assumed.

"He took his anger and frustration out on me. He beat me when he wanted sex and couldn't perform. He beat me if I so much as looked at one of his men. He lied about what we did in bed to make it appear as if he bedded me regularly. The only reason he didn't share me with his men was because he feared they would learn I was a virgin.

He didn't want his reputation as a virile lover ruined."

"Why in the hell did he marry you if he couldn't use you like he wanted?"

"I was so very young," Dawn said slowly. Memories of the naive girl she'd been made her eyes grow misty. "Billy hoped my youth would invigorate him, but it didn't. His men didn't suspect he was half a man. He kept me around as proof of his virility. He lied about what he did to me in bed, but I was grateful he refused to share me with his men."

The more Cole heard, the more he wished he could resurrect Billy Cobb and give him the beating of his life. He wanted to crush Cobb like an insect, pull him limb from limb, inflict excruciating pain.

"Why didn't you leave during one of Cobb's absences? You could have gone to the law."

Dawn gave a snort of mocking laughter. "I was fifteen. Billy terrified me. I was afraid of what he'd do to me if I left and he caught me. Besides, I had nowhere to go. I feared the law would jail me simply because I was Billy's wife. If I ran to my father, he would return me to Billy or sell me to someone just as brutal. As I grew older and wiser I realized I had to escape or risk death beneath Billy's fists. I tried to run away a few times. I didn't get far. Billy always found me and beat me so viciously I couldn't move for days."

Cole couldn't bear to hear another word about Dawn's suffering under Cobb's harsh treatment. When she started to sob softly, he pulled her into his arms, cradling her against him.

"Don't cry, love. Forget Cobb. He'll never hurt you again. He's planted in Boot Hill, exactly where he belongs."

"But there are others like him," Dawn hiccupped. She was thinking of her future. Once Cole left, she'd be stalked by scum every bit as evil as Billy. Sam and Spider were still out there somewhere. Where could she go to escape them?

"They won't get their hands on you," Cole promised. He'd already decided he couldn't leave Dawn alone and unprotected. He hadn't worked out the particulars, but an idea was forming in his brain; an idea that would place Dawn far from harm's way. All he had to do was to get her to agree. And even if she didn't agree, he'd do whatever was necessary to insure her safety.

Dawn wanted to believe Cole, but she knew how men operated, and there were more Billy Cobbs in this world than Cole Websters. Besides, what could Cole do to protect her once he moved on to another job? Nothing. Absolutely nothing.

"Trust me," Cole said, observing Dawn's skepticism.

"Trusting doesn't come easily when I've experienced the vile things men are capable of."

She rolled away from Cole and felt a twinge of discomfort between her thighs. The tiniest of groans escaped her lips. Cole heard and suffered a pang of guilt.

"Are you sore? You should have told me you'd never been with a man before. I could have been gentler."

"Technically, that's not true," Dawn said, recalling Billy's hands on her and the things he'd done attempting to stir his manhood to life. She'd hated every second of it.

"It's true as far as I'm concerned," Cole said, rising abruptly. "Lie still. I'll see what I can do to make you more comfortable."

Cole poured water from the pitcher into a bowl, found a soft cloth in the cupboard and returned to the bed. "Spread your legs, love."

Dawn hesitated too long for Cole's liking. He knelt between her thighs and held them open with his knees while he brought the wet cloth against her center. He cleansed her with gentle thoroughness. Then he washed himself, aware of her eyes upon him and the redness staining her cheeks. When he'd finished he set the bowl aside and smiled at her.

"Better now?"

Dawn nodded, shifting her gaze away from that part of him that had suddenly and quite visibly grown larger. Not only was she comfortable, but his touch had created a wanting inside her. Now that she knew the kind of pleasure Cole was capable of giving her, she couldn't help wanting it one more time before he left her forever.

Cole slid into bed and gathered Dawn against him. His hands went to her breasts, covering them possessively, then pushing them up to accept his kisses. Dawn felt her nipples swelling as Cole tugged them between his teeth and sucked them, first one then the other into his mouth. She moaned. She felt as if her body no longer belonged to her. Cole had awakened her to passion and she was eager to experience that wondrous feeling again. She held his head against her forcibly as he suckled her, listening to his hoarse groans, answering them with small breathy sighs.

Abruptly Cole released her, reluctantly putting distance between them. "I'm sorry, love, I shouldn't be doing this. You're sore. This is your first time. It's just that . . . dammit, I want you again."

Dawn moaned with disappointment as she felt the warmth of Cole's body leave her. She reached for him. "No! Don't leave me. I want you, too. I've been denied this kind of tenderness all my life."

Cole gave her a smile that warmed her soul. Then his hungry mouth covered hers. He kissed her endlessly. His hands roamed over her, stroking her throat, her breasts, her belly. He caressed her hips, the pointed tips of her breasts, her swollen, aching sex.

Dawn could feel the explosive power building within him. The ripe tip of his thick sex rubbed against her, making her aware of his need. She touched him. Tentatively at first, but when Cole closed her hand around him she couldn't resist stroking the velvet hardness pulsing against her palm.

"Oh, God." His big body shuddered and he closed his eyes, ecstasy racing through him as he allowed her to stroke him, pitching his hips upward as he thrust himself against her palm. He allowed her to continue several agonizing minutes before shoving her hand away. He was breathing hard, gnashing his teeth against the urgent need to possess her.

"No more! I need to come inside you now!"

Rearing up on his knees, he spread her legs

wide. Thrusting forward and upward, he pushed his bulk inside her. Abruptly Dawn lost the ability to reason, responding spontaneously to her body's needs as Cole thrust and withdrew, bringing her effortlessly to the brink of madness. The exquisite torment went on and on—until with a hoarse cry she found that final, climactic fulfillment. Waves of emotion rippled through her as she dimly heard Cole cry out her name.

Moments later Cole rolled to his side, bringing Dawn against him. His chest heaved as he fought for breath. Not since his beloved Morning Mist had he felt like this with a woman.

Dawn snuggled against Cole. Words were unnecessary; her body spoke volumes about the wonderful things Cole had made her feel. She had saved up enough memories to last a lifetime. Tomorrow Cole would go on his way and her dreary existence would continue as if he had never entered her life. She would have no money, no way to support herself, but she'd get by. She was tough. She'd survived Billy's cruelty all these years, hadn't she? She closed her eyes and let sleep claim her.

Cole felt Dawn relax against him, heard the even cadence of her breathing and realized she had fallen asleep. It was just as well, he thought. He didn't know how she would react to the plan he had devised for her and would just as soon wait until tomorrow to broach the subject. It would create a tremendous upheaval in her life but it was something he had to do. Unless he assumed responsibility for her, her future didn't bear thinking about.

What kind of life could Dawn expect after he left? Every man in the territory would want to make her his whore, and he couldn't allow that. His plans for her future were far better and much safer than anything she could arrange for herself. He slipped into slumber content to have settled Dawn's future so handily, at least in his own mind.

"Is anybody home?"

A loud pounding on the door woke Cole from a sound sleep. He sat up groggily, aware of the warm, fragrant woman curled beside him, and of bright sunshine streaming through the cabin.

"Cole! Answer me. Are you in there?"

The doorlatch rattled, and seconds later the door swung open. With sunlight streaming behind him, only the outline of the man's body could be clearly seen. He was big, rugged, and wore guns on his hips. He paused a moment in the doorway, hands poised above his guns as he studied the situation. He spied Cole in the bed and relaxed.

"Well, I'll be damned. Never thought I'd find you in bed this late in the morning. You sick or something?" As yet he hadn't seen Dawn lying quietly beside Cole.

"Morning, Sandy. Wondered when you'd show up," Cole said, dashing gritty sleep from his eyes. He started to throw aside the blanket, realized that Dawn was awake and staring at the door in horror, and pulled it back into place.

Sandy strode into the cabin and approached the bed. The huge smile died on his face when he saw the small female figure trying her darndest to hide beneath Cole's body. Embarrassed, he flushed and looked away.

"Uh, sorry, Cole, didn't know you had company. I'll just wait outside for you. Sorry, ma'am," Sandy said, tipping his hat in Dawn's direction. He turned abruptly and hurried out the door.

Holding the blanket to her naked breasts, Dawn sat up slowly. "Who was that?"

Cole stretched and grinned. "That long drink of water is my partner, Sandy Johnson. I've been waiting for him to show up. He's been out tracking Cobb's gang. He must have followed them to Dodge. He probably checked in with the sheriff and learned I was out here. I'll get dressed and go talk to him. Call us when breakfast is ready."

"You want me to cook breakfast for him?" Dawn squeaked in horror. "After the way he found us together?"

"Sandy is a grown man, love. I'm sure nothing he's seen surprises him. You'll like him, I promise."

Cole dressed quickly and went outside. Dawn dressed more slowly, wondering how she would ever face Cole's partner. Calm finally returned when she realized she'd probably never see Sandy Johnson or Cole Webster after today.

"The sheriff gave me directions to the cabin," Sandy said when Cole joined him outside. "He didn't say you had a woman with you."

"Dawn is Cobb's wife."

"Didn't know the bastard had a wife. Sheriff Tayler said Cobb was planted in Boot Hill, and

121

that Duke Riley is in jail waiting for his hanging. I followed Riley, Pickens and Lewis to Dodge. Have you seen anything of Pickens or Lewis?"

"I didn't want to kill Cobb but he gave me no choice. Pickens was here. He caught me off guard. Plugged me in the shoulder. I'm pretty sure I wounded him. Haven't seen hide nor hair of Lewis, but I'll bet anything he's not far away."

"They want the loot from the train robbery. Have you recovered it yet?"

"Found it yesterday." Cole didn't explain why it had taken him so long to find the stolen money, and Sandy didn't ask.

"What about the woman? Is she mixed up in all this?"

"Leave Dawn out of it," Cole growled dangerously. "She's innocent. She was brutalized by Cobb during all the years of their marriage. She had no part in those robberies."

Sandy sent Cole an assessing look. "Don't get your dander up. I'm not accusing her of anything. Our job is to recover the money, and we've done that. It's the sheriff's job now to bring the gang to justice."

Dawn stuck her head out the door and announced breakfast. Sandy took a good look at her and whistled softly. "A damn good-looking woman, Cole. Half-breed, if I'm not mistaken." He shook his head in bewilderment. "You surprise me. It's not like you to get involved with a woman while on an assignment. If she's Cobb's woman, he probably shared her with his men. You're usually more discerning about who you bed."

Never had Cole wanted to hit anyone more in

his life. But Sandy was his friend and probably knew him better than any other man. "Dawn isn't what you think," he said through clenched teeth. "She and Cobb were married five years, but technically she was an innocent until I . . . Never mind, the particulars won't interest you. Come inside and meet her for yourself. She's a tolerable cook, you won't be disappointed."

Dawn set biscuits, eggs and ham before the hungry men and turned away to get the coffee.

"Dawn, meet my partner, Sandy Johnson."

Dawn acknowledged the introduction with a quick nod. She was afraid to meet Sandy's gaze, fearing he'd condemn her wanton behavior with Cole. She did note that he was a handsome man perhaps a year or two older than Cole. The color of his hair fit his name. And his face and hands were tanned to nearly the same sandy shade as his hair.

"Howdy, ma'am," Sandy said, removing his hat respectfully and setting it on the knobby back of his chair. "That food smells mighty good."

"Sit down, Dawn," Cole invited when Dawn seemed reluctant to join them.

Dawn perched on the edge of a three-legged stool which Cole pulled up to the table, her gaze fastened on her plate as she nibbled at her food. Had she bothered to listen she would have learned that the men were more concerned about the return of the money to the railroad than they were about her.

"Frank Williams will be tickled to see that missing money," Sandy said as he shoveled a spoonful of eggs into his mouth.

"I reckon there's a bonus in it for us."

"I won't turn it down," Sandy said with a grin. "Wonder where we'll be sent next."

"I know where I'm going," Cole said, surprising Sandy. "I'm taking a leave to visit my twin sister and her family in Oregon City. When you take the money to Wichita, you can tell the boss I'm taking a year off from my duties. It's been a long time since I've taken a vacation, and there's something I need to do."

Dawn heard Cole's last words and stopped eating, the fork poised midway to her mouth. This was the first she'd heard about Cole taking time off. Was this something he'd just decided? Did it have anything to do with her?

Sandy glanced from Cole to Dawn, guessing more than Cole gave him credit for. He sensed something intense flowing between them that not even Cole was aware of, and wasn't sure he approved. He and Cole had been friends too long for him not to worry and wonder about this outlaw's woman Cole seemed so protective of. What did he have in mind where Dawn was concerned?

"So you're taking time off to visit your family," Sandy repeated slowly. "Would you care to tell me the truth?"

Cole sent Dawn a quick glance and shook his head. "Not now. I do intend to visit my sister . . . eventually. If you're finished with breakfast, I suggest we go outside. I don't want to bore Dawn with our business."

Sandy rose, adjusted his hat on his head and turned to Dawn. "The breakfast was good, ma'am, thank you kindly. If I don't see you before I leave, take care of yourself."

"Thank you," Dawn said, still shaken by Cole's words. "It . . . it was nice meeting you."

"What's this all about, Cole?" Sandy asked when they had walked a safe distance from the cabin. "It's not like you to decide things on the spur of the moment. Does your leave have anything to do with the woman?"

"More or less," Cole admitted. "I can't leave Dawn here unprotected. Not with Pickens and Lewis still on the loose."

"What the hell does that mean? You're not planning to stay here with her, are you?"

"Not hardly," Cole scoffed. "I'm taking her where I hope she'll be safe. Then I really do intend to visit my sister. But I'll need a year to do it all. Tell Frank I'll be eager to go wherever I'm needed when this little matter is settled."

Sandy glanced toward the house. "Where are you taking her? Does Dawn know about your plans?"

"I haven't spoken with Dawn yet. Once I do, she'll realize it's for her own good. She's better off with her own kind."

"Her own kind? Are you talking about Injuns?"

"I'm speaking about Indians," Cole corrected. "Running Elk, to be specific. She'll be safe with him. Some young buck will be delighted to take her for his mate."

"Thank God," Sandy said with a heartfelt sigh. "For a minute I thought you meant to marry the girl yourself. I've never known you to act rashly about anything."

"I'll never marry again," Cole said with such conviction that Sandy had no reason to doubt him. "I'm taking Dawn to Running Elk and that's the end of it."

Chapter Seven

Dawn watched from the doorway as Sandy rode away from the cabin. Cole had returned to the cabin briefly for the sack of money and Sandy had stowed it in his saddlebag before heading back to town. Dawn was still surprised that Cole hadn't left with his partner and didn't know what to make of it. She waited until Cole reentered the cabin to broach the subject.

"Why did you stay? If you're worried about me, you needn't be. I can take care of myself."

Cole sent her an oblique look. "Sit down, Dawn, we need to talk."

"About what?"

"About your future."

Dawn bristled as she plopped down into the nearest chair. "My future isn't your concern."

"It is now."

"Why, because you bedded me? You took nothing from me, Cole. I gave to you freely and expect nothing in return. You're not responsible for me."

"I'm making you my responsibility. Pickens and Lewis will be back. If not them, then other men will come sniffing around for reasons that have nothing to do with money."

Dawn's chin lifted. "I'll manage. I've decided to take the reward money after all. You did say it was mine, didn't you?"

"Yes, if you'll take it. But seven hundred dollars won't get you far, or last very long. Face reality, Dawn. You're a half-breed. It's not going to be easy to provide for yourself in a world such as we live in now. You'll probably marry again, but you should weigh your choices carefully before settling down again. I'd hate for you to get tangled up with another Billy Cobb."

All this talk about her future was making Dawn's head ache. Didn't Cole know she had already considered her options? She'd never marry again, that much she knew. She'd had enough of abusive men to last a lifetime. If all men were as kindhearted as Cole it would be wonderful, but men like Cole were few and far between. And they weren't interested in marrying someone like her.

"I don't see why that should matter to you," Dawn replied. "Go to Oregon. Visit your sister. You'll soon forget I ever existed."

"I can't do that," Cole said softly. His eyes were hooded, revealing nothing of his inner thoughts. "I've come to a decision, Dawn, one I hope you'll accept."

Dawn went still. She didn't like the sound of

that. She was her own woman now. She wasn't required to follow the dictates of any man.

"*You've* come to a decision," Dawn repeated with a hint of sarcasm. "Shouldn't I be the one to decide my future?"

Cole shook his head. "Not since . . . not since I learned just how innocent you really were. Just listen to what I have to say."

Dawn rose abruptly and went to the window. She'd spent five years in this isolated cabin, without friends or human contact except Billy and his men. She'd grown to hate this place and what it represented. She looked forward to leaving, but she was not planning to go to any destination Cole had in mind. Their moment of shared bliss had been incredible, but she was astute enough to realize that Cole had bedded her because she was available. He cared about her future because basically he was a good person. His love was reserved for his dead wife.

It wasn't as if she loved Cole, she told herself. She hardly knew him. He had taught her passion and she was grateful, but she wasn't sure she'd ever trust a man with her life.

She did wish, however, that after they parted he'd not forget her easily. Cole would be haunting her memories the rest of her life. It seemed only right that he should remember her at least for the space of a single week.

"Dawn, are you listening? Don't you want to know what I've decided?"

Dawn turned from the window to stare at Cole. "Go ahead and have your say. Not that it will matter one way or the other. What I do after you leave is entirely my decision." She returned her gaze to the scene outside the window.

Suddenly Dawn was aware of Cole standing behind her, so close she could feel his warmth seeping into her. She wanted to lean back against him, to hear him say she was going to be all right, to feel safe and protected. Instead she stood rigid, shoulders squared, chin high. She refused to accept his pity. Not even when he placed his hands on her shoulders and turned her to face him did she give him the satisfaction of knowing that his nearness affected her in ways that disturbed her. Once Cole left, her life would never be the same.

"I'm leaving tomorrow, Dawn, and you're coming with me."

"What! That . . . that's ridiculous."

"No, it makes good sense. I'm taking you where you'll be safe. Where I won't have to worry about you once I return to my job."

Now Dawn was really confused. It sounded as if Cole intended to drop her off somewhere like unwanted baggage. "I don't want to go to Oregon."

"I'm not talking about Oregon."

Dawn hadn't really expected that Cole would take her to his sister, but she couldn't conceive of another place he could take her where she'd be safe. "I don't like this game, Cole. This is my life you're talking about. Speak your piece, then leave like you planned."

He led her over to the bed and sat her down. Then he began pacing back and forth in front of her. "I think I've mentioned that I was married once to a woman named Morning Mist. She was beautiful, sweet, kind . . . well, never mind, that's not important. Morning Mist was killed in a raid upon her village while I was away. When I returned and learned her fate, I couldn't bring myself to return to the White world.

"Running Elk, Morning Mist's brother, asked me to stay with his people. I spent four years with the Sioux, learning to live with my grief. They taught me skills that I would never have learned otherwise. I left when Running Elk decided to move his people to the reservation."

Dawn was moved by Cole's story but couldn't see how it affected her. "What is the point in all this?"

"As I've said before, you're too innocent, too vulnerable to be left on your own."

Dawn bristled indignantly. "I'm not helpless. I can hunt, fish, plant a garden and glean edible food from the forest. I don't need a man."

Cole ignored her protest and continued his explanation. "Running Elk is a good man. He's like a brother to me. You will fit in with his people and in time learn to adjust to a new way of life. Running Elk will treat you well and find a good husband for you."

The color drained from Dawn's face. "I know nothing about Indians, their culture, or the lives they lead. How can you expect me to fit in with people who are foreign to me? Besides, I don't want a husband."

"You said you speak the Sioux tongue."

"Not fluently. My mother taught me what little I know. I don't want to live with Indians. You can't make me do something I don't want to do."

Cole stopped pacing and sat down beside Dawn. "I've thought long and hard about this. It's the only solution. I believe you'll feel more secure with Indians than with Whites. Half-breeds are despised by White society. I can't bear the thought of you being abused and tormented by society because of the color of your skin. You're coming with me and that's final. Pack up your belongings, we'll go into town later today and buy tickets on the first train to Cheyenne. From there we will make our way by horseback to the Red Cloud Agency."

"I can't believe you've planned all this without my approval. I'm not going anywhere with you." She started to rise, but he grasped her hands to prevent her from leaving.

"You have no choice. I've already accepted responsibility for you and I want a clear conscience where you're concerned. If I hadn't bedded you . . ."

"If you hadn't bedded me you would have ridden out of here and promptly forgotten me," Dawn supplied.

"Perhaps. But that's a moot point now. What's done is done. I'll never marry again, I decided that a long time ago. There will be other women, but none who mean anything to me. I'm telling you this so you'll know that I'm doing the best I can for you under the restrictions I've placed upon myself. What I'm saying, Dawn, is that I can't marry you, and I want you to understand it's not because of what or who you are but what and who I've become since Morning Mist's death."

"I have no desire to marry a man I hardly know.

131

I've tried marriage, it isn't for me. Taking my virginity is not a valid reason for accepting responsibility for me. It could have happened at any time. I'm grateful it was you and not one of Billy's men."

Cole stared at her. At her sweet face, so like Morning Mist's it took his breath away. Her long black hair, blue eyes and dusky golden skin seduced and enticed him. He didn't usually take advantage of innocent woman, but just looking at Dawn made him ache to make love to her again. Her red lips were moist and lush and incredibly tantalizing. Despite her slimness, her breasts were full and firm. Her earthy beauty was rare and highly erotic.

"I wholeheartedly agree," Cole said earnestly. "That fact makes my obligation even more pressing. It will work out, love, you'll see."

"Don't call me that," Dawn said, refusing to look at him. "I've never been anyone's love in my life. I'm not as innocent as you think. Billy did . . . things to me that I can't even talk about. After a while, when he realized he couldn't perform with me no matter what he did, he resorted to beatings."

"Forget Cobb," Cole said angrily. "No man will ever hurt you like that again. I'm going to make sure of that. You'll be fine with Running Elk. He will treat you like a sister and see that other men respect you."

Dawn's eyes grew misty. No one had ever cared about her enough to want her happiness. Yet something inside her resisted Cole's plans. He had no right to organize her life for her.

"I'm sorry, Cole, I won't go. I know what you're doing. You're salving your conscience where I'm concerned, but I don't want you to feel guilty about what we did."

"The hell I am!" Cole cried, leaping to his feet and jerking her up with him. "Conscience has nothing to do with my decision." Those words were not exactly true, but Cole preferred not to admit that his guilt over bedding Cobb's widow was enormous. But he wasn't sorry it had happened. Hell, no! He'd enjoyed their mating, and was glad he'd been the one to initiate her to passion.

"Listen to me, Dawn," he said more reasonably. "Just try it for a while. If you don't fit in, or if you hate it, you can leave. I'll tell Running Elk you're free to leave whenever you wish. Just give it a chance."

Cole wanted to say more, but Dawn's nearness was having its usual effect upon his body. They were standing so close he could feel the tips of her breasts pressing against his chest. The thickness of their clothing did little to protect them from the scorching heat arcing between them. Taking an aggressive step forward, Cole pulled her further into his embrace. He stared at her hard, unblinking. Green eyes flashing. He wanted to kiss her so damn bad he ached.

Dawn went still, the line of her spine rigid. Did Cole think he could use sexual persuasion to bring her around to his way of thinking?

Then all thought fled as his mouth came down hard on hers. His kiss deepened. Her lips softened beneath his for a brief moment as she opened her mouth and touched his tongue with hers. Then reality returned and she pulled away. In aching silence she watched him drop his arms and step back.

"Your method of persuasion won't work," Dawn said. Her breathlessness belied her words.

He searched her face; his intent gaze plumbed the very core of her soul, recognizing something she feared to admit. A reluctant smile turned up the corners of his mouth. "That kiss wasn't meant as persuasion. I wanted to kiss you. Regardless of what you say, you're going to accompany me to Running Elk's village."

"Cole, this is—"

". . . The right thing to do. Pack your personal items. Cobb's horse is a good one. He can serve as your mount. Does he have a name?"

"Billy called him Wally, don't ask me why."

"Wally and Warrior can travel with us on the same train. Old Betsy will find a happy home at the livery. Can you be ready in an hour? Perhaps we can get a train out of here yet today."

Dawn glanced around the ramshackle cabin, seeing nothing she cared to take with her as a reminder of her former life. Except for the clothing Cole had bought her and a small memento from her mother, she had no personal effects. She could flee this place with no regrets if it wasn't for the way Cole was bullying her into leaving. He'd made it perfectly clear he didn't want her for himself, so why wouldn't he just leave? He complicated her life and disordered her thoughts.

When Dawn stared at him mutinously, Cole said, "I mean it, Dawn. You have one hour to gather your belongings." Then he strode out the door without waiting for an answer.

One hour later Dawn and Cole rode away from the cabin. Dawn didn't look back once. She was leaving behind no fond memories, nothing she'd miss or regret. But that didn't mean she'd meekly follow Cole. She didn't want to live with Indians. She might look like an Indian, but in her heart she didn't feel like one. It was disheartening to realize that she belonged to no particular race or culture. She was a product of two cultures, despised by both Indians and Whites. Billy had been right when he'd said she was worthless to anyone.

"Try not to worry, Dawn. Trust me."

Dawn trusted no man. Let Cole think what he wanted. She might get on the train with him, but that didn't mean she'd get off with him. Somewhere between Dodge and Cheyenne lay open country. It would take little effort to escape Cole, and that was exactly what she intended to do.

They left the mule at the livery when they arrived in Dodge and continued on to the railroad station. The Union Pacific wasn't due to arrive until noon the next day. Cole bought tickets and arranged for their horses to be transported with them on the same train.

"What do we do now?" Dawn wanted to know. She wasn't accustomed to living in town, and people made her nervous.

"I'm going to check in with the sheriff and see if he's had any luck finding Lewis and Pickens. Then I'm going to find out if Sandy has left town yet. Why don't you go to the Dodge House and get us a couple of rooms? I'll meet you there later."

Dawn jerked hard on the reins. Wally danced to a stop. Cole reined in beside her. "What's wrong?"

"You want me to get rooms at the hotel?"

"That's right. I won't be long. When I return we'll take supper at the hotel. If Sandy is still in town maybe he'll join us."

"Cole, I don't think you realize . . ."

Her words were lost to the wind. Cole had already kneed his horse toward the sheriff's office. Dawn watched him move away with trepidation. Didn't he realize the position in which he had just placed her? Apparently he had forgotten who and what she was. Unwilling to succumb to her fears, Dawn turned Wally toward the Dodge House.

Cole's thoughts had already turned in another direction. He was still worried about Pickens and Lewis. Had they heard yet that the train loot had been recovered? Were they still in the vicinity?

As luck would have it, Cole ran into Sandy outside of the sheriff's office.

"Sheriff Tayler is not here," Sandy said after greeting Cole.

"I'd hoped you hadn't left yet," Cole replied, angling Sandy back inside the sheriff's office where they could talk. "Do you know if Tayler's seen anything of Lewis or Pickens?"

"The deputy told me Tayler formed a posse early this morning. A rancher spotted them on his land just east of town."

Cole grinned, somewhat relieved by the news.

136

"That's welcome news. After you left, I worried that they might trail you to Wichita and ambush you along the way. They're in desperate need of that money."

"I already thought of that and took care of it. I sent the money to Wichita on this morning's train. There's an armed guard on board just in case. I'm leaving tomorrow morning. If I'm ambushed they won't find a damn thing."

"I have a much safer idea. Spread the word tomorrow that you've sent the money on ahead by train. By then it will be too late for them to do anything about it and there will be no reason to ambush you."

Sandy laughed. "You always were smarter than me. What are your plans? Did you talk Cobb's widow into going to your Indian friend's village?"

"More or less," Cole said, heaving a sigh that was full of misgivings. "We leave for Cheyenne at noon tomorrow."

"Are you sure you're doing the right thing? You really haven't given this much thought." He slapped Cole on the back. "Come on over to the Longbranch, I'll buy you a drink. You look as if you could use one."

"I reckon a stiff drink wouldn't hurt me," Cole admitted. "I sent Dawn over to the Dodge House to get a couple of rooms for us. Maybe I ought to check in on her first. I'll meet you at the saloon in a few minutes." They parted at the door, Sandy heading for the saloon while Cole made his way toward the Dodge House.

*　*　*

Dawn tethered Wally to the hitching post in front of the hotel but didn't enter immediately. She didn't belong in a place like this. Prejudice was a fearsome thing. Cole was the only man who didn't ridicule her for being part Sioux.

Taking a deep, steadying breath, Dawn squared her shoulders and pushed through the door. She walked directly to the front desk and rang the bell, ignoring the people milling about the lobby. The clerk appeared from the back room. He took one look at Dawn and sneered at her from the corner of his mouth.

"We don't rent rooms to Injuns or half-breeds. This is a respectable hotel."

Dawn heard titters behind her and quelled the urge to turn and run. "I'm with Mr. Cole Webster, the railroad man. He sent me to engage two rooms for the night."

"I don't care who you're with, lady. Mr. Webster is welcome any time, but not squaws. Try the flophouse down the street. Sometimes they let people like you in."

Dawn's face turned a dull red. She was so embarrassed she wanted to melt into the woodwork. Everyone was looking at her as if she were something dirty. She was grateful they didn't know she was Billy Cobb's widow. If they did, they would be doing more than laughing at her.

"Did you hear me, lady?" the clerk repeated for the benefit of his audience. "Get out of here, you're disturbing our respectable guests."

It didn't take Cole long to realize what was happening when he entered the hotel lobby. His fury was almost palpable as he strode toward the front desk. The clerk saw him and blanched, frozen in place by the potency of Cole's anger.

"Did I hear right?" Cole asked in a voice that sent terror into the clerk's soul. "Did you or did you not tell the lady she wasn't welcome here?"

Dawn turned at the sound of his voice. Relief came instantly, and her expression must have shown it, for Cole's smile was reassuring.

"It's hotel policy, sir," the clerk whined. "No Injuns or half-breeds allowed. I'm just doing my job."

"The *lady*," Cole stressed, "is with me. We need two rooms for the night. Do you have a problem with that?"

People standing around the lobby leaned forward to hear the clerk's reply. Dawn saw them and tugged Cole's hand. "It's all right, Cole. We can spend the night at the cabin. I don't mind."

"I mind," Cole said, sending their audience a scathing glance. It was enough to send the onlookers scattering. He turned back to the clerk. "Now, about those rooms."

"We're rather crowded and—"

Cole swung the register around and signed his name. "I'll have the keys now. Adjoining rooms, if any are available."

The clerk licked moisture onto his dry lips. What this man would do to him if he failed to comply didn't bear thinking about. He'd always heard that redheaded men had ferocious tempers and he was too cowardly to test the theory.

"Of course, sir. Two adjoining rooms. That will cost a dollar extra." He selected a pair of keys, placing them carefully in Cole's hand.

"Fine. Is there a bathing room the lady can use?"

"Just down the hall from your rooms."

"I'll bring our bags in after the lady is settled in her room," Cole said. He reached in his pocket, pulled out some bills and tossed them down on the counter. "I'm paying in advance." Then he took Dawn's elbow and steered her toward the stairs.

A tense silence prevailed as they ascended the stairs. When they reached the landing, Cole checked the keys for the room numbers and turned to the right. They passed the bathing room, which Cole pointed out, before halting before room number seventeen. He unlocked the door and followed Dawn inside.

Dawn walked into the room and stopped dead in her tracks. The room was almost as large as her entire cabin. The bed was huge, with a lovely floral quilt and real feather pillows. The draperies at the windows were made of velvet, or what Dawn assumed velvet might look like. The wood floor sported a colorful braided rug, and the room held more furniture than she'd ever seen in one place.

"What's wrong?" Cole asked, puzzled by Dawn's silence. "Don't you like it? Perhaps we can trade rooms if you like mine better than yours."

"It's . . . too fine," Dawn said reverently. "I've never seen anything like it. My father's cabin was little more than a hovel. Billy's cabin was no better. I'll wager an Indian tent is more comfortable than what I'm accustomed to."

Cole's head dipped in acknowledgement. "Tipis can be amazingly comfortable. I've lived in one for many years with no complaint. I reckon you'll grow to appreciate their adaptability to climate and seasons."

"I've never lived in anything even remotely comfortable. Pa thought only of his own comfort, and Billy didn't care."

Cole could well imagine the small, defenseless girl living with a brutal father who cared little for her. "Forget the past. I promise your future will be brighter. Meanwhile, enjoy the room, take a bath, do what you like. I'm meeting Sandy at the saloon for a drink. When I return, we'll all have dinner together in the hotel dining room."

"Why don't you and Sandy dine without me?" Dawn suggested. "I'll have something in my room."

Cole sent her a speaking look. "I'm not ashamed to be seen with you, Dawn. We'll eat together. I'll bring your bags up before I join Sandy."

Cole spun on his heel and left before Dawn's protest reached her lips.

Dawn had to admit she felt better after bathing in a real bathtub, washing her hair and donning one of the attractive dresses Cole had purchased for her in Dodge. She was sitting by the window watching the sunset when Cole knocked on her door. He must have returned to the hotel some time ago to bathe and change, for when she opened the door she saw that his burnished hair was still damp and he had donned clean clothes.

"Sandy is waiting in the dining room," Cole said as he eyed her appreciatively. "That dress becomes you. We'll buy you some new clothes in Cheyenne, but you'll probably prefer to wear deerskin tunics and leggings once you become accustomed to them. They are far more comfortable than anything you can buy in a store."

"I'm ready," Dawn said, not really certain she meant it. After the fiasco in the hotel lobby, she wasn't certain she wanted to make another spectacle of herself, but hiding in her room would be cowardly. And she had promised herself that once she was rid of Billy Cobb she'd never act in a cowardly manner again. She was free now. She need never fear Billy Cobb or his kind again. She was beginning to realize that she was capable of anything with Cole beside her.

Dawn nearly lost her nerve when she walked into the elegant dining room of the Dodge House. The room was crowded with people, most of whom stopped eating and gawked at her the moment she entered the room on Cole's arm.

"Don't let them bother you," Cole said when he felt her hand tighten on his arm. "They're jealous because you're so beautiful. Ah, there's Sandy. He's already secured a table for us."

The dinner was more enjoyable than Dawn had expected it to be. Sandy was attentive and jovial and pretended not to notice the curious stares aimed in their direction. Dawn ate with gusto. Most of the delicious food Cole ordered was new to her. If her appetite continued like this, she wouldn't remain skinny for long. She wondered if Cole would like her better with more meat on her bones, then dismissed the thought as irrelevant. Once she and Cole parted, he would not even know how thin or fat she grew.

"I'm lighting out of here at dawn tomorrow,"

Sandy announced as he finished the last of his coffee. "Are you sure you won't come with me, Cole?"

Cole glanced at Dawn, then back at Sandy. "Very sure. I'm taking Dawn to my friend Running Elk, then paying a visit to my sister and her family. I haven't seen them since I visited four years ago. Ashley and Tanner are the only family I have now. I've prepared a letter requesting a leave of absence. I'd appreciate it if you'd deliver it to Frank Williams for me."

"Sure thing," Sandy said, pocketing the letter Cole handed him. "I reckon we can get by without you for a spell. Keep in touch. Where should I have the boss send your bonus?"

"Have him send the money in care of Tanner MacTavish, Oregon City, Oregon. It will be safe with Tanner until I claim it. I've invested most of my savings in Tanner's logging business and he banks the profit in my name. I reckon I've accumulated a tidy sum by now. Logging is a lucrative industry in Oregon Territory, and Tanner was one of the first to take advantage of it."

"I want to get an early start tomorrow so I reckon I'll hit the sack. Take care of yourself, Cole. You, too, Dawn."

He tipped his hat and walked away.

"Let's get out of here," Cole said as he rose abruptly.

He wanted Dawn all to himself. He wanted to make love to her again even though he knew he shouldn't. He wanted to lose himself in her sweet body until he grew dizzy with passion. If he was smart he'd bid her good night and leave her at her door. If he surrendered to his needs he'd not be able to leave her with Running Elk and walk away. No, he had to curb his desire now, before it was too late. Before Dawn wanted more from him than he was willing or prepared to give.

Chapter Eight

Dawn stared at the door separating Cole's room from hers, trying to decide whether she was happy or sad that he had left her without so much as a kiss. She knew their closeness at the cabin had been a mistake but she hadn't thought Cole would regret it so soon. At least he'd been honest with her about his motivation in making love to her. It was lust. Pure lust. He didn't want attachments of any kind while his memories of Morning Mist were still vivid in his mind.

Dawn had no intention of complicating either Cole's life or her own by clinging to a man who didn't want her. Nor was she going to allow him to arrange her life. Still recalling all those emotions and feelings that Cole's loving had inspired in her, Dawn undressed and crawled into bed. Sleep was hard-won but it finally came.

Cole wasn't so lucky. As he tossed and turned in his lonely bed, his thoughts were consumed with Dawn. He pictured her naked in his arms, her hair, thick and black as the darkest midnight, creating tongues of fire against his skin. He had expected a woman knowledgeable in the art of sex and found a virgin.

He wanted her again. Now. But he couldn't take the chance of impregnating her. Not when he was leaving her with Running Elk so that she might find a husband among his warriors. He glanced toward the connecting door, thinking it would take very little effort to open that door and crawl into her bed. Would she welcome him? Somehow he thought she would, and that made him feel even more like a heel. Cole didn't want Dawn to learn to depend upon him. She'd be on her own soon, and he wasn't the kind of man to offer hope where none existed. Dawn would be far better off with a man who could love her with his whole heart. Someone who was not haunted by a woman whose death he refused to accept. He neither wanted nor needed another love.

Sleep finally carried Cole away to his dreams, none of which were particularly reassuring. No matter how hard he tried to separate Dawn and Morning Mist in his dreams, they merged into one being, becoming the heated center of his desires.

At ten o'clock the following morning Cole appeared at Dawn's door to take her to breakfast. Her meager belongings were already packed, and she was becomingly dressed in a gray traveling dress with a small cape.

"I've already spoken with the sheriff," Cole said as he picked up her small bundle and guided her down the stairs. "He's received the reward money. I took the liberty of buying you a small reticule to carry it in." He handed her a small cloth bag, which Dawn tucked into her pocket.

"Thank you. Did the sheriff's posse catch Sam and Spider?"

"They got away," Cole said sourly. "But the posse is riding out again today to look for them. Tayler thinks Pickens and Lewis are heading for more lucrative parts. It's too hot for them in this area. I hope he's right. Are you ready for breakfast? It's a long ride to Cheyenne and the stops will be brief. Did you sleep well?"

"I've never slept in a bed like that," Dawn said as Cole seated her at an empty table in the dining room. "It was almost too comfortable." What she didn't say was that she would have slept better with Cole beside her. "How did you sleep?"

"Just fine," Cole said without conviction. Had his dreams been less confusing, his words might have been true.

After a leisurely breakfast they strolled to the train station. Cole had already made arrangements for the horses and they were tethered nearby, waiting to be loaded onto the train when it arrived.

Two men huddled against the wall at the far end of the long brick station house, hats pulled low, their unshaven faces indistinct in the shadow.

"Dammit, Spider, I hope you heard right about

the train carrying a gold shipment. If you ask me, it's going to be a mite dangerous riding that train."

"I heard the station manager talking, Sam. He said the train was carrying a shipment of gold coins to the bank in Cheyenne. There's no turning back. We already have our tickets and we've made arrangements for our horses to ride in the stock car. If we get off at the town before the pass, we'll still have plenty of time to set up an ambush."

Spider cast a wary glance around him and went still. "Say, ain't that Cobb's wife waiting for the train?"

"Damn! Just our luck. Where do ya reckon she's going?" Sam stared at Dawn, then grinned. "Cobb's hot little piece is looking damn good." His attention sharpened. "Ain't that the railroad detective with her? Wonder why they're together? Do you reckon she's sleeping with him?"

"Maybe we'll get another chance at her if she's boarding the same train. We got cheated out of our money, but maybe we can still get something for our trouble."

"Yeah," Sam said, sneering. "I owe that railroad man for shooting me. Still hurts something fierce. I gave as good as I got, though. Plugged him in the shoulder. As for that little half-breed, I got the hots for her. Would have had her a long time ago if old Cobb hadn't been so damn jealous."

"Here comes the train," Spider hissed as the train pulled into the depot. "Let them board first. Keep your hat pulled low so they don't recognize us. All we have to do is keep out of their way for a day or two. No railroad detective is gonna stop me from pulling off this job."

They waited until all the passengers had boarded before ambling down the line of cars, hats pulled low, faces averted. Dawn and Cole had entered the first passenger car so they bypassed that one and entered the second, choosing a seat at the rear of the car.

"Do ya think the railroad man saw us?" Spider wondered.

"Naw. He suspects nothing," Sam said with confidence. "He probably doesn't even know there's gold on board. We'll get off at La Junta like we planned and beat the train to the pass. That gold is as good as ours."

"Do ya think Dawn will be glad to see us now that Cobb's gone? I got a powerful hankering for her."

They exchanged looks. "We ain't dumb, Spider. I reckon we'll find a way to have both the woman and the gold."

Weary after a restless night aboard the train, Dawn perched on the edge of the seat, looking out the window and listening to the harsh metallic clatter of the wheels, dreading the uncertain future that awaited her. She had hardly slept last night. It wasn't until Cole had put his arm around her and pulled her head down on his shoulder that she had slept at all.

"Relax, Dawn," Cole urged. "You're not going to your death, you know. Trust me to know what's best for you."

His rather arrogant statement sent anger surging through her. "Why should I trust you? I don't want your pitty. We both know how anxious you are to get rid of me in a way that will salve your conscience."

Cole had the grace to flush. Dawn had come too close to the truth. "That's not entirely true. Your future is important to me. I want your promise that you'll stay with Running Elk long enough to get to know him and his people. Who knows? You may find a good man to love."

"I'd just break any promise I made," Dawn said truthfully.

Disgruntled, Cole directed his gaze out the window. If he had any sense he'd disclaim responsibility for Dawn. She neither wanted nor appreciated his concern. Finding her a virgin had been a shock, one that called for special consideration. Walking away from the situation, as he had done in the past when he found himself in a difficult position, was unthinkable. He was under no obligation to provide for Dawn's future, but something about the abused waif had struck a responsive chord in him. He was going to do his level best to see her settled without compromising his own freedom.

The train traveled north and west into Colorado, making scheduled stops along the way. At various stops Cole bought food for them to eat on the train. In between stops Dawn dozed fitfully, fighting the dust and heat drifting through the open windows. They had left the plains and were traveling into high country now. The train had just made a scheduled stop at La Junta to discharge passengers, and they were to have a longer stop that evening at Pueblo to get a hot meal. Dawn looked forward with relish to stretching her legs.

Cole remained alert despite the stifling heat and mingled odors of dust and stale sweat. They were passing through a particularly desolate stretch of low-rising foothills and grasslands when Cole felt the hairs rise at the back of his neck. His attention sharpened but he saw nothing, heard nothing out of the ordinary. Everything seemed as it should be, but his instincts screamed danger. Glancing at Dawn, he saw that she was dozing and decided not to awaken her as he carefully rose and strolled through the passenger cars.

There were only two passenger cars, and everything seemed in order. Passengers were either reading, dozing or talking quietly to their seat companions. He recalled seeing two passengers debark at the last stop and retrieve their horses from the stock car, but saw no cause for concern. He continued down the aisle, presenting his credentials to the conductor standing at the rear of the second passenger car.

"A railroad detective," the conductor said with cautious enthusiasm. "Were you sent to protect the gold shipment? I don't think that's necessary. Two armed guards are riding in the baggage compartment. Rumor has it that Billy Cobb is dead and his gang has scattered."

"You heard right. I killed Cobb myself and recovered the stolen money. But as for the rest of the gang, two men are still at large. I reckon I'll just mosey on back to the baggage compartment and have a look."

"Suit yourself, Mr. Webster," the conductor said as he adjusted his stance to the swaying train.

Suddenly the train slowed to a crawl, and warning bells went off in Cole's head. He grabbed the conductor's arm before the man could amble off. "Why is the train stopping?"

"Nothing to get excited about. This is a particularly dangerous spot. We're beginning our incline into the mountains and the tracks are set on a narrow ledge. The engineer usually takes extra precautions to prevent an accident."

His explanation didn't satisfy Cole. His instincts hadn't failed him yet. He released the conductor and continued toward the baggage cars. "I'm going on back to talk to the guards."

Taking a shortcut, Pickens and Lewis had reached the narrow pass two hours ahead of the train. It was a perfect place for a train robbery. The town of Pueblo lay ahead; behind and around them were nothing but lofty mountains. They tethered their horses in the trees along one side of the incline and crept down to the tracks. It took over an hour to roll heavy rocks and dead logs into place. When they heard the train rattling along the tracks, they hid in a rocky crevice and waited.

The engineer saw the barrier as he rounded a blind curve but was unable to stop in time. He plowed into the barricade, derailing the engine and both passenger cars. By the time the train settled into the dust, Pickens and Lewis, saddlebags slung over their shoulders, had scrambled into the baggage car. The two guards were sprawled on the floor, too shaken to protect themselves. They were shot in cold blood, one dying instantly and the other seriously wounded.

Cole had just passed through the second of three baggage cars when the train derailed. He was thrown against the side of the car, jolted but not hurt. He knew exactly what the derailment meant, particularly in this isolated place.

The sudden jolt sent Dawn hurtling into the aisle. She landed hard, stunned and shaken. Her first concern once her senses returned was Cole. She had been dozing when he'd wandered off and had no idea where he had gone. Then she saw the conductor picking his way down the cluttered aisle, assisting passengers back into their seats and answering questions.

"What happened?" Dawn asked when he reached her seat.

"Don't know, ma'am. I'm heading up front to find out now."

"Have you seen the man traveling with me?"

"You mean that railroad detective? Saw him a few minutes before the derailment. He was heading toward the baggage car. We're carrying a gold shipment to Cheyenne. Don't worry, ma'am, it's well guarded."

Dawn felt a sudden chill. Intuition told her that Cole was in danger. Without a thought for her own safety, she hurried toward the baggage cars, shoving and pushing her way through the tangle of excited passengers trying to find their scattered belongings.

"Hurry," Sam called as he and Spider shoved sacks of gold coins into their saddlebags. "Take as much as you can carry and hightail it back to the horses while I look for Dawn. The passengers are probably too shaken up to offer much resistance."

He bent to his work, until Spider hissed a warning. "Someone's coming."

"Already?" Sam flattened himself against the wall beside the door, waiting for it to open. He heard the latch rattle, lifted his gun by the barrel and brought the butt down hard when the door opened and a man stepped through.

Cole would have been more alert had Dawn not surprised him. He sensed someone behind him and heard Dawn call his name just as he opened the door to the baggage car. He turned to warn her to go back. In that split second he was struck down.

Instead of running away, Dawn gave a cry of alarm and rushed to Cole's side. He was lying between cars, in imminent danger of falling between the coupling and rolling down the steep incline. Unfortunately, her intention of helping Cole was thwarted when hands reached out and dragged her into the baggage car.

"Well, I'll be damned," Spider said with a grin. "Look what the wind blew in. You sure saved us a lot of trouble, honey. Good to see ya again. Did ya miss us?"

Dawn was stunned to see Spider and Sam. "How did you get here? What did you do to Cole?"

Sam grinned. "We rode the train, same as you. The railroad man ain't dead yet," he said as he raised his gun and took deliberate aim at Cole's head. His bullet went wild when Dawn careened into him, spoiling his aim.

"Ya little bitch! I oughta—"

"People are coming, let's get the hell out of here," Spider urged when he heard footsteps and loud voices rushing toward them. "Bring the half-breed."

"No, I'm not going anywhere with you!"

"Ya got no choice," Spider said as he dragged Dawn with him through the baggage car and out the door. "Jump!" he ordered as he and Sam wrestled Dawn to the ground and dragged her into the trees. Seconds later the engineer, conductor and angry passengers burst through the door and started shooting at the fleeing figures.

"Don't shoot!" someone shouted. "They got a woman with them."

Dawn dragged her feet, trying to slow them down, to no avail. She was thrust up into the saddle in front of Sam and held on for dear life as they broke from the trees and sped away from the train wreck.

Cole came groggily to his feet, aware of the ruckus around him. Gunshots echoed through his aching head as he staggered to the doorway and peered out. Squinting against the setting sun, he saw two horsemen riding into the hills. One horse carried two passengers. A man and a woman, her petticoats billowing around her legs. A shudder went through Cole as he recalled turning to warn Dawn seconds before his head exploded. He spared a glance at the dead guard and noted with relief that the second man seemed to be stirring. He knew they would be taken care of and that he had more important things to think about.

Dawn. Lord, how could one tiny woman cause so much trouble?

The conductor stopped to offer aid, and Cole took the opportunity to ask about Dawn, although he feared he already knew the answer. "Have you seen the lady traveling with me? Is she all right?"

The conductor sent Cole a pitying look. "I'm sorry to be the bearer of bad news, Mr. Webster, but the outlaws took your lady. After the derailing, I saw her heading toward the baggage car. The bandits took the gold and dragged the woman away with them."

Cole didn't waste time on small talk. He had to get to his horse quickly. Warrior would be shaken up, but it would take more than a derailment to frighten the stalwart stallion.

"I'm going after them. Board the lady's horse at Smith's Livery in Pueblo. I'll pick him up later."

"You going alone, mister?"

"There are only two of them," Cole said with a grimness that made the conductor shiver. "I'm an expert tracker. They won't escape me."

The Cole who rode Warrior away from the narrow pass wasn't the same Cole who had boarded the train. From the depths of his saddlebags he had retrieved Indian moccasins, breechclout and deerskin shirt. His legs above his knees were bare to his powerful thighs, and he had braided an eagle's feather earned through feats of bravery in his burnished hair. His face, painted in garish stripes, was harsh and taut with purpose, his muscles rigid with determination. Cole Webster no longer existed.

156

Shadow Walker

Shadow Walker rose from the ashes of his past to take Cole's place. The war cry that left his lips as he rode after the outlaws sent fear racing through the hearts of those gathered to watch him ride off. Most had heard of White Indians but few had seen one—until now. Somewhere into the rugged mountains rode a redheaded Indian with vengeance on his mind and murder in his heart.

Dawn tried to throw herself from the horse, but the large, burly Sam was too strong for her. He held onto her and kept her upright in the saddle as they bounced over a rocky trail that climbed steadily upward.

"Where are you taking me?" Dawn flung over her shoulder as she struggled in Sam's ruthless grip.

"To a cave where we'll be safe," Sam said, leering at her as he rubbed his arm against her breasts. "We hid out there with Cobb a time or two. We even left supplies in case we ever needed them again. You'll like it. It's nice and dry and has a pile of blankets we can share. You can show us all the little tricks Cobb liked to brag about. His stories about you made our mouths water."

"He lied!" Dawn protested.

"I don't think so. Cobb told us how you and him would hump all night and you'd still want more. Me and the boys used to wonder if Cobb was man enough for you. We often discussed what we'd do to you if we ever got you alone."

"We're almost there," Spider said as he rode up beside them. "We can hole up in the cave a day or two, then take off for healthier parts."

Spider took the lead. Sam followed close behind. It was full dark when Spider reined to a halt. They had reached their destination. Dawn's untrained eyes could detect nothing remotely suggesting a cave or any other kind of hideout. There was no cabin, no lean-to, no narrow openings in the rock. Nothing but empty spaces, lofty mountains and rocky ledges.

"Get down," Sam said, shoving Dawn from his winded mount as he dismounted. She fell heavily to the ground. He made no effort to help her regain her feet. "Are ya sure this is it?" he asked, turning to Spider.

"It's right in front of your face," Spider said.

Dawn saw nothing but bushes, trees and steep rocky inclines. She watched closely as Spider walked his horse behind the thick tangle of shrubs and disappeared from sight. A few minutes later Sam shoved her forward.

"Follow Spider. I'm right behind ya."

Dawn spied the opening. It was concealed behind thick bushes. It was large enough to admit men and their horses too. Sam waited for them inside.

"Here we are, all nice and comfy," Sam said for Dawn's benefit. "The cave goes way back. We can even build a fire without fear of it being seen. There's a stream a couple hundred yards farther back and a place to keep the horses." He nudged Dawn and winked. "We'll have plenty of time to find out how hot you really are."

"They'll find you," Dawn said with more conviction than she felt. This place was too well hidden for anyone to find.

"Who will find us? That railroad man?" Sam gave a hoot of laughter. "It will take an expert tracker to follow our trail. And if I ain't mistaken, them were storm clouds gathering in the north. Our tracks will be washed away before morning. It will take a damn Injun tracker to find us, and even then I ain't sure it can be done."

He lit a match to some dried twigs soaked in coal oil that had been stored there for that purpose and held the makeshift torch aloft. "Let's go farther back into the cave so we can build a fire and fix some grub. I'm starving."

"Me, too," Spider echoed, "but I reckon Dawn here can ease my appetite a mite." He gave her a gap-toothed grin as he shoved her forward.

They followed a winding path down a long passageway. Dawn stumbled along, taking careful note of their progress. Somehow she would escape this place and these men. Her desperate situation infused her with strength. She'd meant it when she'd vowed never to become a victim again.

At the end of the passageway the cave widened into a large dry room with a sandy floor. Dawn noted signs of recent occupancy. Blankets were scattered around, a few pots lay near a cold firepit flanked by firewood, and bundles of supplies had been placed against a dry wall. She could hear gurgling water somewhere nearby.

Sam led the horses toward the sound of water, and Spider built a fire, which provided sufficient light for Dawn to get her bearings. What she saw did nothing to ease her fears. Everything necessary for survival was here: shelter, food, blankets, fuel.

But would she survive?

"Fix us some grub, Dawn," Sam said when he returned to the cavern. "There's canned beans and some other stuff yonder in those bags." He tossed a sack at her feet. "Here's coffee, flour and bacon. Fetch water, Spider."

Dawn found the coffeepot and filled it with the water Spider had fetched. Once the coffee was boiling, she mixed up biscuits, opened cans of beans and fruit, and fried bacon. An hour later the men were shoveling food into their mouths while Dawn watched with a marked lack of appetite. Once their bellies were full they sat back and grinned at her, their thoughts turning to appetites that had nothing to do with food.

"Take off your clothes, Dawn," Spider ordered. "Cobb told us you had the sweetest pair of titties he'd ever seen on a woman. We wanna see them for ourselves."

"Yeah," Sam chimed in. "I ain't never had a half-breed before. I heard they're hotter than all get-out." He grasped Dawn's arm and pulled her onto his lap. "Need any help getting out of them duds?"

Dawn clawed at him when he tore away the neckline of her dress. He fell back with a howl of rage. Taking advantage of the respite, Dawn jumped to her feet. "Don't touch me! Did either of you help me when Billy beat me senseless? Did either of you pull him off me? No, you enjoyed watching him brutalize me. You're all animals. I want nothing to do with either of you."

Turning abruptly, she raced toward the dark

passageway leading back to the entrance of the cave. She'd take her chances with wild animals before sacrificing herself to the human animals inside the cave.

"Catch her!" Spider cried.

Sluggish after their meal, they were not as fleet of foot as Dawn. Plunging into the dark passageway, Dawn hugged the wall, feeling her way as she went. The night was dark; she could smell dampness and rain. Thunder rumbled overhead. No light appeared at the entrance to guide her steps. Suddenly the wall fell away beneath her hands and she realized that she had come across a crevice or tunnel running perpendicular to the main passageway.

Without hesitation she ducked inside, propelled by the pounding footsteps behind her. Immediately she was pitched into a blackness more suffocating than anything she could imagine. It was like being thrust into the bowels of hell. Seconds later Sam and Spider pounded past. Spider held a torch, but to her immense relief neither man stopped long enough to inspect the tunnel she had ducked into. She dragged in several shallow breaths to calm her speeding heart.

She hoped they would think she had reached the entrance, and prayed they wouldn't remember the tunnel when they failed to find her. Crouching low, Dawn forced herself to remain calm. She had no idea where this tunnel led. Fear of the unknown kept her from exploring the dark corridor.

The pounding rain hindered Shadow Walker but did not stop him. He was a relentless tracker.

161

He followed the bandits' tracks into the mountains, past towering trees and racing streams. When the rain began, he looked for signs other than the tracks that had washed away with the downpour. He found what he was looking for in bent twigs and disturbed bushes. And in scraps of cloth torn away from Dawn's clothing. It was long past dark when he stopped abruptly beside a tangle of dense bushes.

The back of his neck prickled; his body was tensed as he listened. Awareness spoke to Shadow Walker, telling him that he had reached the end of his journey. Shadow Walker reined Warrior in sharply. The stallion danced sideways in the pounding rain as Shadow Walker studied the signs. At length his sharp gaze settled on the thick bushes growing out from the steep incline ahead of him.

A smile curved the hard planes of his lips as he dismounted and slipped behind the tangle of shrubs. He found the opening into the cave and entered. Nothing stirred. Shadow Walker harkened to the sounds of silence, to the forces of nature, to the wind and the rain. And he sensed evil.

Shadow Walker paused just inside the mouth of the cave, letting his eyes adjust to the darkness before continuing. He carried a rifle in one hand. His other hand hovered above the knife at his waist. Then he heard pounding footsteps and smiled grimly. Moments later a pinpoint of light appeared from the darkness of a narrow passageway. Balancing on the balls of his feet, Shadow Walker waited. Acting rashly might endanger

Dawn, and he couldn't let that happen. If they had harmed her in any way, he would make their deaths as unpleasant as possible.

Shadow Walker hugged the wall as two men burst into the outer cavern. They stopped abruptly, unaware that they weren't alone.

"The bitch couldn't have gotten this far," Spider spat angrily. "She must have ducked into a side tunnel."

"We'll find her," Sam growled. "When we do, she'll wish she hadn't run. Come on, let's go back."

Shadow Walker could see them clearly now, outlined by the light of the torch Spider held. He stepped out from the wall. "Stay where you are."

The sound of another voice so unnerved the men that they froze in their tracks. "Who's there?" Sam's voice cracked from fear. Neither man was exceptionally brave.

"Your worst nightmare," Cole said, stepping into the circle of light.

"Son of a bitch, a damn Injun," Sam said, diving for his gun. His hand never reached the barrel. Cole's knife spun away from his body, landing squarely in Sam's heart. He was dead before he hit the ground.

"Throw down your guns," Shadow Walker ordered as Spider stared at his dead partner.

"Don't shoot," Spider said as he unbuckled his gunbelt with his free hand and let it drop to the ground. He still held the torch aloft with the other. "What do ya want? I got money. I'll split it with ya."

"Where's Dawn?"

"Dawn?" His eyes narrowed as he stared hard

at Shadow Walker. "Who are you?" Suddenly comprehension dawned. "You're that railroad detective! What are ya doing dressed like a damn Injun?"

"Where's Dawn?" Shadow Walker repeated.

Spider gulped convulsively. He felt as if he were staring death in the face. Acting on pure instinct and raw fear, he tossed the torch at Shadow Walker and made a mad dash toward the cave entrance. Shadow Walker's rifle barked just before he deftly caught the torch. Spider fell face down and lay still.

Chapter Nine

From the cloying darkness of her narrow hide-away, Dawn heard a gunshot and stiffened with panic. She could see nothing, hear nothing except the sharp echo as it ricocheted from wall to wall. For the space of a heartbeat she considered stepping into the main passageway and risking exposure, but fear immobilized her. She retreated deeper into the tunnel, hugging the wall, listening for the sound of approaching footsteps.

Shadow Walker stared at the two dead bodies dispassionately. Two brutal deaths might have bothered Cole Webster but they didn't faze Shadow Walker. It was astonishing how effortlessly he had reverted to his Indian ways after nearly four years of living in White society.

Holding the torch high to light his path, Shadow Walker stepped over the bodies and proceeded down the long, winding passageway. His one consuming fear was that he was too late to save Dawn. He failed to notice the side tunnel and passed by without giving it a second glance, entering the central cavern a few minutes later. A fire still burned in the firepit. Shadow Walker was stunned at the cozy setup the outlaws had maintained. He spied the saddlebags immediately and knelt to inspect the contents. Glittering gold coins spilled out of the cloth bags. He shoved the coins back inside and resealed the flap. Then he moved deeper into the cavern, discovering the spring and horses. Dawn was nowhere to be found.

Desperation rode Shadow Walker. Close inspection of the cavern failed to reveal a single clue to Dawn's whereabouts. He recalled hearing the outlaws mention that Dawn had escaped, and they were looking for her. He knew she hadn't left the cave, for he would have seen her. There was but one option available to her. Dawn had to be hiding somewhere within the dank reaches of the cave.

Turning on his heel, he retraced his steps, this time taking time to inspect both walls of the passageway. He stopped abruptly before a gap in the wall, noting the existence of another tunnel. Intuition told him that was where he would find Dawn. He called her name, hoping she would recognize his voice.

Huddled just inside the entrance of the tunnel, Dawn caught a glimpse of moccasins and bare legs. Indians! The thought of being found by hostile Indians terrified her nearly as much as being held by outlaws.

She saw a flickering light coming toward her

and feared she had been discovered. She retreated deeper into the tunnel. The unmistakable sound of mice and other burrowing animals brought her to an abrupt halt. But the advancing light and un-known danger spurred her on. Then she heard someone call her name and froze. The voice was neither Spider's nor Sam's. It couldn't be the In-dian calling out to her, she decided, shaking her head to clear it of nonsensical thoughts. She knew no Indians and none knew her. Catching her breath, she retreated deeper into the tunnel.

Shadow Walker called Dawn's name again. He could hear her harsh breathing, sense her fright, and wished to put a stop to her heedless flight. Suddenly he heard her scream, and his heart pounded out of control. He sprinted forward, eat-ing up the distance between them. When he held the torch up, his heart nearly catapulted out of his mouth.

Dawn clung to the lip of a crevice with the numb ends of her fingertips. The ground had fallen away beneath her and she had stepped off into thin air. She had reached out wildly, grasping a rocky ledge and clinging to it. But she was slipping fast, and would soon plummet to her death. She closed her eyes a brief moment to pray, and when she opened them he was standing before her.

His massive legs, bare to his breechclout, tensed powerfully as he set the torch down and knelt to grasp her arms. He pulled her up slowly, effort-lessly, swinging her around to safety and clasping her against the hard wall of his chest.

Seeing nothing but the war paint smeared

across his face, the eagle feather in his hair, Dawn struggled in his arms, trying to escape this new menace.

"Dawn, stop it! It's Cole. I'm not going to hurt you."

"No! Don't touch me!"

He gave her a little shake. "Calm down. Look at me. It's Cole."

Dawn's blue eyes widened in disbelief as Cole picked up the torch and raised it so she could see his face. "Cole . . ." She recognized his burnished hair first. Then his eyes, gleaming like emeralds in the darkness. "Oh, my God. I thought you were . . . How did you find me?" She peered cautiously around him. "What happened to Sam and Spider?"

"They'll never hurt you again. I'll explain everything when we get back to the central cavern." Holding the torch aloft, Cole led her back along the tunnel to the main passageway, and from there to the central cavern, toward the dull glow of ashes in the firepit. "Sit down while I stir up the fire."

Dawn dropped to her knees on a blanket, watching Cole as she tried to reconcile his appearance with that of the Cole Webster she knew. She hardly recognized him wearing Indian garb, his face painted in garish colors. She was quick to admit that he made an impressive sight. "Do you have an Indian name?"

"I am known as Shadow Walker among the People. It feels good to become Shadow Walker again. While I was pursuing the outlaws I almost forgot I was White." He finished with the fire and settled down beside her. "Are you cold?" he asked when he felt her shiver against him.

"I don't know what I am. I can't stop shaking. Are you sure we have nothing to fear from Sam or Spider?"

"They're both dead." His voice held a brittle edge. She could tell he felt little remorse over the deaths.

"You killed them?"

"Yes. We'll take them to Pueblo tomorrow and turn over the gold to the local sheriff. He'll see that the gold gets to its rightful destination. It will take a few days to clean up the tracks and get the trains running again. We might have to spend several nights in town."

"Do we have to stay here tonight?"

"It's a gully washer out there. At least we're safe and dry in here."

Being alone with Cole in this isolated place was daunting. Dawn licked her lips, searching for words. "Are you hungry?"

He gave her a heart-stopping smile. "Starving. Those two scoundrels had a sweet setup here. Is there something you could fix without going to too much trouble?"

"There's coffee in the pot next to the fire. I can heat some beans and fry more bacon." She started to rise.

Suddenly Cole noticed her gaping bodice, and its significance hit him hard. He grasped her hand and pulled her back down. "Wait. Did those bastards hurt you?" His words were tautly spoken from a mouth that had turned grim.

"No. They filled their bellies first. Then, when

they tried to . . . hurt me, I escaped. Thank God you were able to track them, for I don't know what I would have done had they found me."

Cole didn't even want to think about their filthy hands on Dawn's golden flesh. "I'm sorry, Dawn, I should have protected you better."

"It wasn't your fault." She rose abruptly. "I'll fix something for you to eat."

After the remnants of the hasty meal were set aside, Cole went to fetch a bucket of water. When he returned, Dawn was stretched out on a blanket, staring into the dancing flames.

"You should get some sleep. It's been a grueling day." He moved off to fix his own bed.

Dawn jerked upright, reaching out to him. "Don't leave me."

"I'm not going anywhere, love."

"Lie next to me."

Cole gave her a hard look, then moved his blanket next to hers. "Are you sure?"

"I need you beside me tonight. I can't recall when I've ever felt so alone or been so frightened." In all her life no one had cared about her. Cole made her feel safe and protected.

Cole lay down beside her and drew her into his arms, pulling the blanket up over them. Heaving a ragged sigh, Dawn melted against him.

"It's been rough, hasn't it, love? Now you understand why I wanted to see you safely settled. I wanted a better life for you, and I think Running Elk's people will help you find it."

Dawn didn't want to hear about Running Elk. Not with Cole holding her, making her feel safe and wanted. "I shouldn't be depending on you like this."

"I don't mind. Just as long as you don't make a habit of it." He'd meant it as a joke, but Dawn took his words literally. She stiffened and pulled away.

"I'll try to remember that."

He cursed his insensitivity and tried to bring her back into his arms. He succeeded, but it wasn't the same. There was a wariness about her now that hadn't been there before.

"I'm sorry, love, but you know there can be nothing permanent between us. I care for you, but it wouldn't be fair to burden you with a man still obsessed with his dead wife."

"Have I asked for more?"

"You've asked for nothing. I wish . . ." His sentence fell off. He had no idea what he wished. Unless it was to kiss Dawn. He knew he shouldn't, but he couldn't help himself. One kiss and then he'd stop.

He tightened his grip on her shoulders, lowered his head and kissed her. Gently, softly, on her slightly parted lips. He hardened instantly and knew he wouldn't be satisfied with just one kiss. He wanted to be inside her to feel her tighten around him. He wanted to watch her eyes widen as he pushed deeper and deeper. He wanted to take her with his fingers, with his mouth, and hear her cry out. His grip on her tightened, and he felt her quicken against him.

He raised his head and stared at her. Her eyes were pleading and softly misted with emotion. She made a tiny sound in her throat that he understood, and he kissed her again. When he ended the kiss and attempted to pull away, she held him fast.

"No, don't stop. Keep on kissing me."

"I shouldn't, it's—"

". . . what I want. I need you tonight. I need to feel that I'm alive. To forget what Sam and Spider wanted to do to me."

How could he resist? His member was hard and distended and pressing against her thigh. He wanted her; he wanted to erase all the ugly memories of the past hours from her mind.

Cole rose above her, carefully pushing aside the torn edges of her bodice until her magnificent breasts were exposed. They gleamed a dull gold in the firelight, and Cole lowered his head to take a dusky nipple in his mouth.

Throbbing pleasure ebbed and flowed over her as his mouth caressed and suckled her, filling her with hot anticipation. She felt warm dampness pool between her legs and was shaken by the depth of emotions whirling through her.

Words were unnecessary as she helped him strip away her clothing. Then he laid her back against the blanket as he quickly peeled off his own clothing. He pressed their naked bodies together, moaning from the sheer pleasure of hot flesh meeting hot flesh. He kissed her again and again, and when Dawn was nearly dizzy, his mouth left hers for other, more intimate places.

With greedy laps of his tongue and tiny, teasing bites, he lavished excruciating attention upon the generous mounds of her breasts. Dawn arched beneath him, begging him without words to come inside her, to finish this endless torture.

"I know what you want, love," Cole whispered against the sweet tip of her breast. "And it will come, but not yet. There is so much more I want to show you and do to you."

Very gently he slid a finger inside her. Her warmth tightened around him and he fought to control his sharp response. He closed his eyes, inserted a second finger and delved deeper. He was shaking all over from forced restraint. Then he pulled his fingers out very slowly and thrust them into her again. She cried out, her hips lifting off the blanket.

"Please!"

"Shush." His hot breath against her breasts made her tremble and quake with unbelievable feelings.

Then he moved slowly down her body, allowing his fingers to open her as his mouth found her. Dawn went rigid with shock. When Billy had tried to do these things to her, she had fought and accepted a beating rather than acquiesce to his sick needs. With Cole she felt wild elation, not revulsion. He was kissing and caressing a part of her that was private and personal, a part she had denied Billy Cobb, and it felt incredibly satisfying.

His hands slid beneath her, lifting her to his mouth. "Sweet," he murmured, and his heated breath against her most intimate place sent her into a rush of pleasure.

"This . . . isn't right," Dawn said between spasms of burgeoning rapture.

"It is if we want it to be."

Embarrassment rendered her mute as Cole plied his tongue diligently, exploring her, suckling

173

her. She knew she was hot and wet where his mouth worked its magic on her, but he didn't seem to mind. Then coherent thought fled as her body became an instrument through which Cole gave her pleasure. She moaned and arched her back. Her legs trembled, her body shook.

"That's it, love," he whispered. "Press yourself against my mouth. You're almost there. I can feel your legs tensing, your muscles tightening." His tongue darted in and out of her. "Do you like that? Yes, I can tell you do." Her muffled scream told him she adored it.

Realizing she was close to the edge, he slipped his fingers inside her while using his tongue to lave the hard little nub nestled amid her moist folds. It was too much for Dawn. She fragmented, crying out again and again as her blood thickened and incredible feelings pounded through her. Cole's infinite patience had cost him dearly. His control was all but shattered.

"I'm going to come inside you now," he said in a husky voice Dawn hardly recognized.

Still reeling from pleasure, Dawn felt herself stretch and fill as Cole pushed himself inside her.

"You're so tight," he groaned as he fit himself snugly within her. With little effort he could have climaxed immediately, but he wanted to bring Dawn once again to shuddering rapture, this time while buried deep inside her.

Again and again he thrust into her, until she was panting and pounding his shoulders with her fists. He kept up the grueling pace, letting the pressure build, lifting her high, forcing her legs up and her thighs wider. Dawn matched his rhythm, thrashing wildly beneath him, her little cries and gasps urging him to greater heights.

He could hold on no longer. All the demons of hell were driving him to climax. But he was a stubborn man. He wanted to take Dawn with him to ecstasy. He eased his fingers between them, into the soft damp folds above that place where his manhood filled her, and found the pebbled source of her pleasure. With thumb and forefinger he plucked and massaged the tiny nub, until her hips were lifting against his beguiling fingers and explosions racked her body. He waited until her body's movements subsided before climaxing explosively.

Consumed with unspeakable pleasure, Dawn felt Cole harden and thicken inside her, heard the harsh rasping of his breath, and welcomed the warm spill of his seed against the walls of her womb. If she never experienced Cole's love again, she would always have this night to remember.

A sudden coolness seized her when Cole rolled off her. But it was blessedly short-lived as he dragged her into his arms.

"I didn't hurt you, did I? I'm not an animal like Cobb. Sweet Lord, Dawn, you sure know how to make a man forget he's a gentleman."

"You didn't hurt me," Dawn said with a smile. Her heart was still pounding, and she felt flushed all over. She had never imagined that making love could be such an earth-shattering experience. Billy Cobb would have made it an abomination had he been able to perform the act with her.

Cole settled her deeper into his embrace. "You should sleep. Pueblo isn't far, but the Red Cloud

Agency is a good fourteen days' ride to the north. You'll need your strength."

How could she sleep with Cole's arms around her, his warm body pressed against hers, and the memory of the splendid heights he had taken her to still so vivid in her mind she could taste them?

She tried to sleep, truly she did. So did Cole. Unfortunately, their two healthy bodies made a sham of their good intentions. When Cole's body had recovered itself and clamored for another taste of Paradise, he turned to her in the night, and she welcomed him. They made love again. Slowly this time, savoring each other like fine wine. Even then they weren't sated. Shortly before dawn Cole turned to her again and she responded eagerly. He lifted her atop him, and she rode him like a stallion. The end came abruptly, carrying them to ecstasy. They fell asleep in each other's arms.

"Time to get up, love," Cole said as he nudged Dawn awake..Dawn muttered groggily and pulled the blanket over her head.

"Come on, Dawn, I've been up for hours. The rain has stopped, and I need to take the bodies and money to town and make a report."

Grasping a corner of the blanket, Cole whipped it away. Dawn screeched as cool air hit her naked flesh. She jerked upright. She was still flushed from his loving, and he noted places on her body where his mouth had marked her golden skin. Just thinking about their night together made him instantly hard. He turned away with regret. As much as he wanted Dawn again, there wasn't time.

"There's water by the fire. Wash and dress while I take care of the bodies and the money. There's food by the firepit. I've already taken the horses from the cave and staked them outside."

"You've done all that while I was sleeping?" Dawn asked, amazed that she had slept so soundly.

Cole gave her a cocky grin. "You were tired."

Dawn's gaze slid over the length of him, realizing that he looked different than he had last night. "You're no longer dressed like an Indian, and the war paint is gone."

"I don't want to scare the townspeople when we ride in with two dead men. I'm Cole Webster now, Pinkerton detective assigned to the railroad. But you haven't seen the last of Shadow Walker. There are times when it's both more practical and more comfortable to travel as Shadow Walker."

"Shadow Walker frightens me," Dawn admitted.

His eyebrow shot upward. "And Cole Webster doesn't?"

"Sometimes he frightens me too."

"Neither man would ever hurt you, Dawn." He cleared his throat, fearing he had admitted too much. "Will you be all right alone?" She nodded. "I'll return shortly." He hefted the saddlebags containing the gold and disappeared through the passageway.

Dawn washed and dressed quickly. She wished she had her split leather skirt for riding, but it had been left behind on the train. She didn't realize how hungry she was until she spied the plate of beans, biscuits and bacon resting beside the fire-pit. She ate ravenously, aware that she had barely touched her food the night before. While she waited for Cole to return, she braided her long hair into some semblance of order.

"All set," Cole said when he returned a short time later. He retrieved a flaming branch from the fire and kicked out the dying blaze. Then he picked up the sack of food he had purloined from the outlaws' stash, directed Dawn to bring the blankets and led the way through the passage.

Midway down the tunnel Dawn saw the faint light from the cave's entrance and felt a welcome relief. She was more than eager to leave this cold, dark place of death. If not for Cole this cave might have become her tomb.

They came out into sunshine so bright that Dawn had to close her eyes against the nearly painful burst of light. When she opened them again she gawked in awe at the stark splendor of the landscape. The surrounding mountains, hills and valleys held a desolate, fierce beauty all their own.

"The horses are tethered nearby," Cole said as he extinguished the torch and tossed it aside. "Follow me."

They found the horses contentedly munching grass. Dawn recoiled in revulsion when she saw two blanket-clad figures draped over the back of one of the horses.

"There is nothing to fear from dead men. I can't leave them here to be devoured by carrion, although Lord knows they probably deserve it."

He helped her mount the spare horse and tossed

the saddlebags containing the stolen gold across Warrior's withers. "We should reach Pueblo before nightfall."

That was what Dawn feared. They would be that much closer to the place where Cole intended to abandon her.

When they reached Pueblo, the town was already aware of the train robbery and derailment. The stranded passengers and baggage had been transported to town, and the animals in the stock car had been taken to the livery.

Cole dumped the bodies and gold off at the sheriff's office, made his report and promptly left. But when he tried to engage a room at the town's only hotel, he found it filled to capacity with stranded passengers waiting for the next train through town.

"What do we do now?" Dawn asked when Cole informed her of the situation.

"No sense waiting around town for the next train. We've got a lot of ground to cover to reach the Red Cloud Agency. We'll find Running Elk camped somewhere in the area. I'll buy supplies for the trip, then retrieve your horse and our baggage. We'll keep a spare horse to carry our supplies. Had there been room at the hotel, we might have waited, but it will take some time to clear the tracks and I see no reason to delay."

No reason at all, Dawn thought but did not say. The sooner Cole got rid of her, the better he'd like it. It didn't take a wizard to know that.

The sun was slanting low in the western sky when they left Pueblo. Cole had purchased a two-week supply of food and sturdy riding clothes for Dawn. Everything was packed away on the spare horse. Dawn was happy to be mounted once again on Wally. She did wish, though, that she'd had time to take a bath in town. When she mentioned it to Cole, he told her they would camp tonight on a fork of the Arkansas River, where she'd be able to bathe.

Cole found a perfect campsite just as the sun disappeared behind the mountains. The night was warm and balmy, since they hadn't climbed into the higher elevations yet, and Dawn hurried to the shallow pool Cole had pointed out to her. While she bathed, Cole hunted small game for their supper. When Dawn returned from the river, Cole had a plump rabbit cooking on a spit.

"Shall I make biscuits?" Dawn asked as she sat beside the fire to dry her hair.

"Relax, I'll do it."

"You can cook?"

"I've done my share." He mixed biscuit dough while Dawn ran her fingers through her long hair to work out the tangles. Her sinuous motions mesmerized Cole, making his fingers itch to take over the chore for her.

Unaware of his intent perusal, Dawn arched her back, fanning her hair toward the fire. The simple motion pushed her breasts forward against the thin cotton of her shirtwaist, drawing an involuntary groan from Cole.

She has no idea how seductive she is, Cole thought as he watched her stretch like a cat. Firelight played upon her skin, turning it to warm honey, and her ebony hair gleamed like black satin. She looked delicious enough to eat, and Cole knew from experience that she tasted sweet all over. They had shared incredible passion in the cave the night before, and Cole yearned to experience it again. He tried to justify his hunger for Dawn by calling it lust. His mind accepted that explanation, but his heart was more difficult to convince.

Dawn fell asleep with the coffee cup in her hand. She awakened briefly when Cole took it from her and carried her to her bedroll. The urge to join her beneath the blanket was strong, but he resisted with admirable restraint. Each time he made love to Dawn he realized how imperative it was that he find a place for her with Running Elk. Cole couldn't handle a permanent relationship. He wanted freedom to live with his memories of Morning Mist.

They traveled north through eastern Colorado. The weather remained hot and dry, with occasional cloudbursts cooling things down when the heat became unbearable. They kept to the eastern slopes of the Rockies, riding long days and usually finding adequate campsites near rivers and streams. They encountered few travelers, but those they did meet repeated rumors of a huge army of Indians gathering for battle. The battle was in retaliation for General George Custer's expedition into their lands. They claimed he'd started a gold rush into the Black Hills in direct violation of their treaty.

Cole despised the White man's greed and began to have second thoughts about thrusting Dawn into an unsettled and dangerous situation. But until he spoke with Running Elk, his plans would remain unchanged. He prayed that Running Elk would not join his allies. Running Elk was a wise and compassionate leader and would do what was best for his people.

Dawn knew little about Indian troubles. Billy had mentioned them from time to time, but she'd never paid much attention. Until now. Hearing about a brewing war sent fear spiraling through her. How could Cole endanger her life like that?

They had stopped for a cold lunch and were resting with their backs against a tall spruce tree. Dawn ate in thoughtful silence, then blurted out, "Perhaps you should leave me in the next town." Earlier that day they had encountered a traveler who spoke in hushed tones about a huge gathering of Indian nations at the Little Big Horn. "I don't want to be caught in the middle of a war."

"We've come too far to turn back now," Cole replied. "I trust Running Elk. I'm counting on him to remain cool and not rush off to join something that could mean the end of his people. I won't leave you if danger exists."

Dawn snorted derisively. "I don't believe you. I know you want to be rid of me. I don't blame you. I'm not your responsibility."

"If I wanted to get rid of you I would have left you at the cabin." He stared at her, wanting to kiss her but knowing what it would lead to. He seemed to have damn little control where Dawn was concerned. He took her hand and pulled her to her feet. "Time to go. I want to make our next campsite before dark."

Dawn sighed. No matter what Cole said, she knew he wanted to be rid of her. She wished that the fierce, handsome Shadow Walker would return and make love to her the way he had in the cave. For some unknown reason Cole Webster avoided her like poison.

Chapter Ten

One morning Dawn awoke to find Shadow Walker staring at her. He was dressed in breechclout, moccasins and deerskin leggings. His chest was bare, covered only by a thick mat of curling red hair. The breechclout barely concealed the taut cheeks of his buttocks and the thrust of his sex, and Dawn found herself blushing.

"Why are you dressed like that?" she asked, unable to remove her gaze from his powerful masculine form. This half-naked savage was Cole Webster; however, he wasn't the Cole Webster she knew.

"We're in Indian territory. Shadow Walker will be familiar to the Indians we may encounter. I rode with the Sioux long enough to gain a reputation. Our safety may depend upon that reputation. From now on, it would be wise to think of me as Shadow Walker. Does my Indian guise bother you?"

Dawn swallowed reflexively. Bother her? Yes, in more ways than one. Didn't he realize how his very presence affected her? Didn't he know she never would have given herself to him if she hadn't felt it was right? He hadn't made love to her since that night in the cave, and she could only assume that he was trying to impress her with the fact that he didn't need her.

"If you think transforming yourself into an Indian is necessary, then I have no objection. I rather like you this way."

Two days later they encountered their first Indians. A small tribe of Oglalas passed them on their way to the Little Big Horn River in Montana Territory. Shadow Walker spoke with the chieftain and learned that the rumors about a huge army of Indians gathering on the Little Big Horn were true. He was greatly relieved when he learned that Running Elk had not yet joined the rush to the Little Big Horn.

They camped in a small glade that night. The long days of riding were taking their toll on Dawn, and Shadow Walker had begun stopping earlier each day to allow her ample time to rest. She usually fell asleep over their meal, which helped Shadow Walker uphold his vow to keep his hands off her. No matter how desperately he wanted to make love to her, he knew it would complicate their lives. The sooner she forgot him, the better off she'd be.

The following morning Shadow Walker became aware that they were being followed. When he saw a band of garishly painted Indians crowning a nearby hill, he hissed a warning to Dawn. "Don't look back, we're being followed."

Dawn resisted the urge to turn her head toward the danger. "Are we in trouble?"

"I'm not sure. Until they ride close enough for me to identify, I won't know. They could be renegades."

Dawn paled at the word "renegade." Did the Indians mean them harm? Would Cole's guise as Shadow Walker save them?

"Here they come," Shadow Walker warned as the renegades charged down the hill toward them. He calmly drew rein and waited. Dawn pulled Wally in close beside him.

The renegades surrounded them, whooping and eying the packhorse with interest. Shadow Walker brought Warrior around to challenge the leader. He recognized the squat Sioux renegade immediately. He and a group of Dog Soldiers had left Running Elk's tribe when the chief took his people to the reservation. Speaking fluent Sioux, Shadow Walker boldly challenged the leader.

"Why do you stop us? Don't you recognize me, Horned Owl? I am Shadow Walker, brother-in-law to Running Elk."

Horned Owl stared at Shadow Walker, his ugly face revealing surprise. "It has been a long time, Shadow Walker. I heard you had left the People."

"I have returned," Shadow Walker said. "I seek Running Elk's village."

"Bah, Running Elk is a cowardly old woman. He hides on the reservation instead of fighting for the right to live free." He thumped his chest with his forefinger. "Horned Owl will not let the White-eyes take our lands without a battle. Will you join our fight, Shadow Walker?"

"I sympathize with your cause, Horned Owl, but I have important business with Running Elk."

Horned Owl's dark gaze settled disconcertingly on Dawn, liking what he saw. "Is the woman yours?"

"The woman is called Dawn. She travels with me to Running Elk's village. She carries Sioux blood in her veins."

"A half-breed. No matter, I will buy her from you. I have many horses; name your price."

Dawn moved closer to Shadow Walker. She was surprised at her ability to follow most of the conversation. It had been many years since her mother had taught her the language, but little by little the words took on meaning.

"Dawn is not for sale."

Horned Owl gave him a malevolent look. "We will discuss terms over a pipe. Come, you will accompany us to our campsite."

Horned Owl spoke to his men, who immediately surrounded Shadow Walker and Dawn.

"What are we going to do now?" Dawn asked, trying not to panic.

"We're going to go with them," Shadow Walker said. "Don't worry, I'll not let them hurt you."

Surrounded by the renegades, they rode a good two hours before arriving at a small encampment consisting of a dozen tipis. A few women and children moved about the rather decrepit village as several skinny dogs ran out to greet them. Shadow Walker thought it a pitiful example of the Indian villages he had known during his years with the People.

Horned Owl dismounted. Shadow Walker slid from Warrior's back and helped Dawn to dismount. They followed Horned Owl to a lodge decorated with paintings of deer and elk. He ducked inside. Shadow Walker and Dawn followed.

"We will discuss terms now," Horned Owl said without preamble as he lowered himself to the ground and settled against a backrest covered with skins. Shadow Walker and Dawn sat crossed-legged across from him.

Dawn shifted uncomfortably beneath Horned Owl's avid scrutiny. She trusted Shadow Walker to get them out of this fix, but Horned Owl's interest in her was worrisome. Why had she allowed Shadow Walker to drag her into this wilderness? She felt no kinship with Indians despite her mixed blood.

"There is nothing to talk about," Shadow Walker said. "Dawn is not for sale."

"You are my captives," Horned Owl reminded him. "I have the power of life or death over you."

"I am of the People," Shadow Walker declared. "I was adopted into Running Elk's tribe and earned my name through acts of bravery. Killing me will bring no honor to you."

Horned Owl lapsed into a thoughtful silence. "What you say has the ring of truth, Shadow Walker. I left my tribe because I was unwilling to settle on the reservation, but I have done nothing to bring dishonor to myself or the People. I fight for the right to live free while others accept worthless treaties that are broken time after time. I have no quarrel with you. You may leave."

Shadow Walker was too canny to take Horned Owl's words at face value. The renegade wanted Dawn, and Shadow Walker realized that the situation called for diplomacy.

"Dawn and I will leave immediately," he said.

Dawn was so relieved she jumped to her feet. Then she saw Shadow Walker's stony expression and knew a moment of fear.

"You may leave, Shadow Walker, but the woman stays. I have taken a great liking to her. I will ease myself between her thighs tonight."

Dawn could remain silent no longer. "No! I'm going with Shadow Walker."

"Be quiet, Dawn," Shadow Walker hissed in warning. "Don't let him know you're upset."

"You're not going to let him have me, are you?" she whispered.

He sent her an exasperated look. "Not in a million years." Shadow Walker knew there was only one way to save Dawn from Horned Owl's clutches. Desperate times called for desperate measures. He could always force an armed confrontation, but that wouldn't necessarily guarantee Dawn's safety. He must avoid doing anything that would endanger her.

Horned Owl sent Dawn a quelling look. "You are much too bold. I will teach you to curb your tongue."

"Sorry, Horned Owl, Dawn is not yours for the taking. I am well schooled in Sioux laws."

Horned Owl shifted his gaze to Shadow Walker. "What trick do you play, Shadow Walker?"

"No trick, Horned Owl. Dawn is my wife. It is against Sioux law to take another man's wife unless there is a divorce. There has been no divorce. Even now Dawn could be carrying my child." The moment those words left his mouth he was struck by the truth of them. They had made love twice. Either time could have resulted in pregnancy.

Horned Owl's dark gaze swept over Dawn with an intensity that frightened her, settling disconcertingly on her stomach. "You lie!" he screeched. He didn't like being thwarted.

A muscle twitched in Shadow Walker's jaw. "I do not like to be called a liar."

"And I do not like to be taken for a fool."

They stared at one another, recognizing an impasse. If Horned Owl killed Shadow Walker and took his woman, he'd bring dishonor upon himself and become an outcast among his own followers, some of whom had been friendly with Shadow Walker during his sojourn with the People. It was true that Horned Owl was a renegade, but he'd never defied Sioux laws and still considered himself one of the People.

"You will be our guests tonight," Horned Owl said, ending the confrontation. "I will think on what has passed between us and give you my decision tomorrow."

"There is nothing to decide," Shadow Walker said, "but we accept your hospitality." He rose abruptly. "Show us where we may sleep."

"Come, I will take you." They followed him to an empty tipi a short distance away. "Yellow Dog has walked the spirit path, he no longer needs his lodge. You may sleep here tonight."

"Do you think he'll let us go?" Dawn asked after Horned Owl strode away.

"He has to. He's not a bad man, just a hotheaded one. He refused to join Running Elk on the reservation and took a small band of Indians who believed as he did with him. He creates havoc with the soldiers by striking their columns and stealing supplies. I can't really blame him. Indians have been driven from their homes and forced to survive on unfavorable land where game and food is scarce. Horned Owl feels that retaliation is called for."

"You told him we were married."

"I hope you don't mind. I had no choice. I could have fought for you, but it would have served no purpose. I might have been killed, and then I'd be no good to you."

Dawn gave him a slow grin. "Now you're thinking like Cole Webster. I would expect Shadow Walker to be more daring."

"Even a fierce warrior has to think with a cool head sometimes. It sounds like you are inordinately fond of Shadow Walker."

Dawn gave that statement careful thought. She had been made love to by both Cole Webster and Shadow Walker. They were inseparable in body and mind. But she had to admit she greatly admired the bold savage who claimed her as his wife. Though he had lied for a good reason, she felt a little bit resentful. Marrying her was the last thing either Cole Webster or Shadow Walker wanted.

"From what I've seen, Shadow Walker is a dangerous man. But so is Cole Webster. I'd want neither man for an enemy." And either one for a lover, she thought but did not say.

Before Shadow Walker could form a reply, a feminine voice hailed them from outside. When Shadow Walker gave permission to enter, an elderly woman bearing a steaming bowl of venison stew ducked inside. She handed them two shallow spoons made of buffalo bone and left.

"Are you hungry?" Shadow Walker asked as he sniffed the rich aroma rising from the bowl. Dawn nodded. "Sit down, there's enough for us to share."

Dawn ate ravenously, finding the stew delicious. When they finished, Shadow Walker left to get their bedrolls, returning a few minutes later with blankets and a skinful of water.

"Horned Owl invited me to smoke with him. I don't want to anger him by refusing. One never knows what a hothead like him will do. I've brought some water so you can wash. Don't wait up, I may be late."

Dawn watched him leave, wondering if she'd ever grow accustomed to Indian culture. Horned Owl seemed so fierce, so foreign. She hoped Running Elk wouldn't be half so fierce. At least at the cabin she had known what to expect from one moment to the next.

Dawn washed up quickly, placed the bedrolls across from one another and debated whether or not to remove her clothing. Deciding it was safe to remove her split skirt and shirtwaist, she quickly disrobed and climbed between the blankets in her shift. Within minutes she was sound asleep.

It was very late when Shadow Walker returned to the lodge. He entered quietly so as not to disturb Dawn, shed his breechclout and moccasins and crawled into his bedroll. But sleep would not come. Today he had claimed Dawn as his wife and he wanted to do all the things a husband had a right to with a wife. Restraining his natural instincts to make love to Dawn had taken a toll on him. He couldn't understand this aching need and liked it even less.

After experiencing Morning Mist's love, he found that no woman had appealed to him in the same way as his wife. An occasional coupling when the urge became too strong to resist had satisfied his male needs. Until Dawn came along, no woman but Morning Mist had touched his heart. He liked women, enjoyed them fully in every way; he just didn't want to become attached to a woman again. It would make him feel unfaithful to Morning Mist.

Shifting restlessly in his bedroll, Shadow Walker felt the layers of his resolve melt away. His man's flesh had grown hard and uncomfortable, his need a raging inferno. Rising, he realized he could no longer resist the allure of Dawn's sweet body. He stood over Dawn, staring down at her, his eyes glowing softly in the darkness. He could no more deny the passion churning within him than he could stop breathing.

Dawn awoke with a start. She felt Shadow Walker's presence as if he had touched her. Pale fingers of moonlight filtered through the smokehole at the top of the tipi, giving her an unrestricted view of the man looming over her. He was gloriously nude and proudly male. Every superb inch of him was hard, from his thickly muscled chest to his fully distended sex. It rose like a marble pillar from a rust-colored thicket. His legs were spread wide with typical male arrogance, and Dawn thought he'd never looked more appealing.

Shadow Walker knew the moment that Dawn had awakened. Dropping to his knees beside her, he whispered three words that made Dawn burn.

"I want you."

Dawn had no idea what he would do if she refused; she never even considered it. She wanted him. She wanted all that he offered. On all the lonely nights to come she could pull out this memory and savor it. She held out her arms.

"I want you too."

Their loving was hot, fierce, wildly intoxicating. He made her feel beautiful and wanted instead of an outlaw's leavings. Her body thrummed to his kisses. Not an inch of her golden flesh was ignored as he used his hands and mouth to bring her to shattering climax. And when their bodies were rested, he began again. They fell asleep in each other's arms, both aware that their time together was drawing to an end.

Shadow Walker was gone when Dawn awakened the following morning. She dressed quickly and stepped outside. She saw him with Horned Owl. They were deep in conversation. Dawn approached them cautiously. She relaxed somewhat when she realized they were discussing the buildup of Sioux and northern Cheyenne on the Little Big Horn.

"It's a lost cause," Shadow Walker argued. "If the Sioux insist upon this fight, it will be the beginning of the end of the People."

"Too many treaties have been violated," Horned Owl claimed. "The recent expedition into the sacred Black Hills to seek gold is the final insult. It demands retaliation. Soon I will take my followers north to the Little Big Horn to join the great chiefs."

"I cannot stop you, Horned Owl. I can but advise you to remain calm."

"Running Elk calls you brother, but you are still a White man. Trust me to know what is best for my people."

"I pray that Running Elk is more willing than you to listen to reason. Are we free to go now?"

Horned Owl gave him a sour look, still envious of his claim on Dawn. "Go. If you tire of your woman, I will take her off your hands. I can afford to be generous."

"That won't happen, Horned Owl. Thank you for your hospitality."

"I hope you and your woman found a peaceful rest last night," Horned Owl added, giving Dawn a sly look. "I passed your lodge in the night and heard your cries. I envy you your lusty mate."

Dawn made a choking sound, too embarrassed to look Horned Owl in the eye. She hadn't realized that she and Shadow Walker had been so vocal. She felt profound relief when Shadow Walker turned her toward their tipi.

"I didn't know anyone had heard us," she said, patting her flaming cheeks. "It must have been quite enlightening."

195

"Natural body functions do not embarrass Indians. Making love to one's wife is expected."

"I'm not your wife," Dawn reminded him. She turned away so quickly she missed the thoughtful look on his face.

Later that night, as Shadow Walker made love to Dawn, he all but forgot that she wasn't actually his wife. But he'd not forget again, he swore to himself. In a day or two they would reach Running Elk's village, and he intended to make sure the young braves knew she was available. Dawn's happiness was important to him. He deeply regretted his inability to give her the love she so richly deserved, but that was how it must be.

Refusing to become involved with another woman had become an obsession with Shadow Walker. He had lived with Morning Mist's memory too long to take another wife now. He enjoyed making love, but only if his heart wasn't involved. He had explained all this to Dawn because he didn't want her to draw false conclusions about their relationship. She was too sweet to tie herself to a man who could give her only a small part of himself. She deserved far better than he could offer her.

And he did not want to risk fathering a child on Dawn. He could picture no one but Morning Mist as the mother of his children. Since that was no longer possible, Shadow Walker decided to leave producing children to his twin sister.

Horned Owl allowed them to leave his camp without incident. Dawn didn't relax until they had left the small village far behind. Even then she kept looking back, expecting to see Horned Owl and his band of renegades pounding after them.

Three days later they found Running Elk's village sitting in a valley at the western reaches of the Red Cloud Agency. Dawn was overwhelmed by the exuberant welcome extended to Shadow Walker and surprised to see how well-loved he was by Running Elk's people. She wondered what he had done to earn their respect. Then she saw a handsome Indian approaching and knew instinctively that it was Running Elk.

Running Elk clasped Shadow Walker's shoulder and greeted him effusively. "Welcome, brother! Many moons have passed since I last set eyes on you. What brings you to my camp?"

"It's a long story, Running Elk. I seek a favor from you. But first, I'd like you to meet Dawn. Her mother was of the People. She can speak and understand your tongue, but not fluently." He turned to Dawn. "Dawn, this is my good friend, Running Elk."

Running Elk searched Dawn's face. Then he grinned at Shadow Walker. "I am pleased that you have finally taken my advice and found a woman to love. It is good. Your heart has been empty too long."

"No, you misunderstand. Dawn is not my woman."

Shadow Walker's denial of their relationship, no matter how tenuous, struck a blow to Dawn's pride. They had been together several weeks now. They had made love; his tenderness had been a balm to her battered body and bruised ego. He had filled the dark corners of her despair with hope. But if he didn't want anyone to know they had been intimate, so be it. She wouldn't burden him with her caring.

Running Elk shifted his gaze between Dawn and Shadow Walker, astute enough to realize there was more between the couple than met the eye. Dawn was a beautiful woman. She resembled Morning Mist, yet he could see vast differences. Dawn's eyes were mirrors into her soul. Running Elk instinctively knew that Dawn had suffered more than any woman should be made to suffer. Morning Mist had known nothing of suffering. She'd been pure of heart and mind, a loving and lovable creature. Intuition told him that Dawn had known little happiness in her life.

"Come share my food. Spring Rain will be happy to see you."

"How are Spring Rain and your children?"

Running Elk pointed out two naked boys playing nearby with a group of children. "Spring Rain is well. And the boys grow strong like their father."

"Have you taken a second wife yet?"

Running Elk nodded enthusiastically. "I have joined with Spring Rain's younger sister. Sun In The Face is already carrying my child." He touched a brilliant strand of red hair woven among his own raven locks and smiled wistfully. "Had Flame become my wife as I wished, I would have no need for a second wife. I still wear her talisman."

"Unfortunately, my sister was already married. She and Tanner were meant for one another."

"Enough of reminiscing. Bring Dawn to my

lodge. My wives will see that she is made comfortable while we talk and smoke."

Dawn followed enough of the conversation to know that a woman named Flame—could it be Shadow Walker's sister?—had captured Running Elk's heart. The story sounded intriguing, and she vowed to question Shadow Walker the first chance she got.

"Running Elk has invited us to his lodge," Shadow Walker told Dawn in English. "His two wives will make you welcome."

They followed Running Elk to his lodge, where Shadow Walker was greeted by a woman he addressed as Spring Rain. She was no longer in the first bloom of youth but was still lovely. A much younger woman came out of the tipi and shyly greeted Shadow Walker and Dawn. She was pregnant, and Dawn assumed she was Running Elk's second wife.

Running Elk gave instructions to Spring Rain and then invited Shadow Walker to join him as he squatted down in front of the lodge. Spring Rain brought two backrests from inside the tipi, and Sun In The Face fetched the pipe.

"I will fix food," Spring Rain said.

Dawn had no idea what she was supposed to do until Sun In The Face shyly touched her arm and offered to take her to a place where she could refresh herself. Dawn's gaze flew to Shadow Walker, and when he nodded, she walked off with the Indian woman.

Running Elk passed the pipe to Shadow Walker, who took a deep drag of the aromatic tobacco and handed the pipe back. At length, Running Elk said, "I am curious, Shadow Walker. Why did you bring the woman to me?"

"First I must explain about Dawn and how I came to know her," Shadow Walker began. "Then you will understand why I seek your help."

Shadow Walker launched into an explanation, leaving out nothing except details of his intimate relationship with Dawn. That was between him and Dawn and no one else. But Running Elk was no fool. He understood more than he was told.

"You feel responsible for Dawn," Running Elk observed. "Perhaps you are not being truthful with yourself. Dawn is very beautiful. It would be easy to fall in love with her."

"You know there will never be another woman for me after Morning Mist. She is enshrined in my heart. Dawn deserves a man who will love her as she deserves to be loved. She has suffered pain and degradation at the hands of men. It is my hope that you will find a good husband for her."

Running Elk took another drag on the pipe and inhaled deeply. When he exhaled, the smoke drifted upward in a blue cloud. When it cleared, Shadow Walker was surprised to see that Running Elk was frowning. "Have I said something to displease you?" he asked.

"I am saddened by your failure to let my sister find peace. You have kept her alive in your heart too long, my friend. She has been dead a very long time. She would want you to find happiness with another woman. Have you tried to open your heart to Dawn?"

"I am not ready yet. Dawn understands this and accepts it."

Running Elk stared at Shadow Walker for several long minutes, carefully choosing his words. "Have you taken Dawn to your mat?" Despite the personal nature of the question, he expected Shadow Walker to speak openly and honestly.

Shadow Walker flushed and looked away, refusing to answer. His silence told Running Elk what he wanted to know. "Since Dawn is a widow, there is no stigma attached to her yielding to you."

Shadow Walker thought it best not to divulge the state of Dawn's virginity to his friend. Bedding a virgin and then leaving her to another would make him sound like a callous bastard.

"Are you willing to accept Dawn into your tribe?" Shadow Walker asked. "I had hoped you might take her as your second wife, but since you already have a second wife, perhaps you can find a young warrior in need of a mate."

"Is that what you wish?"

"It is how it must be."

"Then so be it. But I would ask one thing of you in return."

"Anything."

"Remain here through the winter. I have missed you."

Shadow Walker wanted to refuse but couldn't find it in his heart to do so. Running Elk had given him sanctuary when he'd been shattered by Morning Mist's death. He had allowed Shadow Walker to heal at his own pace, had become friend and teacher to him. But remaining here would present serious problems. He knew it would be easier to make a clean break with Dawn. Remaining would only provide opportunities for them to indulge in their lust for one another. It was going to be a challenge, but he would honor Running Elk's request and remain with the People until spring.

"I will stay until the snow melts from the mountains. Then I will travel to Oregon to visit my sister."

Spring Rain arrived with their food, and discussion ceased as they dug into the steaming bowls of venison stew and thick slices of frybread.

Dawn felt strange as she accompanied Sun In The Face to the stream to freshen up. Sun In The Face was friendly and eager to please, and as she chattered, Dawn felt more comfortable with the Sioux tongue. There was still much she didn't understand, but she supposed she'd learn in time.

"No one will bother us here," Sun In The Face said as Dawn knelt at the stream and splashed water on her face and neck. "It is the women's bathing place. Is Shadow Walker your man?" she blurted out with unaccustomed boldness. She flushed and apologized when she realized she had overstepped the bounds of politeness.

"It's all right," Dawn said. "I am not offended. Shadow Walker is not my man. He brought me to Running Elk because I had nowhere else to go and he thought I would be happy here."

"Things are not always good on the reservation, but I believe you can find happiness with us. All the young warriors will vie for your attention. Soon you will have many suitors to choose from."

"I'm not sure I want a husband. I am a widow. My marriage was not a happy one."

"Trust Running Elk to choose someone suitable." She gave Dawn a shy smile. "Perhaps he can persuade Shadow Walker to join with you, even though Laughing Brook will not like it. She has waited many years for Shadow Walker."

Dawn felt a sudden chill. She had given little thought to the possibility that Shadow Walker had a woman waiting for him. Was that why he was so anxious to see her wed to another?

Chapter Eleven

Dawn was invited to share the lodge with Running Elk and his family, but when Shadow Walker pointed out that Dawn was a widow and should be given her own tipi, Running Elk agreed. Dawn watched with admiration as the women erected her new home within the circle of the camp. When they had finished, they carried in all the supplies and utensils necessary to set up housekeeping. In a very short time the tipi was comfortable and homey.

Shadow Walker was also to have his own lodge, and when the women finished erecting Dawn's, they began work on Shadow Walker's. Dawn felt somewhat lost when she thought of occupying the tipi by herself. She and Shadow Walker had been together so long she didn't know how she was going to sleep without him nearby.

Shadow Walker approached Dawn, thinking he'd never seen her looking so forlorn. "You can't be unhappy already; you haven't been here long enough to form an opinion. What do you think of Running Elk and his wives?"

"Running Elk seems . . . very nice, and his wives are friendly." Suddenly she clutched his arm in desperate appeal. "I'm not comfortable with these people, Shadow Walker. I'll be alone after you leave."

"I'm not leaving until spring. By then you'll have met a young man you fancy. You may even be married." He frowned. Why did he find that notion disturbing?

She sent him a fulminating look. "I don't want to marry again."

"All men aren't like Cobb. Running Elk will find a good man for you. And I'll be here to help."

Dawn looked away, unwilling to show him how much his urgency to be rid of her hurt. From the corner of her eye she saw a woman approaching. She was older than Dawn, perhaps in her late twenties, and more voluptuous. As she drew near, Dawn noted how the woman's eyes clung to Shadow Walker.

"Welcome home, Shadow Walker. I have missed you." Her eyes held an invitation as old as Eve.

"It is good to be back, Laughing Brook. Have you met Dawn?"

Laughing Brook barely looked at Dawn as she acknowledged the introduction. "Is she your woman?"

"No. You know no one can replace Morning Mist in my heart."

"I have waited a long time for you to return."

"I'm surprised you haven't remarried. There are any number of warriors who would appreciate a wife such as you."

"There is only one warrior I want," she said with sly innuendo. "Come to my lodge tonight. I will cook for you."

Dawn bristled with jealousy. It shouldn't matter who Shadow Walker took to his bed, but it did.

"Not tonight. Running Elk has invited us to share his meal. Maybe another time."

"Another time," she agreed, tossing a smug smile at Dawn as she turned and strolled away.

"She doesn't like me," Dawn said.

"You're imagining things. Laughing Brook has no reason to dislike you."

Dawn thought differently but did not belabor the point. It was obvious that Laughing Brook wanted Shadow Walker. Dawn would have pursued the subject of Laughing Brook if Spring Rain and Sun In The Face hadn't stopped by to take her to the bathing place. Later, she was to take the evening meal with them.

Dawn ate with the women after the men had been served. It seemed strange that men and women didn't eat together, but there was much she had to learn about Indian culture. She helped with the cleanup while Shadow Walker and Running Elk smoked and talked.

"An unsettling rumor has reached my ears, Running Elk," Shadow Walker said at length.

"What rumor is that, my friend?"

"I encountered Horned Owl and a group of renegades a few days ago. I also spoke with a chieftain taking his people north to the Little Big Horn. There is talk of retaliation against the army for injustices done to the People. Is it true that the Sioux Nation is gathering at the Little Big Horn in preparation for a battle?"

Running Elk nodded slowly. "Your ears have not deceived you, Shadow Walker. Too many treaties have been broken, too many false promises given. The recent invasion into our sacred hills cannot be tolerated. We must show the White-eyes they cannot treat us with blatant disrespect."

"I do not like what I'm hearing, Running Elk. Surely you are too wise to take your people to the Little Big Horn. Remain here. Stay out of the fight. It can only lead to the beginning of the end for the People."

Running Elk stared off into the distance, his expression bleak, his dark eyes hollow with sadness. "The beginning of the end has already come. Whites are running over our lands like ants upon an anthill. There is no stopping them. They will not be happy until the People are herded like animals onto inhospitable lands. We have no hope if we do not retaliate."

"I sympathize wholeheartedly, and pray our lawmakers will recognize the plight of the People. Meanwhile, you are treading on dangerous ground by massing together and forcing a fight."

"We do this to appease our pride and our honor. My people will rally to their leaders. The summons came from the Hunkpapa chiefs, Gall, Rain

In The Face, and Crazy Horse and Low Dog of the Oglalas. Thousands of Sioux and Cheyenne will answer the call."

"Are you saying you will join the hordes preparing for battle? There is scant hope of defeating Custer's Seventh Cavalry."

"You are wrong. We will annihilate them," Running Elk said confidently. "Our people will gather in great force. The cavalry will be lured out to meet us and they will taste defeat."

"Then what? Say the People are victorious. There is bound to be retaliation."

"It will be as Wakantanka wills."

"What can I do or say to persuade you to remain at the Red Cloud Agency? I beg you, do not participate in this folly. The thought of your death pains me."

"I do not wish to cause you pain, but honor demands that I join the great chiefs in their endeavor. In the spring I will take my people to the Little Big Horn. If it results in my death, I will die with honor."

"What about your wives and children?"

Running Elk winced as if in pain. "They will understand and honor my decision to die as a warrior should."

"I am sorry, Running Elk, but I cannot accept that. While I am here I will continue to voice my objection."

"And I will do as my heart directs. Now that that's settled, let us discuss Dawn. She has just arrived, but already there is much speculation among the young warriors. Stands Alone has asked to court her."

"Stands Alone," Shadow Walker mused thoughtfully. "I remember him. Is he of good character?"

"He is a fine warrior. A bit young, but he will be good to Dawn. She will have many warriors to choose from if he doesn't appeal to her."

"Yes, of course," Shadow Walker muttered without enthusiasm.

He was beginning to have second thoughts about leaving Dawn, knowing what he did now about Running Elk's decision to join the masses gathering at the Little Big Horn. There was bound to be violent retaliation after the battle, and Dawn would be drawn into the middle of a dangerous situation. How could he leave her to that kind of fate? He decided to delay as long as he could before making a decision. Meanwhile, he'd see what developed between Dawn and the young men courting her.

Time passed with alarming speed. The days were growing cool and the nights frosty. Dawn wasn't unhappy, but neither was she content. She suspected she'd be reasonably happy as long Shadow Walker remained with her. Spring Rain and Sun In The Face took her in their care, teaching her about her mother's people and their culture. Stands Alone had begun to court her, but she had no interest in the warrior. Yapping Wolf, older and more seasoned than Stands Alone, also expressed interest in her. Dawn found him fierce and frightening and tried to avoid him, but he was persistent in his pursuit of her.

Shadow Walker watched the developing situation with growing interest. He thought Stands Alone inoffensive, if somewhat immature, but considered Yapping Wolf boastful and cocky. The way Yapping Wolf strutted and preened before Dawn irritated him greatly. He decided to speak to Dawn about the aggressive warrior the first chance he got. That chance arrived one day when Dawn went down to the stream alone to fetch water.

"Dawn, wait, I'll walk with you," he said as he caught up with her. "How are you getting along?"

"Do you really care?" Dawn asked with little enthusiasm.

"What kind of a question is that? Of course I care."

Dawn kept on walking. Oh, yes, she knew how much Shadow Walker cared. He cared so much he barely knew she existed these days. It nearly killed her to watch Laughing Brook make a fool of herself over him. She wondered if the lovely widow was sharing his bed. A lusty man like Shadow Walker wasn't likely to remain celibate, not with Laughing Brook around to appease his needs. Dawn smiled a secret smile. If Laughing Brook thought Shadow Walker would marry her, she was in for a rude awakening. No one knew better than Dawn how committed Shadow Walker was to his dead wife's memory.

They had reached the stream now, and Dawn set the waterskin down and turned to face Shadow Walker. "Is there something else you wish to say to me?"

"I've noticed that Stands Alone is courting you. What do you think of him?"

"He's a nice boy," she said with marked indifference.

"He's older than you. But I think you're right. He's not right for you. Neither is Yapping Wolf."

Dawn's temper flared. "I thought you wanted me to find a husband. I'll choose whomever pleases me."

"Are you saying you actually like Yapping Wolf?"

"What if I do?" She'd not give Shadow Walker the satisfaction of knowing she didn't like the fierce brave.

"Then you have less sense than I gave you credit for. He has a cruel streak in him, not unlike Cobb. He'll not treat you kindly."

"Let me be the judge of that."

He grasped her shoulders, dragging her up against him. "Dammit, Dawn, I care what happens to you."

Dawn gave a mirthless laugh. "No one cares what happens to me. I'm here because you insisted. You wanted me taken off your hands and now you're trying to tell me what to do. Go find Laughing Brook, I'm sure she'll adore your advice."

Shadow Walker stared at her, seized by the sudden urge to kiss her. He had missed her. Missed the warmth of her sweet body, the tantalizing softness of her lush lips. But continuing their intimacy wouldn't have been right.

"Laughing Brook means nothing to me. Had I wanted her I could have had her years ago."

"That's right, you don't want a wife. You prefer to live with memories of the past. Unfortunately, memories can't warm your bed. You use women like Laughing Brook to satisfy your male needs and fill your empty moments."

"My empty moments can never be filled by women like Laughing Brook, not even temporarily," Shadow Walker confessed. He pulled her closer, his gaze intense and probing as he looked deeply into her eyes. He cupped her face with his hands and brought his mouth down on hers. Dawn felt as if she had waited forever for this kiss.

He kissed her endlessly, his mouth hot and hard, his tongue deeply seductive. His breath was warm and tasted of mint. Fire licked through her when his tongue touched hers. He began to caress her breasts, and Dawn felt the resulting heat clear down to her tingling center. When he stopped kissing her, she uttered a small cry of disappointment, but quickly recovered.

"Why did you do that?"

"I've wanted to kiss you for a long time. You can't imagine how difficult it has been for me not to touch you. You deserve far better than I can offer you. My heart isn't free. I'm not ready yet to give up my memories of Morning Mist."

Dawn tried to turn away, but he held her captive in his embrace. She had to fight her body's reaction to him. "Then you have no say over whom I marry."

"I've been thinking about the battle that's brewing and have begun to entertain second thoughts."

"About what?"

"Running Elk is determined to take his people to the Little Big Horn. A battle will be devastating to the Sioux. There will be violent retaliation. You won't be safe here."

"Where will I be safe?"

Shadow Walker grew thoughtful. "I don't know. I'll think of something."

Dawn turned away. "Don't bother. I've relied on you long enough. I'll stay here and take my chances with one of the men courting me. Yapping Wolf seems most eager to join with me."

"You can't marry Yapping Wolf."

"Why not?"

"Because I won't let you."

"You can't stop me."

He gave her a slow smile. Dawn should have known by his expression that he had something devious in mind. "It's been over two months since we made love. You should know by now if you're pregnant."

She swallowed convulsively and shook her head. "Pregnant?" Oh, God, she knew so little about woman things. Her mother had never gotten around to telling her before she died. Could she be pregnant? "I . . . I . . . of course I'm not pregnant." Lord, she certainly hoped she wasn't.

Shadow Walker should have been relieved, but the opposite was true. What in the hell was the matter with him?

"I have to get back," Dawn said, reaching for the waterskin. "Spring Rain will wonder why I've been delayed."

"Let me help you," Shadow Walker said, bending to dip water into the bag.

They walked back to camp together, parting at Running Elk's lodge. Shadow Walker wanted to say more but decided this wasn't the right time.

Perhaps he should have a word with Running Elk about Dawn. Then a small party of warriors asked him to go hunting, and he decided a hard ride was just what he needed to clear the cobwebs and Dawn's arousing scent from his head.

"Shadow Walker is handsome, is he not?" Sun In The Face said as she joined Dawn. "He is every bit as brave and strong as Running Elk. He will make some woman a wonderful husband."

"Shadow Walker wants no wife," Dawn said with an abruptness that sent Sun In The Face's eyebrows upward. "He's made that perfectly clear on more than one occasion."

"I think you would like to be his wife," Sun In The Face observed. "I believe you love him very much."

Dawn went still. Love? Did such a thing exist? What she felt for Shadow Walker was difficult to label. Billy had totally subjugated her. When freedom had come unexpectedly, she'd vowed she'd never place herself in another man's keeping. But Shadow Walker had shown her there didn't have to be pain between a man and woman. There could be tenderness in intimacy, and caring. And joy. Was that love? She wasn't sure. She did know that she cared about Shadow Walker more than she had thought it possible to care for anyone.

"It matters little what I feel for Shadow Walker," Dawn said at length. "I would not burden him."

"Yapping Wolf and Stands Alone offered Running Elk many horses for you. They are both greatly respected by the People. Will you join with one of them?"

"I don't know," Dawn said truthfully.

They parted then. Dawn returned to her lodge to work on the doeskin tunic Spring Rain had given her. She was sewing beads and feathers on the butter-soft garment according to the Indian woman's directions. Bringing the tunic into the sunshine, she sat cross-legged in front of the tipi and diligently plied her needle. A short time later a shadow fell across her and she looked up, surprised to see Yapping Wolf standing over her.

"I have been waiting to speak with you alone," he said, dropping down beside her. "It is time we speak of our relationship. I want you beneath my blankets. I have offered Running Elk ten horses for you. I do you great honor by offering so large a number. A man's wealth is measured by his string of horses. Stands Alone cannot offer half that number."

"What did Running Elk say?" Dawn asked curiously.

"He said I must speak to you directly. He is not your guardian and therefore cannot speak for you."

"I hardly know you," Dawn demurred.

"You have been married before and are no stranger to a man's body or his needs. I am young and lusty; I will give you fine children and provide for them. My feats of bravery have been sung around the campfire." He pounded his chest importantly. "I am a better man than Stands Alone."

Dawn could not deny that Yapping Wolf was a handsome man, albeit a boastful one. He was strong and tall and powerfully made. But in her opinion he couldn't hold a candle to Shadow Walker.

"I cannot give you my answer now," she hedged.

Yapping Wolf rose to his feet, drawing her up with him. "If you are worried that I will not please you between the blankets, let me prove myself now. I am eager to bury my mighty lance deep inside you. You are a widow; there will be no stigma if we satisfy our lust." He tried to draw her inside the tipi but she resisted.

Dawn saw the ridge beneath the fabric of his breechclout and recoiled in alarm. "I cannot do what you wish. I need time to adjust to my new home and acquaint myself with the People before I decide upon a mate. I mean you no disrespect, Yapping Wolf, but I'm not sure I wish to marry again. Remaining a widow isn't so bad. I understand Laughing Brook has been a widow for a very long time."

"It is different with Laughing Brook. She is waiting to join with Shadow Walker."

They spoke earnestly for several minutes, unaware that Shadow Walker had returned and was watching them. Running Elk stood beside him, measuring Shadow Walker's reaction. When Shadow Walker started forward to intervene, Running Elk held him back.

"Do not interfere, brother."

"What if Yapping Wolf hurts her?"

"Look around you. There are people all about. Yapping Wolf will not risk the tribe's wrath by doing something foolish. He is merely following my instructions. He offered ten horses for Dawn, and I told him to take his offer to Dawn. Dawn is a widow and has the right to choose her own mate."

"She can't accept him. He's not right for her."

"I think you protest too much. I will make certain Dawn is not mistreated."

"I'm having second thoughts about leaving Dawn with the People, unless you change your mind about traveling to the Little Big Horn in the spring."

"I cannot do that."

"Retaliation is bound to be swift and violent."

"I will protect Dawn as I would my own wives and children."

"Good intentions are not enough."

Running Elk searched Shadow Walker's face. "I believe your unwillingness to leave Dawn speaks of what is in your heart."

"You're wrong."

"Then let her choose a mate. If you truly don't want Dawn and wish her well, take Laughing Brook to wife. I spoke with her just today and she is more than willing."

"Perhaps I will," Shadow Walker said recklessly. At least Laughing Brook wouldn't tug at his emotions. "I think I'll go find Laughing Brook," he said, casting a surreptitious glance at Dawn and Yapping Wolf, who were still engaged in conversation.

Running Elk smiled as Shadow Walker stalked off. He knew his friend better than Shadow Walker knew himself. Shadow Walker was more interested in Dawn than he'd admit. Running Elk recognized a jealous man when he saw one. He couldn't wait to see what developed and thought it all great entertainment.

From the corner of her eye Dawn saw Shadow Walker approach Laughing Brook, who had just emerged from her lodge. They spoke quietly a few moments, then Laughing Brook took his hand and led him inside her tipi. He hesitated briefly, then shrugged and followed her inside. Dawn's heart sank. Had she been wrong all along? Was Shadow Walker more interested in the widow than he'd let on? She excused herself abruptly, having had all she could take of Yapping Wolf, and ducked inside her lodge.

Alone with Laughing Brook, Shadow Walker wondered what in the hell he was doing with her when he'd rather be with . . . Damn! What was he thinking?

"I saw you speaking with Running Elk," Laughing Brook said as she sidled close to Shadow Walker. "Did he tell you I am eager to join with you?"

"You know I'm not staying," Shadow Walker said in an effort to discourage her. "Eventually I must return to my own people."

"Spring is many moons away. I am willing to accept your terms if you will be mine alone for as long as you remain."

"It wouldn't be fair to you, Laughing Brook. I can never love a woman like I did Morning Mist."

"I can ease your body," Laughing Brook murmured as she rubbed up against him. "At one time you sought my favors." She reached down between their bodies to cup him beneath his breechclout. He hardened in her hand.

Shadow Walker didn't even try to stifle the groan that rose in his throat. It had been a while since he'd had a woman, and Laughing Brook certainly knew how to arouse him.

They dropped to the sleeping mat in mutual

consent, limbs entwined as Laughing Brook clutched him in almost desperate need. Her legs fell open to better accommodate him. When he hesitated, she clawed at him.

"Please," she whimpered, arching up against him.

Shadow Walker felt his desire shriveling and spit out a curse. At a time like this he should be thinking of Laughing Brook and her lush charms instead of dreaming of Dawn's slim body. This was a mistake. He wanted to prove to himself that any woman could assuage his lust, but all he'd proven was how wrong he'd been. Somehow Dawn had gotten under his skin.

"I'm sorry, Laughing Brook," Shadow Walker said as he untangled himself from her clinging limbs. "This is a mistake."

"It wasn't always a mistake," Laughing Brook said, pouting. "You've taken my body many times and enjoyed it."

"That was also a mistake. I used you, knowing I would never take another wife."

She laughed harshly. "Now you are talking like a White man. I am a widow. It is my lot in life to be used by the single men of the tribe. It is the way of things. But none made my heart sing like you do."

"I'm sorry, Laughing Brook," he repeated.

She stared at him through narrowed lids. "It's that half-breed, isn't it? I've seen how you look at her. If you want her you should join with her instead of denying what you feel."

"You're wrong," Shadow Walker denied.

"Would I bring Dawn to Running Elk if I wanted her myself?"

Somewhat mollified by his words, Laughing Brook decided to bide her time. Shadow Walker was a lusty man. Sooner or later he would come to her.

Shadow Walker left the tipi in a contemplative mood. Being unable to couple with Laughing Brook had been discouraging. He couldn't ever recall having had that problem before. He left Laughing Brook's lodge and walked down to the stream where he could be alone to think.

Dawn hummed to herself as she picked the last of the berries growing in a thicket Spring Rain had pointed out that morning when they'd come down to the stream to bathe. The day had turned warm after a frosty night, and Dawn wondered if it was to be their last warm day before winter set in.

This trip to the stream to pick berries had a dual purpose. Not only was she fond of the succulent fruits but she needed time alone to think. Yapping Wolf's arrogance had been upsetting. She knew that Indians counted their worth in the number of horses they owned, but Yapping Wolf's wealth did not impress her. She felt nothing for the warrior. If she had to accept anyone it would be Stands Alone, whose gentle nature appealed more to her. But neither man excited her as Shadow Walker did.

Moving from bush to bush, she tried not to dwell on Shadow Walker and what he was doing with Laughing Brook. Was he making love to her at this very minute? Dawn wondered, willing the ache in her heart away.

Shadow Walker sat on a fallen log, searching his brain for answers that were not forthcoming. Reverting to his Indian identity felt comfortable, yet he knew it was only temporary. His sojourn with the People would end come spring. He seriously doubted he'd ever return to the wilderness again as Shadow Walker. If Running Elk joined Crazy Horse at the Little Big Horn and a battle ensued, it would be the end of the Indian way of life as he knew it. Then his thoughts turned abruptly to Dawn. How could he leave her to face danger alone? What choice did he have?

Suddenly he became aware of a noise behind him, and his attention sharpened. One had to be careful these days. Danger lurked around every corner. He rose cautiously and concealed himself behind a thicket of shrubbery. He spied Dawn bending over a berry patch, a basket half filled with ripe berries at her feet. Shadow Walker was torn. Should he leave as silently as he'd appeared or make his presence known? The choice was taken from him when Dawn sensed his presence and grew still.

Dawn knew it wasn't a wild animal, for she felt no danger. Nevertheless, the back of her neck tingled with awareness and her heart thudded against her breast. She knew who it was before she turned in his direction. She spoke his name aloud.

Shadow Walker stepped boldly into view. "How did you know it was I?"

"I just knew." Her gaze traveled the length of his

powerful form. He was bronzed all over from the sun and his hair shone. His breechclout did little to conceal the bold thrust of his manhood or the taut mounds of his buttocks.

Shadow Walker stepped closer. "I saw you talking to Yapping Wolf earlier. Have you decided to join with him?"

"I'm still considering it."

"He's not the man for you."

"Would you prefer I choose Stands Alone?"

Shadow Walker realized he could see no man but himself making love to Dawn. "I don't think he'd make you happy."

"I'm leaning toward Yapping Wolf," Dawn said to test his reaction.

His reaction was immediate and violent. He pulled her into his arms and brought his mouth down on hers. His kiss was hungry, almost punishing, sending the pit of her stomach into a wild swirl. When his tongue demanded entrance, she opened to him. Her resistance seemed to ebb as his tongue ravished and probed, tasted and dueled. Her body felt heavy, hot, driven mad by this green-eyed savage who had taught her body to need his. When he finally released her mouth, Dawn staggered backward, stunned by the brilliance of his passion.

"Why are you doing this?" she asked shakily. "Wasn't Laughing Brook enough for you?"

Shadow Walker groaned in dismay, aware that she had seen him entering Laughing Brook's tipi.

"Nothing happened between Laughing Brook and me."

She gave an unladylike snort. "I don't believe

you. Laughing Brook is quite shameless in her pursuit of you. And you seemed willing enough to join her in her lodge."

He gave her a slow smile. "Are you jealous?"

Dawn flushed and looked away. She wouldn't give him the satisfaction of knowing how much seeing him with the provocative widow had hurt her. Shadow Walker had given her no hope of becoming more to him than an intimate friend, so why should she feel jealousy?

"Dawn, look at me." He grasped her chin and raised her face to his. "I didn't make love to Laughing Brook because I kept wishing it was you in my arms. I want you, Dawn. God help me, for I cannot help myself."

"No, don't!" she cried, shoving his hands away. If he touched her she'd shatter. But it was already too late. His hands slid down her body, cupping her bottom and bringing her against the hard thrust of his erection, and she was lost.

Chapter Twelve

Shadow Walker lowered Dawn to a bed of soft moss without breaking contact with her mouth. The hungry urgency of his kisses sent spirals of fire through her. They were both panting as he kissed the pulsing hollow at the base of her throat, nibbled on a pink earlobe, and pressed his lips to the tops of her breasts visible above the vee of her blouse.

"God, you're sweet," he breathed against her lips. "I've missed you. I've missed this."

Dawn's first thought was to deny him. But that thought quickly died, lost in the heat of Shadow Walker's kisses. His taste was so familiar. It was like an addiction. The more he kissed her, the more kisses she wanted. Within seconds she was responding to the compelling demand of his mouth, clinging with desperation, hungrily yielding to the magic of his touch.

He began undressing her, removing her clothing piece by piece. Dawn was too caught up in her own passion to utter a word of protest. Then she was naked and he was kissing her again, one hand kneading her breast, the other cupping her mound, delving a finger through soft down into the velvety cleft already moist for him. The heel of his hand rubbed teasingly against her tiny sensitive nub of passion as Dawn arched up against him.

"You want me as badly as I want you," Shadow Walker whispered against her lips.

Dawn opened her mouth to deny his words, but nothing came out save for a low, anguished moan.

He carefully inserted another finger inside her. His own body tightened painfully in response to the heat building inside her. When her body arched violently against his probing fingers, he wanted to thrust inside her, but he forced himself to be patient.

"You're so beautiful. All smooth and soft and hot," he murmured against her lips. "Your breasts are magnificent." His free hand cradled a breast, grazing his thumb lightly over her raised nipple.

Dawn shivered with delight and moaned as a jolt of pure longing shot through her. Though Shadow Walker wore little to remove, his breechclout became a barrier between them. She pulled at the offending garment, telling him what she wanted without words. He rose slightly and slipped it off. His manhood sprang free, rising high against the taut ridges of his belly. Dawn swallowed convulsively as she reached out to touch him.

Shadow Walker went rigid, grasping her hand and moving it up and down in a motion he found pleasing. Then his mouth sought the pert peak of one breast. His tongue flicked at it with sensual strokes, then he sucked deeply. Dawn felt the pull in that secret place between her legs. She felt hot and damp, pulsing with desperate need.

His hands were never still. He stroked her hips and thighs, her breasts and between her legs. A tortured groan escaped her lips.

"Soon, love, soon," Shadow Walker gasped as jagged spears of desire pierced him.

"Now," Dawn pleaded. She could not bear another moment of this exquisite torture.

He merely grinned as he removed her hands from his member, slid down her body and nudged her legs apart. She felt his warm breath whisper over her intimate flesh and went rigid with wanting. His tongue flicked over the swollen petals of her sex as he lifted her hips to his mouth. He tasted and licked, delved and explored with wild abandon. The sweet torment went on and on—until with a hoarse cry she shattered. Before the last spasm left her body, he rose to his knees and thrust into her, triggering a second climax nearly as violent as the first.

Shadow Walker went still, staring down at her in wonder. Her second climax surprised him. "I love watching your face when you climax," he said in a voice made raw with passion. The pressure of her tremors against his sex was driving him mad.

His muscles were taut, his expression stark as

he flexed his hips and drove into her, again and again, his loins pumping vigorously. Her fingers dug into his shoulders as he held her suspended in the flames of her climax. He rode her hard and deep, one pounding thrust after another. With a hoarse shout, he spilled his seed inside her, and still he continued. Finally his thrusting motion stopped and he rolled off her onto his back.

Dazed, Dawn stared up at the sky. She felt as if she had been catapulted above those lofty clouds to touch the sun. Her body still burned from the searing heat. She turned her head toward Shadow Walker and found him looking at her. She flushed and tried to cover herself with her discarded clothing.

"Don't," he said, staying her hand. "Let me look at you a while longer."

"What if someone comes along?"

"They won't. We're well off the beaten path. You're very beautiful. You remind me of . . ." His words trailed off.

". . . Morning Mist," Dawn whispered, beginning to hate the woman Shadow Walker still loved. "She's dead."

Shadow Walker's lips thinned. Being reminded of his loss hurt.

Dawn sat up and began dressing. "This shouldn't have happened. I'm going to be another man's wife soon. It would be better for both of us if you left before spring. You're too much of a temptation. You brought me here to find a new life for myself; why can't you leave me alone?"

Why, indeed? Shadow Walker pondered. Since he didn't want Dawn for himself, he should leave her to someone else and find temporary pleasure with Laughing Brook. Unfortunately, he didn't want Laughing Brook. And the thought of Dawn with Yapping Wolf or any other man did not sit well with him. In fact, there was no way he would let Dawn waste herself on Yapping Wolf. Even if he had to . . . Sweet Lord, what was he thinking? There was only one way to prevent such a thing from happening, but was he ready to commit to another permanent relationship? Shadow Walker pondered long and hard on the situation at hand.

Dawn was dressed and ready to return to camp when he reached a decision. He leaped to his feet and grasped her arm, preventing her from leaving.

"I can't allow you to join with Yapping Wolf."

"Perhaps I've decided to join with Stands Alone."

"You can't marry him, either."

Dawn bristled indignantly. "Whom do you suggest I marry?"

"Me."

Dawn went still. "What did you say?"

"I know I said I'd never marry again, but you're my responsibility. The only way I can protect you is to marry you myself."

Dawn continued to stare at him. He stood proudly naked and unashamed of his nudity. She thought he was the most magnificent man she'd ever seen. Marrying him would be the culmination of all her dreams. But she, better than anyone, knew that dreams seldom came true.

"I realize now that leaving you with Running Elk would be a mistake," he explained. "I had no idea things would turn out this way. I'd be leaving you in a dangerous environment and it wouldn't be right. We'll be married as soon as we return to civilization. I'll take you to my sister. She'll look after you when I leave."

"When you leave?" Dawn repeated dully. "And of course you *will* leave."

"I'll give you my name, Dawn, but don't expect me to hang around and act like a doting husband. What we have right now is all we'll ever share. We enjoy each other's bodies and like one another. We're lucky to have that much in common."

"Lucky, indeed," Dawn said in a voice taut with anger. "What will I do after you dump me with your sister?"

Shadow Walker shrugged. "I hadn't thought that far ahead. Why must you do anything?"

"No, thank you, but I decline. I'd rather take my chances with Yapping Wolf. At least he wouldn't be an absentee husband."

"You're refusing me?" Shadow Walker was astounded. "Laughing Brook would jump at the chance to join with me."

"Then marry Laughing Brook," Dawn shot back. "I don't want you, Shadow Walker. I want all or nothing from the man I marry. A close second behind a dead wife isn't enough for me. I prefer to marry someone who will give me his whole heart." She turned away.

"I told you before my heart is not free to . . ."

Dawn walked away without looking back. Her own heart was breaking, but she'd never let Shadow Walker see how much his words had hurt her. She had been married once to a man who didn't love her and she refused to make the same mistake twice. Perhaps she'd choose Stands Alone for a husband. He mooned over her like a lovesick puppy. At least he wouldn't dump her with relatives and disappear to pursue a life separate from hers.

Exasperated, Shadow Walker watched Dawn stalk away. What did she want from him? He'd give her everything she desired except his heart. They were good together in bed. He had just made love to her, and already his body wanted her again. He picked up his breechclout, tied it on and started back to camp. He had no idea what he would do next. He couldn't protect Dawn if she didn't want to be protected.

The weather turned cold. Shadow Walker was forced to don his deerskin shirt and leggings for warmth. It would snow soon. Running Elk had given him a buffalo robe to wear as a wrap when the weather turned bitter. Dawn had finished her tunic and wore it now. Shadow Walker thought she looked fetching in Indian garb. But then, she looked fetching in anything she wore—or didn't wear.

Shadow Walker was currying his horse one morning when Running Elk approached to speak with him. "Dawn has agreed to join with Stands Alone," Running Elk said. "She's requested that I ask Dream Spinner to name a propitious date for their joining."

"Damn her!" Shadow Walker spat from between clenched teeth.

"Why does that make you angry? I thought it was what you wanted."

Shadow Walker gave him a sheepish look. "Of course it's what I wanted. Dawn has made her choice, I'll abide by it." He turned abruptly and walked away before Running Elk saw how deeply he was affected by Dawn's decision.

Running Elk smiled knowingly as he watched Shadow Walker stalk away.

Winter blew in with a vengeance. Most days Dawn huddled in her lodge to escape the bitter cold. She saw little of Shadow Walker these days. Whenever she did see him he was with Laughing Brook. It appeared as if he was courting the widow, and Dawn tried not to care.

Dawn waited for Dream Spinner to name a date for her joining with Stands Alone. After reading the bones he tossed upon the ground, Dream Spinner named a day that coincided with the full moon, only two weeks away. Running Elk was told, and a feast was planned to celebrate the joining. According to Dawn's calculations, it would be February 20.

Despite Shadow Walker's words about accepting Dawn's decision, he nevertheless was livid when he heard the news and expressed his anger to Running Elk. "Damn her! She cannot join with Stands Alone! He will not make her happy."

"Perhaps I should have advised her to accept Yapping Wolf's suit," Running Elk said with restrained levity.

"You know how I feel about that match."

"Did you not bring Dawn here to find a mate from among my people?"

Shadow Walker gave him a mutinous look. "I've

231

changed my mind. There is a dangerous situation brewing on the plains. I prefer to settle Dawn where she will be safe."

"You must speak to Dawn. I had no say in her decision."

Shadow Walker thought it over and decided to follow Running Elk's advice. It was time to confront Dawn and talk some sense into her. Living conditions here were more abysmal than he had imagined. Food was scarce, and the cows promised by the government failed to arrive. Shadow Walker went hunting every day with the men but more times than not came back empty-handed. There weren't enough blankets to go around, and the situation would only grow worse as winter progressed. Even more disheartening was the knowledge that Running Elk planned to join the warring Sioux at the Little Big Horn.

Huddled in a blanket, Dawn sat in her lodge trying to keep warm. She felt alone and unwanted. In a few days she would be Stands Alone's wife, and despite his obvious infatuation, she didn't love him and never would. Damn Shadow Walker! Didn't he know how much she was hurting? She clutched her stomach, fighting the terrible nausea that had plagued her the past few days. Sometimes it was so bad she went running from the lodge to spew out her guts.

Dawn sighed despondently. For her, happiness seemed unobtainable. First she had been Billy's victim, and now she was going to wed a man she didn't love and live among people with whom she felt no kinship despite her Sioux blood. Suddenly she heard footsteps crunching in the snow. She hoped it wasn't Stands Alone.

"Dawn, it's Shadow Walker. I'd like to speak with you."

Dawn stiffened. She hadn't been alone with Shadow Walker in weeks. She'd watched him pay court to Laughing Brook and died a little inside each time he entered the widow's lodge. Her stomach gave another lurch, and she gulped back the bile rising in her throat.

"Is it important? I'm not feeling well."

That was all Shadow Walker had to hear to prompt him to burst into the tipi. "You're ill?" His concern was genuine. "What seems to be the trouble? There's a doctor on the reservation if you need one."

Dawn shook her head. "It's just a stomach upset, it will pass. What did you wish to talk about?"

Shadow Walker dropped down beside her. "It's not too late to tell Stands Alone that you can't join with him. I'll speak to him myself if you wish me to."

"Why would I want you to do that?"

His gaze pierced clear through to her heart. "Because you don't love him."

"How do you know that?"

"I just know. I was wrong. You don't belong here."

"Where do I belong?"

Shadow Walker was silent so long Dawn wanted to bash him. There wasn't a man alive more stubborn than Shadow Walker. She wanted to tell him so, but another need took precedence.

Sickness clawed at her gut and she leaped to her feet.

"Where are you going?"

Dawn clapped a hand over her mouth and rushed from the lodge. She barely made it to the edge of the woods before losing the contents of her stomach. Afterward, she leaned against a tree, too weak to return to her lodge. She was unaware that Shadow Walker had followed her until he picked her up and carried her back to her tipi.

"Do you want to tell me what is going on?" he asked after he set her down on her mat and brought her some water.

"N . . . nothing. I don't know what's wrong with me."

Shadow Walker searched her face, his eyes narrowed thoughtfully. "I'm going to ask you a personal question, Dawn, and I expect a truthful answer."

Dawn had no idea what he was talking about.

"When did you have your last woman's time? Was it before or after we made love in the woods?"

Dawn's eyes widened as comprehension dawned. Her voice faltered. "After," she lied. She didn't want a man who didn't want her.

"How long have you been vomiting?"

"Not long." Another lie.

"Any other signs? Are your breasts more sensitive than normal?"

Just this morning Dawn had wondered why her breasts hurt when she was getting dressed. They seemed fuller, too. There was only one way she could answer Shadow Walker's question. "No, I have no such symptoms."

"Are you sure you're not pregnant?"

"Positive."

He dropped down beside her and grasped her shoulders. "Don't lie, Dawn. If you're expecting my child, I'll not let you wed Stands Alone. I won't have another man raising my child."

"Damn you!" She shrugged off his hands. "You don't want a child any more than you want a wife. You offered me your name but not your love."

"You know the reason. I'm not ready to love another."

"And I'm not pregnant. My illness is not serious."

Shadow Walker didn't believe her. If she truly was pregnant, time would reveal the truth. But by that time she would be married to Stands Alone. How could one small woman give him so much trouble?

"Will you tell me if you find you are mistaken?"

"Why?"

"Dammit, Dawn, don't provoke me. If you still insist upon joining with Stands Alone and you are carrying my child, you'd damn well better be prepared to give up your child after you bear him."

Having said his last word on the subject, he stormed from the tipi, leaving Dawn with much to think about. Could Shadow Walker take her child from her if indeed she was pregnant? Dawn wondered pensively. Could she pass the child off as Stands Alone's babe? The answer was a resounding no. Stands Alone was a good man; he didn't deserve that from her.

Dawn touched her breasts, testing their sensitivity. She flinched when the twinge of pain told her that Shadow Walker had guessed the truth before she had. All signs pointed to pregnancy. Shadow Walker would be leaving in the spring, about the same time Running Elk took his people to the Little Big Horn. All she had to do was keep her secret to herself until Shadow Walker left.

Unfortunately, joining with Stands Alone was no longer feasible. Somehow Dawn had to make him believe she wasn't right for him without revealing her secret. With any luck, her pregnancy wouldn't show for several months yet. She couldn't be more than two months along now.

Dawn sought out Stands Alone the following day. The weather had moderated somewhat and she suggested a walk. He eagerly agreed.

Shadow Walker watched them stroll toward the river, his face contorted with rage. He wanted to follow but resisted the urge lest it make him appear jealous, which of course he wasn't. It was just that he took his responsibility for Dawn seriously. Dawn didn't belong with Stands Alone, and he simply didn't want her to make a mistake.

Dawn paused on the path and turned to Stands Alone. He was young, she thought, and would have no trouble finding another woman. "I never meant to hurt you, Stands Alone, but I've changed my mind about joining with you."

Stands Alone stiffened. "Have you decided to accept Yapping Wolf's suit?"

"No, that's not it at all. I'm not ready to marry again. You know I was married before and that it was an unhappy marriage. My husband abused me physically and mentally."

"I would never do that."

"I know, but marriage frightens me. I'm sorry. I'm not even sure I will remain with the People. I don't belong here."

"Will you leave with Shadow Walker? He did not seem pleased with our joining."

"No," she returned shortly.

His handsome face contorted in thought. "I do not understand."

Dawn didn't know what she would do after Shadow Walker left in the spring. Alone and pregnant, her future in the White world was even more dismal. She pondered her situation a long time, wondering if she was wrong not to marry Stands Alone. Indians loved children. Perhaps he would accept Shadow Walker's babe as his own. Still, that kind of subterfuge didn't sit well with her. Perhaps she should just have her child and join with Stands Alone afterward if he still wanted her.

"I wish to wait. If you still want me in a few months, I'll join with you."

Stands Alone's face lit up. "I will still want you. When you are ready, I will be waiting."

Dawn wished she could love Stands Alone. He was young, kindhearted and good-looking. She could do a lot worse. Then she thought of Shadow Walker and wished he wasn't so stubborn. Many people who lost a mate remarried after their time of mourning. Shadow Walker's mourning surpassed the bounds of normal behavior. Unfortunately, Shadow Walker couldn't see that for himself.

* * *

"What did you say to Dawn to make her delay her marriage?" Running Elk asked when Shadow Walker stopped by later that evening to talk and smoke.

"When did she decide that? When I spoke with her last, she was determined to join with Stands Alone. I saw them go off together earlier today."

Running Elk filled his lungs with smoke, then slowly blew it out. "She came to me while you were hunting and told me she is not yet ready to take another husband."

Shadow Walker accepted the pipe from Running Elk, took a satisfying drag and exhaled slowly. "Did she explain the reason for her decision?" Shadow Walker thought he knew. His gut told him Dawn was pregnant.

"That was all she said. Stands Alone has vowed to wait for her until she is ready."

"He is wasting his time."

"Time will tell."

The weeks passed with frightening speed. March found Running Elk making preparations for their departure to the Little Big Horn in April. Dawn remained aloof from everyone, guarding her secret zealously. Not even Sun In The Face, with whom she was closest, guessed her condition. The nausea had passed and she showed no other signs of pregnancy, except that her breasts had grown larger. Her stomach was still quite flat and she hoped it would remain so for a few more weeks. She avoided Shadow Walker whenever possible, but she felt his eyes on her as she moved about the camp.

Dawn feared that he suspected she was pregnant. Fortunately, he had nothing on which to base his suspicions. And she meant to keep it that way. One day Shadow Walker made a special effort to speak to her in private.

"Running Elk is taking his people to the Little Big Horn soon."

"I know." When Shadow Walker left, she would have no one. "I suppose you are preparing for your journey to Oregon."

Shadow Walker gave her an oblique look. "I've changed my mind. I've decided to accompany Running Elk to the Little Big Horn. I have to try to talk some sense into the leaders there. If I can convince them to disband, a great tragedy will be avoided."

Dawn was stunned. "You're not leaving?"

"Eventually, I must. But I cannot leave before I try to talk some sense into the chiefs. They have to realize how disastrous a battle will be for them. Even if they win, they will lose."

"Is that the only reason?" Dawn asked hopefully.

"What other reason could there be?"

Disappointed, Dawn turned away. Why couldn't Shadow Walker forget Morning Mist and learn to love another woman? It hurt to know that she had nothing to offer a man like Shadow Walker. He had seen her at her worst and certainly had no illusions where she was concerned. Her maidenhead had been intact, but little else about her was pure. Shadow Walker knew everything there was to know about her and found her unworthy of his love. It was as simple as that. Why couldn't she accept it?

The entire camp was in upheaval. The weather had turned mild for April, and the exodus to the Little Big Horn was to begin the next day. Dawn's possessions were all packed. She continued to wear her comfortable deerskin tunic, moccasins and leggings instead of her regular clothing. But she had carefully packed the garments she had arrived in, should she need them. Right now, that possibility seemed remote. She had the reward money Shadow Walker had insisted she take, but how long would that meager sum last a woman with a child to support?

Dawn arose early on the day set aside for their departure. Spring Rain and Sun In The Face arrived to help her dismantle her tipi so it could be loaded on a travois for transporting to their new location. She understood it would take many, many days to reach the Little Big Horn and prepared herself for a long journey. To save wear and tear on the horses, she was told the women and older children would walk the entire distance, and she hoped she would hold up under the grueling march. If Sun In The Face, who was heavily pregnant, could endure it, so could she.

Shadow Walker stopped by to ask if she was packed and ready to leave. Dawn assured him she was. Then Stands Alone arrived and Shadow Walker left, his face dark as a thundercloud. Stands Alone helped harness her horse and load the dismantled tipi on the travois. Then he left to join the young men of the band, who rode ahead to scout the way.

Dawn tried not to show her displeasure when she saw Shadow Walker helping Laughing Brook load her travois. A jolt of jealousy pierced her, and she tried to look away, angry with herself when she could not. When Shadow Walker looked her way and saw her watching him, she jerked her head around so fast it made her dizzy. She tottered and clutched her horse's mane until the dizziness passed.

Sun In The Face saw and came to her aid. "Are you ill, Dawn?"

"No, I'm fine. I grew dizzy for a moment but it has passed."

The Indian woman gave her a skeptical look. "Are you sure? I've noticed you aren't quite yourself lately. Does it have anything to do with Shadow Walker? Are you sorry you didn't join with Stands Alone?"

If you only knew, Dawn mused silently. "I'm fine, really. I could not join with Stands Alone . . . not now."

Before Sun In The Face could question her, the signal was given to move out. Dawn had no idea what this journey held for her, or what she'd find at the end. Only time would tell.

Chapter Thirteen

The first days of the journey north to the Little Big Horn were tedious and uneventful. Dawn joined the women and children, who trudged along on foot. The men hunted game to supplement their diet of pemmican and other dried food that had been prepared in advance of their journey. The weather remained unsettled and capricious. One day dawned cold and dry and the next warm and wet with the promise of spring. They band of travelers awoke to frost and newly fallen snow on more than one occasion.

They reached the Powder River four weeks after they had left the Red Cloud Agency. Because the horses were weary, Running Elk called a two-day halt, and they raised their tipis on the bank of the river. Dawn was so travel-weary she was incapable of moving. She stared at the dismantled tipi and wondered how she was going to manage. Knowing that Spring Rain and Sun In The Face were as tired as she, she didn't have the heart to ask for help.

Shadow Walker appeared at her side, his voice rough with concern. "Are you all right?"

"I'm tired, but so is everyone else."

"They're used to this, you're not. I'll help you."

"I thought you'd gone hunting with the men."

"I changed my mind." What he didn't say was that he was worried about Dawn. Her complexion was pasty and she appeared weary unto death. The march had been difficult for her, and they still had a long way to go.

"This is woman's work," Dawn said as Shadow Walker set the lodge poles into place.

"I choose to make it my work today. You're tired. I'll build a fire as soon as the tipi is erected. Rest while you can; the remainder of the journey won't get any easier."

"I didn't realize Indians led such hard lives. Women in particular."

"You're not cut out for this kind of life. I should have realized that before I brought you here. Do you intend to remain with Running Elk after I leave?"

"Perhaps."

"Are you still thinking of marrying one of your suitors?"

"Perhaps."

"Dammit, Dawn, you're the most aggravating female I've ever known! Don't you realizing marrying me would have solved all your problems?"

"Marrying you would present more problems than I could handle."

"Do you want to explain that statement?"

Beneath her robe, Dawn touched her stomach. The slight bulge still wasn't large enough to give away her condition, but she knew her babe rested beneath her heart and was comforted. Shadow Walker must not know. If he did he would insist on marrying her even though he didn't want a wife. "You don't want a wife, and I want all or nothing from a husband. Thank you for your help. I couldn't have put up my lodge on my own."

He stepped inside, holding the flap open for Dawn to follow. "I'll build a fire. You'll be cozy and warm in no time. I'll see that food is brought to you so you won't have to trouble yourself."

She watched him leave to gather firewood, thinking his body had grown harder and more honed, his features sharper during these months spent with the People. While he was gone she spread out her mat and sat down, pulling the blanket around her shoulders. She felt suddenly drained. A nagging pain in the middle of her back had bothered her off and on during the day, and she stretched, trying to ease the pressure.

Shadow Walker ducked through the entrance, carrying a load of wood. "This should be enough to last until we resume our march." In no time he had a cheery fire going, then he directed his gaze at Dawn, frowning when he noted her pinched features. "Are you sure you're all right?"

"Very sure. I think I'll take a short nap."

Shadow Walker was truly concerned. He decided to speak to Spring Rain after he left Dawn and have her look in on Dawn later. He blamed himself for placing Dawn in a situation for which she was ill-prepared. If she wasn't so damn stubborn, they both could have been on their way to Oregon now.

Dawn fell asleep almost immediately. She felt warm for the first time in days. If not for vague pains in her back and low in her stomach, she would have slept into the night without awakening. She awoke with a start as a sharp pain shot across her stomach. A moan slipped past her lips, and her hands flew to her middle. She was deathly afraid that something was amiss with her baby. Five minutes later another pain struck, more powerful than the first.

Dawn was moaning and writhing on her pallet when Spring Rain called out a greeting and entered with Dawn's supper. She saw Dawn clutching her stomach and flew to her side.

"What is it, Dawn? Are you in pain?"

"My baby! I think I'm losing my baby," Dawn cried between pains.

For a moment Spring Rain was too stunned to speak. She had had no idea that Dawn was expecting a child and knew that no one but Shadow Walker could be the father. "I will summon the midwife."

"Hurry, please hurry."

It seemed like hours before Spring Rain returned with the midwife, but in truth only a few minutes had passed. But Dawn knew it was already too late to save her child. She had felt a warm gush between her legs and smelled the metallic odor of blood. The tiny, fragile life inside her had been expelled from her body.

The midwife pursed her lips and wagged her head from side to side when she examined Dawn. "It is too late." She called for water, and Spring Rain hurried to do her bidding. She returned a few minutes later with Shadow Walker.

Shadow Walker dropped to his knees and smoothed the hair away from Dawn's pale face. "Why didn't you tell me? Did you think I would be angry?"

"I didn't want you to feel obligated."

"Is that why you called off your joining with Stands Alone?"

"Go away, I don't want you to see me like this."

Shadow Walker stood abruptly. The least he could do was honor her wish . . . for now. "I'll be back later." He ducked outside and stood there shaking. He would have given his life to prevent this from happening.

Dawn began to cry softly. She had wanted Shadow Walker's baby, had looked forward to holding his child in her arms. All she felt now was painful emptiness. She had lost both Shadow Walker and his baby.

Spring Rain tried to comfort her while the midwife worked over her. When the water was heated, Spring Rain bathed her and tucked her between clean blankets. "Sleep," she said, "it is the best medicine. I will return later."

Dawn was alone. She didn't feel like sleeping. She felt lonely and bereft. Had her child lived, she would have had one human in this world who would love her unconditionally. Tears dampened her cheeks. She knew she would never have another child. Shadow Walker didn't want her, and she'd have no other man. She was sobbing quietly when she suddenly realized she wasn't alone. Assuming that Spring Rain had returned, she said, "There really is no reason to sit with me, Spring Rain. There is nothing anyone can do now."

"You shouldn't be alone." The voice was not that of Spring Rain.

"Shadow Walker!" She turned her face away. "Are you here to rebuke me for not telling you about the baby?"

"No. I feel your loss as keenly as you. Had you seen fit to tell me, I would have tried to make the march easier for you." He crouched down beside her. "Try to sleep. It is likely we will remain here a day or two longer than Running Elk planned. Sun In The Face went into labor tonight. Her child will be born before morning."

"Will she be all right?" Dawn asked anxiously. Her own painful loss was still fresh in her mind.

"Spring Rain says all is as it should be." He slipped off his moccasins, leggings and shirt and slid under the blanket beside her.

"What are you doing?" Dawn cried.

"I'm not going to hurt you. I just want to lie beside you and keep you warm." He wanted to tell her that it was his child she'd lost, that he grieved along with her, that many women died from childbed fever and he wasn't going to let it happen to Dawn, but he said none of those things. "Relax, sweetheart. I'm here if you need anything."

Dawn tried not to attach hidden meaning to Shadow Walker's words. She knew he was a kind man. But she couldn't help feeling that she had disappointed him.

"I'm sorry about the baby. I didn't want this to happen. I wanted your child."

"We'll talk about this later, when you've recovered from your ordeal."

Was that a catch in his voice she heard? Dawn wondered as she drifted off to sleep.

Shadow Walker's anger was tempered by his relief. Had he known that Dawn was pregnant, he could have watched over her. But she had deliberately lied to him, and that made him angry. Yet his relief that she was all right made his anger seem insignificant. He gathered her fragile body in his arms and held her close.

They resumed the march to the Little Big Horn three days later. Dawn was still weak, and Shadow Walker refused to let her walk with the others. He placed her on a travois behind his horse and tucked a blanket around her. Despite the care she received, she did indeed develop a fever, which drained her of what little strength she had left.

Sun In The Face had delivered a healthy baby boy and by the time the march resumed, she was ready to trudge along with the other women, carrying the newborn babe in a cradleboard. Dawn envied the sturdy Indian woman, and when she mentioned her own lack of stamina to Shadow Walker, he told her she had been frail to begin with, whereas Sun In The Face hadn't had to suffer through years of beatings and deprivation.

After a week, Dawn's fever abated and she felt strong enough to join the other women, but

Shadow Walker only allowed her to walk for short periods each day. The rest of the time she rode Wally. Shadow Walker insisted that her meager weight would place no extra stress on the sturdy horse, who already pulled a heavy travois.

Three weeks passed and Shadow Walker made no effort to leave Dawn's tipi. When he slid beside her each night and held her in his arms, she felt happy and content. As the days sped by, Dawn knew it would soon be time for Shadow Walker to leave, and she wondered how she would bear it. Just thinking about life without him made her exceedingly sad. One night she confronted Shadow Walker about his sharing her bed.

"Why are you still here? I am well now, I don't need your help or your pity."

"I'm the cause of your illness. Caring for you is my way of making amends. Once we reach the Little Big Horn we will be joined according to Indian rites."

Dawn's chin tilted stubbornly. "I won't marry you." She paused, daring to ask a question she knew was far too bold. "Do you love me?"

A subtle turbulence moved across his features, was visible in the depths of his eyes. "Love? Love comes but once in a lifetime. I care for you. Isn't that enough? I will see that your needs are met."

"It isn't enough, Shadow Walker." Dawn's distrust of men was so deeply ingrained she feared that Shadow Walker would abandon her after he tired of her. She was astute enough to realize that only love would bind Shadow Walker to her, and since his heart rejected love, she couldn't trust him to keep his word. Besides, an Indian marriage would not be legal in White society. Once he grew tired of her, he would surely leave her.

Shadow Walker's temper exploded. "Dammit, Dawn! Stands Alone can't have you. You belong to me! You carried my child. I was your first man and I'm damn well going to be the last."

He roughly turned her to face him. The fire inside the tipi had burned to embers, but she could still see his face. His expression was fiercely possessive. His intent gaze probed deeply into her very soul. She lowered her eyes lest he discover the love she guarded so fiercely. She had to be strong, she told herself. Shadow Walker's lust for her was frightening. His possessiveness was overwhelming and irrational. His sole reason for marrying her was to keep another man from having her.

"I don't belong to you! I don't want to belong to any man ever again. I learned my lesson the hard way. Billy taught me that possessiveness can be cruel and hurtful."

He gave her a little shake. "I'm not a cruel man. You have nothing to fear from me. I know you enjoy our lovemaking. We have that in common."

To prove his point, he brought her against him and kissed her. Kissed her until her head spun and she grew dizzy. Unlike Indian women, she could not bring herself to sleep naked so she usually donned one of her shifts before going to bed. Shadow Walker's hands slid under the hem of the flimsy garment, slowly lifting it as he lightly skimmed her legs and hips with his palms. Her shift was whisked up and off before she could utter a protest.

"What are you doing?"

"I want to make love to you. Are you healed enough to take a man inside you?"

A miscarriage so early in pregnancy wasn't like giving birth to a full-term child. She had healed a long time ago. But making love now might result in another pregnancy. Shadow Walker admitted he didn't love her; she should put a stop to this now. Unfortunately she wanted him. A woman in love wasn't always rational.

"I am healed enough to take a man, but I fear another pregnancy."

Shadow Walker searched her face. She had said she'd wanted his child. Had she been lying? "I know what to do to prevent conception. Your body isn't strong enough yet to carry another child. Relax; if I hurt you, let me know."

His mouth came down on hers. His kiss was tender, yet fraught with a ravening hunger that startled Dawn. If he'd been bedding Laughing Brook all these months, he shouldn't be this eager. His need was so urgent his body was shaking from it.

A low moan escaped Shadow Walker's throat. It seemed like forever since he'd loved Dawn. He'd pretended to court Laughing Brook merely to make Dawn jealous. When Dawn had called off her joining with Stands Alone, he'd been jubilant, thinking his ploy had worked. He wondered why he couldn't utter the words that Dawn wanted to hear. He should have accepted Morning Mist's death by now and moved on with his life. Why did loving another woman make him feel as if he were betraying Morning Mist's memory?

Dawn's body grew flushed beneath Shadow Walker's hands and mouth. Her breasts swelled and her nipples pebbled into tight buds as he licked and sucked them. His fingers stroked and teased, working their magic from below. Parting the swollen petals of her sex, he found the sweet entrance and probed deeply. Dawn moaned, arching into the pressure of his searching fingers. She gritted her teeth, teetering on the brink of climax, but it was too soon. She wanted to give Shadow Walker the same kind of pleasure he was giving her. When he made as if to raise himself above her, she pushed him down and slid her body on top of him. He looked at her askance.

"I want to know your body in the same way you know mine."

She lowered her mouth to his flat male nipples, mimicking the way he licked and sucked hers. Her mouth moved lower, across the rigid muscles of his belly, lower still. His breath caught in his throat.

The crisp thatch of hair tickled her nose as her mouth slid past his groin to more enticing territory.

"Oh God!" Bolstered by his hoarse cry, she closed her hand over his erection. Starting at the base, she ran her tongue over its entire length, ending at the engorged tip, where a tiny drop of liquid hung like a precious pearl. She touched it with her tongue, and Shadow Walker bucked violently.

"Stop! You're killing me." He dragged her up the length of his body until she straddled his hips. "Ride me, love. Take me inside you and ride me."

Grasping his sex, Dawn raised her hips up and slowly lowered herself, taking all of him inside her. She gasped, not in pain, but from the sheer rapture of being penetrated so deeply.

Shadow Walker went still, thinking he had hurt her. "Should I stop?"

"No! Don't stop. It feels . . . wonderful."

"You're so tight and hot. I could stay inside you forever."

He began to move. Slowly at first, grasping her hips and bringing her down to meet his upward thrust. Then the wildness seized him. He raised his head and sucked a nipple into his mouth as he thrust violently into her soft center. The pull on her nipple and the friction below drove her into a frenzy.

Shadow Walker didn't know how much longer he could hold on. His body was drawn as taut as a bowstring. He was so close to the edge, a tiny nudge would send him hurtling into oblivion. "Come to me, love. Come . . ."

Dawn needed no prodding. Her body was his to do with as he pleased. She felt the vibrations begin from somewhere deep inside her, radiating to every part of her body. She matched him thrust for thrust, throwing her head back and crying out her pleasure. She exploded violently, overcome by raw sensations so intense they defied definition. Shadow Walker continued thrusting until the last tremor left her body, then he gave a hoarse shout and lifted her off him, spewing his seed onto the ground.

"That was . . . incredible," he gasped as he struggled for breath. Of course, it would have been even more incredible had he spent himself inside her. "I didn't hurt you, did I?"

"No, you didn't hurt me." She nestled against him, already half asleep.

Dawn awakened a short time later to a clamoring inside her body. Her skin burned and her nerve endings tingled with awareness. Soft lips covered hers in a gentle kiss.

Shadow Walker.

She smiled and kissed him back, bringing her arms around his neck.

"I want you again," he whispered against her lips. "I can't seem to get enough of you."

"Didn't Laughing Brook satisfy you?"

"I haven't had another woman since meeting you. Lord knows I tried to make myself desire Laughing Brook, but my body refused to obey. A blue-eyed waif with magnificent breasts kept interfering."

"I don't believe you," Dawn scoffed. "You're too hot-blooded to reject Laughing Brook's offering."

"I speak the truth," he said solemnly. "Forget Laughing Brook. Will you let me love you again?"

"I'd be disappointed if you didn't."

He gave her a cocky grin. "I don't ever want to disappoint you."

"You never do."

He kissed her endlessly, bringing her body to aching arousal with his hands and mouth.

"Lie on your side facing me and bring your leg over my hips," he instructed in a voice that exuded sensuality. "That's right." He touched her between the legs. "Ah, you're wet already." They were fused from breast to groin as he eased inside her. For a time their coupling was slow and easy. Then his blood ran too hot to control and he began sliding in and out in hard, swift stokes. And suddenly he was there.

"It's too soon!" he cried, fearing he'd leave Dawn behind. He brought his hand between them and found the tiny bud of her desire. With the pad of his thumb he rotated it gently, slowly bringing her to the same peak of excitement he had already attained. "Now!" he hissed as he felt her rushing toward climax.

Dawn reacted powerfully to his words, trembling with the force of her explosion. A few seconds later Shadow Walker cried out hoarsely and withdrew, spilling his seed on the ground.

"You're mine," Shadow Walker growled as he hugged her possessively. "You'll join with me when we reach the Little Big Horn."

Dawn did not hear him. She had already fallen asleep.

The mountains and valleys were ablaze with color. Wildflowers carpeted the fertile ground, and the verdant mountains were lush with new foliage. The loss of her child still plagued Dawn. She kept wondering what her child would have looked like had he lived. The child would have been a son, of course, with Shadow Walker's burnished hair and strong body.

They reached the Sioux village on the banks of the Little Big Horn River the first week in June. Dawn had never seen so many Indians gathered in one place.

"There must be thousands gathered here," she

said to Spring Rain as they paused at the top of a hill to look down upon the village.

"Running Elk said at least three thousand Sioux and northern Cheyenne warriors are gathered here. We are among the last to arrive."

Soon they reached the place on the riverbank that Running Elk had chosen for their campsite. During the next hours, activity was at a fever pitch as the women raised their lodges and settled in. Soon campfires dotted the area, and the aroma of food wafted through the air.

Shadow Walker appeared at Dawn's elbow. He had come to ask if she needed help erecting her lodge. "There is a council meeting tonight," he said as he began unloading the travois. "Chiefs Crazy Horse, Gall and Low Dog will be there, and I'm going to try to talk them out of this folly."

"Do you think it will do any good?" Dawn asked as she watched him set the lodgepoles in place.

"It can't hurt. The army is bound to learn about the huge force preparing for battle and will try to trap the largest group of hostile Indians ever to gather in one place. I may be very late tonight— don't wait up for me."

"I don't think it is wise for you to continue to share my lodge. You'll be leaving soon, and the People will consider me a loose woman for living with you."

"I don't care what the People think. You won't be here to worry about it. You're leaving with me."

"Damn you! You have no right to tell me what to do."

"You think not?" He smiled at her and stepped back to admire his work. "There, it's finished. All you need do is arrange our sleeping mat."

Dawn hated his overbearing arrogance. She was preparing to give him the sharp edge of her tongue when he walked away. "Impossible man," she complained to his departing back.

A short time later, Sun In The Face brought Dawn a pure white tunic richly embroidered with beads and feathers. It was so lovely Dawn felt unworthy to touch it.

"What is this for?"

"For your joining with Shadow Walker," the Indian woman said shyly. "Laughing Brook is very angry."

"I never said I'd join with Shadow Walker," Dawn countered. Did she have no say in her own future?

"Shadow Walker told Running Elk to prepare a feast. It is to take place tomorrow night. Here," she said, placing the tunic over Dawn's arm. "It is yours. Be happy. Shadow Walker deserves happiness. He has grieved for Morning Mist longer than is healthy. It is time he found someone to love."

Dawn stared at the butter-soft doeskin, marveling over the incredible craftsmanship of the embroidery. She rubbed it against her cheek, painfully aware that her marriage to Shadow Walker would not be legal in the White world. She wasn't stupid. Once they returned to civilization, Shadow Walker would dump her with his sister and forget about her.

Shadow Walker wanted no legal or emotional attachments. He was taking precautions to prevent her from conceiving his child, she thought with resentment. If he intended to make their marriage legal, he wouldn't be so determined to waste his seed on the ground.

"Shadow Walker doesn't love me," Dawn insisted. "He loves a memory. I can't compete with a dead woman."

Sun In The Face laughed softly. "Where did you get that idea? One day you will learn the truth."

Shadow Walker stood in the middle of the large circle, addressing the great Sioux and Cheyenne chiefs. His voice was low yet forceful, his expression grim as he tried to convince them to disband and go back to their reservations.

"I speak out of love for the People," he said earnestly. "My wife, Morning Mist, was Sioux. She was killed in a raid, and I still grieve for her, so you know I do not speak with a forked tongue. I genuinely care about what happens to the People even though I must return to my own kind soon.

"Go back to your homes. Even if you are victorious, the retaliation will be swift and violent. Many lives will be lost and much blood shed. You will be driven to barren lands and forced to eke out a meager existence for your families."

Chief Crazy Horse spoke for his colleagues. "It is too late to retreat. This will be the greatest battle of all time. Never have so many warriors gathered in one place. The army can come but they will suffer humiliating defeat. We must do this to save our sacred hills. Too many treaties have been broken. Solemn vows given in trust have been disregarded.

"I know you, Shadow Walker. You are a brave

warrior and good friend to the Sioux. But this is not your fight. Take your woman and go back to your own kind. It is not right for you to fight against your people."

Defeat sat heavily upon Shadow Walker's shoulders. Crazy Horse spoke for all the chiefs; the agreement was unanimous. A battle was inevitable. Soon he must remove Dawn from danger. He would let her rest a few days while he made arrangements to leave.

After the council adjourned, Shadow Walker approached Running Elk. "Can I not convince you to leave while there is still time? Has nothing I've said moved you?"

Running Elk clasped Shadow Walker's shoulder. "I believe that everything you say will come to pass but I cannot walk away from this battle. These are my people. I will not be called coward."

"No one in his right mind would ever call you coward. I will stay and fight with you."

Running Elk gave him a sad smile. "No, you must heed Crazy Horse. Take your woman and go. Dawn does not belong here and neither do you. This is not your fight."

Shadow Walker felt a grinding pain in the pit of his stomach. He knew that Running Elk spoke the truth, but it was difficult to watch an old and respected friend rush headlong to certain death. For even if death did not come with this battle, it would still come.

"I will do as you say," he said. "We will leave after the joining ceremony."

"The women are preparing a great feast. All the chiefs and their people have been invited. They will bring food and participate in the ceremony. Do not disappoint me, Shadow Walker."

"You wish me to join with Dawn and I will not disappoint you. I wish it also."

Dawn was still awake when Shadow Walker returned to their lodge. Assuming that she was asleep, he quietly shed his breechclout and crawled between the blankets. He drew her against him, taking care not to awaken her. Holding Dawn all night seemed natural now. He wondered how he had survived all those cold, lonely nights without her. His lust for her was enormous, and he intended to satisfy his craving as often as possible until the time came for them to part.

"What did the council decide?" Dawn asked.

"I thought you were sleeping."

"I couldn't sleep until I learned what happened."

Shadow Walker sighed heavily. "Nothing happened. My words had little effect upon men who have been pushed too far to retreat. But I had to try."

"I suppose you'll be leaving soon."

"*We'll* be leaving," he corrected, "but not right away. You need to rest before attempting another long journey. You're still weak."

"Sun In The Face gave me a tunic today. It's so beautiful, I could never wear it."

"But you must. It's for our joining tomorrow."

"Why are you doing this? A marriage between us is a farce. It will not be legal in the White world."

"Humor me. I'm still Shadow Walker. In Shadow Walker's world it is not only right, but legal. I took you, got you with child, and must obey tribal customs. Running Elk expects us to join, and I will do what I must to keep his regard. In the eyes of the Sioux and Wakantanka, we will be husband and wife."

"What if I decide to remain with the People?"

"It matters not what you want. Both Crazy Horse and Running Elk advised me to take you away from here. They realize their days are numbered. You have no choice. We will leave together in one week. Now go to sleep. All this talking makes me weary."

Shadow Walker was far from weary. He wanted Dawn. He always wanted her. But she was still recovering from her miscarriage, and tonight she needed rest more than she needed him rutting between her legs like an animal who couldn't control himself. She wasn't as strong as he would like, and it worried him. Was she still grieving over the loss of their child? he wondered. She exhibited all the signs, and he was an expert when it came to recognizing grief.

Chapter Fourteen

It was time. Shadow Walker would come for her
and she'd become his wife in the presence of hundreds of Indians, and it would mean absolutely
nothing. It hurt to think that Shadow Walker was
going through with this merely to appease Running Elk.

Dawn ran her hands over the soft doeskin of her
tunic. It was the loveliest garment she'd ever
owned. Fringed and embroidered, it hugged the
slim proportions of her figure to perfection. Com-
plementing the tunic were pure white moccasins
and leggings, which Spring Rain had presented to
her this morning after they returned from the
bathing place. Dawn was still admiring the lovely
workmanship of her outfit when the tent flap flew
open and a woman burst in without asking permission.

"Laughing Brook, what are you doing here?"

"You will never join with Shadow Walker! You have no right to take what is mine." Her face was contorted with hatred as she stalked Dawn, brandishing a knife in her right hand. Dawn recoiled in alarm.

"What are you going to do?"

"What I should have done when you first arrived. I've wanted Shadow Walker since the day Morning Mist died."

Stall for time, Dawn told herself as she tried to remain calm. "You know Shadow Walker will not remain with the People. If you joined with him, you would not have him long before he returned to his own kind."

Laughing Brook gave Dawn a sly grin. "Do you think I'm not capable of persuading Shadow Walker to remain with me? He left once and returned. If he joined with me, I would convince him to remain forever. He enjoys my body more than he enjoys yours."

"You're a fool. Running Elk told Shadow Walker to leave, and he will do as Running Elk wishes."

Brandishing the knife, Laughing Brook lunged at Dawn. Dawn lurched sideways, avoiding the vicious slash of Laughing Brook's knife. How long could she dodge the enraged woman? Dawn wondered as Laughing Brook whirled for another attack. Bracing herself against the lodgepole, Dawn visually measured the distance to the entrance, wondering if she could move fast enough to avoid being slashed to shreds.

"I know all about the babe you lost," Laughing

263

Brook taunted as she moved in for the kill. "I don't believe the babe was Shadow Walker's. Whores seldom know which man placed his seed inside them."

Laughing Brook leaped forward, trapping Dawn against the lodgepole. She saw Dawn look over her shoulder and glanced behind herself, stopping dead in her tracks when she saw Shadow Walker standing just inside the tipi.

Shadow Walker had arrived to escort Dawn to the feast. When he saw Laughing Brook standing before Dawn in a threatening manner, he quickly placed himself between Dawn and the jealous widow. "What is the meaning of this?" he thundered. His voice was as hard as his expression. "What are you doing here, Laughing Brook?"

Hiding the knife in the folds of her tunic, Laughing Brook was all innocence as she smiled at Shadow Walker. "I came to wish your bride well. I will leave now." She sidled past Shadow Walker and ducked out the entrance.

"What happened here?" Shadow Walker asked as he reached for Dawn. "Did Laughing Brook hurt you?"

Dawn decided not to reveal the ugliness she'd discovered in Laughing Brook. No harm had been done, and she saw no reason to mention the violence that Laughing Brook had intended.

"I'm fine. It's as Laughing Brook said. She wanted to wish me well."

Shadow Walker searched her face. "Why don't I believe you?"

"Forget it. Whatever Laughing Brook intended is of no consequence."

Shadow Walker wasn't convinced, but there was no time to dwell on it. The drums were beating in a wild rhythm, summoning people from every campsite along the Little Big Horn to the festivities. "It's time to go." His gaze slid down her body, then back up to her face, pleased by what he saw. "You're beautiful. But something's missing."

"Missing?"

He removed the headband adorned with a single eagle's feather from his own head and placed it on hers. He stood back and smiled his approval.

"It looks better on you. Come, the People are waiting." He held out his hand.

Dawn slipped her hand in his, feeling the warmth and strength of his grip clear down to her toes. He looked so handsome, she thought. He was dressed in pure white. His shirt was embroidered with beads and feathers and thickly fringed in the same manner as hers. The shirt ended below his slim hips, where the fringe met the tops of his white leggings. His moccasins were as elaborately adorned as his shirt. The pristine white of his clothing provided a startling contrast to his deep tan. He looked every bit the proud savage despite his bronze hair and green eyes.

The size of the crowd gathering for the festivities was daunting. Dawn clung to Shadow Walker's hand as a path opened for them. Dream Spinner awaited them in the center of a circle that was at least fifty deep.

They paused before the shaman, the focus of attention. Dream Spinner waved his medicine stick and a rattle made of bones, mumbling words

265

that made little sense to Dawn. Abruptly the chanting ceased. As if on cue, the People sat cross-legged on the ground. Shadow Walker grasped Dawn's hand and seated her between Running Elk and himself. Then the feasting and dancing began. Warriors danced around a huge firepit, others sang of their brave deeds. At times women joined the dancing, which grew wilder and more frenzied as the evening progressed.

Shadow Walker touched Dawn's arm and she turned to him. His eyes had turned a dark, impenetrable green; his face was stark with undisguised hunger. She felt as if her bones were melting.

"Are you ready to go?" he whispered against her ear.

Dawn looked at him questioningly. She'd been waiting for their wedding ceremony to begin. "I thought we were to be joined tonight?"

"It is done," he said, smiling. "The shaman blessed us and the People are feasting in our honor. We need only to enter our lodge together to be married."

"Th . . . that's all there is to it?"

Shadow Walker nodded slowly. "Will you come with me now? I have waited as long as I can." He rose and held out his hand.

Compelled by the promise his eyes held, she gave him her hand. He pulled her to her feet, and amid much hooting and laughter, he lifted her in his arms and carried her to their lodge. He set her on her feet and closed the flap, shutting out the night. Ahead of them lay long hours of sensual pleasure, of exploring one another, of taking and giving, mouths and bodies joined in mutual need.

They undressed one another slowly, partaking freely of the love play that led to the deepest level of rapture allowed by the Gods of Love. Shadow Walker made love to her twice without stopping. Then they slept, awakening shortly before dawn to make love again. This time Shadow Walker was so carried away he couldn't withdraw in time and spilled himself inside her. He hadn't intended for it to happen, but passion had sabotaged his good intentions.

Dawn felt as if her entire world were wrapped around this one man. He was in her heart, her soul, her very pores. Why couldn't he love her? she silently lamented. Why did their relationship have to be all one-sided? She knew he hadn't withdrawn the last time they'd made love, and she fervently prayed that his seed had found fertile ground. She wanted some small part of him to treasure after he left her.

Preparations were begun the following day for their departure. It took several days to say their good-byes, gather provisions and plan their route. Before they left, Shadow Walker decided to try one last time to convince the great chiefs to disband and return to their lands. Chief Sitting Bull had arrived and a council meeting was called for two days hence, which was June 21. Unfortunately, Shadow Walker had no better luck convincing Sitting Bull than he'd had the first time he'd addressed the council. He returned to the lodge and told Dawn to be ready to leave the following day, June 22.

"Sitting Bull was no more receptive to my plea

than were the other chiefs," Shadow Walker said with a hint of sadness. "It is time for us to leave."

Dawn offered no argument. Tension was high within the village. An air of fatalism prevailed among the People. She was aware that Shadow Walker was right in taking her away, that her safety depended on leaving this place. She would go with Shadow Walker and make a life for herself in whatever place he left her.

"Where are we going from here?"

"To Bozeman. It's not too great a distance away, and we should be able to join a wagon train passing through to Oregon. It's an arduous trip, but I think you're well enough now to endure it."

He slipped off his breechclout, moccasins and shirt and joined her beneath the blanket.

"Where do you intend to dump me?"

"We're both going to Oregon," Shadow Walker said with a frown. "Who said I was going to dump you?"

"Aren't you?"

"My sister and her husband will make you welcome," he hedged.

"I wish—"

"Dammit, Dawn, you talk too much. How can I love you while you're haranguing me about something that's too far in the future to predict?"

Something unspoken lingered in the air, and Dawn tried to banish the intrusive thought that once they left the village Shadow Walker would shed her just as quickly as he had just shed his clothing. He didn't want a wife. He pitied her, and pity wasn't enough for her.

*　　*　　*

The entire village turned out to bid them good-bye the following day. It was June 22. The Indian forces gathered at the Little Big Horn were awesome in their very numbers.

Dawn was overwhelmed. She felt an ominous stirring within her breast and despaired for these people with whom she shared kinship but little else. She glanced at Shadow Walker, amazed by his transformation this morning. The fierce Shadow Walker, garbed now in white man's clothing, had disappeared with the dawn. Cole Webster, every bit as handsome, strong and fierce as Shadow Walker, was the same man yet somehow different.

"May Wakantanka protect and guide you," Running Elk said, grasping Cole's forearm in a gesture of friendship.

"And you, brother," Cole returned.

Suddenly their attention was diverted by a scout riding toward them. He rode as if the devils of hell were after him. He headed into Crazy Horse's camp, reining his horse in sharply when he spied the great chief talking to Sitting Bull and Gall.

"It is Man Who Loves Horses. I will find out what is going on," Running Elk said as he hurried off.

"What do you think has happened?" Dawn asked fearfully.

Cole had his suspicions but didn't voice them. A few minutes later Running Elk returned, his face set in grim lines. "What is it?" Cole asked anxiously.

"You must leave immediately. The Seventh Cavalry has been spotted a day's march away. We must prepare for battle."

"General Custer," Cole said slowly, recalling the name of the man in charge of the Seventh Cavalry. He hated to leave but realized he must. In all the time he'd lived with Running Elk, he'd never turned against his own kind. No matter how sympathetic he felt toward the Indian cause, he believed this battle was wrong. There would be no winners no matter who won.

"My prayers go with you," Cole said. He was torn by the desire to remain and appalled at the thought of the blood that would spill in this place.

He lifted Dawn onto Wally's back, attached the leading reins of the packhorse to his saddle, and then mounted Warrior. He exchanged a look of complete understanding with Running Elk, then slapped the reins against Warrior's rump. Dawn dug her heels into Wally's sides and followed, turning back once to wave at Spring Rain and Sun In The Face.

They camped that night near a stream. Cole made love to Dawn beneath a full moon. She sensed his melancholy, which made their loving poignant and intense. She shared his despair for reasons of her own. Certainly she felt sadness for the People's plight, but it was her own uncertain future that loomed large and frightening before her. Soothing Cole with her body was the only way she knew to reach out to him. She took him inside her, using their passion for one another as a balm for all their hurts.

Sometime during the following day, June 24, they paused on a ridge and watched as the Sev-

enth Cavalry thundered toward the Indian encampment. Cole's face was grim when the last of
the soldiers disappeared in a cloud of dust.

"How soon will they reach the Little Big Horn?"
Dawn asked.

"It depends. If they ride all night they will arrive
at dawn tomorrow. If they stop for the night they
won't arrive until nightfall tomorrow."

Dawn couldn't suppress the shudder that
passed through her body. "There are so many of
them."

"There are nearly three thousand Indians gathered on the Little Big Horn," he reminded her. "All
we can do is pray that each side will show mercy
to the other."

Five days later they reached Bozeman. The
town was in an uproar. Word had arrived that very
day about the massacre at the Little Big Horn.
General George Custer's entire Seventh Cavalry
had been annihilated by a large force of Sioux and
northern Cheyenne, with little loss of life for the
Indians. Ignoring his scouts' warning of overwhelming numbers of Sioux and Cheyenne
camped in a huge village on the Little Big Horn,
General Custer had ridden to his death.

With feelings running high against Indians,
Cole decided not to wait around for a wagon train.
He would take no further chances with Dawn's
life. He did not explain to Dawn their need for
haste as they rode through town and camped in
the hills overlooking Bozeman.

"I'm going back to town for supplies," Cole said.
"We're not going to wait for a wagon train. The

trail to Oregon is easy to follow. I've traveled it before."

A frisson of fear passed through Dawn. "What is it? Why did we leave town so abruptly? Why don't you want to wait for a wagon train?"

"You were in town long enough to know what is going on. The People annihilated the Seventh Cavalry. Whites are going to take out their anger on anyone carrying Indian blood."

Dawn's eyes widened. "You mean I . . ."

"They will act first and ask questions later. I don't know if I could save you once they set their sights on you." He tried to make her understand without hurting her. "You have Indian blood. That makes you the enemy of people with little tolerance or sympathy for the Indian cause."

Dawn lowered her head to hide her tears. "Will it always be this way?"

Cole stared at her bent head and wanted suddenly to kill all those who would harm her. He pulled her into his arms. "I fear it won't change for a very long time."

She looked up at him. "Do you think Running Elk and the others are safe?"

"We can pray that they survived. Will you be all right here for a few hours? Our supplies need replenishing, and I want to purchase a wagon and oxen. I don't want to leave you alone any longer than necessary."

"I'll be fine. Just hurry back. I don't like being alone."

It was true, Dawn realized. It seemed as if she'd been lonely the bulk of her life. She had preferred loneliness to Billy's company. When he had sought the safety of the cabin between holdups, she became the victim of his abuse. With Cole as a companion, she knew that even if he didn't love her she would suffer no abuse, and he would protect her with his life. It wasn't in Cole's nature to be abusive to a woman. He could be hard and unyielding, but never would he deliberately hurt her.

"No more than I like leaving you out here unprotected," Cole replied. "I'll leave my rifle for you." He propped the gun against the tree. "I'll be back by nightfall."

"What if you're not?" she asked anxiously.

"I will be," he said with a determination that eased Dawn's fears considerably.

After Cole had left, Dawn hunkered down beneath a tree to wait for him. She was so tired. The journey had been exhausting, and this was only the beginning of a much longer trek over mountains and rivers. She didn't want to dwell on her future once they reached Oregon. She had no idea how long Cole would remain with her. She sighed despondently and rested her head against the tree trunk. She was tired, so tired . . .

Dawn awoke to dark shadows and a deep sense of fear. She didn't know how long she'd been sleeping, but darkness had crept in on silent wings while she dozed. She stirred from her lethargy to gather wood and kindling for a fire. She found matches in Cole's saddlebag and struck a light to the pile of dried grass she'd placed beneath the kindling. Once the fire was blazing nicely, she rummaged through the supplies for fixings to prepare supper. She planned to have a hot meal prepared by the time Cole returned.

Dawn glanced nervously into the shadows surrounding the campsite as she worked, trying to dispel the feeling of anxiety she couldn't seem to shake. The odor of sizzling bacon drifted on the breeze, drawing unwanted attention to the campsite. She heard a twig snap and whirled around, hoping to see Cole. The welcoming smile died on her lips when she saw two riders enter the circle of light and dismount.

"Well, well, what do we have here?" A big man sporting a scruffy beard eyed her through overbright eyes.

"It's a woman, Mace," the second man said, grinning lasciviously. He was tall and thin and wore a patch over one eye.

"Reckon she wants some company, Gil?"

"What do you want?" Dawn asked, edging toward Cole's rifle resting against the tree.

Gil squinted at her through his good eye. "Damn! It's a squaw. Her people put out my eye." He stalked her, forcing her to retreat. "Where is your man? Was he at the Little Big Horn? A lot of good men were killed by yer people."

"I wouldn't reach for that rifle if I were you," Mace warned as he snatched the gun out of her reach. While Mace held Dawn's attention, Gil slipped behind her.

"My husband is hunting, but he'll be back soon," Dawn said with bravado. "Leave now, while there's still time."

"Ha," Gil hooted. "Yer man probably took off when he heard us coming. Savages are all cowards. Look what they did to General Custer at the Little Big Horn." He stepped closer, peering at her owlishly. "Well, I'll be damned. Blue eyes. Looka there, Mace, she's a half-breed. Her mother probably rutted with some White man. Are you a whore like your mama, honey?"

Dawn backed away, right into Mace's arms. She screamed as he clamped her against him. "Got ya!" he laughed, enjoying Dawn's helplessness. "I ain't never had a half-breed. The last woman I had was a worn-out whore in Cheyenne. I'm gonna enjoy this." His hand slid upward to her breast, squeezing it hurtfully.

"No!" Dawn cried, anger exploding within her. "No man is going to hurt me again!" She sank her teeth into Mace's arm. He howled in pain, slackening his grip long enough for her to whirl around and knee him in the groin.

"Little bitch!" he gasped, staggering to his knees.

Gil swung his arm back to wallop her, and Dawn braced herself for the blow.

"Hold it or you're a dead man."

"What the hell!" Gil whirled toward the voice. He started to reach for his gun, saw that Cole already had him in his sights, and dropped his hands.

"Toss your gun down and move over by your friend."

"Cole, thank God you're here," Dawn said, weak with relief.

"Are you hurt?" His voice was rough with concern.

"No."

"You, on the ground," Cole said, gesturing at Mace, who was still on his knees clutching his groin. "Throw your gun over here." They both complied, staring warily at Cole's Colt .45. "Now get on your horses and ride. If I see your faces again I'll shoot first and ask questions later."

"Hell, we didn't hurt yer squaw, mister," Gil whined. "We were just being friendly like."

"This woman is my wife," Cole said with emphasis. "You'd do well to remember it."

"What are ya, an Injun lover? Haven't ya heard what happened at the Little Big Horn?"

"I heard. Now get the hell out of here."

"What about our guns?"

"You just lost them. Dawn, check their horses and see if they have rifles. If they do, remove them."

"Now wait a damn minute," Mace growled. "You can't leave a man without protection."

Dawn removed their rifles from their saddle boots and moved to Cole's side.

"I can and I will. Would you prefer that I take you to town and turn you over to the sheriff? I wouldn't be surprised if you're both wanted by the law."

"No need to turn us in to the sheriff, mister, we're going." They sidled past Cole, scrambled onto their horses and took off.

Cole watched them leave, not relaxing until long after they had disappeared. After ample time had elapsed, he turned to Dawn, searching for injuries. "Are you sure you're all right?"

"I'm fine."

A grin hung on the corner of his lips. "What did you do to Mace?"

Dawn returned his grin. "I made him sorry he

touched me. When he put his hands on me, all I could think of was Billy. I wasn't going to let him hurt me, so I did what I had to."

"I'm sure you would have handled the other one with the same efficiency and courage had I not appeared on the scene."

"Maybe," she said doubtfully. "I was still mighty happy to see you. What kept you?"

"I had a hard time finding a wagon. I finally located one in need of repair. The blacksmith promised to have it ready tomorrow afternoon. I had no trouble buying the supplies or oxen. I left them with the wagon." He sniffed the air. "Is that bacon I smell? I could eat a bear."

"Oh, the bacon!" Dawn removed the smoking frying pan from the fire. "It's a little burnt, but I'll wager it tastes better than bear. I'll open some beans, and I think there's a can of peaches left."

They ate in silence. Cole wolfed down his food while Dawn picked at hers. When they had finished, Dawn began cleaning up. Cole watched her with a hunger that had nothing to do with food. When she started off toward the stream with soap and towel, he called out, "Don't go too far."

The night was cool, but Dawn felt in need of a bath after being touched by Mace. She stripped off her riding skirt and shirtwaist and waded into the water wearing her shift. The water in the mountain stream was colder than she'd expected, and she washed quickly. She had goosebumps the size of Montana by the time she was finished. She was walking out of the water when she spied Cole. He was waiting for her on the bank with a blanket. When she reached him, he wrapped the blanket around her, lifted her into his arms and carried her back to their campsite.

"I can walk," Dawn protested.

"I'd rather carry you." He set her on her feet beside the fire and stripped off her shift. "Let's get rid of this. It's soaking wet. I gathered your clothes while you were bathing and brought them back to the campsite." He surrounded her again with the blanket, scooped her up and carried her down with him to the bedroll he had arranged for them to share.

He placed his guns within reach, removed his pants and shirt and covered himself and Dawn with a second blanket. "Are you still cold?"

Cold? Dawn was burning. Since leaving the Little Big Horn she'd been too exhausted to do anything but curl up against Cole each night and go to sleep. She had missed the joining of their bodies, missed his kisses, his hands on her. "How could I possibly be cold with the heat of your body warming me?"

"God, I've missed you," Cole murmured against her hair.

"I've been right here with you," she reminded him.

"I haven't touched you in days. You were so exhausted I couldn't bring myself to disturb you. I'll not disturb you now if you're too tired or upset. Those two bastards must have frightened you. When I saw Mace's hands on you I wanted to kill him."

"I'm glad you didn't. I've had enough of killing and violence. Just make love to me. Make me forget you're going to leave me."

278

"Dawn, I . . ." What could he say? That he didn't intend to leave her after his visit with his sister ended? That he loved her? He'd already told her he couldn't love again, and he didn't like lying to her.

"No, don't say it. I know what you're thinking. I know that your heart isn't free to love. And I'll have no man who can't love me as fiercely as I love him. Make love to me now. Let me pretend that we're truly man and wife and you'll never leave me."

Her impassioned words smote his conscience. He'd always scorned men who used women, yet wasn't he doing just that with Dawn? Not since Morning Mist had his body united so completely with that of a woman. He craved Dawn fiercely, but did he love her? He didn't know how to deal with her feelings for him. It was more of a burden to him than a blessing. Then his thoughts scattered when Dawn pulled his head down and kissed him. Once their lips meshed, lust made a shambles of his conjecturing. All his senses centered on the woman in his arms.

Dawn opened her mouth to him as he ravaged her with his tongue. She felt cool air touch her skin as he unwrapped the blanket, giving him free access to her body. He kissed and licked her breasts, finding them deliciously swollen, their nipples sweetly ripe. He groaned; his arousal was pleasurably painful. The pulsebeat in his sex matched the one pounding in his throat.

His fingers caressed the soft petals of her woman's flesh. She was wet and swollen, her juices bedewing his fingers. Suddenly he could

279

wait no longer. He gave an explosive sound and flung himself atop her, parting her thighs. "I need you," he muttered against her lips. "It's been too long. Too long . . . Oh, God, I need to . . . I can't wait . . ."

He plunged, hard, deep.

She cried out and arched sharply upward.

Heat and need blotted out every other thought as he thrust wildly, lifting her buttocks to meet each savage thrust. It was as if he couldn't get enough of her, couldn't move fast enough or thrust hard enough. When he needed more, he lifted her legs and put them over his shoulders, opening her to him and taking her as he'd never taken her before.

"Cole! I can't! Oh, God!" She was sobbing now, driven so close to the edge she feared she'd explode. Then she did. So intensely she died a little before regaining her senses.

Cole pounded into her again and again, galloping at full speed toward his own climax. When he came, he spent himself inside her, too overcome to withdraw.

Chapter Fifteen

Cole returned to Bozeman the following day to pick up the wagon and oxen he'd purchased the day before. The wagon was ready as promised. Cole would have paid the blacksmith and left immediately, but the man was in a garrulous mood.

"It's a damn shame what happened to General Custer," he said, shaking his head sadly. "The man is a hero. Rumor has it the army is sending out patrols to avenge his death. Reprisal has already begun. Soon there won't be an Injun left alive to give us any more trouble. Every chief will be forced to surrender his people and be jailed or executed."

"That's what I'm afraid of," Cole muttered.

"What did you say?"

"Nothing important. How about the Indians? How great were their losses?"

"News travels slow, but I heard their losses were light. They hightailed it back to Powder River country with their wounded and dead."

"Thanks again for finishing the job so quickly," Cole said. "I'll bring my oxen around and hitch them to the wagon. I want to be on the trail as soon as possible."

"You going it alone? Wagon trains come through here regularly throughout the summer. One just passed a few days ago. You might be able to catch it if you're so all-fired determined not to wait for the next one."

"Thanks. I'll keep that in mind."

An hour later Cole was on his way back to the campsite to get Dawn.

He found her sitting beneath a tree, holding the rifle across her knees. She jumped up to greet him and then turned to inspect the wagon. It wasn't as large as a Conestoga but built along the same lines. The bed was deep enough to hold all their supplies, and the white canvas top looked sturdy enough to keep out the worst of weather.

"I've filled the water barrels and stowed all the supplies. Since we don't have any furniture or personal belongings to transport, there is plenty of room for us to sleep inside during foul weather. When the weather is good we can sleep under the stars."

Dawn thought sleeping under the stars with Cole sounded wonderful.

They easily located the trail. It was deeply rutted from hundreds upon hundreds of wagon wheels and worn down by the feet of emigrants heading west.

The first several days passed without their seeing a single soul. Later they encountered an occasional traveler or two. The trail grew rough as they climbed into the high country. Two weeks into their journey they overtook the wagon train that had left Bozeman several days ahead of them. Cole conversed with the wagon master, who invited them to join the train. Cole hurried back to tell Dawn.

"Do you think it's safe?" Dawn asked worriedly.

"These people don't even know what happened at the Little Big Horn," Cole said. "They might not find out for weeks yet. By that time they'll have come to know you, and your mixed blood won't matter to them."

Dawn wasn't as convinced as Cole. "Are you sure it's the right thing to do?"

"It's far safer traveling with a group. When wagons break down, there is always someone to help with repairs. We'll try it. If it doesn't work out, we'll leave and go it alone."

Days turned into weeks. The trail didn't get any easier. Wagons broke down. People got sick and died. Throughout it all, the women of the wagon train treated Dawn with cool reserve. Most had either experienced or heard about Indian brutality and held half-breeds in the same contempt as savages. Dawn kept to herself, depending upon Cole for company. She knew that whatever friendship the emigrants extended to her was because of Cole.

Cole made himself indispensable in many ways. He hunted for the entire wagon train, dividing his catch equally among the families. He helped wherever he was needed and was approached whenever a level head was needed. Dawn found herself falling more deeply in love with him every day. They still made love regularly, with Cole carefully spilling his seed outside her body. Dawn's hope that she carried Cole's child was dashed when she had positive proof that she wasn't pregnant. She supposed it was for the best, but mourned the children she'd never have.

Dawn learned that Cole had sent a telegram to his sister from Bozeman, alerting her to his visit, and she wondered if he had mentioned the fact that he was bringing a woman with him who wasn't his legal wife. Whether he had or hadn't, she was still leery of meeting Cole's family. Would they like her? One thing was certain: When Cole left, she had no intention of imposing on Cole's sister.

Dawn wondered if Cole's sister was prejudiced against Indians. Would the fact that Dawn was a half-breed make her any less welcome in Ashley's home? How would Cole introduce her? Legally, she wasn't Cole's wife. Would his family consider her Cole's whore? So many questions, so few answers. All she could do was wait and see.

The journey over the Oregon Trail ended six arduous weeks from the day they left Bozeman. They left the wagon train at Oregon City, bidding good-bye to their traveling companions, some of whom were traveling north to Washington. The rest would continue west to the Oregon coast.

They left the wagon and oxen at the livery to be sold and rode their horses to the MacTavish house. Cole seemed to know the way as they turned down several winding streets, heading toward the outskirts of town.

"Don't the MacTavishes live in town?" Dawn asked

"They built a large house close to the sawmill a few years ago. It's not far."

They turned down a narrow road cut out of a forest of towering pine, Douglas fir, spruce and cedar. A short time later the house came into view. Solidly built against a backdrop of thickly forested hills, the rustic two-story structure had a rough wooden exterior that blended perfectly with its surroundings. Dawn's mouth gaped open as they approached the house. Never had she seen a house so large or splendid.

"It's beautiful—and so big," she said, clearly awed. She didn't belong in a place like this.

Cole laughed. "Ashley thought so too, but it's what Tanner wanted for her. He insisted on building her the finest home this side of the Mississippi."

"He must love her a great deal," Dawn said wistfully. "Were they childhood sweethearts?"

"Hardly," Cole said, vastly amused. "Ashley was denied a place on a wagon train because she had no husband or family, so she paid Tanner to marry her."

Dawn's mouth gaped open in disbelief. "She paid for a husband? That must have taken a great deal of courage."

"There's more. You don't know Ashley. When she makes up her mind to something, she'll let nothing stand in her way. I'd been jailed at Fort

Connie Mason

Bridger for a crime I didn't commit, and Ash was determined to clear my name."

"Did she? Clear your name, I mean."

"In a way. Unfortunately, she was captured by Running Elk before she reached the fort. He saw her and believed she was the red-haired medicine woman promised to them in a shaman's dream. She was called Flame by the People."

"Your sister was a captive? How did she get away? Did you rescue her? No, you couldn't have, you were in jail."

"That's another story. Tanner came to the fort seeking help from the army to rescue Ashley and ended up breaking me out of jail. We found Running Elk's village but became captives ourselves." His voice broke and he grew pensive. "That was where I met Morning Mist."

"How did you escape? And how did you became such good friends with Running Elk when you were his captive?"

"I met Morning Mist and fell in love. My affections were returned, and we were joined according to Indian customs shortly afterward. But that's only half the story. Do you recall seeing the hank of red hair woven in Running Elk's hair?" Dawn nodded. "It's Running Elk's good-luck charm, a talisman from Ashley to bring him good fortune. Ashley gave him a hank of her hair, and he's worn it ever since. Ashley and Tanner were allowed to leave the village, but I wanted to remain with Morning Mist. Then something happened and I had to leave."

"What was that?"

"The man responsible for the murder I was accused of came to the village to trade with the People. I took him back to the fort to stand trial and to clear my name. I didn't want to be a wanted man the rest of my days. My case was reopened and I was found innocent. It all took longer than I had expected, and I was unable to return to Morning Mist as quickly as I would have liked."

He paused, finding it difficult to continue.

"During my absence the village was attacked by Crow raiders. Morning Mist was slain in the raid. She carried my child."

Dawn felt his pain as if it were her own.

"That was eight years ago," Cole continued. "Running Elk suggested that I stay with his people during my time of mourning. I learned skills I would have never learned on my own. I owe Running Elk and the People a great deal."

"Why did you leave?"

"Running Elk moved his people to the reservation. It was time for me to leave. I found a job with the Pinkertons, then made a brief trip to Oregon to visit Ashley and Tanner. I've spent the past two years on special assignment with the railroad."

"Thank you," Dawn said.

"For what?"

"For telling me. It helps to understand you better. Morning Mist must have been a very special woman. I wish . . ." Her words drifted away.

Cole searched Dawn's face, suddenly unable to recall Morning Mist's beloved features. It frightened him. Morning Mist's image had been with him so long he couldn't imagine life without it. Yet at this moment he could recall nothing but how much he enjoyed making love to Dawn, how sweetly she clung to him and called his name when he brought her to climax. He shook his head, trying to dispel the gnawing hunger for Dawn that was always with him.

They had reached the house now, and Dawn watched with trepidation as a flame-haired woman darted out of the door to greet them. She was so beautiful the sight of her nearly took Dawn's breath away. Dawn felt dull and lifeless compared to the brightness and sunlight Cole's sister exuded. She was a feminine version of Cole.

Cole leaped from his mount and held his arms wide. His sister rushed into his open arms, her green eyes awash with tears. Cole hugged her tightly, and Dawn wished she held only a small part of the love he felt for his twin.

Dawn stood apart, watching the poignant reunion between brother and sister. There was a strong bond there, she reflected, and she suddenly felt like an intruder. She wondered if Cole's hair had ever been as bright a red as his sister's. Living flame was the only description Dawn could think of to describe Ashley's hair. It was no wonder Running Elk had considered her some kind of goddess.

Ashley and Cole parted, their hands clinging as they stared at one another. "You've changed," Ashley said. "Your face is older, harder." She tested the muscles of his forearms and laughed. "Your body is harder, too. Shame on you for waiting so long between visits. It's been four years! You've yet to see your new niece. You left before she was born."

"I'm here now," Cole said. "God, I'm glad to see

you." He gave her another quick hug. Ashley's gaze slid past Cole to Dawn, noticing her for the first time.

"You're not alone," she said, surprise coloring her words. "Where are your manners, Cole? Who is your companion?"

Ashley's eyes, so like Cole's in color and shape, glittered with curiosity. The last time she'd seen her brother he was still grieving for his dead wife. When she'd suggested that Cole should find another woman, he'd told her he'd never remarry, never have a child now that Morning Mist was dead. Ashley had believed that time would heal his broken heart. But as the years passed and Cole remained single, she'd despaired of his ever finding another woman to love.

Cole moved to Dawn's side. "This is Dawn. My . . . wife. Dawn, this is Ashley, my twin sister."

"Your wife!" Ashley exclaimed, shocked and delighted. "I never . . . why didn't you write that you had remarried?"

Dawn sent Cole a startled look. How could he introduce them as husband and wife when they weren't really married? What would Ashley think of her when she learned the truth? "I'm happy to meet you," she said, finally finding her tongue. "I hope I'm not imposing."

Ashley remembered her manners once her shock passed. "Nothing of the sort. It's about time Cole found someone to love. You're a pretty little thing. Come inside, you must be exhausted after so arduous a journey."

"Where is Tanner?" Cole asked as he followed Ashley inside the house.

"He and Price are at the sawmill. Our son is going to follow in his father's footsteps. He accompanies Tanner to the sawmill every chance he gets, even though he's only six."

"And my niece? How is she?"

"Lily is fine," Ashley said.

"Lily is a little lady now, all of eight years old. Tanner spoils her outrageously."

"She probably has her mother's temperament," Cole teased. "Does she have red hair like you?"

"No, thank God. It's black as sin, just like her father's. Pierce's hair is more like yours. Not flaming red, more the color of mahogany. You'll see them soon."

Dawn could find no words to describe the house. Her entire cabin would fit in the parlor. She was surprised to find no fancy furnishings, nothing pretentious. There were good sturdy pieces polished to a high luster, overstuffed sofas, comfortable chairs and thick carpets on the floor.

The rooms she could see were spacious and comfortable. Nevertheless, the house boasted more luxury than Dawn was accustomed to and it intimidated her a bit.

"I'll bet you're starved," Ashley said, taking note of Dawn's slim figure. "Have you been starving your wife, Cole? She's thin as a rail."

"I've always been thin," Dawn said, absolving Cole of all blame.

"I'll show you to your room. You can rest while I ask the cook to prepare something to hold you over until supper. We have our main meal in the evening, when Tanner returns from the mill.

Come along." She led the way up the stairs, chattering as she went.

The bedroom was huge and attractively furnished. The focal point was a large four-poster bed covered with a patchwork quilt. The rest of the furnishings consisted of washstand, desk, dresser, two chairs and wardrobe, all highly polished and built for comfort.

"I hope this will suit you," Ashley said anxiously. "It's the best guest room in the house."

"It's . . . perfect," Dawn said, noting the magnificent view from the window.

Ashley turned to Cole. Her eyes held a mischievous sparkle. "Would you like separate rooms?"

"I'll share my wife's room," he said, sending his sister a cocky grin.

"I thought you might." Ashley's answering grin was every bit as cocky as Cole's.

"There's a bathroom down the hall," Ashley said. "With a water closet, bathtub and running hot and cold water. Tanner thought of everything. He dug a well and built a windmill to pump water into the house. There's even a coal burner in the cellar to heat the pipes that carry hot water."

"Hot water," Dawn repeated, clearly impressed. "And a water closet. I never imagined such indulgence. It must have cost a great deal to build in those luxuries."

"The lumber business is very successful. Tanner exports lumber all over the world. Did Cole tell you that he's grown quite wealthy from his investment in the business? Now, if you'll both excuse me, I'll check with the cook. Meanwhile, take a hot bath, it will relax you after your long trip. Come downstairs in about an hour."

"Why did you tell her we were married?" Dawn asked when they were alone. "I don't like lying to your sister."

"Did you want me to tell her we're sharing a room without benefit of marriage?"

Dawn's blue eyes widened, then narrowed. "You wouldn't! We don't *have* to share a room. You could have taken another room. Surely a house this size has more than one guest room."

"There are several, if I recall correctly. And I have no intention of sleeping alone while I'm here. We've been sleeping together for several months now. A few more weeks can't make any difference. Now, would you like that bath Ashley mentioned?"

"In hot water," Dawn said longingly. "It sounds wonderful."

"Come, I'll show you where it is." He held the door open and ushered her down the hall to the bathroom.

The modern bathroom boggled Dawn's mind. She'd seen nothing to compare to this kind of luxury. While the tub was filling with water, Cole showed her how to work the water closet. There was also a sink with hot and cold running water. When the tub was full, Cole left, affording her privacy to use the water closet and undress.

Dawn sank into the tub, letting the hot water caress her skin. She found a bar of fragrant soap in a soap dish and worked up a rich lather. Suds dropped into her eyes, and she reached for the washcloth she'd seen draped over the tub.

"Are you looking for this?"

Dawn started violently. "Cole, I didn't hear you come in." She snatched the washcloth from his hand, expecting him to leave. Instead, he began unbuttoning his shirt. "What are you doing?"

"Tanner built the tub big enough for two. I'm going to share your bath." He stripped off his shirt and stepped out of his pants.

Dawn stared at him. As often as she'd seen him naked she still found something new to admire about him each time he disrobed. Everything about him pleased her. Still, bathing in the same tub with him was a new experience. Did men and women normally bathe together or was Cole pushing the limits of decency? She decided to ask him.

"Is this considered decent behavior?"

"To me it is. Tanner must think so too. Move over, I'm joining you."

Water splashed over the sides of the tub as Cole eased his big body into the water, settling across from her.

"Look at the mess you're making! Your sister won't be pleased."

"I'll clean it up." He took the washcloth from her nerveless fingers. "I'll wash you first, then you can wash me."

He worked up a rich lather and began with her foot, working his way up her leg to the dark triangle at the apex. He didn't linger there but moved to the other foot, slowly working the lather upward. When he reached her sweet center, he dropped the cloth and parted her with his fingers.

"Cole! What are you doing?"

"Exactly what it feels like." His finger slid inside

her. He closed his eyes, savoring the tightness and warmth of her sheath as it closed around his finger.

"You shouldn't do that. What if someone came in and saw us?" If he stopped she would die.

"I locked the door." He slipped a second finger in beside the first. Then he began working them in and out of her, smiling when she groaned and lifted her hips to meet his questing fingers.

"Relax, sweetheart," he whispered. "Not so fast." He had become painfully aroused in a very short time, just as he always did when he was with Dawn. When had making love to Dawn become necessary to his well-being? he wondered distractedly. "I know what you like. Trust me to give it to you." With his free hand he caressed her breasts, rolling each nipple between forefinger and thumb, watching passion transform her lovely features. God, he loved seeing her like this, hot for him, only for him.

Dawn was burning. Not even the cooling water could douse the fire Cole had ignited in her. She was clinging to the edge, driven nearly senseless by Cole's deft fingers and hands. Then abruptly his hands left her body. She cried out in deprivation, wanting him to continue, wanting his fingers in her, on her. "I know what you want, sweetheart," Cole said as he lifted her and brought her onto his lap facing him. He shifted slightly and thrust upward, impaling her with his sex. He was rock hard and heavy, but he slid into her effortlessly.

Grasping her hips, he brought her down hard, thrusting his loins upward at the same time. Over and over he repeated the rhythm, her softness squeezing him as his juices swelled and filled him. "Hurry, sweetheart, come to me." His voice was strangled, his face contorted with urgency. When his mouth fastened on her breast, suckling her, she went wild.

She felt her climax beginning clear down to her toes. Her head fell back, her mouth opened in a silent scream as her body convulsed again and again, giving him everything he asked for, everything she had to give.

Cole's climax commenced before Dawn's ended. When he would have spent his seed outside her body, she refused to allow him to withdraw. Clamping her legs around his hips, she slid as far down onto his manhood as she could get without causing herself pain. Cole gave a hoarse shout and exploded inside her, his fierce convulsions spilling nearly all the water out of the tub onto the floor.

"Why wouldn't you let me withdraw?" Cole asked when his breathing slowed to a steady pounding.

"I wanted you inside me as long as possible."

He gave her a shuttered look. "That was foolish of you and reckless of me." He lifted her off him and set her aside. "We've been lucky thus far. I've tried not to get you with child. It's nearly time to go downstairs. I'll clean up here while you get dressed."

Fifteen minutes later Dawn and Cole walked downstairs together. Ashley was waiting for them. She took one look at Dawn and couldn't help smiling. Dawn's face was flushed and her breathing still hadn't returned to normal. It wasn't difficult to imagine what the two had been up to. Cole had the sated look of a cat who has just lapped a saucer of cream.

"Did you two get a chance to rest?" Ashley asked with feigned innocence. "I hope the bed was comfortable."

"You know damn well we didn't rest," Cole replied, sending Ashley a wicked smile.

"Cole!" Dawn cried, embarrassed by his impudence.

Ashley laughed gleefully. It was wonderful seeing Cole like this. After his last visit she'd begun to fear that Cole would never recover from Morning Mist's death. Now it was obvious that he loved his new wife, and nothing could have pleased Ashley more. Cole hadn't mentioned Dawn's mixed blood, but it wasn't difficult to tell she was a half-breed. The intriguing combination of blue eyes and golden skin made her beauty riveting.

"Don't be embarrassed, Dawn. Cole always was outspoken. You can't begin to know how pleased I am to see him this way. I feared he'd never recover from Morning Mist's death. It left him devastated." She saw the haunted look in Dawn's eyes and immediately regretted her candid words. "Forgive me. I didn't mean to bring up the past."

"There is nothing to forgive, Ashley. I know all about Morning Mist and how much Cole loves her."

"*Loved* her," Ashley corrected. "Morning Mist is dead. I'm pleased Cole has found another woman to love. He loves you very much, I can tell."

Dawn bit her bottom lip to keep it from trembling. "Ashley, I—"

"Enough of this kind of talk," Cole interrupted. "When am I going to see my niece?" Talking about love made him nervous. He'd only just begun to explore his feelings for Dawn and still didn't understand the strong emotions she stirred in him. He wasn't sure he wanted to.

"If I'm not mistaken, that's Lily now," Ashley said. "She was upstairs doing her lessons. "

The words were no sooner out of Ashley's mouth than a compact bundle of energy came bounding down the stairs. She slid to a halt, dark curls bouncing, when she saw Cole and Dawn.

"This is your Uncle Cole and Aunt Dawn," Ashley said, urging the child forward. "Make your curtsy, sweet."

Lily curtsied clumsily, then smiled beguilingly at Cole. One day she was going to drive men wild with her flirty green eyes and stunning smile, Dawn thought. No wonder she was the apple of her father's eye.

"Pleased to meet you, Lily," Cole said as he bent and kissed the little girl's cheek. "Did anyone ever tell you you're a little charmer?"

"Only my daddy," she chirped. She turned her attention on Dawn, studying her gravely. "Is Aunt Dawn your wife?"

"She is," Cole said, giving Dawn a quick look that could have meant anything.

"She looks like an Indian," Lily remarked with the innocence of a eight-year-old.

Ashley blanched, embarrassed to her toes.

"I'm half Indian," Dawn said, filling the void left in the conversation.

"I'm sorry," Ashley said. "Lily is a curious child."

"It's all right. I'm accustomed to being looked at oddly. The only time my heritage wasn't remarked upon was during my stay with Running Elk and his people."

Ashley gave Cole a tongue-lashing for his omission. "Why didn't you tell me you'd returned to Running Elk's village?"

"I'll explain later," Cole said as he set Collette on her feet and seated himself at the table. "I'm starved."

Between mouthfuls, Cole told Ashley an abbreviated version of their visit to Running Elk's village. He purposely skipped over the part about taking Dawn to the reservation with the intention of leaving her with the People.

"We heard about the battle at the Little Big Horn," Ashley said. "Was Running Elk there? Did he participate in the battle? I'm sorry you could do nothing to prevent the Indians from going on the warpath. I'd hate to see harm come to Running Elk and his people."

"I haven't heard a thing except that a battle took place and the Seventh Cavalry was soundly defeated. Running Elk still wears your talisman. He believes it will protect him. I pray it does."

They fell silent, each consumed by his own thoughts and worries. Finally Ashley asked, "Where did you meet Dawn? How long have you been married? Is she one of Running Elk's people?"

"A lot has happened that you don't know about," Cole hedged. "Running Elk asked me to remain until spring, and I agreed. I hoped if I stayed I might still talk him out of joining Crazy Horse and the other chiefs at the Little Big Horn. Dawn and I even traveled to the Little Big Horn with them so that I could plead with the chiefs to return to their reservations. Nothing I said made them change their minds."

"What about Dawn?" Ashley pressed, wanting answers that Cole seemed unwilling to give. "I know she's a half-breed. You never did say where you met her."

Dawn stared at Cole curiously, wondering what he would tell his twin.

"I met Dawn in Dodge City."

Ashley waited for him to continue. When he didn't, she asked, "Is that all you're going to tell me?"

"For the time being."

The closed look on Cole's face told her it was pointless to pursue the subject. When Cole wanted her to know, he'd tell her.

Dawn swallowed past the lump in her throat and concentrated on her food. She wondered why Cole didn't tell Ashley the truth. Was it up to her to tell his sister that they weren't really married after he left?

Chapter Sixteen

Dawn was favorably impressed with Tanner and envied the deep and abiding love he and Ashley shared. Somewhat older than Cole, Tanner was handsome in a dark, dangerous way, with hair as black as sin and eyes the color of newly minted silver. Dawn was intrigued by his soft Southern drawl. She questioned Cole about Tanner's roots when they were alone.

"Tanner is a Southerner," Cole explained. "Ashley told me they got along like oil and water at first. But their love proved too strong to allow different beliefs to come between them. Their love has survived many obstacles."

Dawn sighed wistfully. She'd die for a love like that. Why did she have to love a man who couldn't love her in return?

"They're very lucky."

"Ashley had been content with being a spinster until she met Tanner. She'd been jilted once by a fiance who loved money more than he loved her. Before she came West she taught school in Boston. She sold the house our aunt left to her and arranged to travel with a wagon train. There was a mixup about her name, and the wagon master refused to let a single woman travel with his outfit. It proved to be quite an adventure, but happily it turned out well at the end. She met her true love, and I couldn't be happier for her. Ashley and I have always been close, even when separated by thousands of miles."

"I envy Ashley."

"Tanner and I have a lot in common despite having fought on opposite sides during the war," Cole continued as if Dawn hadn't spoken. "We both lost wives. Tanner's wife killed herself. She'd been brutally raped and couldn't live with the shame. Her death made a bitter man of Tanner. He hated all Yankees. He was in jail when he and Ashley met. But as their love grew, Tanner was able to put his past behind him."

"He must love Ashley a great deal." Dawn regretted being unable to reach Cole on that level. His past was still very much a part of him.

Cole and Tanner spent every day except Sunday at the mill. Since school had let out for the summer, young Price was free to tag along. Dawn tried to make herself helpful to Ashley, who did just about everything in the house that had to be done except for the cooking.

"Tanner wanted to hire household help," Ashley

confided one day while they were working together in the small garden behind the house, "but I didn't want the house overrun with strangers."

Dawn wondered if Ashley considered her, Dawn, a stranger. She wondered what Ashley and Tanner would think when they learned that Cole expected Dawn to make her home with them after he left.

"It must be wonderful having a real home," Dawn said wistfully.

"Where do you and Cole plan to settle? It would be wonderful if he decided to stay in Oregon. Tanner wants to deed Cole a piece of land so he could build a house for you."

"You'll have to ask Cole," Dawn said noncommittally. "I think he plans to return to his job with the Pinkertons. He enjoys his work a great deal."

Ashley rested her hands on the hoe she'd been using and stared at Dawn with concern. "But that job takes Cole all over the country. What will you do while he's on assignment? Where will you live? Does he plan to drag you from town to town?"

Dawn bit the soft underside of her lip while she sought an answer that would satisfy Ashley. Nothing came to mind. Finally she said, "I'm not privy to Cole's plans. And we haven't been together long enough for me to read his mind."

Ashley was thoroughly perplexed, as well as upset, with her brother. Married couples were supposed to share everything, yet Dawn appeared to know nothing about Cole's plans for their future. Cole was exceedingly secretive about his wife and his marriage, and it bothered her. Ashley was curious about the whole situation, but she set her misgivings aside. Her twin had no reason to lie to her.

"I'm sure it's just an oversight on Cole's part," Ashley said. "Maybe he hasn't decided yet where to settle. I'm sure he doesn't intend to leave you alone months at a time while he's on an assignment."

Dawn said nothing, for the truth hurt. Not only did Cole intend to return to his job but he had every intention of abandoning her. He would leave her with his sister and go about his business without his conscience bothering him. All he'd ever wanted was to settle her somewhere safe. White society didn't recognize their Indian marriage, so he had no reason to claim her or to remain with her. He could go on as before, cherishing his freedom, his heart cold and empty except for his memories of Morning Mist.

When Dawn remained mute, Ashley decided it was time to have a talk with her brother. But first she'd talk it over with Tanner. She broached the subject that night as they cuddled together in bed. Throughout the years of marriage, their romance hadn't died, it just grew better. Their lovemaking was as intense and rewarding as ever.

"I'm worried about Cole," Ashley said, nuzzling Tanner's neck.

"How so?" His hands skimmed her body, which was still as slim as a girl's.

"Something's been bothering me. Dawn isn't as happy as a new bride should be. Cole doesn't confide in her."

"I asked Cole to stay on here. He's learning the lumber business amazingly fast. I could use a man like him. He already owns a share of the business."

"What did he say?"

"He didn't say anything. I got the impression he intends to move on soon."

"There are problems in that marriage," Ashley said worriedly.

"Your brother and Dawn share a bed and appear to be intimate lovers. What worries you, love?"

"I don't know. I hate to interfere, but if Cole won't confide in me, I'll be forced to speak with him."

"Your brother doesn't need to explain himself to you or anyone else."

"He does if it concerns an innocent girl. I know Cole. I'm his twin. I can sense when he's troubled."

"Let them be," Tanner advised. "Cole hasn't said a word yet about leaving. Wait until he comes to you with his problems before you jump to conclusions. Now," he said, pulling her against his hard body, "how about giving your starving husband some attention?"

"Starving? You put away too much food at dinner tonight to be starving."

"Did I say anything about food? Live up to your name, sweet Flame. Make me burn."

Ashley laughed. Whenever Tanner used her Indian name she could expect a night of extraordinary passion.

He didn't disappoint her.

In another bedroom, Cole had just finished making love to Dawn. She lay atop him, replete, but she sensed his withdrawal, not just from her body at the moment of climax, but mentally as well. He seemed miles away.

"What is it, Cole?" she asked anxiously.

"I've been here four weeks now." His tone betrayed nothing of his thoughts, but Dawn knew what was coming.

"You're leaving," Dawn said without surprise. "Where will you go?"

"I'm concerned about Running Elk. I have to find out what happened to him and the People after the battle."

"Am I going with you?" She should have known better than to ask.

Cole refused to look her in the eye. "You'll be safer here with my sister. She and Tanner think the world of you."

"You're not coming back." It was a statement rather than a question.

Dawn could not see his expression in the darkness but she felt his rejection keenly. She would have been surprised at the uncertainty and confusion on his face had she been able to see it. Cole had searched his soul for an answer to his dilemma and come up empty-handed. He'd fought against his growing feelings for Dawn and was losing the battle. Placing distance between them was the only way he could come to grips with his dilemma. He needed to find out if the time had finally come to bury his memories of Morning Mist and move on. He hoped the solitude and peace he'd once found with the People would help him find the answers he sought.

"I can promise nothing more than what I've already given you. I know it's damn little, but I need to resolve the uncertainties that plague me. I can't do it unless I distance myself from the temptation of your body. My obsession with you haunts me night and day. I loved once; I'm not sure I can love again."

"I'll not settle for anything less than your whole heart," Dawn said, disheartened by his words. If Cole couldn't love her, she didn't want him. "Lust isn't a bad thing but it's not enough to base a marriage on. I want more. I want a lifetime of commitment. You're right, you should leave now. I hope you find what you're looking for."

"You'll remain here with Ashley," he said firmly.

"Am I to wait for you to return?"

"I . . . yes."

"What if you never return? I refuse to impose upon your sister's charity."

Unspoken words hovered between them like a silent mist, encompassing Dawn in a shroud of resentment. Cole had used her like his whore for months. Now he was leaving, proving how little he cared for her. He'd made her love him. Why couldn't he find it in his heart to return even a tiny portion of that love?

It wasn't as if she hadn't known beforehand that his heart wasn't free to love, she told herself. He'd made it clear that he would never love again. But she'd kept hoping, praying for a miracle. Now it was too late to wish for anything but his speedy departure.

Cole reached for her. "Dawn, I . . ."

Dawn scooted out of his reach. "No, don't touch me. What a fool I've been. You'll never use me again, Cole Webster. Shadow Walker claimed me as his wife, but Cole Webster used me as his whore."

"Dammit, Dawn, it's not like that."

"How is it, Cole? I'm not the same girl you met in Dodge City. That girl and I share the same distrust of men but little else. In you I thought I had found a trustworthy man, but you are no better than Billy Cobb. You don't abuse me physically, but there are times I'd rather suffer physical abuse than be used just to satisfy a man's lust. I can never be more than a warm body to you. After Billy, I thought nothing could hurt me again, but I was mistaken. Somewhere on this earth dwells a man who will love me."

She turned her back on him. Cole felt the finality of her words as keenly as he felt her coldness. He deserved the scorn she'd heaped upon him. Unfortunately, the thought of Dawn with another man made him crazy with jealousy. He turned her around to face him, his face dark and seething.

"If this is our good-bye, I want more than a cold shoulder from you."

"It's more than you deserve."

"Damn you!" His mouth slammed down on hers, hard, determined, implacable. He kissed her until her head spun and her legs trembled. "You know we both want this!" he said, panting harshly.

"I don't want you. I don't want this," Dawn shot back. "I want nothing more to do with you."

"We'll see about that." Cole had no idea why he was acting so unreasonably. He was being a bastard and knew it. He was finding that guilt was an emotion that destroyed one's good sense. Jealousy fed his obsession for Dawn. It wasn't right for a man to want a woman so badly he'd deny everything he held dear, all his precious memories, to have her.

"Don't touch me!"

"I'm going to do more than touch you, sweetheart. When I finally come inside you, you're going to remember it all the rest of your days. I'm going to make you as wild as you make me."

Before Dawn could protest, he'd pinned her to the mattress with his body. Then he proceeded to live up to his promise. He slid down her body and shoved her legs apart, holding her in place with an arm across her hips as his mouth found her hot center. Dawn fought against the restraint, but his strength was too great for her. His mouth and tongue possessed her with an intensity she'd never known in him. She resisted fiercely, until all fight left her and she arched into his mouth with shameless abandon.

But he didn't let her climax. Time and again he brought her to the brink, then left her wanting and mindless. Tortured beyond endurance, Dawn finally begged between sobs for him to finish it. He smiled darkly as he slid up her body and thrust into her. She climaxed immediately. He was still hard inside her. Then he began anew, arousing her till she twisted and writhed beneath him. This time they came together violently. Cole stayed inside her until she'd drained every last drop of seed from him. Then he withdrew and left the bed.

Cole spent the remainder of the night sprawled beneath the stars, making his bed under a tree. He stared at the dark sky, wondering if Dawn hated him enough to forget him. A blackness inside him had driven him to do things he knew he'd regret later. He'd wanted to hear Dawn beg him to stay, to hear her say she loved him. Instead, he had turned her against him, telling himself it was what he wanted.

Dawn required more of him than he could give her. He needed to find answers to his doubts before he could dedicate his life to her. He'd done that once with Morning Mist. Until his doubts were resolved, he could make no commitments.

Silent tears ran down Dawn's cheeks long after Cole left. He had forced a response from her against her will, and she'd never forgive him for that violation. She had always given to him freely, but this time he'd taken what he wanted. She was truly on her own now. She refused to avail herself of Ashley and Tanner's hospitality when she was nothing to Cole but his whore.

Cole found Ashley alone in the dining room early the following morning. "I need to talk to you, Ash."

"Sit down and have some breakfast. Tanner left early. He said he'd meet you at the mill."

Cole sat but didn't bother filling his plate with food. "I'm leaving."

Ashley dropped her fork. "So soon? We're just getting to know Dawn. I'm going to miss her."

"Dawn isn't coming with me."

Ashley gave him a startled look. "I don't understand."

"I'm leaving Dawn with you and Tanner, if you don't mind."

"Of course we don't mind. But why?"

"I'm returning to Indian country to find Running Elk."

"Why must you keep running back to Indian country? I never could understand your preoccupation with Indian life. You're white, Cole, you belong with your own kind. I couldn't wait to leave Running Elk's village behind."

"I'm not going to stay, Ash. I need to return for my own peace of mind. I need to find myself, to come to grips with . . . certain things."

"Do those things concern Dawn?"

"You always seem to know what's in my head."

"Do you love Dawn?"

"I don't know. It's something I intend to find out."

"How do you expect to get answers while you're hundreds of miles away? This separation could very well end the relationship between you and Dawn."

"If you asked her right now, Dawn would tell you she hates me," he said cryptically.

"What did you do to her?"

He flushed and looked away. "Ask Dawn."

"Oh, Cole, why did you marry Dawn if you don't love her?"

"It's a long story."

"I have time."

"Suffice it to say, I felt responsible for Dawn. I'd killed her husband. She had no one. Half-breeds are treated with little regard, and she had no way to support herself. I decided to leave her with Running Elk, hoping she would find a husband from among his people, someone who would love her as she deserved."

"This is all very confusing. You said Dawn is your wife."

"Circumstances demanded that we marry. We joined according to Indian customs."

"What circumstances?" Ashley questioned relentlessly.

"You don't give up, do you? Very well, if you must know the truth, I'll tell you. Dawn carried my child. I felt it was the right thing to do."

"Dear God! What happened to the child?"

Pain hardened Cole's features. "Dawn lost our babe. She received repeated beatings from her husband during their marriage and wasn't strong enough to carry the babe to term."

"Thank God you killed the bastard," Ashley said fiercely. "How could you think of leaving Dawn at a time when she needs you more than ever? She carried your child. You should have married her legally as soon as you reached civilization."

"Dawn doesn't want a husband whose heart isn't free to love. I care for Dawn more than I've cared for any woman since Morning Mist. But I feel as if I'm being unfaithful to Morning Mist's memory."

"The hell with memories!" Ashley swore. "Memories can't keep you warm at night, or give you children. I don't know you anymore, Cole. You've grown hard and stubborn, and far too cynical. Put the past behind you. You need a flesh-and-blood woman to share your love."

"Perhaps you're right, but I still have to make

this journey. I need to know if the feelings I have for Dawn will survive a separation."

"You're a fool, Cole. Dawn might not be waiting for you when you return . . . if you return. No matter what you decide, I'll always consider Dawn my sister-in-law. She'll have a home here for as long as she cares to remain."

"That's all I wanted to know." He hugged her hard. "I'll go to the mill now and say my good-byes to Tanner."

Ashley sat for a long time after Cole had left, wondering if she'd ever been as stubborn or hard-headed as her brother. The relationship between her and Tanner had been fraught with obstacles, but their problems seemed tame compared to Cole's. His unwillingness to admit he loved Dawn was downright stupid. Men! When would they grow up and accept the inevitable without a fight?

Dawn entered the dining room, interrupting Ashley's ruminations. She sat down, a pale ghost of herself.

"Are you all right?" Ashley asked anxiously.

"Cole's leaving."

"I know, he told me. Don't fret, he'll be back."

Dawn's lips turned down into a grimace. "I don't want him. He's used me for the last time. I have some money. I've decided to move to town after Cole leaves. I don't want to impose on you any longer than necessary."

"You're not imposing. You're Cole's wife; you're welcome to stay as long as you like."

"I'm not Cole's wife." Dawn watched Ashley carefully, expecting her to exhibit disgust, or at the very least, surprise. When neither was forthcoming, Dawn qualified, "I'm Cole's whore."

"Don't you dare call yourself that name!" Ashley admonished angrily. "You were married in an Indian ceremony."

"Cole told you?"

Ashley nodded. "Just this morning. He should have married you again in front of a minister as soon as you reached civilization."

"Cole isn't ready for that. I doubt he'll ever be ready. What else did he tell you?"

"He told me about . . . the baby. I'm sorry. You must have been devastated."

"Cole joined with me for the sake of our child. He didn't want me. He's never wanted more than my body. He doesn't love me enough to marry me legally. He still grieves for Morning Mist. I've lived too many years with a man who cared nothing for me. I won't let that happen again."

"Cole will come to his senses and realize you're what he wants."

Dawn shook her head in fierce denial. "By that time it will be too late. I'm not waiting around for him to decide whether he wants me in his life or not."

"Please don't do anything you'll regret," Ashley advised. "Stay here as long as you like. Don't rush off without thinking this over carefully."

"I've thought of nothing else all night. I ask only one thing of you. Don't tell Cole about our conversation, or my intention to leave."

"Dawn, I don't think—"

"Please! Promise me! I don't want Cole badgering me about staying with you."

"Very well, if it means that much to you," Ashley

said. "What will you do? Where will you go?"

"I'll find a job in town. I'll do whatever is necessary to survive."

"You love Cole a great deal, don't you?"

Dawn smiled wanly. "I love him with my entire being . . . and hate him with equal fervor."

"My God, what did he do to you?"

"Ask Cole. Excuse me, I can't talk about this anymore." She rose abruptly and departed hastily, leaving Ashley with her mouth hanging open.

A short time later Ashley rode to the mill to confront Cole. "What did you do to Dawn?" she demanded harshly.

"What did Dawn tell you?"

"Nothing! She told me nothing. My God, Cole, how could you hurt her? You're not the brother I remember."

"I've changed in many ways," Cole said, "but I've never lifted a hand to Dawn. I don't abuse women."

"I know that. But there are other ways to hurt a woman. She told me she was your whore."

Cole winced. "I won't deny our relationship was based on strong mutual attraction, but we care deeply for one another. Dawn was never my whore. She was married to Shadow Walker. She carried his child. He gave her all he could give of himself. And so did I."

"You talk as if you're two people!" Ashley charged.

"In some ways I am."

"You're being stupid, Cole. One day you'll wake up. I pray it's not too late."

"I didn't say I won't return," Cole hedged.

"Meanwhile, Dawn will be safe here with you and Tanner."

Ashley didn't correct him. She had given her word to Dawn and she meant to keep it.

"Finding Running Elk is important. He's been like a brother to me. I'm worried about him. Besides, a separation from Dawn will help me decide if what I feel for her is love or lust. Wanting her is like a sickness, and it frightens the hell out of me. But I don't want Dawn to suffer in any way because of my indecision. I want her to have my share of the profits from the mill during my absence."

"I hope you find what you're seeking," Ashley said, turning away. "For the first time in my life I'm disappointed in you."

"I'm sorry, Ash. Dawn deserves a man whose heart isn't torn by conflicting emotions. I need to learn where my heart lies before committing myself."

"Save your apologies for Dawn," she flung over her shoulder as she stalked away. "Good-bye, Cole."

There was a catch in Cole's voice. "Good-bye, Ash."

A week after Cole left, Dawn packed her few belongings and informed Ashley that she was leaving.

"Where will you go?" Ashley asked. "You'll always have a home with us. Not because of Cole but because we think of you as family."

"But I'm not family," Dawn said with finality. "You know what I am to Cole. I can't continue to impose upon you and Tanner. There must be someone in Oregon City willing to give me a job. I have some money. Enough to last until I find work."

"Cole made arrangements for you to receive his share of the profits from the mill during his absence."

Dawn stiffened. "I don't want his money."

"We all consider you Cole's wife. He'll return, mark my words. Cole and I are twins; I feel the same things he feels. He's confused right now. In time he'll discover he loves you."

"I no longer love Cole," Dawn lied. "I'll leave tomorrow."

Ashley realized there was nothing she could do or say to change Dawn's mind. In her own way, Dawn was just as stubborn as Cole. "Promise you'll keep in touch. Tanner and I are here if you need us. You'll always be welcome in our home."

"Thank you," Dawn said sincerely. "After Billy died I always intended to make a new life for myself. Were it not for Cole's interference, I would have. I'll keep in touch. You're the closest I've ever had to a relative or friend. Until Cole burst into my life I had no one . . . no one . . ."

Dawn rode Wally into town the following morning. She inquired about work at the general store first. By the time she'd asked at every store and shop on one side of the street, including two dress shops, a milliner, two feed stores and a hardware store, she was becoming discouraged. Some shop owners had been downright nasty, implying that her mixed blood made her unemployable.

She had no better luck with the shops on the opposite side of the street. Most shop owners looked at her as if she were something dirty. By late afternoon the only businesses Dawn hadn't visited were the saloons and dance halls.

Dawn's rumbling stomach told her she hadn't eaten since breakfast, so she entered one of the restaurants. She was met at the door by a waitress who looked her up and down and said they didn't serve Indians. Rather than cause a scene, Dawn left. To appease her hunger, she bought an apple from the grocer and munched on it as she considered her options. By now she had grown desperate. She knew she could always return to the MacTavishes but wasn't ready yet to admit defeat. She didn't want to spend her life dependent upon the generosity of others.

The thought of becoming a burden to the MacTavishes drove her to do something she wouldn't have considered under normal circumstances. She ducked into the nearest saloon and asked for work. Cully Porter, the owner of the Watering Hole, looked Dawn up and down, liked what he saw and hired her on the spot.

"What are my duties, Mr. Porter?" Dawn asked, grateful to have found honest work.

Cully Porter gave Dawn his most affable smile. "Serving my customers according to their needs," he said with sly innuendo. "Men are drawn to women with pretty faces. Flirt, encourage them to buy drinks, and join them if they ask."

Dawn blanched. "I don't drink."

Cully laughed. "Don't worry. The girls are

317

served watered-down drinks. What's your name, honey?"

"Dawn. Dawn Webster," she said without thinking. It seemed logical to use Cole's last name since she couldn't bring herself to use Billy Cobb's name. And using her father's last name was equally repugnant to her.

"Do you have a man, Dawn?"

"A man?" Dawn was immediately leery. "I'm unmarried, if that's what you mean." She wasn't sure she understood his line of questioning.

"You have no protector?" His smile was almost predatory.

She still didn't understand. "My parents are dead. I'm on my own. I'm grateful for the job. I'll not disappoint you. Can you tell me where I might rent a room?"

He gave her a sly smile. "I'm sure you won't disappoint me. As for a room, didn't I tell you a room comes with the job? My girls find it convenient to live close to their work. In addition to room and board, you'll be paid a small salary." His eyes lingered on her breasts. "But I predict you'll make enough from tips and . . . overtime to compensate."

Dawn was too excited about finding a job that included room and board to dwell on the meaning of Cully Porter's cryptic words.

Chapter Seventeen

Cole left the train at Cheyenne. He'd had a long time to think during the lonely trip, and the longer he pondered, the more confused he became concerning Dawn. No other woman, including Morning Mist, made him feel as Dawn did. And he wasn't sure he liked that. He'd lived with memories of his lost love for so long that discarding them now seemed almost sinful.

After collecting Warrior from the stock car, Cole found the nearest Western Union and sent a telegram to his office. Because of his unsettled future, he had decided to resign his job. He'd already been gone longer than he'd expected, and his employer deserved to know his plans. And honestly, he had no idea when if ever he'd return to his former line of work. He was seriously considering Tanner's offer to work at the mill upon his return to

Oregon City, if . . . when he returned. His decision depended solely upon the strength of his feelings for Dawn.

Cole heard some distressing news in Cheyenne. The Sioux had been given no time to celebrate their victory at the Little Big Horn. In July a thousand northern Cheyenne, on their way to join the great Sioux leader Crazy Horse in Powder River country, were beaten back by Colonel Wesley Merritt's Fifth Cavalry at War Bonnet Creek. The defeated Cheyenne had turned back to the Red Cloud Agency.

On September 6, General Crook attacked a Sioux village near Slim Buttes, forcing the surrender of Chief American Horse. Shortly afterward, weapons and ponies were confiscated from tribes residing at all agencies. The final humiliation came when the Sioux were forced to give up the sacred Black Hills and all hunting rights outside the redefined reservation.

Cole wondered whether Running Elk had found sanctuary in Powder River country or had been forced to return to the crowded Red Cloud Agency. A week of hard riding should put him in Powder River country. Ten days if the weather turned nasty. The thought of Running Elk without weapons with which to hunt and no ponies to ride was disheartening. Indians took great pride in their ponies and hunting skills. Without them they would be reduced to begging the government for sustenance. The government had the Indians exactly where it wanted them, Cole thought bitterly.

The days were growing colder. Cole wakened most mornings to find the frozen ground glazed with frost. To ward off the biting cold, he wore a full set of buckskins and fur-lined moccasins, tossing a buffalo robe over his shoulders for extra warmth when needed.

The first Indians Cole encountered were a pitiful sight. He spoke with their chief, Crazy Dog, and learned that they were fleeing north to Canada. Cole was saddened to learn that just days before a column led by Colonel Miles had tracked down a defiant Sitting Bull and his Sioux followers at Cedar Creek in Montana Territory. When Sitting Bull refused to return to the reservation, the column attacked. Two thousand Sioux surrendered after a two-day battle, but Sitting Bull and a few followers escaped to Canada. Crazy Dog told Cole that those chiefs who hadn't been accounted for by the army were heading for Canada, just as he was.

Cole asked about Running Elk and was told that the chief hadn't taken his people to the reservation, that he was still hiding in Powder River country, or possibly already on his way to Canada. Cole thanked Crazy Dog and continued on his way. He hoped he wouldn't have to chase Running Elk all the way to Canada, but he would if he had to.

A week after his encounter with Crazy Dog, Cole entered Powder River country. It was late October by his reckoning and the first snow had already fallen. His supplies were dangerously low, and he had to take precious time from his journey to hunt fresh game. Cole still hadn't found Running Elk when he ran into an army patrol. Cole made up a story about being a trapper, which Lieutenant

Conrad believed. Conrad told Cole that the Army had launched a winter campaign to bring the remaining defiant Indians to heel. His patrol was on the trail of Chief Sitting Bull, one of the greatest warriors of the northern plains, and any other dissidents they might encounter.

The knowledge that the army was hot on Running Elk's trail spurred Cole on. If he didn't find Running Elk soon, the army would. Fortunately, Cole had an edge on the army. He knew all the places in Powder River country where Running Elk might hide. Some were so remote and secluded that Cole was certain that only an expert tracker could find them.

Two days later Cole stumbled upon Running Elk's camp. Despite the near blizzard raging around them, the entire village was a beehive of activity. Preparations were in progress for a long journey, and Cole could only assume they were preparing for a trek to Canada.

Cole was challenged as he rode into the narrow valley nestled between two hills. Once he identified himself, he was allowed passage into the camp. His name was passed from person to person, until it reached Running Elk. The chieftain came out of his lodge to greet him.

"You come at a bad time, brother," Running Elk said, frowning. He appeared wan and troubled. "Our people are being hunted like animals. The army wishes to deprive us of our weapons and ponies and to force us onto government lands where we must depend upon them to provide our meat and blankets. The reservations are too crowded to support so many. People are sickening and dying in increasing numbers."

"I feel your pain," Cole said. "I spoke with Crazy Dog a few days ago. He is taking his people to Canada. Is that your plan?"

Running Elk shivered as a chill wind lifted the edges of his robe. "Come inside my lodge. First we will share a pipe, and then I will speak of our plans."

Cole followed Running Elk inside the tipi. He spoke briefly to Spring Rain and Sun In The Face before settling down beside his friend.

"What brings you to Powder River country?" Running Elk asked curiously. "Where is your woman?"

"I was concerned about the People," Cole said. "Were many killed at the Little Big Horn?"

"Our losses were surprisingly small. I told my warriors that it was a good day to die as I led them into battle. The bluecoats came on us like a thunderbolt. We retreated to give our warriors time to group together, then we charged. The White warriors dismounted, holding their horses' reins with one arm while firing. Their horses were so frightened that they pulled them all around. A great many of their shots went up in the air. It was a good fight. The White warriors were brave, but we were braver and stronger."

"Reprisals have been swift and bloody, just as I predicted. Many of the great chiefs are already in custody. Never again will their power be as great as it once was. I fear for you, Running Elk."

"Do not fear, my friend. I will die as I have lived . . . with honor and courage. We cannot survive without weapons or ponies; that is why I am taking my people to Canada. Even as we speak, preparations are in progress for our departure."

"Winter is already upon us. The journey will not be without difficulties."

Running Elk nodded gravely. "I am aware of that. The council has taken everything into consideration and decided that we must make the journey. Even if we die, an honorable death is preferable to being trampled into compliance by White men. What of you, my friend? I sense that your marriage isn't all I had hoped it would be."

"If it's not, it's entirely my fault. I'm not yet ready to accept another woman in Morning Mist's place. I left Dawn with my sister. I'm not certain when I'll return. I'd hoped to find the answer to my dilemma here."

"You will find nothing here but emptiness and desperation."

"Perhaps I should go on a vision quest."

"A vision quest is not necessary. The answers lie within your heart."

"My heart is too full of Dawn to think clearly. Then, when my mind clears, I feel guilty for harboring such thoughts. Replacing my beloved Morning Mist with another seems sinful."

"Memories cannot keep you warm on cold nights. You have taken Dawn's body and shared her mat."

"We share a physical relationship too pleasurable to accurately describe. When I make love to Dawn I feel as if I've waited for her all my life. She's like an obsession. My need to possess her suffocates me. I had to get away. I needed to find answers that elude me when I'm with Dawn."

"Do you expect to find them here?"

"I hoped I would."

Spring Rain handed Cole a bowl of steaming stew, and he ate distractedly, not even realizing he was chewing and swallowing. When the meal was finished, Running Elk invited Cole to share his lodge with his family. Cole realized it would be an imposition to stay in the already crowded tipi and declined.

"Laughing Brook would be pleased to share her lodge with you," Running Elk said slyly. "You can take her as your second wife, if you so desire. Laughing Brook would not object. I would offer you a lodge of your own, but at present there are none to spare."

Cole did not remark on Running Elk's words as he rose to leave. "How long before you start your journey north?"

"Soon. Each day we remain increases our danger."

"I will leave you to your rest," Cole said. "Sleep well, my friend."

Cole ducked out of the lodge, intending to make his bed in the snow as he'd been doing every night on the trail. He was leading Warrior to the corral nearby when he heard someone hail him. He turned, not surprised to see Laughing Brook approaching. He continued unsaddling Warrior as he waited for her to join him.

"I knew you would return, Shadow Walker. I've been waiting for you. Why is your woman not with you?"

"I left Dawn in Oregon with my sister. I did not

want to subject her to another long journey."

"Your concern is commendable." Her voice held a hint of sarcasm. "Nevertheless, it pleases me that you have returned alone. Come," she said, grasping his hand. "It is cold out here and you need a place to sleep. Will you share my mat tonight?"

Cole started to protest, then changed his mind. Bedding Laughing Brook might be exactly what he needed right now. What better way to test the depth of his feelings for Dawn? Could he experience with any other woman what he'd shared with Dawn?

"Are you sure I am welcome in your lodge?" Cole asked.

"Very sure. Come, the night grows cold and my fire is warm."

Taking up his saddlebags, Cole followed Laughing Brook through the village to her lodge. She ducked inside and he followed. She took his saddlebags and placed them against the wall of the tipi.

"Have you eaten?" Laughing Brook asked. Her sultry smile promised untold delights, and Cole felt himself harden and thicken.

"I shared Running Elk's meal."

Laughing Brook spread out her sleeping mat, then turned to Cole. Her high cheekbones were tinged with color beneath the gold tones of her skin as she gave Cole a seductive smile. Cole's manhood jerked as her little pink tongue flicked out to moisten her generously curved lips. Her eyes glowed darkly with desire as her hands picked at the lacing on Cole's shirt.

"I can do it," Cole said gruffly as he pulled off his shirt.

"Let me help," Laughing Brook whispered as she fumbled with the laces on his trousers. Before she had finished, Cole was throbbing painfully. It had been a long time since he'd had a woman, and he hadn't forgotten how passionate and knowledgeable Laughing Brook was. Her hands lingered on his groin, cupping and stroking, clearly impressed by the length and strength of his sex.

Cole grasped her wrists. "I can finish undressing myself."

Laughing Brook gave him a saucy grin and whipped her tunic over her head in one fluent motion. Her body was lithe and sinuous, more seductive than he remembered. Her skin was a shade darker than Dawn's, and she was voluptuous in ways that Dawn was not. But her breasts and flat nipples were quite ordinary compared to Dawn's magnificent breasts.

Suddenly Cole realized he was thinking about Dawn when he should be concentrating on the woman he had every intention of bedding tonight. When Laughing Brook dropped to the sleeping mat and reached out to him, he hesitated only a moment before joining her.

Boldly Laughing Brook caressed him between his legs. "Your mighty lance is eager to sink into my flesh," she teased. "Come, my warrior"—she opened her legs and spread herself with her fingers—"unleash your weapon."

Glistening pink folds of moist feminine flesh beckoned to Cole. He looked away, suddenly and unaccountably repulsed. She was wet and eager for him; her heavy thighs were bedewed with her honey. The image of Dawn's slim, shapely thighs and tender woman's flesh flashed before his eyes, and disgust at what he was about to do killed his desire. How could he bed another woman when Dawn was the only woman he wanted? Sweet Dawn. Beautiful Dawn. She had known far too much pain in her young life and had somehow risen above it. The heavy weight of guilt rode him relentlessly. It had nothing to do with his past, or with Morning Mist, and everything to do with Dawn and his future.

Suddenly Cole knew what he wanted, what he yearned for. Running Elk had been right. There was no need for a vision quest. The vision dwelled within his heart, in Dawn's smile, and in the love he felt for her, a love he was finally able to accept without guilt or self-recrimination. He was free now, free of ghosts, free to embrace a future with Dawn. Of course he would never forget Morning Mist, nor did he want to. His memories of her were precious. But memories must be relegated to their rightful place in his life. Dawn was his future. Morning Mist was his past. And Laughing Brook was neither.

"Hurry, Shadow Walker," Laughing Brook urged. "It has been too long since I felt your strength inside me."

Abruptly Cole rose to his feet. He wasn't the kind to deliberately hurt a woman, but desire had died inside him as surely as his love for Dawn had been revealed. "I'm sorry, Laughing Brook, but I can't do this."

Her gaze fixed on his sex, still vibrantly alive

and pulsating. She smiled. "You can do this very well. Memory has not deserted me. Come to me." She arched her back, offering him everything she had to give.

Cole reached for his trousers. "I cannot share your mat. I do not wish to be unfaithful to Dawn."

Laughing Brook frowned. "White men have strange ways. I will become your second wife."

"I am not allowed two wives."

"Do not return to your White world, Shadow Walker. Come north with us. You are familiar with our ways; it will be no hardship for you."

"Though I have lived with your people many years, I do not truly belong. I will help Running Elk prepare for the journey north, then I will return to Oregon . . . to Dawn."

Cole was fully dressed now. He apologized to Laughing Brook one last time before he bent to retrieve his saddlebags.

"Wait! Where are you going? You will freeze before morning if you sleep outside in the snow and cold. I envy Dawn your love and loyalty but I do not wish your death. Share my lodge as a friend."

Cole hesitated. Her words seemed sincere, and it was freezing outside. Snow was piling up fast. "Very well. I appreciate your offer. Just understand that friendship is all I'm willing to share with you."

"I understand," Laughing Brook said as she pulled on her tunic. "We will share my mat for warmth."

"I will sleep apart from you. Give me a blanket if you have one to spare."

Laughing Brook had still harbored hopes that

329

Cole would make love to her, but now she recognized the finality of his words. With visible regret, she tossed him the blanket he'd asked for. "Sleep well, Shadow Walker."

Snow continued to fall the following day. The only comfort Cole gained from it was the sure knowledge that the snow would gain Running Elk precious time while it delayed the army's pursuit of him and his people. Mounting snowfall presented a new problem to Cole. If he didn't leave immediately he wouldn't get out of the mountains before spring. Fortunately, he had learned what he had traveled all this way to find out. Running Elk was safe. Soon he would be in Canada, where the army could no longer follow. He could live there in peace, in full possession of his weapons and ponies.

Two days later Cole bid Running Elk a sad farewell. In his heart he knew it would be the last time he would ever see his friend. The tribe was ready to begin its dangerous trek north to Canada. Cole was eager to return to Dawn now, and prayed she would forgive him for acting like a damn fool. Ashley had pegged him right. He'd been existing on memories far too long. It was time he put the past behind him where it belonged. He longed to return to Dawn, a flesh-and-blood woman he'd come to love more than his own life.

Please God, don't let it be too late.

Dawn's work at the Watering Hole was exhausting. She was forever ducking men's groping hands while trying to maintain a modicum of dignity.

She was but one of several bar girls who worked for Cully Porter, none of whom had offered her more than token friendship. Dawn tried to keep an open mind when she saw the other women take men upstairs, but it was difficult for her to imagine having a different man every night. The only man she wanted was Cole, and he didn't love her.

Dawn had worked at the Watering Hole a full month before Cully Porter hinted that she should consider entertaining men upstairs in her room after working hours. Mouth agape, Dawn stared at him as if he'd lost his mind.

"Why would I do that?"

Porter gave her a disgusted look. "All the girls do. It's part of their benefits. And I get half their earnings, in case you're thinking of keeping it all for yourself." When Dawn looked shocked, he said casually, "I'm sure I mentioned that it's part of your job. So far I've not made a damn cent off you. Why do you think I provide my girls with rooms?"

Dawn swallowed convulsively. "You never said a word about . . . about that to me."

"I assumed you knew what I was talking about when I said you'd earn extra money on the side. Servicing customers is part of the job. You're neither blind nor innocent. You've seen Milly and the other girls take men upstairs after working hours."

"All I agreed to do was sit and talk to the customers and urge them to buy drinks. I'm not a whore," Dawn all but shouted.

Milly sauntered over from her position at the bar, having overheard the conversation. "Do you think you're better than the rest of us?" she asked harshly. "Look at you! You're half savage. I bet you don't even know who your pa was."

"I'm sorry, I didn't mean to insult you. But I've never done anything like that in my life and I'm not going to start now. I'll pack my belongings and leave first thing in the morning."

"Now hold on," Porter said. "My customers like you. They would miss you if you left. Stick around awhile, maybe you'll change your mind. One day some man will appeal to you." Suddenly his eyes narrowed. "Hey, wait a damn minute. You're not a virgin, are you?" Dawn bit her lip and looked away.

Suddenly Porter laughed. "I thought not. You wouldn't be working here if you were. You're just holding out for bigger stakes. Very well, I'll play your game. But if you don't start earning your keep soon, I'll choose for you. You've got to start sometime."

Dawn was speechless long after Porter walked away. She didn't realize that Milly had remained until she spoke.

"Wise up, Dawn. You're no innocent. Besides being a half-breed, you're too skinny for most men's tastes. We all work for Cully and we all earn more on our backs than we earn in wages. You're damn lucky he's giving you a little leeway to be choosy. But mark my words, one day he'll grow impatient and force you to take a man to your bed."

Dawn was too shocked to think, let alone reply. Cully couldn't do that, could he? During the weeks she'd worked at the Watering Hole she'd made a point of acting detached and unavailable. Most of the men who frequented the saloon were rough lumberjacks looking for a good time, and she wasn't about to make herself available to them.

What Dawn didn't realize was that her natural distrust of men and cool detachment gave her an air of mystery that drew Cully's customers to her like moths to a flame. They vied for her attention, placing bets on who would be the first to bed the sultry half-breed.

All the bar girls had Sundays off. After much soul-searching, Dawn decided against visiting Ashley and Tanner on her free day. She had withheld her visits all these weeks because she'd been too ashamed to reveal her place of employment, even though she was putting in an honest day's work for honest pay. She couldn't bear having Cole's family think badly of her, so she remained in her room on her day off.

As the weeks passed, Dawn began to despise her job. The customers were getting harder to handle and becoming bolder. Smiling at those same men whose hands she had to slap away from various parts of her body became a disagreeable chore. Cully Porter watched her like a hawk, his eyes narrowed in disapproval when she refused to bed men offering good money for her body.

After giving the situation careful thought, Dawn decided it was time to quit her job and live off her savings until something more respectable came along. Something happened that night to change her mind. Tanner MacTavish entered the Watering Hole with a man Dawn recognized immediately. Sandy Johnson! What was Sandy Johnson doing in Oregon? she wondered. She watched in trepidation as they seated themselves at an empty table and continued their conversation. Dawn wanted to turn and flee as fast as her legs would carry her. She dreaded being seen in her present circumstances by two people close to Cole.

As luck would have it, Porter appeared at Dawn's elbow just at that moment, making flight impossible.

"Now there's two likely looking gents," Porter said slyly. "Tanner MacTavish owns the largest logging operation in these parts." He gave her an ungentle shove. "Go on, sit with them. Keep them buying drinks."

"No, I can't. They're . . ."

Her words stuttered to a halt as Porter grasped her arm and pulled her along to Tanner's table. "You gents look lonely," Porter said, smiling obsequiously. "Meet Dawn, she'll take care of all your needs. Whatever takes your fancy, gents, Dawn will see that you get it. In any way you wish," he added with a wink. Before he left, he whispered in Dawn's ear, "Give them whatever they want, understand?"

Acute embarrassment pinkened Dawn's cheeks. What would Tanner and Sandy think of her? She already knew the answer to that question. They would think she was a paid whore.

Tanner found his tongue first. His fierce frown told her he was not pleased to find her here. "What is this all about, Dawn? Do you work in this place? Why haven't you been out to see us? Ashley has been worried sick about you."

"I'm sorry. I meant to visit but never got around to it." She licked her suddenly dry lips. "This is not what it appears. I work here, but not as . . . it's not what you think. I'm not a whore!" she blurted out.

"I never said you were," Tanner said, unamused. "I'll speak with Porter. You're coming home with me tonight. You know damn well Cole wouldn't be pleased with your choice of employment."

Dawn's eyes blazed with anger. "Cole left me! Had he cared about me he would have taken me with him. I won't live on your charity. This might not be the most respectable work in town, but it was all that was available to me."

Dawn looked away, refusing to meet Tanner's gaze. By doing so she looked straight into Sandy Johnson's startled eyes. His expression held pity. Pity she neither wanted or needed.

"Hello, Dawn, it's nice to see you again."

"I didn't mean to ignore you, Sandy. What are you doing in Oregon? Did you come to see Cole? I suppose Tanner has already told you he left over four weeks ago."

"It just didn't seem right working without Cole," Sandy explained. "He's been my partner ever since he joined the Pinkertons. When I heard about his resignation I decided to join him and try my luck in Oregon."

"Cole resigned his job?" Dawn asked with surprise. "I didn't know that. Cole rarely confided in me."

"I've offered Sandy a job and he's accepted," Tanner said. "He's staying in one of the cabins at the mill. He can decide if he wants to make it permanent when Cole returns."

"I hope you're prepared for a long wait," Dawn said bitterly. "It's unlikely Cole will return any time soon."

"I disagree with you," Sandy said with conviction. "I think Cole has too much to lose by not returning." His steady gaze held hers, making Dawn want to believe. "I think he'd be disturbed to find you working in a place like this. Tanner is right. You should return home with him."

"I'm perfectly capable of taking care of myself," Dawn declared hotly. Why must every man she met try to arrange her life?

"Is Dawn taking care of you, gents?" Porter asked as he paused beside their table. He glared at Dawn. "You haven't ordered drinks yet. What will it be?"

Both Tanner and Sandy ordered whiskey neat.

"Are either of you gents going to buy a drink for the lady?"

Tanner shot Dawn a look that spoke volumes about his displeasure.

"Give the lady what she wants," Sandy said. Porter left without taking Dawn's order, well aware of what his bar girls were allowed to order and what they'd get.

"I don't feel comfortable leaving you here," Tanner said, glowering darkly.

"It's my choice, Tanner." Though Dawn had been planning to leave until Tanner arrived, now sheer stubbornness made her change her mind. It was too much. No man was going to order her around.

Just then a lumberjack hailed Dawn from the next table. He was obviously drunk. Porter was standing next to him, egging him on. "Hey, Dawn, you free tonight? I've got an itch only you can scratch, if ya ain't already promised to those gents you're flirtin' with."

"Find another woman, Tallman," Tanner growled in a voice that left no room for compromise.

Tallman blinked once, then blinked again. He recognized his boss and hastily retreated. "Sorry, Mr. MacTavish," he muttered. "Didn't mean to horn in on your territory."

Tanner had had enough. He'd brought Sandy to the Watering Hole for a quiet drink after his business in town was concluded and had found more than he'd bargained for. He rose abruptly, slapped money down on the table and grasped Dawn's arm. "Let's get the hell out of here. I'll send for your belongings tomorrow."

"Let me go, Tanner. I'm not going anywhere with you. I'm content with my work. I have a decent room and food in my stomach."

"Let her go, Tanner," Sandy said quietly. "Dawn is old enough to know what she wants."

"Thank you, Sandy," Dawn said, pulling out of Tanner's grasp. "Tell Ashley I'm sorry I haven't visited. I . . . I've been very busy."

"Yeah, I imagine you have," Tanner said succinctly. Always the hothead, Tanner had jumped to the wrong conclusion about Dawn's employment. "What are you going to tell Cole when he returns?"

"The truth, *if* he ever comes back." Turning abruptly, she flounced away.

"She's changed," Tanner said sadly. "I'm positive Cole loves her. Ashley thinks he'll return when

337

he realizes what he has lost. I'd hate to be in Dawn's shoes when Cole returns."

"If everything you've told me about Cole and Dawn is true, Dawn has a right to be bitter."

"Has she the right to sell her body?"

"We don't know that she is. Tell you what. You have a mill to run, so I'll keep an eye on Dawn for Cole. Cole is my best friend. He's saved my skin countless times. The least I can do is watch out for his woman. You *are* sure he'll return, aren't you?"

"Ashley believes Cole loves Dawn. She knows her twin better than he knows himself. He'll return. I'd stake my life on it."

From the corner of her eye, Dawn watched Tanner and Sandy leave the Watering Hole. She knew she'd angered Tanner, but he had no right to dictate to her. It hurt to think that he believed she entertained men in her room. He had tried her and found her guilty of sins she hadn't committed. All men were alike, she fumed. She was better off trusting no one. Not even Cole's brother-in-law.

Chapter Eighteen

Sandy Johnson appeared at the Watering Hole the following night. And the night after that. And all the following nights. It soon became evident that the sandy-haired man with a dangerous glint in his eye had a special interest in Dawn. He watched her like a hawk, glaring daggers at any man who dared to lay a hand on her. Cully Porter saw what was happening and assumed that Dawn had finally chosen a man to take to her bed.

"Tonight had better be the night you take that Johnson fellow upstairs," Porter said to Dawn when Sandy entered the Watering Hole at his usual time. "He's not going to wait forever."

Sandy spotted Dawn across the room talking to Porter and headed in their direction. He knew what was expected of him, so he asked, "Can I buy you a drink, Dawn?"

Connie Mason

Porter's eyes narrowed. "You're monopolizing Dawn's time, Johnson. There are others hankering for her company. You're fortunate that Dawn favors you. No one else has paid for her favors tonight. If you can come up with five dollars, she is yours for a couple of hours. The price for all night is twenty dollars."

Dawn's cheeks flamed, and she prayed for the floor to open up and swallow her. Of course it didn't. To her acute embarrassment, Sandy reached into his pocket, pulled out a twenty-dollar gold piece and dropped it down Dawn's bodice. Then he took her hand and pulled her over to a table. Porter followed.

"She's not yours until after working hours," he said. "And no rough stuff. I don't like my girls coming to work the next day with bruises. I'll send over your usual drinks."

Dawn was beyond speech. The color had drained from her face, leaving her deathly pale. Sandy noted her paleness and asked, "Are you all right, Dawn?"

Dawn's head spun dizzily as bile rose up in her throat. She swallowed convulsively. It was the same kind of sickness she'd experienced too often of late. "You must think . . . that is . . . I'm not . . ."

"I don't think anything, Dawn."

"You paid for my . . . my . . ." She couldn't say it. "I've never taken a man to my room. Cully told me I had to if I wanted to keep my job, but I kept stalling for time."

Sandy gave her a sympathetic look. "I never believed you were working as a whore. I've hung around here long enough to know what the men are saying."

Dawn gave him a puzzled look. "What are they saying?"

He smiled. "They call you the ice maiden. They're placing bets on who will be the first to thaw you. I reckon that's me. How late do you usually work?"

Dawn was too startled to speak. She made a strangled sound deep in her throat before finally finding her voice. "You don't expect me to . . . I thought you were Cole's friend."

"Calm down, Dawn. I reckon I put it badly. I didn't pay for the use of your body, if that's what you're thinking. I'm doing this for Cole. If I buy your time, Porter will stop badgering you. I'll go upstairs with you and stay a decent amount of time. If this job is so all-fired important to you, I reckon I can help you keep it."

"You'd do that for me? When we met I got the impression you didn't care much for me."

"I was afraid you'd take advantage of Cole's good heart. But after Tanner explained the situation to me, I changed my mind about you. Cole didn't do right by you. The least I can do is keep you safe for him until he returns."

"You have more faith in Cole than I do," Dawn said with a bitterness that surprised Sandy. "He's not coming back."

"That remains to be seen. Go ahead and circulate. You have to keep your boss happy. I'll be here at closing time."

Dawn felt more at ease that night than any night since taking the job as a bar girl. Sandy's solid presence comforted her. His silent vigil kept the men's hands where they belonged and their lewd suggestions at a minimum. Even Cully seemed content, knowing that Dawn was finally earning him extra money.

Dawn couldn't wait for closing time. She was more exhausted than ever tonight and couldn't fathom why. She'd been much less on edge now that Cully wasn't plaguing her to sell her body. She glanced across the room where Sandy sat, waiting patiently. Most of the girls had already disappeared above stairs with their customers, and no one but Dawn, Sandy and Cully remained in the saloon.

Sandy must have realized that Porter was waiting for him to claim his prize, for he uncoiled his long frame from the chair and took Dawn's arm. "Are you ready?"

"She's ready," Cully said, daring Dawn to disagree. "You can leave by the back stairs when you're finished. Remember what I said about leaving bruises."

"I don't abuse women," Sandy said, eying him coolly. "Come on, Dawn, show me your room."

Once the bedroom door closed behind them, Dawn grew nervous. She really didn't know Sandy well enough to trust him. The only man she'd ever trusted was Cole.

"Relax, Dawn, I'm not going to hurt you. I'll just stay long enough to satisfy Porter. Sit down, you look beat, honey."

Somewhat more at ease, Dawn perched gingerly on the edge of the bed. "I am tired. I haven't been feeling well lately."

Sandy immediately grew concerned. "Should I find a doctor?"

"No, it's probably just a minor upset from something I ate. I'm sure it will pass."

Sandy looked at her strangely. "Are you sure?"

"Of course, what else could it be?"

"I suppose you're right." They talked of trivial things for a while longer, and then Sandy said, "Well, I reckon it's safe to leave now. Get some rest, honey. I'll see you tomorrow."

"Sandy . . . thank you. You didn't have to do this."

He stared at her, his blue eyes strangely disturbed. "I do have to do this. Now more than ever."

After that cryptic remark, he left. But he was back the following night, escorting her upstairs after the saloon closed its doors. The same pattern continued for two weeks. Dawn felt guilty about draining Sandy's finances and insisted on returning the part of the money Cully didn't claim.

Dawn's health didn't improve. Dizziness and nausea plagued her during the early part of the day, and her appetite seemed to have deserted her. She could ill afford to lose weight. Cully had complained about her slimness on more than one occasion.

That night Sandy was late. A few of the customers decided he had tired of Dawn and vied among themselves for the right to buy her favors. A fight broke out. Within minutes the altercation turned into a melee of major proportions, with every man and a few of the girls joining in. Dawn fought her way to the staircase, watching in trepidation as the fighting grew rowdier. Suddenly the brawling crowd overwhelmed her and she swayed on her feet, overcome by dizziness.

Sandy entered the Watering Hole slightly out of breath. He was late due to a problem at the mill, and he feared that Porter's customers might have misread his tardiness. He'd become somewhat of a fixture at the Watering Hole these days, and everyone was aware that Dawn favored him above others. He pushed through the swinging doors and walked into bedlam. He searched the room for Dawn and spied her trying to make her way to the staircase. Relief slammed through him when she appeared to be unharmed. Suddenly she began to sway dizzily and his heart leaped into his mouth. Using his considerable strength, he pushed, shoved and dodged fists until he reached her side.

It wasn't a moment too soon. Dawn began a slow spiral to the ground just as Sandy reached her. He scooped her up and took the stairs two at a time. By the time he reached her room, she was coming out of her swoon.

"What happened?"

"You fainted. I reached you in the nick of time." He placed her carefully on the bed and stood back, staring at her. "Isn't it time you told me the truth?"

"The truth? About what?"

"All the signs are there. You're carrying a child. Is it Cole's?"

Dawn's eyes blazed with anger. Did he think she was capable of giving her body to anyone but Cole?

Sandy recognized the source of her rage, but it was a question he'd felt compelled to ask. "I'm sorry, Dawn. I have to know for Cole's sake."

"Cole was my first and only man. I was never Billy Cobb's wife in the true sense."

Somewhat embarrassed to be privy to such personal information, Sandy looked away, although he already knew that Cole had taken Dawn's virginity. Abruptly he turned back to her. "Do you love Cole?"

Dawn sighed, recalling their volatile parting. "I did at one time."

"You still do."

"I'm not sure anymore. Cole doesn't deserve my love."

"What are you going to do about the babe? How far along are you?"

Dawn recalled the times Cole hadn't withdrawn from her during their lovemaking. Several came to mind. The most recent being the day he'd left. But she could have conceived before that. She thought back, shocked at how long it had been since her last cycle. If she missed another monthly cycle, it would be her third, which meant she must be three months into her pregnancy. She should have realized she was pregnant before now, but she'd been too miserable and unhappy to recognize what was taking place inside her own body.

"I can't be sure. Two or three months." Her chin came up. "Don't worry, I can take care of myself."

"Not while you're working at the Watering Hole. You have to quit now, whether you want to or not. I'll do my damndest to find Cole for you."

"No!" Dawn shot back. "Don't you dare. Cole doesn't want me. He's never wanted me. I'll provide for myself and my babe."

"Cole has a right to know. I'll consult with Ashley, she'll—"

"Don't you dare! I'll leave town if you tell anyone. In fact, leaving town is probably best for everyone. Ashley will insist that I live with her and Tanner once she learns I'm carrying Cole's child. I don't want their pity."

"Be reasonable, honey. Cole will be returning soon. Don't decide anything without consulting him."

"What makes you so certain Cole will return? He's probably decided to join Running Elk. He's accustomed to Indian ways. He even has a woman waiting for him there."

Sandy frowned. He was an old-fashioned man with old-fashioned values. A woman with child needed a man to protect her. She shouldn't be doing the type of work that demanded more of her than she was willing to give. Working at the Watering Hole had all but destroyed Dawn's reputation even if she wasn't actually a whore.

Once Sandy made up his mind, nothing would change it. He was as immovable as a mountain, dependable and loyal. "Pack your things, you're coming home with me."

"What! I'll do no such thing. I can't live with you."

"You can and you will. I'll marry you myself if I have to." His words shocked him, but even as he said them he knew he'd meant them. Cole had used Dawn and deserted her. He should have known she could be carrying his child. If Cole didn't return soon to claim his woman, Sandy would claim her himself and raise Cole's child.

"Dawn, listen to me. I'd never hurt you. I can't leave you without protection, it goes against everything I believe in. You've refused to seek refuge with the MacTavishes, so I'm offering another alternative."

"People will talk."

Sandy let out a string of curses. "And they won't talk about you if you remain here and grow large with child? Use your head, honey. I'm not a threat to you. Can you say the same for Cully Porter? Hell, I'll marry you."

Dawn stared at him. "You'd do that for me?"

"Not just for you, but for Cole. I'll raise his child to the best of my ability."

"I could never be a real wife to you, Sandy, I'm sorry."

"Did I ask you to be?"

Dawn's hands clasped and unclasped in her lap, her nerves stretched taut. "I can't live with you. I'll remain here a while longer, until I reach a decision about my future. Perhaps I won't carry this child to term. I've already lost a child of Cole's. I appreciate all you've done for me, but it's too much to ask of any man. You're a good person, Sandy Johnson."

"You lost one child already?" Sandy asked, aghast. His face hardened. "That does it! You're too fragile to live on your own. I'll give you a week or two to resign yourself to our marriage, then I'm going to announce our engagement."

"Sandy, I can't—"

"No more talk, Dawn. Get some rest. I'll see you tomorrow."

"Wait! Promise you won't tell Ashley or Tanner

about the baby. I want to see a doctor first to confirm my condition."

"Very well, if that's what you want. But sooner or later they'll know you're carrying Cole's child."

After Sandy left, Dawn lay in bed staring at the ceiling, her head in a muddle. Common sense told her that Cole was never coming back. How could she support herself and a child on her meager savings? She could always take the money Cole had offered, but she was too angry at him to accept his charity. She knew the MacTavishes would take her in, but she didn't want to become a burden to Cole's family.

Her thoughts shifted to Sandy Johnson. Why was he taking his loyalty to Cole beyond friendship? Trusting men still came hard for Dawn. She couldn't help thinking that Sandy's proposal masked an ulterior motive. It seemed unlikely that he would give up his freedom without asking for some kind of reward.

During the following week, Dawn discreetly visited a doctor. After a brief examination he confirmed her pregnancy. She was still slim as a willow, so it seemed incredible to Dawn that she was three months along. Except for extremely tender breasts, her body hadn't changed significantly. Her clothing still fit reasonably well, and no one suspected her condition.

While Dawn dangled on the horns of her dilemma, Sandy became convinced that Cole intended to make his absence a permanent one. Taking matters into his own hands, he told Ashley and Tanner that he and Dawn were going to marry. The MacTavishes were shocked at first, still convinced that Cole would come to his senses and return soon. Then Sandy broke his promise to Dawn and told them she was expecting Cole's child. In view of the circumstances, they agreed that Dawn and Sandy should marry.

Ashley and Tanner had come to appreciate Sandy's good qualities. Of course, they would rather raise Cole's child themselves, but if Dawn felt uncomfortable moving in with them, marrying Sandy was the next-best solution. Ashley proclaimed that if she ever saw Cole again she'd have a hard time forgiving him.

The wedding was set to take place a week later. When Sandy told Dawn what he had done, she was furious. But once she calmed down, she realized her choices were limited. What kind of life could a half-breed give an illegitimate child?

Torrential rains inundated the Willamette Valley during the following week. The first day or two, business was conducted as usual at the Watering Hole. But as the rains continued it became more difficult for lumberjacks to cross the swollen creeks. When Sandy failed to show up two nights in a row, Dawn assumed it was due to the weather.

Cully Porter was clearly disgruntled as he eyed the thin crowd drinking and gambling. Drenching rains were bad for business, and he looked for a way to liven things up. From the corner of his eye he spied Dawn. A slow smile stretched his lips. Her protector had been conspicuously absent the last couple of days, and an easy way to earn some extra cash and create a little excitement occurred to him.

"Let's liven things up, gents," he announced in a loud voice. "Most of you have been waiting for a chance to thaw the ice maiden, and I'm going to make that possible for one of you lucky bastards. I propose an auction. The haughty half-breed goes to the highest bidder. The winner can rut with her until dawn, if he has the energy," he said crudely. "Line up, gents, who's going to make the first bid?"

"I will!" called out a muscular lumberjack with arms the size of small oak trees.

Dawn had paid scant heed to Porter's announcement until she heard him mention her name. Her head swung around and her attention sharpened. When she realized what was happening, she took flight. Porter's arm came around her before she made it to the staircase.

"Ten dollars!" the muscular lumberjack shouted.

"You can't do this!" Dawn protested. "I'm not your property to sell. Let me go!"

Porter grinned, his arm tightening around her waist as he swung her around to face the men participating in the entertainment. "Come on, gents. Ten dollars won't even buy a peek at the ice maiden's titties." He cupped her breasts suggestively. Dawn screeched and kicked, to no avail.

"Twenty-five dollars," another man shouted.

From there the bidding progressed rapidly. When it reached seventy-five dollars, some dropped out. But a resolute few remained in the bidding, determined to win the ice maiden.

* * *

Hunched over his horse, Cole was drenched to the skin and freezing cold. Rain fell in solid sheets, making his progress slow and painful. He shrugged his discomfort aside when he pictured Dawn, eagerly awaiting his return. He guided Warrior down the muddy streets of Oregon City, his soaked buckskins clinging to him like a second skin and his hat so saturated with water it had lost its shape long ago. The journey from Powder River country had been long and arduous, but Cole had been spurred by his eagerness to reach Oregon City and Dawn.

He was chilled to the bone and shivering uncontrollably. The cheery light shining through the front window of the Watering Hole lured him, beckoned him, compelled him. He pulled on Warrior's reins. The horse obediently halted, waiting for his master's direction. Some sixth sense drew Cole to the saloon even though common sense directed him to continue on. Common sense lost as Cole reined Warrior toward the saloon. A bolstering whiskey was just what he needed to thaw his frozen bones, he decided as he slid from the saddle and looped Warrior's reins over the hitching post.

Cole pushed through the swinging doors, pausing to get his bearings. What he saw made the blood freeze in his veins. His gaze flew to Dawn, held captive by a man dressed in fancy clothes. Every male inside the saloon was crowded around the pair. Even the poker tables were deserted. The noise was deafening as men shouted out bids, each one higher than the one before. When it dawned on Cole what was happening, the roar in his ears was no less deafening than the shouts of the men calling out bids. The last bid he'd heard was one hundred dollars, and he knew without being told that Dawn was the prize. The thought that he had driven Dawn to sell herself sent a knife lancing through his heart.

A satisfied grin curled Porter's lips as the bidding went to one hundred dollars. This night wasn't going to be as disastrous as he'd thought when he first saw the thin crowd. After the last bid a hush fell over the crowd. Porter opened his mouth to declare the bidding over when a man who had just entered shoved through the crowd.

"Two hundred dollars." Cole's voice had a hard edge to it, as if daring anyone to top his bid. No one did. The man who had bid one hundred dollars looked as if he wanted to tear Cole apart, but when he looked into Cole's glittering green eyes he changed his mind. He drifted away with the rest of the unlucky bidders.

"Did I just hear you bid two hundred dollars, mister?" Porter asked. He hadn't anticipated such good fortune.

"I did."

"Show me the color of your money."

Dawn had been rendered speechless the moment she spied Cole pushing his way through the crowd of men bidding for her favors. She'd thought she'd seen the last of him months ago. Now here he was, coolly bidding for her favors as if she were a common whore. She watched in dismay as Cole counted out the money and shoved it at Porter.

"She's all yours, stranger. I envy you the job of

thawing her out. The only man she's cottoned to is that Johnson fellow."

Cole's glittering green gaze rested on Dawn. Dark currents swirled beneath the fiery centers of his eyes as he searched her face. It didn't take a mind-reader to know what he was thinking. Gathering her courage, Dawn boldly returned his perusal. Who did he think he was? He had no right to judge and condemn her. Her chin lifted defiantly.

"I'm not going anywhere with this man."

Cole smiled. A long, slow smile that contradicted her words. "Oh, yes, you are."

Swinging her into his arms, he started up the stairs. "Which room?" he called over his shoulder.

"Second door on the left," Porter replied as he counted the money Cole had thrust at him. "She's yours for the rest of the night. No bruises or rough stuff," he yelled after them. "And no marks where they'll show."

"Put me down, damn you!"

Cole gave her a scathing glance but said nothing. His face was set in harsh lines, his eyes cold and furious. He kicked the door to her room open and slammed it shut after he entered. Then he dumped her unceremoniously on the bed.

Dawn stared up at him, her face mutinous. "You lost the right to dictate my life when you deserted me."

"Which one of those bidders downstairs would you prefer to bed?"

"None of them! That auction wasn't my idea."

"That fancy man downstairs said you worked here."

"That's right. And don't give me that condemning look. I had to support myself some way. This was the only establishment in town willing to hire me."

He glared at her, his eyes blazing fiercely. "Do you enjoy bedding a different man every night? If I'd known you wanted to take up whoring for a living I would have left you in Dodge City."

Cole's verbal abuse pushed Dawn over the edge. He was leaning toward her, his face inches from hers as he flung his insults. Fisting her hand, Dawn swung at him and was rewarded with a satisfying thud when her fist connected with his jaw. He reared back, turning the air blue with his curses as he rubbed his jaw with the palm of his hand. Dawn's own hand throbbed with pain. The blow might have hurt her more than it hurt him, but it served to cool Cole's temper. Still rubbing his jaw, he sat down on the bed. Dawn scooted as far away from him as possible.

"I'm not going to hurt you. I just want some answers. First, who is this Johnson fellow who bought your favors?"

A bubble of laughter trilled past her lips.

He scowled. "What's so damn funny?"

"You are. Don't you recognize the name of your best friend?"

Cole was shocked into silence. When he found his voice, words literally exploded past his lips. "You're screwing my best friend! What in the hell is Sandy doing in Oregon?"

Outraged, Dawn jerked upright. "Get out of here! Get out now!"

Cole gave her a narrow-eyed smile. "I paid two

hundred dollars for your body, remember. Before you earn your money, I want some answers. I repeat, what is Sandy doing in Oregon?"

"I'm not sure. He said he wanted to try his luck in Oregon. He's working for Tanner."

"Very good. Let's drop that subject for a few minutes. Why did you leave my sister's house? You had my share of the profits from the mill to live on during my absence."

"Was that to be my payoff for services rendered?" Dawn flung at him. "You used me, then discarded me. Your sister is too decent to be saddled with her brother's discarded whore."

A shudder went through Cole. Was that how Dawn thought of herself? Was that why he'd found her selling her body? She'd never been his whore. He had come back from Powder River country to make amends. He was going to make her his wife.

"What's going on between you and Sandy?"

"Sandy is my friend and protector. I . . . I'm going to marry him in a few days."

The words tumbled out before she had time to call them back. She had never actually agreed to marry Sandy, but she probably would have for her child's sake. She didn't want Cole's child to be raised a bastard.

"Like hell you are!" Cole blasted. "Are you sleeping with your 'friend and protector'?"

"That's none of your business."

"I'm making it my business."

"You left me, Cole. You promised me nothing and I asked for nothing. I should have known better than to trust you." What she really meant was that she should have known better than to fall in love with him. "Live in the past, cherish your memories, I don't care what you do. I'm going to marry Sandy."

Something inside Cole snapped. Grasping Dawn's shoulders, he gave her a violent shake. "Are you sleeping with Sandy? You *will* answer me, Dawn."

"No, damn you! No! You're the only one."

A shudder went through Cole. His hands fell to his sides and his chin dropped down to his chest. When he raised his head, his shuttered expression gave away nothing of his feelings. Dawn had no inkling of how hurt and disappointed he'd been on hearing that Dawn was bedding his best friend. At first he hadn't wanted to believe it of her, but now he didn't know what to think.

He gazed down at Dawn, suddenly aware of her waiflike vulnerability. His anger deflated when he realized that he had acted like a bastard in the past. He'd treated Dawn like a possession, afraid to admit his love because of guilt. Unfortunately, he'd come too late to the realization that Morning Mist belonged in that distant part of his brain where all good memories are kept. Dawn was his present and his future. Now that he was finally ready and eager to love Dawn with his whole heart and being, he had lost her.

No, he wouldn't let that happen. He knew Dawn better than he knew himself. She couldn't, wouldn't, take men indiscriminately into her bed.

"What about that auction I walked into tonight?"

"Sandy hadn't shown up for the past couple of

nights due to the flooding. Cully Porter was losing business because of the rain and he wanted to liven the place up. I didn't agree to the auction. I'd never do anything like that."

"Does Cully Porter own the Watering Hole?" Dawn nodded. "Was he forcing you to participate?"

"Yes, but I would have found some way out of it," Dawn said with a hint of defiance.

Cole's fists clenched at his sides. "I'll kill him."

"You won't do any such thing. I've answered your questions, now it's time to answer mine. Why have you come back? Did you find Running Elk? Is all well with him and his people?"

"Running Elk is taking his people to Canada. The government wants to deprive all Indians of their weapons and ponies and force them onto lands that are too small to contain their numbers. Do you know what that means? They'll all die of starvation and sickness."

"Are Spring Rain and Sun In The Face well?"

"They're fine. Indian losses were light at the Little Big Horn."

Dawn couldn't help asking the question that burned on the tip of her tongue. "And Laughing Brook? Was she pleased to see you?"

His eyes were dark and enigmatic. "She offered to share her mat with me."

Dawn lowered her eyes. "I see."

"No, you don't see. I didn't. I . . . I couldn't. I kept thinking of a blue-eyed beauty waiting for me in Oregon. I've finally come to my senses, sweetheart. Am I too late?"

Dawn stared at him, her face pale but determined. "Far too late, Cole. I'm going to marry Sandy."

Chapter Nineteen

Cole refused to believe that Dawn felt nothing for him. He couldn't let her go. Not now, not when the jagged edges of his life were finally coming together. If not for Dawn he'd still be living in the past, grieving for a dead woman who was beyond the ability to return the love he had stubbornly kept alive. From the beginning he had accepted responsibility for Dawn, and now he knew why. It was simple, really. He couldn't let her go because he loved her. Loved her with his whole heart and soul. And she loved him. He'd stake his life on it.

"You're not going to marry Sandy," he said harshly. "You love me."

Dawn's jaw jutted out defiantly. "I *don't* love you. What love I had for you died for lack of nurturing. I'm not Morning Mist, nor will I ever be. You were attracted to me simply because of my

358

resemblance to your dead wife, but I don't want to be a substitute for a dead woman. You freed me from the nightmare my life had become with Billy, and I'll always be grateful. I want a real home, children, stability. But most of all I want a man who will love me."

Cole stared into the volatile depths of her blue eyes and realized how empty and without direction his life had been all these years. Dawn was everything he'd ever wanted. Without her, life had no taste, no scent, no purpose. He'd wallowed in grief for years, lost, incomplete and wanting, and had been too stubborn to realize that his Maker had given him another chance. Dawn was his beginning and his end, with many years of loving in between. But only if she came to her senses and realized they belonged together.

"I love you, Dawn. I want us to be together forever."

Dawn stared at him, her expression blank. "I don't believe you."

Dawn wanted to believe him, but she was frightened that if she remained with him she'd lose him again. She wouldn't be able to bear it a second time. She had a child growing inside her to consider and protect. Cole couldn't be trusted to settle down to a normal life with her and their child.

Desperate to prove his words, Cole caught Dawn up against him. His eyes blazed fiercely as he lowered his mouth to hers. The cool air of the room only heightened the raw heat of his mouth as his hungry kiss shattered her composure. Cole was taking unfair advantage of her vulnerability, stealing her will and making a mockery of her resistance.

Cole deepened his kiss. Dawn fought against succumbing to the passion he tried to coax from her. But it was a losing battle. Her lips parted of their own accord, inviting the sweet invasion of his tongue. The gentle massage of his tongue inside her mouth sent currents of desire spiraling through her. It had been far too long since she'd been in Cole's arms, felt the powerful persuasion of his embrace, experienced the sweet joy of taking his body into hers.

"You want me; I know you do," Cole whispered against her lips.

Her denial sounded hollow to her own ears. "I might have wanted you at one time but I'm not the same woman you left behind. After you abandoned me, I was forced to survive in a world I knew nothing about."

Cole held himself to blame for all her troubles. After he'd left her, she had dug deep inside herself, curled into a shell, shutting her emotions away from the world she now inhabited. He searched frantically for a way to break through the protective shell she'd pulled around herself.

Raw despair drove him as he dragged her against the hard wall of his chest. He kissed her again. And yet again, trying to reach her on a physical level after failing to reach her emotionally. He moved his mouth over hers, devouring her softness, more demanding this time. His kiss was like the soldering heat that joins metals. He showered kisses around her lips and along her jaw, then moved back to her mouth, his lips caressing and demanding, his tongue plunging deeply.

His hands roved freely over her body, causing a curling heat to begin low in her stomach. She felt his lips tugging at her nipple and suddenly became aware that Cole had unfastened her dress in front, baring her breasts to his greedy mouth.

"Cole, I don't want this!" Her trembling voice belied her words.

Ignoring her protests, he raised her skirts and slid his hand through the triangle of soft black curls at the juncture of her legs. His hand grew bolder as he explored the tender flesh between her thighs. He gave her a slow smile when she cried out, thrusting her loins against his hand.

"Tell me you don't want me, love." He slipped one finger inside her.

Dawn's protest became a strangled sob as tongues of fire licked along her nerve endings. Spreading the petals of her sex wider, he slid a second finger beside the first, easing both of them out, then back in. She could feel her wetness welcoming him as he prepared her, and resentment welled up inside her.

"You're not being fair," she cried brokenly. "You know exactly how to make my body want you."

"You'll always want me, love. Don't deny me now. I promise to be the best husband a woman could ask for."

She shook her head in vigorous denial, unable to speak with his fingers working their magic down below and his lips pulling on her nipple.

Suddenly Cole gathered her dress in his two hands and pulled it off her. With a swiftness that left her breathless, he rid her of her petticoats, corset and chemise. Her stockings and shoes were the last to go. Then he quickly shed his own clothing, still damp from the rain. When he returned to her, Dawn tried to roll away, but Cole caught her and held her fast against the raging heat of his body.

"Easy, love, I'm not going to hurt you. I want to love you. I've been dreaming about this moment since the day I left Oregon City."

"You didn't have to leave," Dawn accused.

"If I hadn't left I might never have realized how much I love you."

He stopped her angry retort with his mouth. His seductive kisses sent her senses spiraling out of control. His lips tasted her mouth, then her breasts, sucking them, then sliding his mouth down her stomach to the tangle of ebony curls at the joining of her thighs. Dawn held her breath, fearing he'd notice the slight protrusion where her babe rested beneath her heart, but he barely paused as his mouth found the tiny jewel hidden within the dewy petals of her sex.

Heat throbbed in her belly as he kissed and laved, opening her pink flesh with his tongue so he could take more of her into his mouth. He tugged, nipped and tasted. She felt her moisture flowing, hating herself for responding as she wept into his mouth.

Cole made a ragged sound low in his throat. Then he was parting her legs with his knees, positioning himself between her thighs. He stared avidly down at her. She was open and vulnerable to his perusal. She tried to hide herself with her hands but he pushed them aside. "You're beautiful all over," he said hoarsely. "Don't hide yourself from me. I'm going to spend the rest of my life looking at you and loving you."

Dawn's eyes settled on his arousal, painfully aware of the mindless pleasure he was capable of giving her. Cole followed the direction of her gaze, and his heartbeat accelerated.

"Touch me, love." He dragged her hand to his erection, clasping it around him. He closed his eyes and groaned as violent shudders seized him.

When Dawn tried to remove her hand, he held it captive against him and moved it slowly up and down the length of his sex. She felt the scorching heat of him as he grew and expanded within her palm. Sweet agony seized him as he cried out and flung her hand away. He moved up her body.

"I can't wait! I'm coming inside you, love."

Dawn's body tensed. She wanted to deny her need but could not. He knew exactly where to touch her to make her want him. It had always been thus between them. It was as if their bodies were in complete harmony with one another. She arched upward to meet his thrust, crying out as he filled her to bursting. He fit her like a glove, she thought dimly as warmth flooded her body. She had always loved the feel of his hard-muscled body lying atop hers and the rigid length of him inside her. It was no different now.

Anger prevented Dawn from saying the words Cole ached to hear. He had the ability to reach her body, but he still hadn't convinced her to trust him. Dimly it occurred to her that she could not marry Sandy now that Cole had returned. It would only cause dissension between men who had been friends long before she'd met Cole. It would be best for all concerned if she just quietly disappeared. Then coherent thought fled as her body took over, responding violently to Cole's loving.

Cole increased his rhythm, his movements growing faster, deeper, his muscles straining. Her own muscles began to grow taut. Pleasure rippled over her, through her, sending raw fire spilling into her veins. He was swollen and rigid; she could feel him pulsating inside her. He lifted her, then thrust again and again, his hard hands digging into her hips. His breath was harsh, deep, raw, as he waited for Dawn to reach her climax before allowing his own.

Brilliant fire consumed her, and Dawn felt as if her soul was leaving her body. Felt a great rush of pure rapture spiral through her quivering flesh. She screamed, unaware that she called Cole's name as she exploded convulsively. Cole clawed his way to the crest as his own release overtook him. He threw his head back and shouted.

Reluctantly Cole left her body and rolled to his side. Dawn turned her face away so he couldn't see how deeply his loving had affected her. Cole was the only man who could reach her emotionally, the only man she could respond to physically. The thought of being touched by another man sickened her. Despite his ability to move mountains with his loving, she still feared to place her life and that of her child into his keeping. All she remembered of her father were harsh words and a heavy hand. Then he had sold her to Billy Cobb and her life had become unbearable. Not that she thought Cole would ever mistreat her physically.

But withholding his love would be a far worse kind of abuse.

Perhaps she didn't deserve happiness, Dawn reflected. She should go away, now, before she started to yearn for things beyond her reach. Cole had left her once and he would likely leave her again.

"You can't deny what we have together," Cole said when he regained his breath.

"Are you referring to lust?"

"No, dammit! I'm referring to love. Tomorrow I'm taking you home. We'll be married as soon as arrangements can be made."

"Just when did this great revelation come to you?" Dawn asked with a hint of sarcasm. "As I recall, you weren't interested in loving another woman after losing Morning Mist."

"I went away because I needed to know if I could trust my feelings for you. I'd denied my love for you, fought my own emotions until I was too confused to think straight. It didn't take long to realize how very much I needed you. I missed you desperately. It takes some men longer than others to come to their senses. In my case, memories of a love I refused to let die prevented me from realizing you were my destiny."

Dawn didn't believe him. "Can you honestly say you are over Morning Mist? That her memory won't intrude upon our life if we marry?"

"I can truthfully say I know you're the woman I want."

Those weren't the words Dawn wanted to hear. She needed to hear him say that Morning Mist had been laid to rest once and for all. Her self-esteem was too fragile to be dealt another crippling blow. Billy Cobb had all but destroyed her sense of self-worth, and she needed more assurances than Cole appeared willing to give.

Her silence roused Cole to anger. "What more do you want from me? Morning Mist is my past, you're my future." He saw her tremble and pulled the blanket up over her. "Oh, God, Dawn, what did I do to make you so bitter? What must I do to prove you're the only woman for me?" His arms tightened around her, as if he feared she would disappear. "Get some sleep. We'll leave first thing in the morning."

A pleasure she refused to acknowledge washed over Dawn as Cole gathered her into his arms and pulled her against him. When she was with Cole, he could talk her into anything. But she was stronger now than she'd ever been. Until she could be assured of the kind of happiness she'd only known in her dreams, she would not marry Cole Webster.

Sometime during the night the rain ceased. By morning a weak sun pierced through the watery gray sky, but the promise of rain still remained. Cole slept late, more at ease than he had been in months now that Dawn was back in his arms where she belonged. Accustomed to late mornings after working into the wee hours, Dawn did not awaken early from her exhausted sleep.

A loud pounding on the door startled both Dawn and Cole from a sound sleep. Cole leaped out of bed, struggling into his pants and shirt as the door burst open. Why hadn't he thought to lock it last night?

Dawn sat up in bed, holding the blanket to her chin, her eyes wide and frightened. Then she recognized Sandy, and her fear turned to embarrassment.

"Are you all right, honey? Milly told me about the auction. I'll kill that damn Porter when I get my hands on him." His expression was murderous as his gaze fell on Cole, whose face was buried in the folds of his shirt. "As for you, mister, I'm going to tear you apart limb from limb."

Cole's head burst through the neck of his shirt. "Hello, Sandy." His expression was unreadable but his green eyes glittered fiercely.

"Good God! Cole!" His gaze flew to Dawn. Her face was tinged a delicate pink, and he knew without being told what had taken place in that bed last night. He was happier than hell to see Cole but couldn't help wondering what his intentions were toward Dawn.

"Surprised to see me?" Cole's voice held only a trace of friendliness. "It didn't take you long to claim my woman."

Sandy's eyes widened in surprise. "Now wait a damn minute. I was merely protecting Dawn in your absence."

"Dawn tells me you proposed."

Sandy shot Dawn a quizzical glance. Dawn shook her head, warning him to say nothing about her condition. "Did she tell you why?"

"She didn't have to. Any man would value a woman like Dawn, and you took advantage of her vulnerability."

"You're the one who left her alone and vulnerable," Sandy charged. "I've grown damn fond of Dawn. Marrying her was the only way I could think of to protect her against predators like Cully Porter and his like. You'd been gone so long even your sister gave up on you. I hope you'll correct the mistakes you made now that you're home. With you here, Dawn is no longer in need of my protection."

"Damn right she doesn't need your protection," Cole snarled fiercely. Suddenly he realized he was speaking to his best friend as if he were his worst enemy, and the harshness left his voice. "I'm sorry, Sandy, I know you'd never do anything to hurt me. Thank you for all you've done for Dawn. You can be the best man at our wedding."

"Soon, I hope," Sandy said meaningfully.

"As soon as it can be arranged."

"No!" Dawn protested. She wasn't going to sit back and let Cole arrange her life. He walked in and out of her life at will and expected her to be waiting for him like a pet dog. "I'm not marrying Cole."

"You are so," chimed Cole and Sandy in unison.

"Are you forgetting something, honey?" Sandy reminded her.

Cole's green gaze pierced her. "What is it you're forgetting, love?"

"Nothing! Nothing. . . . Both of you get out of here so I can get dressed."

"I'll wait downstairs for you," Cole said. "We'll leave together."

"No, I have to pack and—"

"No excuses, love. We're riding home together."

"Ashley's house isn't my home."

"It will have to suffice until I can build a house for us. Come on, Sandy, Dawn needs some privacy."

"You might have to wait a long time," Dawn warned. "I want a bath and I'll need to pack my belongings."

"An hour. Meet us downstairs in an hour. Meanwhile, Sandy and I can have a long talk." He sent Sandy a look that suggested there was much his friend had to account for.

"Very well," Dawn sighed, "an hour." Cole should have been suspicious of her easy capitulation.

Once the door closed, Dawn leaped from bed. She washed quickly and dressed in her sturdiest riding clothes. Then she threw the rest of her belongings into a pillowcase and cautiously opened the door. The hallway was deserted. Most of the girls were either still abed or downstairs having their breakfast in the kitchen. She could hear Cole's voice drifting up to her and hesitated with her hand on the doorknob. Was she doing the right thing? she asked herself. How far could she get before Cole found her? What if he decided she wasn't worth following?

What about the baby?

Dawn utterly rejected the notion of telling Cole he was going to be a father. She would have to trust Sandy not to divulge her secret. Cole had to want her for herself, not because she was carrying his child. Indecision sat heavily upon her shoulders. Just hours ago Cole had told her he loved her, that he wanted to marry her and settle down.

He'd sworn that Morning Mist no longer stood between them, that his heart was free to love again. Suddenly Dawn came to a decision.

She would claim Wally from the livery and ride west to Portland. If Cole came after her, she would know he truly cared. If he let her ride out of his life, she was well rid of him. She had a feeling she was being unreasonable and foolish. Maybe her pregnancy made her that way. But she wanted to be sure she was more than a warm body to Cole.

Closing the door softly behind her, Dawn slipped down the back stairs. The livery was but a short distance away. Within a quarter of an hour she was on her way.

Cole tried to relax but couldn't. He worried that he hadn't convinced Dawn that he loved her. What would it take to make her realize she meant everything to him? He glanced at Sandy, noting that his friend was as edgy as he was.

"Perhaps we should have that talk while we're waiting for Dawn," Cole suggested. "Exactly what is there between you and her? Why did you propose, and why did she accept? She flat out refused my proposal."

Sandy sent him a disgruntled look. "You abandoned Dawn. You gave her scant hope for a future with you. For God's sake, Cole, you forced her to leave Dodge City against her will! Why? Was it for your own selfish purposes?" He shook his head. "I just don't understand you."

"I told you why I took Dawn away from Dodge. I planned to leave her with Running Elk, but circumstances made it impossible. I couldn't in good conscience leave her there, with all the trouble brewing on the plains. The Indians were on the warpath. My protective instincts run deep where Dawn is concerned."

"It wasn't your protectiveness that got her with child."

Cole flushed. "You know about that? It was a mistake. Dawn never knew how deeply I grieved when she lost our child. I'm glad you know. Now you understand why I feel responsible for Dawn."

"Do you love her?"

"Deeply. I realized how much I cared shortly after I left Oregon City. It was too long in coming, but I've finally accepted Morning Mist's death. She's part of my past, remembered and loved, but finally laid to rest. She will never interfere with the future I intend to share with Dawn. I want to marry Dawn, to settle down and have children with her. But now Dawn doesn't believe me."

"Do you blame her?"

"No. I blame myself." He stared at Sandy, suddenly wanting answers. "What are you doing in Oregon City? What does Dawn mean to you, and why in the hell did you propose to her?"

"After the home office informed me you'd resigned your job, I felt at loose ends. Without you as a partner, the job no longer held the same appeal. I decided if you liked Oregon well enough to stay, I'd like it too. I turned in my resignation and took the next train west."

"You've answered only half my question."

"I've grown extremely fond of Dawn. Fond enough to want to protect her."

"Is that why you asked her to marry you? Seems like a flimsy reason to me."

Sandy sent him an oblique look. "Did Dawn say nothing to you?"

"About what?"

Sandy was silent so long Cole felt a sinking feeling in the pit of his stomach. Something was wrong, terribly wrong. He felt it in his bones. And whatever it was, Sandy seemed loath to reveal it to him.

"Spit it out, Sandy. What is it you're hiding?"

"If Dawn wanted you to know, she'd tell you. You *did* spend the night in her bed, didn't you?"

Cole was puzzled at the accusatory note in Sandy's voice. "I don't deny it. Nor do I deny asking Dawn to marry me. She refused. She said she was going to marry you. What in the hell is going on?"

"Dawn refused your proposal?" Sandy asked, aghast. "Dammit, Cole, she couldn't have been thinking clearly. The only reason I asked her to marry me was because . . ." His sentence fell off and he dropped his gaze, refusing to look Cole in the eye.

"Go on," Cole gritted out. "You may as well tell me. You asked Dawn to marry you because . . ."

"This should come from Dawn."

Frustration made Cole's voice harsh. "You're supposed to be my best friend. What are you hiding?"

"Dawn is carrying your child," Sandy blurted out. "I asked her to marry me because everyone assumed you weren't coming back and her babe needed a name."

Cole leaped to his feet, stunned. "Why didn't Dawn tell me?" His eyes narrowed. "Unless the child doesn't belong to me."

"I ought to punch you in the nose for even thinking such a thing," Sandy blasted. "You don't know Dawn if you think she'd consort with another man."

Some perverse devil made Cole say, "Obviously she was willing to share your bed when she agreed to marry you."

"You don't know a damn thing, Cole. Our marriage was to be merely a formality to give your child a name. We both agreed we wouldn't share a bed. I could have let Dawn bear your child in shame, but I felt too strongly about your babe being raised without a father or a name."

Cole felt like a jealous fool for doubting Dawn's loyalty. His heart told him she loved him but she had been hurt too many times to trust again. "I'm sorry, Sandy, jealousy does strange things to a man. I just can't figure out why Dawn didn't tell me about the baby. Especially after I asked her to marry me."

"You haven't earned her trust, Cole. Dawn's past life must have been a living hell, if only half of what you told me about her is true. She needs someone who will love her without restrictions, someone she can depend upon. Until now you've given her scant hope of enjoying a future with you. She doesn't want to be second best in your heart."

Sandy's astute observation astounded Cole. How could Sandy know what was in Dawn's heart after so short an acquaintance? Had he, Cole, been blind to Dawn's needs? Had his stubbornness, his refusal to listen to what his heart had been trying to tell him, cost him the only woman with the power to reach inside him and free him from his past?

Suddenly Cole became aware of the passage of time. It was long past the time Dawn was supposed to join them. He glanced toward the staircase, concern creasing his brow. Sandy followed the direction of Cole's gaze, a gnawing suspicion grinding inside his gut.

"You don't think . . . ?" Sandy's question ended abruptly.

"I'd put nothing past Dawn when her mind is set on something." Cole sprinted up the stairs, with Sandy close on his heels.

Cole knew before he flung open the door to Dawn's room that he wouldn't find her inside.

Sandy's concern was apparent. "Where do you suppose she's gone?"

"Damned if I know. When I find her I don't know what I'll do first, kiss her or wring her beautiful little neck. She has more than just herself to protect, she has my child growing inside her. She's already lost one child, what if . . ." Cole nearly choked on the horrible notion that sprang unbidden into his head. "What if she loses this child? She's fragile. She might not survive this time. Oh, God, what have I done to her?"

"I'll help you look for her," Sandy said. "Does she own a horse?"

"She probably boarded Wally at the livery. Let's start there. It's raining again. I have to find her before she freezes, or catches pneumonia. The little fool! What in the world possessed her to leave like this?"

"You can ask her when you find her," Sandy said, urging Cole down the stairs and into the cold drizzle that froze into hard pellets before it reached the ground.

The hostler told Cole that Dawn had been there earlier, and that she'd seemed in a great hurry. He mentioned that she was carrying a bulging pillowcase that she'd tied onto her saddle before she left. No, he didn't notice the direction in which she was headed, nor did she say where she was going. The stableboy volunteered the information that the lady had ridden west out of town, along the Portland road. Cole thought that made sense. Losing herself in a big city was safer than being alone in the wilderness.

"I'm going after her," Cole told Sandy.

"I'll come with you."

"I'm going alone. You return to the house and tell Ashley and Tanner what happened. Dawn doesn't have too much of a head start. I should catch up with her easily."

"Are you sure? You've been traveling for days. You look about done in. Let me go in your place."

Cole sent Sandy a look that would have frozen the ears off a brass monkey. "No. Dawn is my responsibility. I'll find her. Tell Ashley she can start planning a wedding for next week. And tell Tanner I'm taking him up on that offer of a piece of land. I want to start building immediately. Dawn has never had a real home. I want to give her everything she deserves."

"I hope that includes your love," Sandy said sternly.

Cole laughed. "Since when have you become a maudlin romantic, you old fraud? I love Dawn. Without her, my life has no meaning."

"I hope you told her that."

"I did. She chose not to believe me."

"Bring Dawn back, Cole. Now get out of here. I'll relay your messages to your family."

Chapter Twenty

The heavens opened up, pelting Dawn with huge drops of icy rain. She dashed water from her rain-stung eyes and squinted into the sodden half-darkness of the storm-shrouded day. Suddenly a bolt of fire cleaved the heavens, burying itself in the earth. A crash of thunder followed, shaking the ground beneath her. To Dawn it appeared as if God were wreaking vengeance upon the earth and all its creatures.

The narrow road she followed cut a path between lofty pine, spruce and hemlock trees. Due to the inclement weather, muddy roads and swollen creeks and rivers, fellow travelers were conspicuously absent. Dawn urged her horse through the sucking mud as a mixture of rain and ice poured relentlessly down upon her. Lightning streaked across the gray sky and thunder rattled the heavens. With sinking heart, Dawn realized that her reckless flight might very well cost her her life.

God was punishing her, she thought as she pulled her coat closer around her quaking shoulders. She was cold, so very cold. She had made a terrible mistake. Why did she have to be so stubborn? Why couldn't she just rejoice in Cole's return and accept the love he offered? It was time she learned to trust again. Cole had sounded sincere when he'd said he loved her, but some perverse devil inside her had refused to believe him. He had never given her any reason to hope he would come to love her, so why should she believe him? His whole life revolved around a woman he'd sworn to love into eternity.

Dawn shivered violently and huddled deeper into her coat. She was as miserable as she'd ever been. She had effortlessly gone from the frying pan into the fire. For someone who loved a man as deeply as she loved Cole, she'd acted exceedingly foolishly.

Suddenly Wally shied, nearly throwing her. Clinging to his neck, Dawn hung on and searched frantically for the source of danger. What she saw chilled her blood. The bridge spanning a normally quiet and picturesque creek was out, and water was rushing at an alarming speed over the rocky bottom. It was almost as if Fate had ruled against her foolhardy flight, Dawn thought as she turned Wally around. There was nothing left for her now but to return to Oregon City and face Cole's wrath.

Cole was bound to be irate, she reflected dimly. She had deliberately placed two lives in danger, hers and that of her unborn child. She wondered if Cole would be happy to learn he was going to be a father. He had mentioned that he wanted to start a family with her, but she'd been too frightened of being hurt again to believe him.

Cold, relentless rain beat down upon her. She felt bruised all over. Suddenly a bolt of lightning struck so close that Dawn could almost taste the scorching tang of it. Her hair stood on edge, and she felt a prickling along her spine. The crash of thunder that followed spooked Wally. Her horse reared, then took off into the woods, ignoring Dawn's futile attempts to control him. Several tense minutes passed before Dawn had Wally once more in hand and turned him back toward the road, or what she thought was the right direction.

The crude logger's hut that loomed up from the curtain of mist and rain was a welcome sight. At first, Dawn thought it was a mirage. She blinked, then blinked again. When it did not disappear or waver, she offered a quick prayer of thanksgiving and reined Wally toward the shelter. When she reached the hut she hastily dismounted, retrieved the pillowcase holding her belongings and pushed open the unlatched door. The room was dark and cold, but at least it offered some degree of shelter. She dropped the pillowcase on the floor and ducked back outside to see to Wally. There was no shelter for her drenched mount, but the least she could do for the poor beast was to remove his saddle.

But her plans were foiled when another vivid display of lightning and violent crash of thunder

Connie Mason

sent the horse stampeding through the trees.
Dawn couldn't have stopped him had she tried.
She was shivering uncontrollably by the time she
returned to the hut. Evidently the hut hadn't been
used in a very long time, for it was in a sorry state
of disrepair.

The room was sparsely furnished with a small
scarred table, two rickety chairs and a narrow cot.
Dawn's eyes lit up when she spied a blanket neatly
folded at the foot of the cot. Then she spied the
stack of dry kindling and firewood beside the fire-
place and she gave a cry of gladness. Her joy was
short-lived when she realized that without
matches or tinder, the possibility of starting a fire
was remote. But she tried to look at the bright
side. At least she would have a roof over her head
during the height of the storm. And she felt certain
that once the storm abated she'd find Wally
nearby.

Meanwhile, she had to get out of her sodden
clothes. She undressed quickly, shivering violently as she peeled off the wet layers of clothing.
Then she rummaged through the pillowcase until
she found a reasonably dry shift, shirt and skirt.
Once she was dressed, she removed the dusty but
serviceable blanket from the bed and pulled it
around her.

Cole was colder than he'd ever been in his life,
and more frightened. He hadn't caught up with
Dawn yet, and the thought of her out in this storm
made him push poor Warrior to the limit of his
endurance. Her stubbornness appalled him. Her
failure to tell him about the babe she carried made

him furious. It was pure willfulness that had made her endanger that precious life growing inside her.

Thunder and lightning rent the skies, and Cole cursed the capriciousness of winter in Oregon. This infernal rain seemed to have no end or beginning. It just went on and on without any sign of relief. Early this morning it appeared as if the sun was going to break through the clouds, then, as if frightened by the heavy gray clouds, it had retreated and the storm had returned with renewed vengeance.

The road was awash in gluey mud, Cole was covered in grime, and water was running off his slicker, soaking him below the hips.

Suddenly Cole saw something that froze the blood in his veins. The bridge spanning the creek was out. Halting Warrior on the bank of the seething stream, Cole debated whether or not to attempt a crossing. He prayed that Dawn hadn't been so foolish as to plunge recklessly into the creek. But what if she had? What if even as he hesitated she was struggling to survive in freezing water? That thought caused a painful roaring in his head. He hadn't passed her on the road, which led him to believe that she had indeed attempted a crossing. He was about to urge Warrior into the raging water when he heard a noise to his left.

Cole's heart plummeted when he saw a horse burst through the trees onto the road. Wally! Warrior must have recognized his friend, for he snorted a greeting. Wally halted, tossing his head and stomping the mud beneath his hooves.

Cole approached the riderless horse cautiously

lest he frighten the animal away. Wally obliged by waiting patiently for Cole to grab hold of his trailing reins. "Where's Dawn, boy? What happened?"

Of course, the horse couldn't answer, but his flaring nostrils and wild eyes gave Cole a hint of what had happened. It didn't take Cole long to figure out that Wally had been frightened by the violent display of thunder and lightning and had thrown Dawn. That thought was so alarming that Cole put his heels to Warrior and plunged into the woods with Wally in tow.

The next lightning bolt and clap of thunder made Wally go wild, but Cole's will was greater than the horse's. Cole rode through the trees like a man possessed, shouting Dawn's name at the top of his lungs between claps of thunder.

Cole spied the hut through driving sheets of rain, and his heart leaped with fragile hope. He prayed that Dawn had found shelter inside as he leaped from his mount, pausing only long enough to tether both horses to a bush. Just as he took a step toward the hut, a lightning bolt snaked down from the heavens, striking a tree so close to Cole he could smell the acrid odor of burning wood. He had but a moment to call out Dawn's name before a sturdy branch, split by lightning and set aflame, struck him on the head.

The flash of lightning and roar of thunder that shook the hut badly jolted Dawn. It had struck so close, the odor of fire lingered on the damp air long after the last rumble of thunder vanished. Then, in the calm that followed, she imagined she heard someone call out her name.

Curiosity plagued Dawn. She would not be able

to rest easy until she investigated, even if it had been nothing but the howling wind imitating a human voice. Cautiously she pried open the door. The wind was ferocious, catching the flimsy panel and flinging it from her hands. Peering out the door through the nearly impenetrable curtain of rain, Dawn saw little to rouse her suspicion. She was about to turn back inside when the soft nickering of a horse caught her attention. Had Wally returned? She poked her head through the doorway to widen her range of vision and spied two horses tethered to a bush, their heads bent against the driving wind. Wally and Warrior! That meant Cole . . . Then she saw him, pinned beneath a fallen branch, one end of which was still smoking but whose flame had been doused by the rain.

"Cole!" She rushed out of the hut, falling to her knees beside him. He was unconscious. Panic-stricken, she realized she had to get him out of the rain and cold immediately.

The branch was heavy but manageable as she lifted it from Cole's body. He had been struck on the head and bore a lump to prove it. Groaning under the burden, Dawn cast the branch aside and tried to rouse Cole. He didn't respond. He was as still and unmoving as solid rock. And just as heavy. Incapable of lifting him, Dawn did the next best thing. She grasped him under the arms and dragged him the short distance to the hut, thankful there were no stairs to contend with.

By the time she pulled him all the way inside the hut, she was panting from the exertion. Cole still hadn't budged or opened his eyes. But he was shivering uncontrollably. And so was she. She looked longingly at the hearth, wishing there was a way to strike a fire in the hearth before they both froze to death or died of pneumonia. She was wearing her only set of dry clothes and now they were as wet as those she had removed earlier.

Her mind worked frantically. She was desperate enough to try rubbing two sticks together, but fortunately she recalled something that made the attempt unnecessary. Cole always carried matches in a tin in his saddlebags. Cole's pale face provided the impetus she needed to venture out in the raging storm again to get them. She paused but a moment before plunging through the door and into the solid wall of water. The horses snorted a greeting as Dawn approached, but she was too intent upon her mission to spare an answering pat for them.

Dashing the rain from her eyes, she searched through Cole's saddlebags, exclaiming in joy and relief when her hand closed on the tin of matches. Clutching them to her breast like something precious, she ran back to the hut, pushing the warped door shut behind her. Cole lay where she'd left him, pale and unmoving.

Her hands were shaking so badly it took three precious matches before the kindling caught. Minutes later a fragile flame ignited the wood, giving forth a promise of warmth. When Dawn was certain the fire would not die, she returned to Cole. His stillness frightened her. Using a piece of her wet petticoat, she washed the blood from his head and inspected his wound. It did not appear serious. The skin was broken but already scabbing over. Far more worrisome was the blow he'd received to his head.

The small room was heating rapidly. Dawn spread all her wet clothing except for what she wore across the two rickety chairs and on the floor before concentrating on getting Cole out of his clothes. He cooperated not at all, lying like dead weight as she removed his guns and pulled and pushed to strip him of his wet buckskins. When he was nude, she wrapped him in the blanket. After she had made Cole as comfortable as possible under the circumstances, Dawn saw to her own needs. She stripped down to her shift and lay down beside Cole to share his body heat and the blanket. She tried to remain awake, but the events of the day had exhausted her and she nodded off.

Cole was hot. The fires of hell licked at him. He moaned and tried to escape the suffocating heat, but something even hotter than his own burning flesh pressed against him. His head hurt and he moved it cautiously. When he felt strong enough, he opened his eyes. The first thing he saw were walls made of logs. With difficulty he turned his head toward the source of the heat torturing his flesh.

Even with her hair matted against her head and her face smudged with dirt, Dawn was the loveliest sight he'd ever seen. He racked his brain, still foggy and disoriented, but failed to find answers to his questions. Where was he? How had he arrived here, and why did his head hurt like the very devil? Why was he lying naked with Dawn in his arms?

It came to Cole suddenly that the source of scorching heat was Dawn. Her heated flesh had chased the dampness and cold from his bones just as surely as the fire burning cheerily in the hearth. He spied his clothing laid out before the hearth and realized that he had Dawn to thank for that. He could remember nothing beyond chasing through the woods in search of Dawn. Through some quirk of fate, the rescuer had become the rescued. What in the hell had happened?

Dawn sensed movement beside her and struggled to awaken. She was so cozy and warm she resisted as long as she could, but finally she opened her eyes.

"Cole, thank God you're awake. How do you feel?"

"Like I've been struck by lightning." He had no idea how close to the truth he had come.

"You were struck, but not by lightning. A bolt of lightning severed a tree limb and sent it crashing to the ground . . . right on your head."

He touched the lump on his head, and it all came back to him in a flash. "How did I get inside the hut? I'm not a lightweight."

"I dragged you."

He shook his head. "Foolish girl. You could have hurt yourself." He gave her a crooked smile. "It appears I'm nude beneath the blanket."

Dawn flushed. "I stripped you. You were soaked to the skin. Are you sure you're all right?"

"I have one hell of a headache, but I'll survive. More importantly, how are you? Or should I say, how is our babe?"

Dawn released her breath in a surprised hiss. "You know? How?"

"A mutual friend told me."

"Sandy! He promised."

"Why didn't you want me to know? I told you I wanted children with you. Is it so difficult to trust me?"

"You've given me no reason to believe you'd stick around long enough to welcome our child into the world."

He placed his hand on her stomach, finding scant sign of a child growing inside her. She was too slim, and far too fragile, to be carrying a child. "I'll never abandon you again, love. I know I've hurt you in the past, but you've got to believe me when I say I'm ready now to devote the rest of my life to you and the family we'll have together."

His words sounded pretty, but . . . "Why should I believe you?"

He touched her face with a tenderness that made the breath catch in her throat. "Because I love you. Without you I have no heart or soul. If you hadn't come into my life I would have fed upon my grief forever, living with cold memories. I realize now how close I came to destroying myself out of grief for a past love I could never bring back from the grave. Grieving had become a way of life for me. Morning Mist would want me to move on with my life. Finding love again has given my life purpose."

He was so intent, so utterly sincere, Dawn felt all her doubts melting away. "You're happy about the baby?"

"Incredibly happy." He spread his fingers across

her belly, massaging gently. "You're so slim. Are you certain all is well with you and the babe? Have you consulted a doctor?"

She nodded. "I should deliver a healthy baby in six months, if all goes well."

Her last words sent fear racing through his blood. "I could wring your beautiful neck for running away. How could you endanger yourself and our child like that? You've already suffered one miscarriage, you can't afford another. Oh, God, Dawn, if anything happens this time I'll hold myself responsible." He kissed her brow, even though lifting his head caused him excruciating pain.

He lay back with a groan.

"Don't move. You may have a concussion."

"We have to get back to town. Is it still raining?"

She glanced out the window. "No, the storm has moved on. But we're not going anywhere until you're well enough to move." She started to rise, but he held her tightly against him.

"If I'm not moving, neither are you. You've been through a harrowing experience. I should be very angry with you but I'm just damn glad to see you safe and sound. I was supposed to rescue you, not the other way around."

"I'm fine, Cole, really. I'm stronger than I look."

"Maybe so, but I'm not taking any chances with you this time. This babe is going to grow inside you to term. We'll be married as soon as possible. I sent Sandy to tell Ashley that she's to plan a wedding for next week. I've accepted a piece of land from Tanner and hope to build you a grand house before our child is born."

A real home. Someone to love who would love

her in return. A child of her own. Dawn was too overcome with happiness to reply. Leaning on her elbow, she kissed his mouth, loving the unique taste and scent of him. How could she have been so foolish as to run away from the only happiness she'd ever known?

"I love you, Cole," she said. Her voice shook with emotion.

"Thank God," Cole said, sighing raggedly. "Those are the sweetest words I've ever heard. You already know I love you."

Dawn grinned happily as she cuddled close to Cole. Fading light cast eerie shadows into the cabin as the day drew to an end. When her stomach emitted a loud growl, Dawn was reminded that she hadn't eaten since the previous night.

"You're hungry," Cole said. A hint of laughter crinkled the corners of his eyes. "Is there anything to eat in the hut?"

"No, I've already looked. It's been abandoned a very long time."

"There is some jerky and hardtack in my saddlebags. Lie still, I'll get them."

"No! You can't get up. You're not well enough. I'll get them."

"Not unless you knock me out first," Cole insisted. "I'm not going to let a little headache stop me. Maybe I can find something more palatable than hardtack and jerky in my cache of food."

He tottered to his feet, fighting off a wave of dizziness as he pulled on his dry pants and shirt. When he opened the door a blast of cold air caused Dawn to shiver and snuggle deeper into the blanket. Cole wasn't gone long. He returned with a cloth sack. It held several pieces of jerky, some hardtack and a hunk of cheese. Cole sliced the cheese with his knife and divided the contents of the bag between them.

Dawn ate with gusto. When she finished, she sighed and regarded Cole for a long, measuring moment. "Are you really sure you want to marry me? It's not because of the babe, is it? Because if it is, I couldn't—"

Cole stopped her with a kiss. "Hush, love. I'm here because you are in my thoughts night and day. Because my whole life revolves around you. I know I've hurt you but I intend to make it up to you. God, Dawn, I must have been mad to question my feelings for you. I'd want you even if you weren't carrying my child." He kissed her again, hard.

Dawn's bones turned liquid. When he stopped kissing her, she tugged his head back down and leaned up, inviting him to continue. They were sitting on the floor atop the rumpled blanket that had covered them while they slept, and as Cole's mouth devoured hers, she slowly pulled him down with her, until she lay flat, with Cole bending over her, their mouths meshed, her arms clinging to his neck. She wanted to draw his taste inside her, to be savored forever.

Cole felt his control slipping. He wanted to make love to Dawn, to lose himself in her sweet body, but he didn't want to hurt her or their babe. Her face was pinched and wan. Battling the storm had drained her. The life growing inside her was too fragile and precious to endanger. Dawn made a little moaning sound inside her throat when he drew away, and she tried to pull him back.

"No, sweet, I can wait. I won't let my lust harm our babe."

"Cole . . ."

"Yes."

"I love you so very much. Are you sure you won't mind being married to a half-breed?"

"How can you ask such a thing? You've had a rough life, love, and have risen above it. Your beauty is not just skin deep, it goes clear through to your heart. When I look at you I don't see a half-breed. I see a warm, passionate woman with so much love to give it makes me feel unworthy."

"Are you sure Morning Mist's ghost won't haunt our marriage?" She had to know the answer before she gave herself into Cole's keeping.

"Morning Mist is dead, love. She's been dead a very long time. I've agonized over this a great deal. I loved her dearly but I no longer need to exist on memories. I have you. Morning Mist and I were both so very young when we met and fell in love. I clung to her memory simply because I hadn't met another woman who could replace her in my heart. I've finally found that woman, love. I love you, Dawn, only you." He sealed his vow with a kiss.

"First thing in the morning we'll ride back to Oregon City. Ashley and Tanner are probably worried sick about us. They weren't even aware that I had returned. I stopped first at the Watering Hole when I arrived in town. I guess Fate had a hand in bringing me to you when you needed me."

Dawn gave him a mischievous grin. "Before we marry, you have to promise me one thing."

"Anything, love. Anything within my power."

"Promise you will let Shadow Walker come to me sometimes. He's such a magnificent savage."

Startled, Cole regarded her for one long moment. Then he threw back his head and gave a shout of laughter.

AUTHOR'S NOTE

Dear Readers,

Shadow Walker completes my two-book Western series. I hope you enjoyed both *Flame* and *Shadow Walker.* My next book will be a departure from Frontier America. My trip to Morocco has provided me with a wealth of information and ideas for an exciting new story. I've come up with a name that I hope will instill a sense of the times and locale of my book. *Sheik* says it all. I hope you enjoy the exotic, for that's what you'll be getting in *Sheik.*

I enjoy hearing from readers. You can write to me in care of Leisure Books at the address printed on the copyright page of this book. If you'd like a newsletter, bookmark, and an answer, please enclose a self-addressed stamped envelope. It would be a big help if you'd include your address on your letter.

All My Romantic Best,
Connie Mason

FLAME
CONNIE MASON

"Each new Connie Mason book is a prize!"
—Heather Graham

When her brother is accused of murder, Ashley Webster heads west to clear his name. Although the proud Yankee is prepared to face any hardship on her journey to Fort Bridger, she is horrified to learn that single women aren't welcome on any wagon train. Desperate to cross the plains, Ashley decides to pay the first bachelor willing to pose as her husband. Then the fiery redhead comes across a former Johnny Reb in the St. Joe's jail, and she can't think of any man she'd rather marry in name only. But out on the rugged trail Tanner MacTavish quickly proves too intense, too virile, too dangerous for her peace of mind. And after Tanner steals a passionate kiss, Ashley knows that, even though the Civil War is over, a new battle is brewing—a battle for the heart that she may be only too happy to lose.

_4150-2 $5.99 US/$6.99 CAN

THE LION'S BRIDE — CONNIE MASON

Winner of the *Romantic Times* Storyteller Of The Year Award!

Lord Lyon of Normandy has saved William the Conqueror from certain death on the battlefield, yet neither his strength nor his skill can defend him against the defiant beauty the king chooses for his wife.

Ariana of Cragmere has lost her lands and her virtue to the mighty warrior, but the willful beauty swears never to surrender her heart.

Saxon countess and Norman knight, Ariana and Lyon are born enemies. And in a land rent asunder by bloody wars and shifting loyalties, they are doomed to misery unless they can vanquish the hatred that divides them—and unite in glorious love.

_3884-6 $5.99 US/$7.99 CAN

SIERRA
Connie Mason

Bestselling Author Of *Wind Rider*

Fresh from finishing school, Sierra Alden is the toast of the Barbary Coast. And everybody knows a proper lady doesn't go traipsing through untamed lands with a perfect stranger, especially one as devilishly handsome as Ramsey Hunter. But Sierra believes the rumors that say that her long-lost brother and sister are living in Denver, and she will imperil her reputation and her heart to find them.

Ram isn't the type of man to let a woman boss him around. Yet from the instant he spies Sierra on the muddy streets of San Francisco, she turns his life upside down. Before long, he is her unwilling guide across the wilderness and her more-than-willing tutor in the ways of love. But sweet words and gentle kisses aren't enough to claim the love of the delicious temptation called Sierra.

_3815-3 $5.99 US/$6.99 CAN

LOVE FOREVERMORE

MADELINE BAKER

The West—it has been Loralee's dream for as long as she could remember, and Indians are the most fascinating part of the wildly beautiful frontier she imagines. But when Loralee arrives at Fort Apache as the new schoolmarm, she has some hard realities to learn...and a harsh taskmaster to teach her. Shad Zuniga is fiercely proud, aloof, a renegade Apache who wants no part of the white man's world, not even its women. Yet Loralee is driven to seek him out, compelled to join him in a forbidden union, forced to become an outcast for one slim chance at love forevermore.

___4267-3 $5.99 US/$6.99 CAN